Careless Rapture

Dara Girard

ILORI
Press Books, LLC

Silver Spring, Maryland

ILORI PRESS BOOKS, LLC
PO Box 10332
Silver Spring, MD 20914

www.iloripressbooks.com

Originally published by BET Books in 2005 as Carefree

Other Books by Dara Girard

Dear Reader,

I had no intention of creating a series. Really. When I finished my first published book, a mainstream romance called *Table for Two*, I immediately started on a sequel about the best friend of the heroine and called *Gaining Interest*. After that I thought I was done. I'd given a happy ending to two great friends.

But I was wrong. By the end of *Gaining Interest* the Hensons had taken over. Drake, Eric and Jackie soon became the driving force through the books. I hadn't expected this until I started receiving emails asking me "What about Jackie?"

Hmm...yes. I had to find out too and an accidental trilogy fell into place with the publication of *Careless Rapture* (previously published as *Carefree*). Now you can find out what happened to Eric and Adriana after the wedding, what Drake and Cassie are up to and whose heart Jackie threatens to steal.

If this is your first taste of my mainstream work, find your favorite reading spot and enjoy.

Dara Girard

Prologue

Althea Williams hurried through a breakfast of blueberry muffins, scrambled eggs, and a Pepsi, unaware she'd be dead in ten hours. Had she known this, she might have put her time to better use. She might have visited the father she hadn't seen in years or forgiven the sister she'd quarreled with last week. Instead she fought with her ex-husband over car payments, cursed out a clerk at the local Safeway, and spent two hours in the salon complaining about her life.

She returned home under a splattering of stars that seemed frozen in the sky by a late February wind. Her high heels clicked along the crooked D.C. sidewalk as she made her way to her second-story apartment. As she turned the key in the lock, someone called out her name. She swore and turned, then suddenly smiled.

Her killer returned the expression.

Chapter One

Clay Jarrett knew two things about women like Jackie Henson. One, they didn't like to hear the word "no," and two, they could make a man regret saying it. Unfortunately, the moment Jackie walked into his office looking like a willful sprite in a crisp gray business suit with a red scarf artistically draped over her shoulders, he knew what his answer would be: No. And he wouldn't regret it. He'd been a private investigator long enough to rarely regret a decision.

She wasn't a pretty woman, but she didn't need to be. She was cute—and knew it—with straight black hair that reached her chin. She didn't have much height or much of a figure, but her big brown eyes made up for it all. They were warm, wicked, and smart, with a tendency to tilt a little at the ends. At times, this gave her an elfish appearance. Her looks made him think of a fairy tale. He could certainly picture her as an imp causing mischief. It started as soon as she came into his office.

Jackie could hypnotize a man with a gaze. He would have allowed himself to succumb. However, he considered her brothers, Drake and Eric, friends, and would do nothing to jeopardize that relationship. Not even to satisfy a growing curiosity.

Although he knew his answer would be no, he still listened to her request. It only reinforced his initial decision. She wanted him to look for an invisible man. That wasn't his job. Cheating spouses, missing loved ones, courier service? Yes. Chasing a man out of curiosity? No.

He leaned forward, twirling a pen between his fingers. "I can't help you," he said. He tried to sound apologetic, but failed.

"Why not?" she asked, her words more of an accusation than a query.

"Because it's a waste of time." He continued before she could protest. "You have nothing for me to work with. You want me to track down a man with no name, no address, nothing. And your sole basis for this investigation is that a client of yours thinks she's cured."

Jackie's hand gripped the strap of her handbag. "Melanie is an intelligent woman who has been part of HOPE Services for two years. All of a sudden she calls to cancel services, saying she doesn't need us anymore. No ordinary man could have convinced her of this."

He shrugged. "These things happen."

"She's the fifth client in three weeks to cancel services. When I went to visit her, she'd changed. She seemed different. More spiritual somehow, and she kept talking about a man."

"With no name."

Restless, Jackie shifted, frustrated by the bored look on his face. She didn't blame him for not seeing the urgency of her case. Her supervisor, Faye, hadn't paid much attention either. Faye was certain the man was just a boyfriend. That theory was a possibility, since many of their female clients had unreliable boyfriends or husbands that led them astray. But this was different. Jackie was certain and the proof was what she had seen.

The Melanie who answered the door yesterday was not the Melanie she knew. She had Melanie's same angular face, dyed brown hair to cover her gray, and tight mouth that rarely offered a smile because of missing teeth. But her eyes were too bright—not from a spark of health or even the use of drugs, but something completely unfamiliar.

When she had stepped into the apartment, a sickening sense of dread had crawled over Jackie's skin. The room lay bare. All Melanie's furniture was gone, with only a few cushions in its place. All her photographs, trinkets, and valuables were gone. It looked as though her life had been erased. Then she spoke of her spiritual quest and her adviser.

Melanie wouldn't give his name, which had worried Jackie most. She knew going to a private investigator was a drastic measure but she didn't know what else to do. Clay had been her first choice. She'd known him since his sister Cassie married her brother Drake four years ago. They saw each other at family dinners and holidays and were like family. Except looking at him now as he sat across the desk from her, he seemed like a stranger. Probably because in a sense he was.

She still didn't know much about him. His full name, Clarence, didn't suit him properly. It implied a big bespectacled man with an awkward grin and an unhealthy attachment to his mother. Yet the name Clay didn't completely suit him either. Though his skin was the exact shade his name described, he seemed far more unreachable than the common earth beneath one's feet. There was a distance to him. His dark eyes, while always friendly, were never warm. His face, though handsome, was not classically so. It held an ageless, rugged strength as though all his distant ancestors had contributed to its creation—an aristocratic jaw was balanced by a blunt-cut nose. His eyes were his most intriguing feature. Instead of revealing emotions, they seemed to mask them, as though shadows drifted through, altering any true feeling.

The shadows were there now as he watched her with the intense patience of a hawk.

Jackie shifted again, awkward under his penetrating stare. "I can't give you a name because she wouldn't tell me. She just calls him her adviser. She said he was a messenger of a higher power. I said he had to have a last name like a pastor or rabbi. She said he didn't want to be known because his message is revolutionary and if he is known he will be persecuted. So obviously he's not just some boyfriend she's in love with."

He shrugged.

She found his complacency maddening and pounded his desk. "Look, this guy is convincing my clients that they're cured. I need to know who he is and I need to know why."

Clay set the pen down in a quick, controlled manner. His voice remained soft. "I can tell you who he is. He's probably some self-appointed messiah who targets underprivileged individuals with the message that they're not alone, that the universe is fair if they follow his instructions and change their lifestyle. If they do all that he says, then they'll be saved---changed--or whatever the current term of the day is. It's a system that is hard to penetrate once people enter. It's difficult to convince them to leave."

"But why does he tell them this?"

"Because he believes it himself. Is he delusional? Possibly. A con artist? Maybe." He thought for a moment, then shook his head. "But that's unlikely, considering who he targets. He will do this for as long as it suits him."

She folded her arms, then let them fall. "Have you worked on a case like this before?"

"No. "

"Then all this is just a clever guess."

"It's more than a clever guess."

"Why? Because it sounds plausible?"

"Because I know."

"And how do you know so much about a man like this?" she challenged.

He didn't respond right away. Jackie wasn't surprised. Clay was a man as careful with his words as he was with his company, always cautious about what he revealed. He leaned back, appearing casual, though his gaze sharpened. She could not interpret the expression, but it made her skin bristle.

"My sister married one," he said simply, in a gritty voice softened only slightly by the hint of his British background. "An African prophet by way of Brooklyn who'd christened himself Prince. He was well educated in the ways of manipulation and wife-beating and convinced her to be his fourth wife. He later punished her for her sins, then sent her straight to heaven. He was not charged for this...service...because he explained it was part of a ritual and she had fallen and tripped. An autopsy cited this as a cause of death and he was freed. I don't know where he is now. My hopes are his body is floating somewhere being eaten by maggots." The corners of his mouth kicked up in not quite a smile, but far from a grimace. "Unfortunately, we all can't get our wish."

Jackie stared, momentarily speechless. How could he speak so matter-of-factly about his sister's death? She pushed that disturbing thought aside and said, "Then you know this man is dangerous."

He twirled his pen again. "There are a lot of dangerous men out there. Fathers who prey on their children, teachers who prey on their students, boyfriends who prey on their girlfriends. And we're only talking about the male of the species. Do you want to investigate them all?" He pointed the pen at her. "You can't touch him. I suggest you get new clients."

"And do nothing? Just sit around as my clients are persuaded one by one to enter his group?"

Clay tapped a beat on his desk. "What will you do when you find out more about him?" He raised a mocking brow. "Meet him and say, 'Please stop'?"

Her lips thinned. "I don't know what I'll do, but that will be my business, not yours."

He ignored her. "Unless he's taking money by deception, you have nothing." He shook his head before she could argue. "You have nothing to charge him with. You can't charge him with giving hope to the hopeless."

Jackie knew he was right, but refused to back down. "What he's doing is wrong."

"That is a matter of opinion. You can't argue opinions in court. You need facts. There's nothing you can do. Let me suggest this: when you get new clients, warn them about this man."

"I don't even know his name," Jackie said helplessly. She took off her scarf and threaded it through her fingers, agitated. "I have to know something."

"You know what he's offering and that's a start. You don't need to know his name. At this point it's not important. You have a profile. You know how he works, who he targets."

"That's just the problem," she argued. "I don't know how he operates. I don't know how he targeted Melanie. I don't know how he convinced her or what he looks like."

Clay waved his hand. "Forget about the concretes like name and features, that's irrelevant."

She threw up her hands. "Why?"

"Because it's what he does, not who he is, that is the concern. Perhaps he is just an adviser. The next question would be, does he work for someone else—a leader, perhaps?"

Her eyes widened. "You mean there could be more?"

Clay silently swore. He'd meant to put her at ease, not give her more reason to worry. "If you're talking about an occult, there will be plenty more and their job is to recruit followers and take over their lives. However, we're getting ahead of ourselves. Let's suppose for some reason an occult has decided to target people in your program. Have others talked about this man?"

"No, but most aren't as articulate as Melanie. When they want to do something they do it with no explanation. One client, Althea, just disappeared. She called to cancel services and that's the last we heard from her."

"So Melanie is the only link to this man?"

"Yes."

He lowered his eyes. "Hmm."

"What does that mean?"

Clay glanced up. "It means, hmm. It is not meant to be interpreted as anything but a noncommittal response."

Jackie frowned. "Are you this rude to other clients?"

"You're not a client."

She lifted her chin. "I don't see why not. I think you should help me find out who he is."

"And I think you're missing the big picture. Tell your clients about the possible threat and build from there."

She looked at him, appalled. "You want me to protect newcomers and leave Melanie and the others to the mercy of this lunatic?"

"They are grown women who have made a choice."

"No. A choice was made for them. Clients are like family. I have to look out for them. I need to know why he's targeting my clients and what he is after."

Clay started to get annoyed with her stubbornness. "I can't help you."

Jackie nodded. "I understand." She crossed her legs and swung her foot.

He sighed, knowing the battle had only begun. "Is there something else?"

"No."

"Then why are you still here?"

"I think you're under the misconception that I need you. You have a partner, right? Perhaps he will be willing to help me."

Clay smiled coldly, aware of the game she was playing. "Yes, I have a partner. You'll interest him. It doesn't take much to get Mack's attention. Blink your big eyes, perhaps show a little leg, and maybe you'll convince him to help you. It will be very amusing to sit back and watch you waste his time."

Her eyes flashed fire. "How dare you imply that I'm some cunning—"

"I'm not implying," he interrupted quietly. "I'm stating fact. I think you're under a misconception of your own. You think you can manipulate me."

Jackie jumped to her feet. "You're—"

"Sit down."

She glanced at the door. "No."

Clay blinked lazily. "Would you like to make a little wager on who will get there first?"

"I know you're bigger than I am, but I'm faster and I won't stay—"

"Sit down, Jackie." The words were said without anger or even an inflection in tone. The impact, however, was paralyzing. She'd never heard that tone before, chilly enough to cause frost. She realized he hadn't moved. He didn't need to. He was the type of man who could control a room with just a look. The one he sent her now made her reconsider her option.

She sat, more out of curiosity than fear. He'd never inspired fear in her. Her curiosity, however, was growing. She'd never seen this side of Clay before—patient, cold, intimidating. At that moment she knew he was good at his job. He was a natural predator. She watched him absently twirl his pen between long fingers that looked both elegant and deadly. She briefly wondered what it was like to be his prey.

"You made a mistake," he said.

"I know. I shouldn't have come here."

"No, that wasn't your mistake." He set his pen down. "I doubt this will happen again, but let me offer you a warning." He sat forward and clasped his hands together. "Never walk into my office as though you're doing me a favor, question my logic, and then threaten to undermine me by trying to use my partner instead. Unlike TV, we PIs aren't waiting around for some pretty woman to hand us a case that will then send us on a merry-go-round of events where we meet up with one-eyed men and thugs who speak with forty-fives." He held up his hand; she closed her mouth. "We don't accept every case presented to us, we may even suggest another agency or just say no for the client's sake. I know you don't like the word "no." You don't hear it very often and you take it personally." He held up his hand again; she bit her lip and drummed her fingers against the chair.

"Since I know what you don't like, let me tell you what I don't like— women who think they can use me. I don't mind being used on occasion. Especially if I'm in an indulgent mood. It's rare. I work in a business where people lie to me more often than not and try to use me for their own purposes. I choose when that is." He began to smile, knowing what an effort it was for her to keep quiet. "I admire your intent, not your approach. But I'm still saying no for all the reasons I've stated. If you wish to insult me further, my partner should be back in an hour. Are you going to wait?"

She nodded, too angry to speak.

He stood. "I'm going to the vending machine. Do you want anything?"

Jackie shook her head.

"Fine." He left the room.

He went farther than the vending machine by a few blocks, trying to walk until his temper cooled. Damn that woman! She could always make him lose his temper. He didn't know why he let her. He had trained himself to let few things bother him. A quick temper was a definite handicap in his trade. He'd learned to be analytical and calm; he wasn't very calm right now.

He shouldn't have told her about Rennie, his sister. He never talked about her to anyone. Especially not to some brat used to getting her own way. Jackie didn't interact with men, she studied them and used their weakness against them, and he'd just given her one of his. He clenched and unclenched his jaw. He wouldn't be one of those men who fell under her spell. He refused to be enchanted by those bright eyes and charming smile. Then again, she'd never really smiled at him. He shook his head, frustrated. He didn't care. He wasn't going to work with her. She could work with Mack or go elsewhere since she didn't have the sense to leave it alone. But she'd do well to stay away from him.

Nearly a half hour later he returned to the office, hoping she was gone. She wasn't. She still sat in her chair as though he'd hit the pause button when he'd left. He masked his surprise and dropped his coat over the chair. He sat behind his computer.

"I can't afford to fail," she said in a tight, little voice.

Clay glanced up. "I'm sorry?"

"I can't afford to fail. My job is all that I have to prove myself." She stood and walked to the window. "I've been bouncing from here to there all my life and HOPE is the only place where I am in charge. I have real responsibilities. I'm in charge of people's lives and I take that seriously." She turned to him with a rueful grin. "I know you think I'm spoiled, perhaps you're right. Older brothers don't give you a chance to prove yourself and nobody has ever had to depend on me." She walked over to his desk. "At HOPE people do and I will do anything in my power to make sure they are safe. Just for a while, their suffering will ease. I want to be an inspiration to them and let them see that since I have made it, so can they." She leaned on the desk and met his eyes. "I will not sit around while a nameless bastard tells my clients to give up on life, that nobody loves them except him, and to trust no one outside of his community." She took a deep, steadying breath. "I need an investigator. It doesn't have to be you or your partner. You could give me the name of another agency." She gripped her hands into fists. "Or if you don't want to do that then just tell me what to do. Show me the way. Give me the tools and put me on the right path so that I won't waste anybody's time but my own."

Clay sat back and silently swore. He hadn't expected that. A tantrum perhaps, maybe some tears or even a well-executed pout. Not such a solid, quiet conviction. Conviction was something he understood very well. It would be easier to send her away, probably smarter, too. However, no one had ever accused him of that. He looked at her earnest face, trying to convince himself that she wasn't weaving her magic on him, that he had come to the decision on his own based on a quick reassessment of the situation. "All right."

Her eyes brightened. "You'll help me?"

"Yes."

She came around the table and hugged him. "I knew it." She gave him a quick kiss on the cheek. "You scared me for a minute. But I knew you couldn't have been as heartless as you seemed." She pushed some papers aside and sat on the desk. "We're going to work well together."

He cleared his throat, trying to recover from her enthusiastic response. "Yes, well, don't get too hopeful."

"Oh, I know. You don't have to warn me twice." Jackie jumped down. "I am just so happy. I know you'll be able to find him for me."

His partner, Mack O'Donnel, came in, saving him from any reply. Mack stood five-eleven with a body made of mostly muscle and a grin that could be both beguiling and threatening. Forty-five his next birthday, he sported no gray in his thinning blond hair that kept his youthful gray eyes and smooth skin from looking too boyish. A thick, ugly pair of reading glasses stuck out of his shirt pocket. "Hello," he said in a tone he specifically used when in the presence of a pretty woman.

Clay made introductions. "This is Jackie Henson. Jackie, this is Mack O'Donnel."

They shook hands, then Mack looked at Clay, a series of questions in his eyes. Clay only answered one. "She's our new client."

***

After Jackie left, Mack clasped his hands behind his head and grinned. "So I finally got to meet Jackie, your aggravating sister-in-law." He glanced up at the ceiling. "Man, what a pair of eyes. No wonder you never described her. You can't. She's the kind of woman who could strip you naked, cuff you to the bedpost, and steal all your money and you'd thank her for the experience." His hands fell. "Too bad her case is a piece of crap, but she's willing to pay and we're willing to serve."

Clay frowned at his computer. "She's going to hate to discover there's nothing she can do."

"She's a big girl. She'll just have to accept it."

"Jackie doesn't 'just accept' things."

"In this case she'll have to."

Clay stood to get a drink. He saw something red on the ground, picked it up, and frowned. She'd left her scarf. It held her scent. Not the light and fruity scent one would associate with sprites—it was a tangy, spicy aroma like jasmine and orange blossoms, implying a mischief much more carnal than any fairy tale. He crumbled it up and sighed. "She won't."

***

Jackie glanced at her watch and swore. She was running late. Brian wouldn't like that. Brian Croft revered punctuality in all things—when his mail was delivered, when his food was served, when his date arrived. If she hadn't been thinking about Melanie and her talk with Clay, she would have paid closer attention to the time. She sat on the Metro, urging it to move faster than its regular sleep-inducing lull. She could have taken her car, but parking was dreadful in D.C., especially on a Saturday night. It was only recently she'd been able to fully indulge in D.C.'s reputable nightlife. Before, she had been too busy trying to establish herself, and her most creative date was dinner and a movie.

Fortunately, Brian had broken that pattern. He'd taken her to events at the Kennedy Center and dinner on the Potomac. He'd taught her about the finer things in life. She glanced down at her stockings and groaned when she noticed a run. Too bad she couldn't always imitate the finely dressed, coiffured women he was used to. But she would continue to try.

When she finally reached the restaurant, she was surprised to see Brian with a look of preoccupation instead of his usual harried expression. She walked toward the leather-cushioned booth, curious as to what was on his mind. The pensive gaze gave some personality to his boringly handsome, neat features and trim mustache. At times she still couldn't believe he'd been dating her for four months.

She kissed him on the cheek, then sat. "Sorry I'm late. Have you ordered yet?"

He didn't meet her eyes. "No."

"Good, then we can order together." She picked up the menu. "What are you going to choose?"

"I'm getting married."

Jackie turned the page and ran her finger down the selection of pasta. "That sounds good." She tapped her chin. "Let's see what I'll get."

He lowered the menu, forcing her to look at him. "Jackie."

"Yes?"

"I said I'm getting married."

She stared blankly. "That had better be a euphemism for something else."

"It's not."

Her gaze fell back to the menu. "I see."

"I know you're upset."

"Upset isn't the word," she muttered.

"But this is for the best. I'm sorry. You're a great woman, but Darlene and I—"

"Did you say Darlene?" she cut in, her eyes turning to stone.

He nodded.

She snapped the menu shut. "You're marrying your ex-wife?"

He glanced around to make sure no one overheard, conscious of his image. "Yes, we both realized that our divorce had been hasty. We are well suited in all the important areas. That's what counts in a relationship. You and I had fun, but—"

"I understand." She grinned bitterly. "Tom drunk, but Tom nuh fool."

He scowled. "I hate when you talk that lingo. It's common and makes no sense. What does that mean?"

"It means things are not what they seem. I know I'm not as well suited to a man hoping to establish a career in politics. I have no real connections. I'm just a Jamaican immigrant of unknown parentage." She nodded. "Yes, I understand more than you know." She took a sip of her water and glanced around the elegant atmosphere. "I also understand why you brought me here." She placed a finger on the back of his hand and drew little circles. To an outside observer, it looked like a loving gesture; Brian knew it was not. He swallowed, nervous. "It's to deter me from causing a scene. Such as throwing water on you, smashing a plate of food in your face, or even stabbing you with a fork." She patted his hand and withdrew. "You're right. I won't cause a scene."

He visibly relaxed. "I knew you wouldn't."

"No, you didn't. You just hoped so. I can be so unpredictable." She lowered her lashes. "I will be expecting an invitation in the mail."

"I'm not sure Darlene—"

Her eyes glittered. "I will be expecting an invitation in the mail for myself and a guest."

"Yes."

"Don't worry, I won't cause a scene there either. I only want to be there for this joyous occasion." She jerked her glass toward him. He jumped. "Good, you're nervous. That means you have a conscience."

"I don't think you should be too upset. We only dated casually and never even . . ." He let his words trail off, recognizing it wasn't the proper topic for a dinner conservation.

"Well, you certainly made me glad of that."

"Now, Jackie—"

"I suggest you stop talking." She opened her menu and selected an item.

"Why?"

"Because you only encourage my desire to cut out your tongue. I believe they serve tongue here. I would love to chop it into little pieces."

Brian adjusted his collar.

The waiter approached the table. "Are you ready to order?"

Jackie smiled at Brian with freezing disdain. "I hope you brought your gold card. This dinner is going to cost you."

***

Jackie spent most of Sunday morning running errands. She didn't want to be at home—she'd only end up thinking about Brian and getting angry.

Four months she'd devoted to him and he'd dumped her for a woman he'd married before. It was insulting and humiliating. By late afternoon she was finally forced to return home, and halted when she saw Clay leaving her building. She called out his name. He stopped and turned.

Jackie greeted him with a smile, oddly glad to see him. "Hi," she said. "How are you? What are you doing here?"

"I'm fine. I was just—"

"I'm glad I caught you." She raced inside the lobby, then pushed the elevator button. "I've been out all day. So do you have something about the case?" The elevator arrived. She stepped in.

He hesitated, then stepped in also. "No, not yet. Listen, I—"

Jackie shrugged. "Never mind. I know it will take time. We only met on Friday, right?" She didn't give him a chance to answer. "Yes, I should remember because Saturday was dreadful. The day was fine, but that night went to hell—but I won't bore you with the details." The elevator stopped on her floor.

Clay grabbed her arm before she got out. "I only came by to give you something."

"That's fine, I'll take it." She slipped out of his grip and went to her apartment. "But since you came all this way, you might as well come in. I'm sure you can spare a few moments." She inserted the key in the lock.

He glanced at his watch. "Not really. I—"

"Good. I could use the company." She opened the door, and flipped on the lights.

The apartment looked as though it had been ransacked.

Chapter Two

The couch cushions lay across the room, frames were shattered with glass scattered on the floor. CDs, videos, and books littered the ground, two side tables lay upside down with their legs in the air like dead cockroaches.

Clay shoved Jackie behind him with such force that she crashed against the wall. "Stay here."

"Relax." She stepped in front of him "I haven't been robbed. I did this myself. Brian and I broke up."

He surveyed the damage, stunned. "What?"

She walked over a book and picked up a cushion. "I was upset. He's marrying his ex-wife."

"Upset?" he choked. "Looks like you went mad. Did you foam at the mouth as well?"

She sent him a sly grin. "Now that you know what I'm capable of will you help me clean it up?"

"No."

"You can stay and watch, then."

He headed for the door. "No."

Jackie jumped in front of him. "I just need the company, please. You won't have to clear anything."

He sighed fiercely, then took off his jacket. "I'll stay five minutes."

She replaced the cushion on the couch. "Fine."

He crossed the small living room, briefly skidding on broken glass, then glanced out the window. "Not a bad neighborhood."

"Worried about your car?"

"Anyone who takes my car would be doing me a favor." He turned and spotted her curio in the corner. It held an assortment of glass figurines from horses to unicorns, birds to castles to fairies. His mouth kicked up in a quick grin. The touch of whimsy was very fitting.

She placed the last cushion on the couch. "The couch is back to normal. You can take a seat."

Clay did and picked up the remote. "I'm surprised you didn't kick in the TV."

Jackie came out of the kitchen with a broom and duster. "It was tempting." She swept up the glass. "Can you cook?"

He sent her a suspicious glance. "Why?"

"Because you could make lunch while I clean up."

"I only know how to cook dinner."

"What?"

"Never mind." He stood. He was a bit peckish. "I'll see what's in the kitchen."

"It's still early, perhaps we could have brunch."

Clay raised a knowing brow. "I suppose you have a preference?"

"I would love Swedish pancakes, but I'd settle for French toast."

"Wonderful," he said sarcastically. "Two meals that take no effort. You like to make a man's life easy."

"There's nothing wrong with requesting what you like. You know I'll eat whatever you make. I'll even pretend to like it if it's horrible."

Clay grunted and opened the fridge, pulling out a carton of milk.

"So why did you come over?" she asked after a few minutes.

He turned on the stove. "Because I wanted to make one big mistake this week and I thought I'd start with you."

She wagged her finger. "Be nice, little boy, or I'll tell my big brothers on you."

Clay knew it was an empty threat, but didn't want to encourage her to say anything to Drake and Eric about his coming over. "You left your scarf at my office."

"Thanks." She dumped the debris in the trash bin. "That's odd, though. I don't usually leave things. Why would I do that? I must have been more distracted than I thought."

"Or you like to make me suffer."

"It's a possibility. I enjoy annoying you."

"You can congratulate yourself on succeeding."

Jackie grinned at his playful tone and watched as he placed a bowl in the sink and turned on the faucet. The simple movement stretched the fabric of his T-shirt, emphasizing his wide shoulders. She'd never looked at Clay as a man before, just as Cassie's older brother. Now she did. She had to admit, it was a nice view. For a man past forty, he had no right to possess a body that stood over six feet with a tough, lean quality that could give a woman ideas. Not the obvious kind of ideas, something more pervasive, more deceptive, more enticing. He was interesting and that held its own kind of danger. She returned to cleaning, listening to him move about in the kitchen. After a few moments, she said with a note of surprise, "You're a very comfortable man to be around. Even though your head nearly touches the ceiling. "

He glanced up. "A gross exaggeration. I have a few inches yet."

"Well, you're a giant compared to me."

"A stool is a giant compared to you."

"Mind your manners. Some men prefer petite women."

"I know. I've met them."

"But you're not one?"

"No."

Jackie sighed. "Brian liked petite women. His ex-wife is four-eleven."

"How do you know?"

"He told me." She paused. "Come to think of it, he talked about her a lot." She chewed her lower lip. "I suppose that was a sign."

"Hmm."

"Is brunch ready?"

"In a minute."

Jackie rested her chin on the top of the broom. "So why don't you like petite women?"

"I didn't say I didn't like them. I said I didn't prefer them." He pointed to the table with his spatula. "Sit down. Brunch is ready."

She sat at the table. Clay placed a Swedish pancake with peach slices and blueberries in front of her.

She pointed. "What is this?"

He frowned. "What does it look like?"

"Swedish pancakes."

"Exactly. That's what you wanted, right?"

"Yes, but—"

"Then what's the problem?"

"Nothing, but—" She stopped, knowing she was insulting him. She'd been joking about the pancakes, but forgot that men took things literally. Fortunately, having two older brothers helped her to learn how to soothe the male ego. She crooked her finger as though she wanted to tell him a secret. He bent down.

She kissed him on the cheek. "It's wonderful, thank you."

Clay only grunted, but she knew he was mollified.

Jackie took a bite, then moaned in pleasure. "This is delicious. I am now officially your love slave."

He sat. "Have you been drinking?"

She made a face. "Leave me alone. I'm enjoying myself." She closed her eyes and wiggled in her seat. "Hmm. Absolute heaven." She pointed her fork at him. "I didn't know you could cook."

He shrugged. "I get by. Truth is, I have only seven meals I can cook really well. And I learned them all with one purpose in mind."

"What's that?"

He leaned forward and lowered his voice. "To impress women."

"And from that twinkle in your eye, my guess is you've succeeded. I should be offended, but I'm too in awe of your skill. So what are we to have to drink?"

Clay pointed. "I'm sure you have glasses in the cupboard and can find juice in the fridge."

Jackie stood. "You're supposed to supply the drink with brunch."

"I cooked. The rest is self-serve."

Jackie crossed the room, took down two glasses, then opened the fridge. "What would you like?"

"Orange juice."

"I don't have orange juice."

"What do you have?"

Jackie looked at the various containers. "Everything but."

"Grape, then."

Jackie poured the drinks then returned to her seat. "So when do you usually serve Swedish pancakes?" She handed him his glass. "Is it an after-sex treat in the morning?"

"No. They are not good after-sex food for me."

"Why not?"

"I end up eating them alone."

She stared at him. "Why?"

"Because my companion is no longer there."

"Your women leave after sex?"

"Either they do or I do. It's a mutual understanding."

Her eyes widened. "Every time? You never stay?"

He leaned back and thought for a moment. "I find that mornings tend to shine too bright a light on a relationship."

Jackie wrinkled her nose. "But that isn't a relationship if you always leave."

He took a sip of his drink. "You may have a point."

"So when do you serve Swedish pancakes?"

He lifted a brow, skeptical. "I'm not sure I should tell you."

"Why not? You don't have to impress me." She held up a hand, ready to pledge. "And I promise not to share your secrets."

Clay thought for a moment, then nodded. "First I begin with the atmosphere. Dim lights and soft music. I make sure to do all the major food preparation before she arrives. When she comes, I finish up the details, a little sautéing or grilling, so that she can see me in action. After she tells me what a delicious meal I've made, then I serve the pancakes for dessert topped with powdered sugar and strawberries. It tends to tip the scale in my favor."

"What if she doesn't want to have sex with you?"

Clay blinked. "I ply her with wine and have my way with her."

"That's awful!"

He flashed a devilish grin. "It's also not true." He returned to his food. "I don't lead women on. Most women who go out with me want to sleep with me. Let's say I give them a reason to."

"They're grateful for a good meal?"

"I have no aversion to a little gratitude. And you're missing the point. It's what the meal represents—the time and effort that she hopes will translate to other aspects of my life."

"But what about a relationship?"

Clay speared a blueberry. "What about it?"

"What if you meet a woman who wants to stay until the morning? What will you give her for breakfast?"

He scratched his chin. "I'd give her an apple and send her on her way."

Jackie nudged him with her foot. "Be serious."

"I am. Some people prepare for certain catastrophes. I will take my chances that it will never happen."

She sawed a peach slice in half. "A woman staying until morning should not be described as a catastrophe. I don't know why you would think so."

"Because a woman who stays the night will have questions in the morning."

"Questions?"

"Yes. Namely, "Where do we go from here?" or, "When can I see you again?" or my ultimate favorite, "Do you think I'm better than my sister?""His grin widened at her expression. "That was a joke."

"Not a very funny one. Your sense of humor is lost on me."

"That's because you're not a man. You can't help but see a possible relationship every time a woman and man meet. It's understandable. We need women like you out there. Otherwise we wouldn't have families. Fortunately, there are certain types of women who suit men like me."

"Commitmentphobics?"

Clay took no offense to the term. "I'm not hurting anyone and I find my situation preferable than women turning psychotic over being dumped."

"You're right," she admitted reluctantly, glancing around the room. "He wasn't worth it. But I still have hope for the future."

"As you should."

"So you believe in marriage?"

He shrugged. "Sure."

"Just not for you?"

"Not presently, no. Maybe not ever."

Jackie rested an elbow on the table and tugged on her earring. "So you don't mind being alone?"

"In my profession that's almost a necessity."

"Private investigators can marry."

"Sure they can, but can they stay married? There are long hours, things you can't share, things you don't want to." He sighed, his face becoming grim. "I doubt I'll do it much longer, though."

"Getting old?"

He sent her a quick glance. "Yes, I suppose to you I am."

"I didn't say you were old, just—"

"I know what you meant, my feelings aren't hurt. You needn't apologize for making an honest statement. I'm not sure if it's my age or that I'm getting restless."

Jackie studied him, aware of the controlled energy and vitality that belied his age. "I'd say you were restless. Are you going to eat that peach?"

He pushed his plate toward her. She ate the peach then set her utensils down. "Fruit salad."

Clay glanced at her, confused. "I'm sorry?"

"Fruit salad."

"What about it?"

"That's what you should serve the woman who stays the night."

He slowly grinned. "No woman is going to stay the night."

Jackie ignored him. "It's best to be prepared. Make it the day before so you can eat it in bed. And if she doesn't stay, it's a nice food to eat alone with yogurt."

"Why does my sex life interest you?"

"It's not your sex life that interests me. It's your after-sex life." She drummed her fingers on the table. "I just imagine some poor woman staying with you and having nothing to eat in the morning." She patted him on the hand. "Follow my advice, you won't be sorry."

"Hmm."

After eating, Jackie went back to cleaning; Clay sat on the couch watching TV. A few minutes later the phone rang. "Could you get that?" she asked.

He glanced at the phone next to him. "No, this isn't my place."

"Just pick it up, *nuh*."

"Let the machine get it."

She kissed her teeth and reached across him, purposely blocking his view of the TV, grabbed the phone, and put it to her ear. "Hello? Yes, I'm fine. I know. Uh-huh. Right. I'll see you Monday." She hung up. "That was

Faye. She wanted to know if I was okay. I told her about Melanie and she knows I'm concerned, but she doesn't know about you."

Clay stared up at her, trying to ignore that her breasts were at eye level. "I didn't ask."

"Well, I'm telling you anyway." She straightened, then looked down at her blouse. "So did you like the view?"

"There wasn't much to see."

Jackie narrowed her eyes.

"You did ask."

She folded her arms. "I know I have no breasts, but you could have pretended."

"My imagination doesn't stretch that far." He pushed her aside so he could see the TV. "Stop trying to flirt with me to make yourself feel better. You're an attractive woman. You'll find somebody else soon enough."

She picked up her duster.

A news flash came on the screen. Senator Heldon's niece Amanda, a student at George Washington University, had been missing since yesterday. They posted her fresh, lovely face on the screen. The sight of it depressed him. He turned the TV off.

Jackie noticed his grim expression. "Do you think they'll find her?"

"No."

"Why not? It's only been a day. Must you be so cynical?"

"I'm being honest. She wouldn't be the first woman to disappear in this city."

"I hope they find her."

"They probably will, with her legs missing."

Jackie picked up a pillow and hit him on the head. "You're revolting."

He tossed the pillow aside. "If they don't find her soon they'll be looking for a body. That's a fact."

"No, it's not."

"What do you think they'll find?"

"She could have gotten disoriented or kidnapped. Perhaps she'll find a way to escape and show up wandering somewhere. Why are you smiling like that?"

"It's amazing to find people who still believe in fairy tales." He glanced around the room at the fuzzy blue rug and circular purple cushy chair. He wasn't quite sure what color the couch was but it matched the reddish-blue tint of the drapes on the window. The mirrored hooks with etched designs complemented the light-up tulips on the window ledge. Her place was like nothing he'd ever seen before and it fit her completely. She was the most unfathomable thing in the room. A creation from any fairy tale. For a moment he felt like a giant who'd had the misfortune of falling into one.

Chapter Three

"I prefer my fairy tales to your book of constant purgatory," she said.

He shrugged and lifted a picture off the floor. "Is this Brian?"

"No." She shifted awkwardly. "He came with the frame."

He sent her an odd look.

"A girl can dream," she said defensively.

"But to keep—"

She rested a hand on her hip. "Do you have the latest *Playboy*?"

"No."

Her hand fell. "Oh."

He put the frame down. "*Penthouse* is better. Less airbrushing."

"Why do men have to look at naked women?"

"Why do women have to go to the toilet in pairs?"

Jackie rested the broom against the wall. "To rate men, why else?" She winked at his startled expression. "That was a joke."

He leaned back. "I think you should be relieved I like naked women. There are plenty of men who prefer *Playgirl*."

Jackie didn't reply.

He stood and set a side table to right. "So, do you cause this kind of destruction after every breakup?"

"No." She looked around the apartment. It was beginning to look normal again. "I guess Brian was the last straw. Every relationship I have ends on a sour note." She knelt down and gathered her CDs. "One guy wanted me to have cosmetic surgery, another wondered if I'd ever consider wife swapping." She held the CDs to her chest and sighed, resigned. "And then there was Josh."

He fixed the other side table. "What about Josh?"

"He liked to dress in women's clothing. Not in public, just around the house, but that turned me off."

"Yes, I can imagine."

Jackie shook her head. "No, I doubt you can. Picture coming home one day and finding your boyfriend in an orange cable-knit cardigan and fitted skirt."

Clay cleared his throat, trying to keep a straight face. "What did you say?"

"Nothing. What can you say?"

He winked. "You look lovely?"

She giggled then straightened her features. "No, I shouldn't laugh. At the time it wasn't funny. I just stared. He explained that he felt comfortable in women's clothing. I tried to make it work." She held up a hand and shook her head. "But when he wore the stretch lace top and jeans, I had to end it."

"And then there was Brian."

"Right. Who seemed ideal—respectful, good job, great personality."

Clay nodded. "Absolutely perfect except for the tiny flaw of being in love with his ex-wife."

She placed her CDs in her entertainment system.

"You're enjoying this, aren't you?"

"Very much."

"I don't think I like your sense of humor."

"I wasn't being funny. Have you ever wondered why you choose men who end up being such disappointments?"

Jackie's eyes widened in outrage. "Oh, so you're saying this is all my fault?"

"No, I'm suggesting that perhaps you're playing the same game I am."

Her voice tightened. "I don't play games."

" 'Game' is the wrong word." He thought for a moment. "Agenda. You want companionship, but you don't want the commitment."

"I want to get married someday."

Clay knelt beside her and picked up a book. "Just not yet and that's okay. However, you think you should be looking because you're getting older."

"Are you a part-time psychologist?"

He shoved the book on the shelf. "This is just a theory not a diagnosis."

"Well, you can keep your theory to yourself." She tapped her chest. "I invest a lot in my relationships. I really care for the men I go out with. I'm loyal."

He glanced down at her with a smug look. "I met Martin the wife swapper, remember? Thanksgiving dinner."

"So?"

"He was obsessed with the seventies. He talked about threesomes constantly."

"1 thought he was a trivia buff." She rested against the wall and sent him a cool look. "For a man whose idea of a relationship is making sure he has enough condoms and money for a taxi, you have nothing to say."

"You don't have to be in a relationship to give advice. Do you know how many married people smugly talk down to single people about the dating scene, then five years later—when they're newly single—have no idea what to do?"

"You still don't know what you're talking about. You have no idea how hard it is to find a normal, decent, upwardly mobile man who has to meet the Henson brothers' seal of approval."

"They want what's best for you."

She rolled her eyes. "Naturally you'd be on their side. You're as bad as they are."

"Me? What did I do?"

"Drake told me about your pre-wedding advice." She narrowed her eyes. "That you would use his intestines as a noose if he ever hurt Cassie."

Clay smiled, pleased. "I love that line."

She shook her head, defeated. "I can take care of myself and choose my own men. Drake would arrange a marriage for me if he could. He has the perfect man in his mind."

"He wants someone to take care of you."

She knew Drake couldn't help it. Her eldest brother had raised her since she was seven. Their parents died shortly after they'd emigrated from Jamaica. She would never trivialize all that he had sacrificed so she could have a better life. Unfortunately, she had yet to convince him she could make it on her own. They had come so far from poverty; she knew he had a secret fear that she would marry someone who would take her back there.

"I can take care of myself," she said.

"Then why am I here?"

"I wanted company."

He raised a brow. "You can't have it both ways."

"What?"

"You can't play the role of the independent woman and the little sister at the same time. They don't mesh. I've seen you at work with your brothers. You're very good." He glanced around the room and scowled. "Hell, you got me to stay."

She sighed. "You're right. It's a hard habit to break." She wiggled her eyebrows. "Especially when it works."

"Hmm."

They finished cleaning the apartment, then Jackie went through her mail from yesterday. Brian had dropped by and given her the wedding invitation; he hadn't wanted to spend money on a stamp. When she finally opened it, her face turned to thunder.

Clay looked at her. "What happened?"

She waved the invitation. "That bastard!"

"What?"

"Brian sent me a wedding invitation. I asked him to, but *this* was before I asked him to."

Clay stared, confused. "What?"

"That little snot was planning to marry even while he was dating me."

He grabbed her shoulders. "Calm down."

"Calm down! I should rip off his balls and serve them as hors d'oeuvres to his fiancée."

Clay winced.

She grimaced. "Yes, that is a rather disgusting image. I apologize." She took a deep breath, tightening one hand into a fist. "I am so angry."

Clay led Jackie to the couch and gently forced her to sit. "Relax. You're not going to demolish anything after we've just finished cleaning up this place."

Jackie shook the letter. "Not only did he insult me, he's mocking me." She pounded the couch.

Clay sat beside her. "Perhaps he wants to show he has no hard feelings."

"*He* has no hard feelings?"

"I'm hazarding a guess." He shook his head helplessly. "I don't know. Just tear up the invitation and forget about it."

"Do you know when the wedding is scheduled?" She didn't give him a chance to answer. "This Saturday. Do you know how long it takes to schedule a wedding?"

Clay looked at her blankly.

"At least ten months."

He snatched the invitation and tossed it aside. "It could be a simple wedding. Weddings in Las Vegas take no planning at all."

"This isn't being held in Las Vegas," she said through clenched teeth.

"You've discovered the man's an ass. Consider yourself lucky."

She tapped her finger against her chin as a thought came to her. "This weekend, huh? I bet he doesn't expect me to show up."

"And you don't plan to go, so everything's settled."

She sent him a sly glance. "You realize he's offered me a challenge."

"What?"

"This means war." She picked up the invitation and studied its rose and ribbon design. " I will go."

"Why?"

"To show I have no hard feelings."

Clay scratched his head, confused. "You just said you wanted to rip his—"

She made a dismissive gesture. "Yes, I know, but he doesn't need to know that. I'll be gracious and show that I'm above him."

He sat back and stretched his legs out. "That's up to you."

"Of course, I'll need a date. Someone sophisticated, suave, preferably rich. But then again, he would expect that." She rested her elbows on her knees and drummed her fingers together. "I could go with the complete opposite. A man with an interesting career, a bit intimidating and little rough, uncouth but presentable." She leaned back and folded her arms. "But where could I find a guy like that on such short notice?" She slowly turned to him.

Clay stiffened. "No."

"Come on," she urged. "It's just one night."

"No."

She straightened. "All you'd have to do is wear a tuxedo for a few hours, dance with me, then leave."

"No."

"Why not?"

Clay's eyebrows shot up. "Do I need a reason?"

"Yes."

"Not only is your plan juvenile, asinine, and deceitful, it would be a complete waste of my time."

"Do you know the type of women who attend weddings? Lonely women—"

"Who want to shackle the first single man they see."

"Substitute 'shackle' for 'shag' and you'll be right."

"I'm not in short supply of women." He stood and grabbed his jacket. "And presently I've had my fill."

"Just one night. Please." She jumped to her feet. "I'll make it worth your while."

He paused. "How?"

"You tell me."

He grinned maliciously and opened the door. "Perhaps I will," he said, then left.

***

On Monday, Jackie darted through the spring drizzle of a cool rain that slickened streets and accentuated the mingled scent of blossoming trees and car fumes. The swish of wipers and honking horns filled the air, while umbrellas knocked against each other as people raced to work. She rushed into the lobby of her office building and nearly opted to stand outside when she saw William Chavis, an accountant who bored her with his smile and constant attention. She tried to hurry past him and make it up the stairs before he saw her. She failed.

"Jackie," he said, blocking her path.

She offered a brief smile and tried to move around him. "I'm in a hurry."

"This is a quick question. The Cherry Blossom Festival is coming up. Would you like to walk with me along the Tidal Basin?"

Sure, to push you in. "I'm very busy right now." She shook her umbrella, getting water drops on his shoes. "Sorry, excuse me." She dashed into an elevator and sighed with relief. A few moments later, she entered the airless three-room office of HOPE Services, a nonprofit organization that fed homebound people and helped others reenter the workforce. She hoped that in a few years the company would own an entire floor and be nationally recognized. Right now she was content with a job as vice president in charge of finances. It was a step up from coordinator at another nonprofit organization that helped young people with employment. In two years she'd be thirty-five. By then she hoped to develop a program so large and profitable that grant funding would become unnecessary. She knew it was a lofty goal but she was determined.

"Did you have a good weekend?" Patty Jayson asked as Jackie came through the door. She wore a short, curly red wig that complemented her honey skin and brown eyes, but looked oddly out of fashion for a woman of fifty-seven.

Jackie hung up her jacket and umbrella. "I discovered my boyfriend is getting married."

"Is he good-looking?"

Jackie checked her in-box. "Would it hurt your feelings if I ignored you?"

"If he's ugly, who cares? I just think you should look on the bright side of things. Especially now."

She glanced up from her letters. "Why especially?"

"I suppose the news can wait."

"What news?"

Faye Radcliff came out of her back office with the panicked look of a workaholic in crisis. Her conservative gray dress made her look older than her thirty-eight years. Reddish-brown hair fell around her slightly flushed pale skin. "Have you told her?" she asked Patty in her smooth, husky tone.

Patty shook her head. "No."

Jackie's gaze darted between them. "Told me what?" Her shoulders drooped. "Is it bad? Did another client cancel services?"

Faye leaned against Patty's desk. "No, it's worse."

"What could be worse?"

Patty waved her hand. "You're going to wish you didn't ask that."

Faye sighed. "You know Mr. Everton Hamlick, our generous funder? The man who said he'd support us for the rest of his life?"

Jackie nodded with mounting dread. "Yes?"

"His life ended yesterday."

Chapter Four

Jackie fell against the wall. "Somebody killed him?"

Faye shook her head. "No, he dropped dead. He was waving to the mail carrier, then toppled over. And since he has such a nice, close-knit, and loving family," she drawled in a sarcastic tone, "they all swooped in and immediately cut the funds to all his charitable organizations. His recent donation is all we'll ever see." She sighed. "I told him we should have had something in writing."

"The guy was sweet. Unfortunately, he refused to see that not everyone thinks and cares about things the way he does. Or did." Jackie frowned. She hated having to refer to him in the past tense. Mr. Hamlick had become an integral part of their little group and it wasn't only because of his financial help. An older white man with wispy gray hair, he'd always been superbly dressed, with piercing hazel eyes and a booming laugh that shook his lanky frame. She'd miss him.

"It made him unique, but vulnerable. The funeral is next Saturday. Do you want to go?"

Jackie made a face. "And see those vultures? No, thank you."

"Perhaps if they see us, see how much he meant to us and the people we help, they may be persuaded to continue his legacy."

Patty rolled her eyes. "Oh, please. Rich people like that only care about themselves. I wouldn't be surprised if they didn't kill him off."

Faye frowned. "Don't be disgusting."

"I'm not. You're always hearing stories like that—sons killing their mothers, daughters pushing their fathers down the stairs or hiring hit men."

"The man was seventy-six years old. He died of natural causes."

"My dad's ninety and still has a few years left." Patty wagged her finger. "You know there are drugs out there that can make a death look natural." She adjusted her hair. "I know, I read."

Faye opened her mouth; Jackie shook her head in warning. Getting into an argument with Patty could last all morning. Jackie said, "The fact is he's dead and our present grant will never be able to cover all our expenses."

Faye nodded. "We can struggle by for a few months, but after that we'll have to greatly reduce our services."

Jackie pushed herself from the wall. "No, we can't do that. People depend on us."

"What else can we do? Our best plan of action is to meet his family."

"A funeral is a tacky place to ask for money." Jackie affected a wide grin and held out her hand. "Hi, sorry for your loss, but we want your money. Can you write a check?"

Faye scowled. "I wasn't going to ask there. I'd meet with them, then call them later. There must be a bleeding heart in the family."

"You're assuming they have hearts," Patty muttered. "The rich can afford not to."

"What do you have against rich people?"

"I envy the fact that I'm not one." She rested her elbows on the desk and leaned forward. "Do you know what I would do if I had money?"

"Besides generously donating to us?"

Patty waved a dismissive hand. "Yeah, yeah, whatever. If I had money I'd"—she wiggled in her seat and winked—"you know."

Faye and Jackie looked at her blankly. Jackie said, "No, we don't know."

"I'd get everything done." She gestured to the ceiling, then the floor. "Head-to-toe makeover."

Faye folded her arms. "You don't need it. You look fine."

"In a few years time, 'fine' will be the new ugly. By then everyone will have had something done."

"I certainly hope not. Imagine a world of porcelain veneers and silicone butts. That would be a scary world."

"Not if everyone is doing it."

Jackie cleared her throat. "I'm sorry to have to redirect this thrilling and socially essential conversation for more mundane matters, but we need money."

Patty nodded. "See? And if I were prettier, I could get a rich man and help you out. You two should seriously consider that. Men like to help beautiful women."

"I think we're attractive," Faye said.

"You're pretty." She looked at Jackie. "And you're cute. It's not the same. Now if—"

Jackie interrupted her. "Yes, thank you, Patty. But since we don't plan on getting anything done, we need to think of something else."

Faye said, "The funeral is worth a try." She caught Jackie's frown. "Unless you have another idea."

Jackie tapped her chin, pensive. Suddenly, an impish grin spread on her face. She snapped her fingers. "What about that man who used to fund us when Latisha was here?"

Latisha Robins had developed HOPE Services. After seven years as president, she had suddenly resigned, stating family obligations.

"There were a lot of men when Latisha was here," Faye said, too well bred to let complete disdain color her words.

Jackie ignored the implication. "I think his name was Wallace or Wynon or—"

"Mr. Winstead?"

"Yes. He used to be one of the biggest donors. Why did he stop?"

Faye shrugged. "I don't know. She never explained. She left leaving a lot of unanswered questions."

"Perhaps I could persuade him to reinvest."

Faye bit her lower lip, hesitant. "I don't know. Latisha had a certain way of doing business. A bit ruthless, but it suited her."

Jackie waved her hand, unconcerned. "That's fine. We all have our gifts. I'm in charge of funding and I plan to solve this problem. Patty, get me his number, please."

"Are you sure?" Faye asked as Patty searched the database.

"No, I'm not sure, but it's an option. HOPE has grown and those that want to get-their names seen can use this opportunity. At least that's how I'll present it to those who can't just contribute out of the kindness of their hearts."

"Got it!" Patty said.

Jackie wrote down the number, then disappeared into her office. A half hour later, she came out of her office smiling. "I scheduled an appointment with Mr. Winstead."

"Great." Faye smiled, but it didn't reach her eyes.

***

Clay usually didn't mind Monday mornings. This Monday was an exception. The day seemed extra wet and the rush-hour traffic extra congested. Sunday night had been a sleepless one. He'd kept thinking about Jackie. Thinking about her eating Swedish pancakes wearing nothing but a red scarf. That wasn't like him and it was an annoying change.

He entered Hodder Investigations in anything but a good mood, briefly muttering a greeting to Brent Holliday, their part-time secretary, a college graduate with shaggy black hair and green eyes who'd learned early on that PI work was more tedious than he'd thought.

Clay walked into the main office, where Mack greeted him with a big grin he couldn't return. Mack had been wearing that same expression when they'd met years ago in a church. Clay wasn't a religious man, but found comfort in the quiet of the various churches the city provided. He'd been staring at the row of candles on the altar when he saw Mack. He had never seen a guy look so happy leaving confession. Curious, Clay followed him and asked him why. They started talking and had an instant affinity. Mack had been a police officer who was tired of the bureaucracy and at a crossroads in his career. He wondered if he should try for detective or leave the force and work on his own.

Clay understood the dilemma. He had worked with an investigating firm in New Jersey when a case brought him to D.C. After reconnecting with his sister, he'd decided to stay. At the time he'd met Mack he had been working for an insurance-fraud firm. They decided to work together after two drinks at a bar. Fortunately, both were sober enough not to regret the decision.

Mack instantly took to Clay's quick eye and blunt honesty; Clay appreciated Mack's grim police humor and cunning mind. They'd worked together three years now At times Clay wondered how much longer they would continue to do so.

He hung up his jacket, his eyes sweeping the familiar surroundings with little interest. White walls covered the rectangular-shaped room and a large poster of a silhouette of a man in a trench coat hung on the far wall. Mack had a fondness for old PI movies. Presently, he sat at his desk with his legs on the table, staring at his laptop. He was a morning person. Clay learned not to hold that against him. He tossed his keys on the desk, an old pine desk, where one disgruntled worker had carved 'This is hell'. At times, depending on the case, he agreed.

"So, I take it you had a bad weekend?" Mack asked, resting his laptop on the desk.

Clay ran a hand down his face and grunted. "Yeah." He went to the coffee machine and emptied out the pot. It was a daily routine. Mack made coffee. Clay threw it out then made his own. Neither complained. They both knew Mack's coffee tasted like tar.

After fixing his coffee, Clay sat, took a long swallow, then began to feel human again.

Brent entered the room, tapping a file against his palm. "Evans still hasn't paid."

Clay glanced at his watch then held out his hand. "Get him on the phone for me in an hour. I need to schedule a meeting."

Brent's eyes widened with excitement as he handed him the file. "Are you going to rough him up?"

Mack shook his head. "He doesn't have to. Clay walks into a room and suddenly the money appears."

Brent's excitement died. "Oh."

Mack watched Brent leave, then rested his elbows on his chair. He grimaced. "So how bad was your weekend?"

"Bad enough. What does that have to do with anything?"

"I could wait a couple hours before telling you about another case."

Clay tapped his mug impatiently "Tell me now."

"Milton called again."

Clay's tapping increased. "And you turned him down."

Mack shrugged.

Clay's expression darkened. "I thought I told you to double his fee," he said softly.

"I did. He's willing to pay."

"Then you should have said no. He's wasting his money."

"That's not our problem."

"He's wasting our time."

"He's making it worthwhile." He grinned. "If we were really mercenary we could just follow his wife around town and do nothing else."

Clay turned on his computer. "But we're not mercenary."

Mack looked disappointed. "Really?"

"Yes." Clay sat back in his chair. "Explain something to me."

"Ask away."

"How much evidence does a guy need that his wife is cheating on him? What level of denial can explain all the footage away?"

"I think he gets off on them."

His eyes turned cold. "What?"

Mack held up his hands. "It's just a theory."

"That makes a lot of sense. What else could he be doing with those pictures?"

Both men were quiet a moment as they pondered the many uses of the evidence they'd provided. Clay swore. "We're contributing to some guy's fetish? I knew there was something weird about him."

"We don't know that."

"Nearly a year of evidence? Something's going on here. That's way past curiosity or even denial. Did he explain why he wanted us to do it?"

"Same excuse: he wants to 'make sure.'"

"He wants to make sure," Clay repeated with disgust. "Does he want us to give him a room key or perhaps bring back some used condoms?"

"Clay, I don't see why you're upset. This is easy money. Who cares the reason why? You get too involved."

"I don't like when people do foolish things."

"Then you're in the wrong business."

Clay entered his password into the computer. "Perhaps, because I'm the biggest fool of all."

Mack stood and leaned against Clay's desk. He began to grin. "All right. Who is she?"

Clay scowled. "I don't know. What are you talking about?"

"Only a woman can tie you up like this. I should know." He sighed with regret. "It's over with me and Verona."

"She didn't like you seeing Patrice on the side?" Clay said in a dry tone. "Silly woman."

Mack ignored his sarcasm. He tapped him on the shoulder. "You know what? Women should be taught how to share."

"They don't mind sharing if they're told that's what they're doing. You shouldn't let women think you're dating them exclusively."

"Why not? You get more devotion that way."

Clay shook his head, amazed at his partner's logic. "Perhaps you should get married again. Cheating never got you into too much trouble."

"Yeah, imagine that." He folded his arms in bewilderment. "Ten years of marriage, four with my mistress, and my wife divorces me because I don't want to have another kid."

"So how is Megan?"

"Greatest kid on the planet."

"That *kid* is twenty."

"She'll always be a kid to me. Her mother wasn't such a bad woman."

"Which is why you treated her with such respect."

Mack took no offense used to the subtle jabs. "What else is a wife for, but to cheat on? Once women become mothers you can't do certain stuff with them. It seems wrong. Why are you smiling?"

"It's always interesting to hear people justify bad behavior."

"You've never been married."

Clay raised a brow. "Never been divorced either. What's your point?" Since he didn't have one, he let his arms fall. "I did love her, but—"

"Not enough."

"No, that's not it. I think I was just selfish."

"You're going to pay eventually."

"Yeah, I do pay sometimes. Most times I don't have to. . ." He stopped at Clay's expression. "Oh, you mean a different kind of pay."

Clay pointed three fingers in the shape of a gun. "Yes, and you'd better not get caught—"

"Don't worry, that was back when I was a cop."

Clay couldn't help a grin. "That's a relief."

Mack winked. "I was doing my job, buddy. Getting them off the streets."

Clay shook his head.

"So why do you think I'll pay?"

"You have a daughter, yet you're every father's nightmare."

"Hey, if a guy like me comes into my kid's life, I'll be able to spot him."

"And that will be the one guy she wants to marry."

Mack narrowed his eyes. "Are you offering a future scenario or a wish?"

"I'm just saying you can't keep this up."

"Hmm. I wonder . . ." He stopped, then suddenly punched his palm. "Damn it, Clay! I hate when you do that."

Clay lifted a mocking brow. "Do what?"

"Get me to start talking about myself."

"You seem to like the subject."

"What happened this weekend? And if you don't tell me, I'll investigate and find out. It's Jackie, isn't it? You're worried about the case."

"I'm not worried about the case, but it does concern Jackie. She wants to take me to her ex-boyfriend's wedding."

Mack stared, waiting for more. When nothing else came, he shrugged. "So? Go."

"Did you miss the part about this being her ex-boyfriend's wedding? She wants to take me to prove that she's over him or something equally absurd."

Mack shrugged again. "Yes, I heard you the first time. I don't understand the problem."

Clay covered his eyes and groaned. "Oh, god, it's happening."

"What?"

"Everyone else in the world is crazy, except me."

"Your problem is you're not seeing this in the right light. Do you know what kind of women there are at weddings?"

"Don't start. She presented me with that same argument. It didn't work then." He sat back in his chair. "I'd suggest she take you, except I wouldn't want you within twenty miles of any women I know."

Mack rested a hand over his heart. "You wound me."

"You'll recover." Clay leaned forward, reading something on his computer. "I think we're closing in on the Tanya case."

Mack wasn't ready to talk about work yet. "I once met this bridesmaid." He briefly shut his eyes, a smile on his face. "What a night. Did I ever tell you about the bridesmaid at my sister's wedding?"

"Many times."

"And it bears repeating." He held his hands out, cupping the air. "I mean, this woman—"

Clay shot him a cold glance, his patience fading. Mack stopped, recognizing the warning. He cleared his throat and switched topics. "So basically Jackie is still driving you crazy."

"She doesn't drive me crazy."

"After every holiday and family gathering, that's the only name I hear."

"Possibly because she's the only single female there. Your subconscious blocks out the rest."

Mack thought for a moment, then shook his head. "No, that's not it. I think it's because you're interested."

Clay finished his coffee.

"Take her to the wedding."

Clay leaned back in his chair and bit his lower lip, thoughtful. "You're absolutely right. I should chuck all common sense and go along with a shallow, childish deception for a few hours of my life that I will never recapture again. Thank you for making that clear to me."

Mack patted him on the back. "That's the spirit." He sat at his desk. "I'm impressed how you Brits make sarcasm an art form. We Yanks catch it more often than you think."

"How amusing."

Mack sent him a look, unsure whether he was jesting or not. "Gabriella's parents paid us, by the way. They dropped by after you'd left Friday."

Clay hit the PRINT icon on his computer. "You can keep my half."

He sighed. "You couldn't have saved her."

That fact still tore at Clay. It had been a case he'd wished they hadn't taken in the first place. Most PIs got odd cases. Theirs was Gabriella Anderson, a young woman raised a Catholic on Boston's South Side, who'd ended up homeless. She'd received a degree in museum studies and a masters in anthropology. Her family had paid them to check on her every week. See that she was still alive. That was all. He'd wanted to do more and had gotten too close in the process. He'd wanted to get her off the streets. Get her safe. He'd failed.

At quiet moments he could still hear the thrilling sound of her voice, more eloquent than her haggard appearance would suggest. He could remember the expression in her eyes—a color between brown and gray— full of a knowledge about a life few people would admit to. He'd gained that same knowledge as a teenage runaway. She would have turned twenty-nine in three months if she hadn't been found dead in a street alley. It wasn't supposed to end that way. He couldn't get the *what ifs* to stop. He almost welcomed them as ready punishment.

"Let it go," Mack urged. "Take the money. You worked for it."

"She had her whole life ahead of her. She had a master's—"

"Yeah, and she also had a nervous breakdown at twenty-six and continued to spiral down until her family had given up on her. Stick with the facts. We're not in the job of storytelling or of making happy endings. If you want your insides ripped out, start caring too much. I know it's your instinct that gets cases solved,-but be careful not to get too involved. She made choices."

So had he, the wrong one. It wasn't the first time. He'd put Cassie's life in danger by underestimating a predator's affections. The decision to wait so long before interfering still haunted him; he hadn't been focused then. He'd been worrying so much about her relationship with Drake that his real target nearly succeeded.

"You're good," Mack said. "You don't give yourself credit. If you're not careful, you'll burn out."

Clay rubbed the back of his neck. "I think I'm already burned out."

"You had a bad weekend. You're just tired." Mack changed the subject, "Tell me about Tanya."

Clay nodded, relieved to focus on work. "Vincent thinks he saw her in Germantown. At least she's still in the metropolitan area." Tanya was the daughter of a prominent family who'd disappeared with her boyfriend a week ago. It wasn't her first time. At fourteen she'd run off with a teacher. At seventeen she'd at least run off with a guy closer in age, but with the misfortune of having a ten-page rap sheet. He stood. "I'm going to Dupont Circle to talk to him."

Brent came into the room. "I have Evans on the phone," he said with pride.

Clay didn't readily reply. When he did, his tone was without inflection. "Why?"

Brent suddenly looked unsure. "I thought you said you wanted to meet him in an hour."

"No," Clay said patiently. "I said get him on the phone for me in an hour."

"Oh. Well, he's on the phone now."

Clay waited.

"Uh . . . what should I say?"

Clay sighed. "Check my schedule and make an appointment. Better yet, tell him to pay or I'll have to meet with him and I won't be happy."

Brent nodded. "Okay."

"Write that down."

He grinned, pleased. "That's all right. I heard what ..." His words trailed off at the look on Clay's face. He grabbed a pad and wrote down the message. Once Clay looked it over he left.

Mack shook his head. "You realize that kid's an idiot."

"He's not an idiot. He's still learning."

"You'd think a college graduate would know how to think."

"You hired him."

"Yeah?" Mack frowned, remembering his mistake. "He seemed bright and interested. Felt like a good idea at the time. Now I'm not so sure. Let's fire him and get ourselves a coed. Preferably one with a nice—"

"No. He'll learn his way around soon enough." Brent had made a few errors, but Clay was certain that with the right guidance Brent would make a fine investigator.

"Before you leave, I have one more piece of advice."

Clay slid into his jacket. "What?"

"Take her to the wedding."

***

Dupont Circle was an area of lively entertainment and impromptu rallies that would descend down Connecticut Avenue and gain momentum. A neighborhood of galleries, unique stores, and nonprofit organizations, it held its own particular charm. Clay walked down the sidewalk filled with all types of people as the scent of international dishes floated through restaurant windows. Gabriella had called a side street home. As the only woman for blocks, she had been the sole source of people's sympathies and disdain. He briefly stopped at the empty place where she had lived, welcoming the pain of her death.

Loss and death had been a constant shadow over his life. Pain had become a familiar companion—he wasn't sure if he would feel completely alive without it. Clay turned and continued walking, stopping briefly when he saw a homeless man. He dropped five dollars in his cup, waved away the "God bless you," and continued to his destination. Clay had no illusion that the guy could own a home in the wealthy Potomac area and make a living off suckers like him, but it was a habit. One that reminded him of the days he had desperately wished someone would have handed him some money.

An hour later, he left the restaurant brooding about the information Vincent had given him. It wasn't going to take him far, but it was better than nothing. And he could assure Tanya's parents when they called. He shoved his hands in his pockets as he walked past a bridal shop, and thought about Jackie's crazy scheme. She probably would convince some poor git to take her to the wedding. He softly swore, then shrugged. It might as well be him.

***

Jackie went through her closet, searching for something to wear for tomorrow. She knew she couldn't match Faye's elegant style, but she did her best to look professional. Since she'd grown up with only two brothers to guide her, she'd never had the benefit of a sister or mother to emulate. She would wear jeans all the time if she could get away with it, but also knew the importance of projecting the right image. Jackie grabbed a maroon blouse. It reminded her of her third date with Brian—he'd taken her on a boat luncheon and she'd wanted to look casual but elegant. She tossed it aside. Brian was getting married and she had to find a date for the wedding. She couldn't let him think she was someone he could use. She'd show him she could attract other men. Clay was right—it was juvenile, but she wasn't above being a tad immature. The phone rang. "Hello?"

"You're looking for me, aren't you?" The voice was cool in its delivery and precise in its intention. It scared her.

"Who is this?"

"I could give you careless rapture. Do you believe in that? No, not yet, but you will. Don't worry, I'll keep in touch."

He hung up before she could reply. Jackie put the phone down, then rubbed the goosebumps on her arms. Her first instinct was to label him as some pervert. But she knew otherwise. He was the man she was looking for. Melanie's man. And he knew more than she'd suspected. Naturally, the number was blocked. He wouldn't be that stupid. She paced. Had he meant to scare her or warn her? Or perhaps persuade her? But the call hadn't sounded spiritual. She stopped pacing and frowned. He wanted to give her "careless rapture"? It sounded like some disgusting sexual act. He was probably a nut. She jumped when the phone rang again. Instead of fear, she felt anger.

"What do you want?" she demanded.

"I'll take you," Clay said.

"You'll take me? Take some lessons in obscene phone calls, you pervert."

He groaned. "Jackie, its Clay."

Jackie fell onto the bed, relieved. "Oh, sorry. I didn't recognize your voice. You should have said that first."

"Yes. So, if you still want to go to the wedding, I'll take you."

She pumped the air with her fist, but kept her voice level. "That's great. Thank you. You won't regret this."

"I doubt that." He paused. "Did Brian call you?"

"No."

"Why?"

"You sounded scared when you picked up the phone."

"I wasn't scared, I was angry."

"Why?"

Jackie hesitated. "A man called me. He asked if I was looking for him. He said he could give me careless rapture. Sounds disgusting doesn't it?"

"You mean, does it sound like our invisible man or a pervert?"

She sighed, relieved that he understood and didn't make fun. "Yes."

"I'm not sure. Tell me if he calls again."

"I will." She stood, feeling more relaxed. "Now, about the wedding." She gave him instructions, then said, "Be prompt. It's a late afternoon wedding. I don't want to be tardy."

"I won't be late."

Chapter Five

Of course he was late. Twenty minutes, to be exact. Jackie checked her watch again, then continued to pace her living room. When she saw him, she would strangle him or, better yet, use his, sleeves as a garrote. He was ruining her entire plan. If they arrived late, she'd bring more attention to herself. Having a giant like Clay as her escort it was hard to "slip in" anywhere. She had wanted to appear composed, refined, as though she was like all the other guests who had received the invitation months ago. Not as the perpetually late ex-girlfriend Brian had dumped a week ago.

Jackie checked her hair for the third time. It was pulled up in a bun and clasped by a silk flower with a sterling-silver center. She adjusted her moss-green gown then reapplied her lipstick. She checked her watch again. Yep, it was decided. She would kill him.

When someone knocked, she stormed to the door and swung it open. She stared at the man standing there and took a hasty step back as though she'd received a strategic blow. In a way, she had. Clay stood there looking devilishly sexy in a tux with a little yellow and blue budgie on his shoulder.

She pointed. "What is that?"

"It's a bird."

"I can see it's a bird. Why is it there?"

"It won't leave me alone." Clay glanced at the bird who was preening its feathers. "I tried to get rid of it, but it kept coming back." He looked at her. "Reminded me of someone."

She opened the door wider. "Can't imagine who."

"It's probably a pet bird that's lost or escaped from a pet shop. You don't see birds like this flying wild."

"Poor little thing. It has probably mistaken you for a tree."

"Yes, well, she's why I'm late."

Jackie stepped closer, peering at the bird for any telling signs. "How do you know it's a she?"

"Just a hunch."

"We can't take her to the wedding." She rested her hip against the door and narrowed her eyes. "Although if you wore a black eye patch you would make a convincing pirate."

He ignored her and grabbed something hidden from view.

"You bought a cage," she said as he walked in and shut the door.

"I'm leaving her here until we get back."

"You're just a big softy. Oh, look, you bought toys and everything."

Clay set the cage on the table. "Don't you need to finish getting ready?"

"I am ready. I've been waiting for you."

He glanced at her feet. "You plan to go barefoot?"

Jackie looked down, chagrined. She'd been so upset and busy pacing she'd forgotten that tiny detail. "Oh, right." She went to the bedroom and slipped on her shoes. When she came back she found Clay sitting at the table. The bird still sat on his shoulder.

He said, "Go on then, into the cage."

The bird bobbed left to right, but stayed in place. "You're planning to make my life more difficult. Wouldn't be unusual for a female."

Jackie placed a hand on her hip. "Is that right?"

"Excuse me, but this is a private conversation."

"Between you and your bird?"

He laughed. "Me and my bird. Good one."

"What?"

"You know bird means woman, yeah? Guy's got a bird?" He saw her confused expression and shook his head. "Never mind."

"British humor."

"I've been out of England going on over twenty years."

"You're still British."

"Only to you. When I'm there I'm definitely a Yank."

She sat beside him. "I know what you mean. I couldn't go to Jamaica and fit in although I was born there."

"A couple of displaced persons."

Jackie smiled. Usually the thought made her feel odd, different. But Clay's acceptance of it made her feel okay. "Yes." She looked at the bird. "So are you going to convince her to go in or not?"

"She needs a little gentle persuasion." He picked up the bird and stroked its head, then put his hand in the cage. The bird jumped down and waddled about. Clay nodded, pleased. "Good girl." He stood. The bird began to bob up and down, agitated. "I'll be right back." He looked around for something to cover the cage and stopped when he saw Jackie. "What are you grinning at?"

She shrugged innocently. "Nothing."

"Do you have a towel?"

Jackie retrieved a towel and covered the cage. "Let's go before Harriet misses you."

"You're not calling my bird Harriet."

"What would you prefer?"

"Laura."

"That's a silly name for a bird."

"That's what I'll call her until she flies away."

"How do you know she will?"

"She flew away from her first place, she'll do so again."- He pulled something out of his pocket. "I got you this." He slipped a bracelet on her wrist, his hands brushing against her skin with surprising tenderness. She would have expected such large hands to be clumsy, not gentle. It shouldn't matter of course, since he was all wrong for her. "It's not much," he said, "but it's part of the image of us being a couple." He met her eyes, concerned. "You're shaking."

He was dreadfully wrong, completely wrong, sinfully wrong, she reminded herself as her eyes drank him in. "I'm ready."

"I was hoping you'd changed your mind."

"And waste a perfectly good dress?" She grabbed her purse. "I don't think so."

They arrived at the church just in time for the ceremony. Jackie sat next to Clay, trying to ignore the scent of his cologne that made her think of the woodsy fragrance of a forest in autumn. Brief flashes of them lying naked among the leaves filled her mind as she thought of his gentle hands all over her. She pinched herself, forcing her mind to focus. She couldn't entertain such fantastic thoughts about him. Anyone else but him. She sat stiffly, determined not to touch him. If she didn't, she'd be okay.

The cathedral echoed with the melodious sound of a pipe organ while blossoming spring flowers scented the air. The late afternoon sun seeped through the stained-glass windows, casting strips of green, yellow, and red light on the wooden pews and well-dressed guests.

An elderly woman in an orange pinwheel hat and eyes full of wonder turned around to them. She asked, "Oh, isn't it a beautiful church? I'm sure it will be a perfect wedding."

"It should be," Jackie said. "They've had the practice." Clay nudged her. The woman smiled as though Jackie had said something fascinating then looked toward the front.

Jackie toyed with the pearls on her wrist.

"They're not real," he grumbled.

"I know that."

Clay shifted in his seat. He'd been fidgeting since they'd sat down; it wasn't like him and it annoyed her. Every time he moved it enhanced his cologne and his arm brushed against hers. "Can't you keep still?"

He slanted his eyes and glanced her way, but said nothing.

"You needn't look so bored."

"I detest weddings."

She stared at him, amazed. "Why?"

"They're all alike. Except for Cassie's nice, simple wedding, and Eric's justice of the peace. The rest have no imagination."

"What do you mean by that?"

"The ceremony will last more than an hour. Why? I don't know, but it will. Someone will sing 'The Wedding Song' or 'Let's Stay Together,' the pastor will drone on about 'Love is kind, love is whatever,' then a baby will start crying during the exchange of the vows and the mother will ineffectively, but loudly, try to shush it."

"I'm sure it won't be like that."

He glanced at his watch. "*If* they'd get started they could prove me wrong."

Soon the procession began. A singer stood and sang "Let's Stay Together." Jackie refused to look at Clay. Later the bride, dressed in a beaded gown with satin white gloves, descended down the aisle.. The pastor greeted everyone then began I Corinthians' "Love is." Jackie bit her lower lip to keep from laughing. She succeeded until a baby began to cry. Clay nudged her. She covered her mouth and laughed harder. Two women turned, offering stem looks.

"She's overwhelmed," Clay explained, hoping they would mistake her laughter for tears. Jackie closed her eyes. The two women nodded in understanding; their own handkerchiefs handy for such an occasion. He seized her arm and stood. "Excuse us." He whisked her outside then let her go, shoving his hands in his pockets and glancing at a passing Volkswagen. Jackie rested against the railing. After a moment, they glanced at each other, then burst into laughter.

"I can't go back inside," Jackie gasped. "Oh, god, when the guy started singing."

"How about the pastor?" Clay pretended to hold a Bible and said in a formal tone, "'Love is patient, love is kind. It does not envy, it does not boast, it is not proud.'"

Jackie covered her mouth in mock honor. "Dare you mock these sacred words?"

Clay looked down his nose. "I do not mock, my dear. I merely wish people would choose another damn verse. I believe God himself must roll his eyes, thinking, 'Not again.'"

"We're not being kind."

He nodded. "I rather like it."

"What can we do now?"

"Let's go for a walk."

"We have to be back for the send-off."

"Why? To throw stones?"

She playfully pushed him. "You're being mean."

"He is your ex-boyfriend."

A wicked grin spread on her face. "Perhaps tiny pebbles then."

Under a canopy of trees cringing against the wind of an uncommonly balmy day, they walked up the street toward the main road. When they reached the road, they spotted a food cart. Without words they headed toward it.

"What would you like?" asked the vendor, a big man with a bigger smile.

"Mike and Ikes," they said in unison.

He checked his supply, then said, "Sorry, only have one left."

Clay turned to her. "So what are you going to get?"

She narrowed her eyes. "There are words for men like you."

"Come on, little girl. Don't waste the man's time."

For the first time she bristled at the reference. He'd called her little girl before, but this time it vexed her. She wanted him to see her otherwise. She asked for Skittles. Clay paid, then they headed back to the church. Once there, Clay peeked inside and saw that the ceremony was still going. They sat on the top step. Jackie watched shadows drift on the ground and squirrels sprint across the street and under cars. Clay handed her the box of Mike and Ikes. "You can finish it."

She grasped her chest. "Oh, my goodness. You do have manners."

Clay grinned. "No, I just want some of your Skittles."

She sent him a look, then traded candy.

"So if you were to get married, what would your wedding be like?" she asked.

He leaned back on his elbows. "Well, I'd have them play 'The Wedding Song' and then—"

She hit him. "Be serious."

"I don't know. Something quick. Get the deed done and go on with my life."

"Me, too."

He looked at her, surprised. "Really? I thought women liked big affairs. Haven't you dreamed of this moment your entire life?"

"No. I'd like a small wedding and a big honeymoon."

He nodded. "Good idea."

"Yes," she said dryly. "I have them sometimes."

He jerked his head in the direction of the church. "Do you regret coming?"

Jackie thought about it as she felt the breeze against her face and watched a robin dart between the trees. A bus rumbled past in the distance as she glanced down at the cold cement step. She was at her ex-boyfriend's wedding and she didn't care. She didn't feel heartbroken or discarded, and she knew why. Jackie looked up at Clay with his shadowy eyes that at times were so serious, yet could hint at fun, then glanced at his mouth and wondered if it was as tender as his hands. "Not at all."

He patted her on the back, nearly pitching her forward; unfortunately, he didn't know his own strength. "Good, that saves this day from being a total disaster."

"Why did you decide to come?"

"I didn't have a date lined up and thought I might as well go with you."

"So this is a date?"

He shook his head, popping a Skittle in his mouth. "No, this is two people spending a Saturday doing something ridiculous."

Jackie looped her arm through his. "And enjoying ourselves." She smiled.

He felt a warmth move through him. He'd always wanted her to send one of her bewitching smiles his way. But to his surprise something twisted inside him. A feeling he'd never expected. He wanted her. The realization nearly knocked the wind out of him. He could no longer explain his feelings away as a mere curiosity. It was pure lust. He drew away.

"What's wrong?" she asked when he abruptly stood.

"The ceremony should end soon." To his relief they heard the sudden sound of applause from inside the church. The ceremony was over.

***

Gold and silver ribbons draped the reception hall. Classic beaded place-card frames sat on cream-colored brocade tablecloths among frosted votive candles engraved with the couple's name. On each table sat a bouquet of "Black Beauty" roses surrounded by pompom moss. It was a joyously festive event that started with toasts, was followed with a scrumptious meal, and ended with dancing. Jackie and Clay remained seated.

Clay picked up an olive with his fingers. Jackie slapped his hand as he popped it in his mouth. "Stop that. Where are your manners?"

"I'm supposed to be crude."

"Yes, I know, but people are staring."

Actually, only women were staring. She didn't blame them. Clay in a tux was a sight to behold. Only he could take a civilized outfit and make it look almost primitive. Female eyes were magnetically drawn to him. Particularly one pair. She'd been doing so most of the evening. Jackie shifted her chair closer to Clay. She saw the woman stand and for a moment wondered when she would stop. She was at least five feet, ten inches of mostly legs and a chest of enviable proportion.

Jackie jumped to her feet. "Let's dance."

He lifted his glass. "I wasn't hired to dance."

She tugged on his sleeve. "Clay, please."

He set his glass down and shrugged. "Fine." He stood and glanced around the room. "Where is he?"

"I don't know," she said, heading toward the dance floor.

"There's no use dancing if he doesn't see us. I thought you wanted to make him jealous."

"Right now I just want to dance."

He pulled her into a dancer's embrace.

She drew back, shocked by how quickly her body responded to him. Heat flooded her cheeks.

Clay looked at her, confused. "What's wrong?"

"You shouldn't hold me so close."

"Did I hurt you?"

"No, I just think we should have some distance."

He looked at her as though she were a little strange. "Why?"

"That's just the way you're supposed to dance."

"How can we look like a couple if we dance like we're strangers? Just trust me on this." He pulled her close. She hoped he couldn't feel her heart pounding. She had to focus on something besides his arm around her waist, his lean physique, and the woodsy scent of his cologne. She glanced around the room and saw Legs. Jackie sent a triumphant look at the woman.

"Her name is Iyana," he said.

"Who?"

"The woman you're glaring at. She gave me her number."

Jackie looked up at him, shocked. "When was that?"

"Doesn't matter."

She turned away and frowned. "You shouldn't have accepted."

"Why not?"

"Because then you look as though you're being unfaithful to me."

"Would you like me to kiss you?"

Jackie jerked her head back, surprised. "No!" Yes.

Clay shrugged, resigned—he couldn't win. "You're the one who suggested I could meet women."

"*After* the reception, not during." She rolled her eyes. "Some date you are."

"She learned I was an investigator and wondered if I could help her."

Jackie frowned, disgusted he could fall for such a ploy. "That's just a line."

"I know, but it can be interpreted in two ways. We can flirt while still *looking* faithful."

"Looking faithful?"

He nodded. "Yes, her husband's here."

"She's married?"

"Which is of course a turn off. I don't like married women. Their husbands get in the way. And then if the woman has kids, being introduced as Mommy's 'special friend' gets tiresome."

Jackie stared at him, skeptical. "You're making this up."

"I was wondering when you'd catch on."

"Your sense of humor is as warped as Cassie's."

"I guess Eric is the only Henson with a sense of humor."

"A birth defect."

"At least I succeeded with my goal." He smiled.

She liked that expression. It seemed for a moment to wipe the shadows from his eyes and reveal the man underneath. "Goal?"

"I distracted you."

He didn't need to tell a story to distract her, his hands were doing a good job. He held her casually. It was her imagination that made them feel as though they were burning through her dress, heating her skin, and that maybe, just maybe, he held her closer than he needed to. She didn't mind.

He abruptly stopped. "I see him."

"Who?" she asked absently, lost in a daze.

He gently shook her. "Brian."

Who cares? "Oh."

"Come on. It's time to introduce ourselves."

"He saw us in the reception line," she said, not wanting the dance to end.

Clay ignored her and dragged her across the room where Brian stood with friends. Jackie stared at her ex, wondering how she could have dated him for so long. Their relationship would never have progressed. She glanced at Darlene, who spoke to her bridesmaids. She was dainty, cultured, and perfect. Brian's match. Jackie, on the other hand, wasn't the type of woman he wanted and never could be. She'd been silly to think it would have become serious. The truth of that stung. Clay nudged her forward.

"Hi, Brian," she said.

He turned and smiled warily. "Hi, Jackie." The other men melted away, sensing a possible scene.

"I wanted to wish you joy."

"Thank you."

"This is my date, Clay."

Clay shook his hand, then slipped into a British accent, "Hallo. Quite a palava you have here." Jackie's jaw dropped; he ignored her. "But I haven't been to a wedding in donkey's years." He lowered his voice to a conspiratorial tone. "Couple months ago went to a christening. It was so boring I thought of gluing me eyes open. Well, best be off and let you two chat a bit. Bye, love." He quickly kissed her on the forehead. "Look after her for me." He pushed her forward, then left.

Jackie balled her hands into fists, watching him leave. "I will definitely kill him one day," she muttered.

"What did you say?" Brian asked.

She turned to him, smoothing her features into a smile. "Oh, nothing."

"Your date seems like an okay guy. Doesn't seem your type, though."

Her eyes shot daggers at the man now surrounded by a crowd of women. "It was short notice and I thought I needed a change."

"Yes, you deserve that." He took her arm and led her outside to the patio where a string of lights dotted the darkness like fireflies. "You deserve a lot of things." His eyes swept her face. "You look beautiful. Especially with the moonlight touching the crystals in your hair clip."

"Uh, thank you," she said, uncertain.

Suddenly his face crumbled. "Her parents won't give me the money for a few years. I'll have to put my career on hold. Oh, Jackie." He drew her close, then burst into tears. "I don't know what I'm going to do."

Stunned, she tried to pull away. "Get a hold of yourself."

"Oh, god." He sniffed. "I've just made the biggest mistake of my life."

She opened her purse and handed him a tissue. "No, you haven't."

"I have," he said in a gloomy tone. "Perhaps I invited you here hoping you would somehow stop me or force me to stop myself. What am I going to do?"

Jackie patted him on the back as though he were a little boy. "You're going to relax."

He rested against the wall. "I can't believe I married her again. I know she has great family connections and a perfect background. Then there's the money. But I have to wait three years for it. Three years with her before I see a penny." He sniffed again. "How will I cope? She used to nag and nag and nag. She still does." He raised his voice to a falsetto. "'Brian, make sure the maid dusts', 'Brian, hire the lawn company', 'Brian, check the heater to make sure it's at the right temperature.'"

Jackie tried to sound sympathetic. "Yes, but remember all the things you missed when you were apart?"

"I can't remember one thing right now."

"You're just having cold feet."

He looked doubtful. "After the wedding?"

"Yes, once you're on your honeymoon, you'll—"

He shook his head. "No big surprise there—I've already slept with her as a married man and we're going to Pennsylvania so she can buy antiques. What am I going to do?" He held his head then let his hand fall. "I've ruined your life, too. You're dating a man obviously beneath you trying to get over me. I realize there's a raw appeal women have for men like that, but he won't take you far. Don't suffer because of me." Jackie bristled; Brian didn't notice. "I don't know what I will do."

Jackie shifted, growing impatient. "Think of your career, your aspirations. Your wife can help you achieve that."

He thought for a moment, then nodded. "You're right." He began to smile. "Yes, you're right. I've only been delayed, not stopped. I'm glad you came."

Jackie sighed, annoyed. "You've already said that."

"Do you think your date would mind if we danced?"

"Probably not, but I don't think we should. You should dance with your bride."

Brian stuffed the tissues in his pocket. "I've got ten years to dance with her."

"Only ten?"

He looked amazed. "You don't expect us to be married longer than that, do you? The percentage of second marriages lasting is even lower than the first."

"That's a cynical approach to marriage."

"Just honest." He pulled her close and began to move in rhythm to the music. "You know, when I'm on the market for a third wife, perhaps you'll still be around." His voice lowered. "Or we don't have to stop seeing each other at all."

She smiled brightly. "Yes, you're right."

"Good."

"But I walk dogs, I don't date them." She patted his cheek, pleased by his startled expression, and stepped back.

"There you two are," Clay said. "Can't leave you two alone too long." He nudged Brian in the ribs. It was a casual gesture, but applied with enough force to make Brian wince. "Wouldn't want you chatting up my bird, now, would I?"

Brian's eyes darted between them. He lifted his chin, his pride still hurt from Jackie's refusal. "I see that it would never have worked, you can't fake polish."

"Doesn't take much to pass yourself off as a poncy twit. Seemed to impress your wife."

Brian stormed away.

Jackie watched him leave, then turned to Clay, furious. "What the hell was that?"

Clay quickly dropped the accent. "You wanted someone rough about the edges."

"You needn't have made a farce out of it."

"A farce was watching him sniveling all over you."

Her anger turned to embarrassment as she remembered Brian's behavior. "It was awful. To even think I considered him husband material doesn't say much about me. I'm sorry you saw that."

He grinned wickedly, rocking on his heels. "I'm not. Did you accomplish your goal?"

"Well, I wanted him to be regretful, but I didn't expect that." She glanced at the reception hall. "How come revenge never quite works out the way you picture it?" She shot him a steely glare. "Then you had to act like a reject from a Noel Coward play and make me look ridiculous. I shouldn't have come. I'm an idiot."

He nodded. "It's always helpful to identify the problem first. Ow!" He cried when she hit him. He rubbed his arm. "So what are we going to do now?"

"I don't know. What does one do after a hollow victory?"

He tucked her arm through his. "We could play a little game."

"What?"

He nodded to a woman in the corner "What do you suggest I serve her for dinner?"

Jackie snatched her arm away. "Arsenic, for all I care." She headed inside.

Clay grabbed her arm and spun her around. "Do I detect a note of jealousy?"

"No."

He released her. "You were interested before."

She took a step closer, then tilted her head to the side. "You know what would interest me?"

Clay looked down at her suspiciously, aware of the teasing glint in her eyes. "What?"

"What would you cook for me?"

He slowly smiled, shaking his head. "Dangerous waters, little girl."

"I'm not a little girl."

He glanced away, his voice low. "I know that."

She moved closer. "You haven't answered my question."

He stepped back. "I don't plan to."

"Why not?"

His voice deepened. "You know why." He lifted her chin. There was nothing subtle about the gleam of interest in his gaze. "The night suits you, my little mischief maker."

Jackie narrowed her eyes, her voice a whisper. "I don't cause mischief."

"I guess you only inspire it." He bent down, she waited breathless for his lips to meet hers. He kissed her cheek instead.

She stared at him her heart crashing to her feet. "A kiss on the cheek? What was that?"

"A warning. Be careful who you try to bewitch." He turned and walked toward the hall.

"Are you afraid I may bewitch you?"

He glanced over his shoulder and grinned. "No, but you should be," he said, then disappeared inside.

Chapter Six

Nearly a week later, Jackie could still feel the tingle of Clay's lips against her cheek. In her imagination his lips went much lower than that. She dreamed of what it would be like to bewitch a man like him and banish the shadows from his eyes. Just the thought brought heat to her face. She took a deep breath. Today she needed to focus. She adjusted the collar of her blouse and straightened her skirt as she rode the elevator to Payton Winstead's office. Presentation was key. She knew people tended to indulge her as they would a Girl Scout selling cookies because she was cute. However, that wouldn't be advantageous now. People weren't willing to donate large sums of money to a little girl. She gripped her portfolio as the doors opened. To her surprise, she didn't have to wait long before being ushered into his office.

The secretary said he would be with her shortly, then partially shut the door. Jackie took the opportunity to glance around Winstead's office. The style was studied sophistication mingled with unmitigated conceit, displayed by the number of photos of Payton posing with various important people.

"Sorry to have kept you waiting," he said, entering the room.

"Not at all." Jackie stood and shook his hand.

Powerful shoulders offset a sagging middle. He was fully aware of his physical defect and used his striking and prominent features to divert attention away from it. He brushed his russet-brown hair back so nothing could compete with his high forehead and cool brown eyes.

"Would you like anything to drink?" he asked.

"No, thank you." She opened her portfolio. "I'd like to get right down to business."

"Certainly." He settled on the couch. "What do you have for me?"

Jackie sat next to him and dived into her usual sales pitch. She described all that her company offered, adding little anecdotes of successful clients. "I believe you used to donate to HOPE a while back and would like to persuade you to do so again. How can I do that?"

His eyes brightened. "You would like to offer the same arrangements as Latisha?"

Jackie chose her words carefully. "Since I am not aware of how Latisha did business, I can't promise you anything. However, I'm sure we can come to some sort of arrangement ourselves."

"I'm sure we can." His gaze briefly dropped to her legs. "You look very flexible."

Jackie paused. She didn't like the strange emphasis he put on the word "flexible." She stiffened when he leaned back and rested his arm the length of the couch, brushing the back of her neck. "I won't deny that an immediate decision would be helpful." She zipped her portfolio, ready to leave. "Naturally, I will give you time to think this over."

"Don't worry," he said in a smooth tone, "I'm thinking things over right now." His eyes trailed the length of *her* this time. "Making quick decisions comes easily to me."

Right then she didn't care what his decision was. He could take up self-mutilation for all she cared. She gathered her things.

"I think you'll do." He grabbed her wrist before she stood. "Wait, you have fuzz on your blouse." His hand grazed her breast as he removed invisible fuzz.

She lowered her eyes as heat filled her face. Not from embarrassment—rage. Her voice remained cool. "I see."

Winstead interpreted the demure expression as an invitation. His hand dropped to her leg and began its ascent up her skirt. "I'm glad we understand each other." He leaned close, his lips brushing her ear. "My wife's a bitch."

She grabbed his crotch, not enough to hurt him, but enough to cause discomfort and promise more. Her eyes met his. "Yes. Unfortunately, so am I." She lowered her voice, but kept her tone light. "Here is another opportunity to make a quick decision. Do you let go of my leg or do I crack your balls?"

His hand fell.

She stood, her voice composed. "I'm afraid this meeting is over."

He towered over her, eyes blazing. "No one's going to invest in your stupid little program out of kindness. People want to make money, not give it away to lazy derelicts who are a burden to society. This is a big boy's game."

Jackie glanced down at his trousers. "Not that big, apparently. Goodbye." She opened the door.

He slammed it shut. "You've obviously forgotten who you're dealing with."

Jackie grasped the door handle. Whatever he did, she wasn't moving from that spot. "Oh, I know *what* I'm dealing with."

His finger traced the line of her jaw, leaving her skin cold. "And just *what* would that be?"

Jackie boldly met his eyes, but said nothing.

"I can feel you trembling." He began to smile. "You have every right to be scared. I destroyed Latisha and I could destroy you."

Jackie continued to stare, her look of contempt more forceful than words. The willful stance enraged him. He grabbed her arm, his hands like a tourniquet. He whispered, "I dare you to scream."

She quivered inside, every part of her wanting to collapse. She didn't move.

"I get what I want. Latisha didn't quite understand that. We had a nice little arrangement until she wanted to change the rules. I wasn't pleased and let her know it. She's now living under another name in a city where nobody knows her. Plant a few incriminating business transactions, call it blackmail, and a career is destroyed."

"Thank you for that information," she said in clipped tones.

"You don't believe me."

"Yes, I believe you and so do my colleagues who are listening to this conversation right now."

His smug veneer slipped. "Colleagues?"

"Yes. I'm working with Hodder Investigations on behalf of Latisha and they're listening to the wire tap right now. We can overlook this confession if you let me leave now, or you could start getting your lawyers together. You decide."

His grip tightened. She bit her lip to keep from crying out. "Show me the wire."

"It's in a place you will never see. And if you try to find it, I'll bite you until I draw blood." Jackie flashed a grin for emphasis.

He released his grip and took a hasty step back. Jackie spun around and raced out the door.

Once outside, she felt her legs give way. A group of senior tourists grabbed her before she collapsed onto the sidewalk.

"Are you okay?" a man in a bulky D.C. sweatshirt asked.

She gathered strength from their support and comfort. "I just felt dizzy a moment. I'm fine."

A woman in a sun visor patted her hand. "You're probably just pregnant."

Jackie nearly laughed. "Uh, no."

"Ignore her," a husky-voiced woman said. "She's just missing her fertile years."

Jackie straightened and forced a smile. "Thank you." She waved, then walked away, trying to tame the remnants of anger and fear that still gripped her as his hand had. Thank god he believed her lie. She had become an expert liar during childhood and had learned not to show fear. The streets were not kind to weaknesses. It was a place where grown men looked at seven-year-old girls with decidedly adult thoughts. A place where your wits were your greatest tool. If you were weak, you were prey. She couldn't risk that.

When she returned to HOPE Services later that day, Patty and Faye looked at her expectantly.

Jackie walked past them into her office. "Winstead is a definite no," she said firmly, inviting no questions. She closed the, door, then paced, wanting to break something. She hated him for making her feel vulnerable, for reminding her that she was powerless, that men like him did rule the world. Jackie clenched her fists and wished she'd squeezed him harder.

Clay was right, she didn't like the word "no." Perhaps it was West Indian arrogance, but she didn't like being told she couldn't do something. She and her brothers had once been one of those derelicts, as Winstead liked to call them. But they had succeeded in becoming much more. And so would the people she helped. They would become viable citizens. She just needed money. Jackie would find an investor eventually. She wouldn't let HOPE services disappear as many other nonprofits had. She refused to fail.

***

Mack hung up the phone and stared at it in wonder. "What the hell was that?"

Clay sat in his chair with faxes Brent had given him. "Strange call?"

"That was Payton Winstead. He said he would destroy us if we released the tape."

Clay paused. "What tape?"

Mack scratched his head. "Beats me."

"Did he sound sober?"

"He sounded scared—worried. Worried men are dangerous." He folded his arms, pensive. "He could do some damage to our reputations if he wanted to."

"Did you tell him you didn't know what he was talking about?"

"Of course not." Mack clasped his hands behind his head. "I told him he could pay us off and consider the tape erased."

Clay stared, amazed.

Mack raised his hands in surrender. "Hey, it made him relax. I did a good deed."

He frowned. "What if those tapes show up somewhere?"

"Then I'll think of something." He grinned. "I always do."

That night Clay lay on his couch with a beer can resting on his stomach. He flipped through the TV channels for the mind-numbing entertainment it usually provided. Someone knocked on the door. Clay took another swig of beer. He rarely got visitors and figured someone would discover they had the wrong address. They knocked again. And again. He set his beer down and stood. "Who is it?"

"It's me," a female voice replied.

He looked through the peephole, but only saw the back of a woman's head. He opened the door. "Can I help you?"

Jackie turned and smiled up at him. "Hi, you wouldn't believe the day I had."

He stared at her, then softly swore. He still wanted her. He'd hoped the feeling would pass. "This is a bad idea."

She ignored him and walked into the room. "Have you eaten?" When he didn't reply, she nodded. "No? Me neither. We can order in."

He leaned against the door and shook his head, confused. "Wait, wait. What do you mean 'we?' What are you doing here?"

"Have you found anything on my case?"

"No. You gave it to us only a week ago. Don't worry, you'll get your invisible man."

"I know. I was just asking." She looked at the cage in the corner. "Hi, Laura." The bird chirped. She turned to Clay. "That's not why I came."

"Am I supposed to guess or are you going to tell me?"

She tossed her portfolio down and stepped out of her high heels. "I just came to visit."

His brows shot up. "With me?"

"Does someone else live here?" She opened the fridge, grabbed a beer, and took a long swallow. "Mmm, this is good." She licked her lips then set the can down on the large gray trunk he used as a coffee table. "I just need to talk and you're easy to talk to. I used to visit my brothers, but with them being family men now, it's just not appropriate. I thought since you're around . . ." She shrugged. "Do you want to talk about your day first or—" She held up a hand. "Actually, I think we should order dinner first."

"I don't usually have visitors," he said stupidly. He wished his mind would function so he would have something clever to say like 'Get out' or 'Stay the hell away from me.' Unfortunately, a part of him wanted her there despite the fact that she was dangerous to him. He never thought an elf could be dangerous, but she was. There was something too fay, too mercurial about her. Something he couldn't grasp. He didn't like things he couldn't understand, especially women. Especially this woman who could hold his interest even when he didn't want her to. Of course there was the other part of him that just wanted to strip her naked and have sex with her. That made her dangerous, too.

"I know you don't usually have visitors. You need a change." She grabbed a phone book. "What are you in the mood for?"

Clay watched as her skirt inched up her legs as she sat on the couch. She had nice legs even though they were short.

"Clay?"

He glanced up. "What?"

"What are you in the mood for?"

She needed to ask? He shoved his hands in his pockets. "You shouldn't be here."

"Why not? We had fun at the wedding."

He turned away, dragging a hand down his face. He was still trying to recover from the wedding and not kissing her. If he wasn't careful, tonight he would succeed.

"I want to make it up to you, all right?"

He rubbed his fist against his palm. *Tell her to leave. Tell her to leave.* He looked at her. Then again, if his imp was up for a night of mischief, so was he. "Fine, then you'll pay."

Chapter Seven

Jackie shook her head. "No. We'll split."

He folded his arms.

"You're a big guy," she protested, measuring him from head to toe. "I'm sure you eat a lot more than me."

"Probably."

"Actually, I've seen you eat. You'll likely order two meals."

He walked to the door. "Wow, look at that! It's still open. You can just walk out and disappear."

She sighed, resigned. "Okay, I'll pay."

He closed the door. "I want Italian."

"Chinese."

"I'm sorry. Didn't you ask me what I was in the mood for?"

"That was before I was paying."

"I want Italian."

"But you're having Chinese," she said firmly.

"Do I need to clarify what the phrase 'make it up to you' means?"

"I'm paying for dinner."

He rested a hand on his chest. "I'm offering you both my company and my place. The least you can do is pay for a meal I want to eat."

Jackie shook her head.

"Funny how this door keeps swinging open."

She kissed her teeth, annoyed. "Fine, you'll get Italian."

"Actually, I think I want Mexican."

"Clay!"

He laughed. "Italian's fine." He handed her a menu.

Jackie placed the order then picked up her drink. Clay took it from her.

"Hey!"

"This is my beer," he explained. "Yours is the one with the lipstick."

She grabbed her drink and took a sip. "So tell me about your day."

He sat, sinking into the couch. "No."

She shrugged. "Then. I'll tell you about my day." She tucked her feet underneath her. "Last week I found out that our generous funder had died and his family had stopped all future donations. Well, obviously this is a perfect time to panic, but I refused. Patty, our secretary, came up with a ridiculous way to make money. . . Are you listening to me?" she asked when Clay flipped to another channel.

He grunted. "Sure, every word."

She doubted it, but continued anyway. "So I think of contacting previous contributors and encouraging them to donate again. I made an appointment with Payton Winstead. Well, today I discovered he and our former president, Latisha, had a far cozier relationship than I expected. When he touched my leg--"

Clay stopped with the beer to his lips. "He did what?"

"Touched my leg. Although *touched* sounds pretty tame. More like groped and I—"

"What was his name again?"

"Payton Winstead.

He rested his head back and groaned. "Why am I not surprised?"

"About what?"

He turned to her. "That it was you."

"Me? What about me?"

"You gave him our name." When she looked blank, he said, "Did you somehow mention Hodder Investigations when you were with him?"

"I had to," she said without apology. "He was getting a little out of hand. I told him I worked undercover for you and that he was being taped."

"You're an excellent actress. He called and threatened us."

She grimaced. "Oh, no."

"Fortunately my partner is admirably unscrupulous and, well . . . let's just say you gave me and my partner a nice bonus today."

"Then you should pay for dinner."

"You weren't doing me any favors. You could have had us screwed. At least we don't have to worry about any tape popping up." He grinned despite himself. "Very clever, by the way."

"Thank you." She folded her arms, pleased.

His smile faded. "What's this?"

She glanced at her arm, lifting her sleeve higher to see the bruise. "I told you he got out of hand."

His voice hardened. "He grabbed you?"

"No, he groped me. Weren't you listening?"

Clay sat forward. "You got this from him groping you?"

She shook her head. "This isn't from the groping. He got upset with what I did."

"What did you do?"

"I grabbed his balls."

Clay nodded. "If I'd been there, he wouldn't have them. So what happened next?"

"He wouldn't let me leave and...You're getting upset."

"I'm not upset," he said in a quiet tone. His voice belied his eyes where shadows gathered, turning his eyes almost black and so cold she shivered.

"It's no big deal."

"What happened next?"

Jackie looked away, unable to meet his eyes. "He wouldn't let me leave so I made up the story about being undercover."

Clay grabbed a pad and pen. "What's his address?"

"Doesn't matter."

"Fine." He tossed the pad down and twirled the pen. "I can find out myself."

"Oh, leave him alone. He didn't have much to grab." She wanted to make light of the situation, to show she was in control. She didn't need his protection, though a part of her was comforted by it. His presence made the memory less threatening. "I'm all right now."

"Hmm." Clay returned his attention to the TV. Jackie resisted the urge to lean against him He was the kind of man that invited that response. You felt you could trust him. She stood up, suddenly restless, and walked around on the hardwood floor. She glanced at the green patterned rug that barely matched the green couch, walked up to the framed poster of a Cezanne landscape. On close inspection she realized it was a puzzle, as was the Gauguin on the other wall. She caught sight of an unfinished puzzle in the corner.

She turned to him. "You're a puzzle fanatic."

"I'm not a fanatic."

"Why frame them?"

"I like the picture and since I can't afford the real thing, this is my alternative."

She raised a brow. "What's the picture in your bedroom?"

"*Attack of the 50 Foot Woman.*"

"Really?"

He grinned. "I enjoyed putting that together."

"I'm sure you did."

"I flip it over to a van Gogh when I have company."

"You're a sly one. I should be nervous."

He sent her a glance that made her entire body tingle. "Yes, you should be."

She walked to a shelf and saw a green stuffed animal. She picked it up. "Is this supposed to be a dead parrot?"

"It's not dead, it's just resting."

She frowned, confused. "What?"

"I guess you're not a Python fan."

"This is a parrot."

"No, I—" He caught her grin and knew she was teasing. "Cute."

"I know." She curtsied. "Thank you."

Someone knocked on the door. Clay crossed his legs at the ankles, settling farther into the couch. "When you pay, don't forget the tip."

Jackie shot him a glare. "You're obnoxious."

He clicked his tongue. "Name-calling isn't nice, little girl."

She playfully hit him. He grabbed her wrist. She stiffened, fear leaping into her eyes. He let go. "It's okay," he said gently. "I was just teasing you."

"Sorry." She laughed without humor. "I guess I'm still jittery." The person knocked again. "Just a minute," she called. She grabbed her handbag, then answered.

Clay watched her pay the deliveryman, wondering what he would do to make Winstead pay. Some men just had to learn to keep their hands to themselves.

"Let's sit down to eat," Jackie said, closing the door with her hip.

He glanced around him. "I am sitting."

"At the table."

He turned to her. "Why?"

"Because I want to talk and I hate talking to the side of a man's head while he watches TV."

"Set the table and call me when you're ready."

"Are you being overtly annoying or just performing for my pleasure?"

"If this gives you pleasure, I can be a lot worse."

"I can imagine," she muttered as she searched through his kitchen for the dishes. After setting the table, she said, "Dinner is ready."

He sat and noticed she'd given him the ineffective plastic knife and fork while she had steel ones. He just smiled and got his own utensils.

"Why did you become an investigator?" she asked, digging into her chicken penne pasta.

"I sort of fell into it."

"How?"

"It's a long and dull story."

"That's okay, I—"

"Are you satisfied with your work?" he interrupted, not wanting to discuss his past.

"What do you mean?"

"Do you think you do any good?"

She thought for a moment. "Depends on the day. Depends on the person. Some people make progress, which makes you feel hopeful; others keep failing and make you wonder if it's worth it. But I'm not in the business to give up on them even when they give up on themselves." She rested her chin in her hand "Why? Are you not satisfied with yours?"

Not always, but did it matter? A job was a job. Gabby was dead. So were a lot of other women and many more would follow every day. Like the senator's niece who still hadn't been found, despite her parents' pleas and the police search. Some bastard had killed her and didn't care. Life was a lot easier for those who didn't care. He frowned down at his linguini. "It's fine."

"This is my philosophy," Jackie said. "Do a job well, that's the only thing you can control." She frowned. "I really hate it when you smile like that."

"I can't help it if I find you amusing."

"I was being serious."

"I know. That's what's amusing. Your optimistic view of life."

"There is nothing wrong with optimism."

"If you can afford it."

"The last time I checked, it was free."

"For you."

"What do you mean by that?"

"Life somehow works for you. I know you have been touched by tragedy and I would never disregard the level of your suffering, but somehow you were born with a light inside you that is so strong nothing could diminish it. Whereas I--" Clay felt as though he'd always lived in darkness. Like a moth he was drawn to her light, drawn to the promise of warmth, but he wondered if maybe her light would be too bright and he'd burn his wings. Or perhaps his darkness was too fierce for her and would destroy her light. He looked at his food. "Thanks for dinner."

To his relief she let the topic drop. "You're welcome."

Once they'd finished eating, she stood and cleared the dishes.

"Thanks for washing up," he said

Jackie placed the dishes in the sink next to the other dishes soaking there. "I wasn't planning on washing them."

Clay pointed. "There's an apron somewhere in the cupboard. Wouldn't want you to get your blouse wet."

"You can't force me to wash."

"Sure I can."

"I'll break all your dishes."

Clay rested back and folded his arms. "And pay for each one with your sweet little behind."

"You'd probably like that."

"Yeah, and so would you. How many times have you tempted a man to throw you over his knee?"

"Turn around and I'll show you."

He did, expecting a crude gesture. Instead she sprayed him with the hose.

She laughed. "Just one."

Clay stood, soaking wet. "You will regret that," he said, his voice soft with mock threat. He came toward her.

Jackie waved the hose. Her eyes dipped to the wet T-shirt that clung to his muscled chest. It was evident he was a man of brute strength, but she wasn't afraid. She was never afraid with him. "Just try and touch me."

He grinned. "You're going to need a bigger hose if you think that will stop me." He wrestled the hose away and trapped her against the sink, his arms on either side of her. Their eyes met. First in play, it soon turned into an almost tangible desire that threatened to explode between them.

He lifted her onto the counter. "I'm going to regret this."

"What are you doing?" she asked, breathless.

"I'm going to kiss you." He raised a mocking brow. "Scared?"

She grabbed his collar and pulled him close. "Try and make me."

Chapter Eight

He nearly succeeded. The mere touch of his lips sent shock waves of a sensation so foreign yet so thrilling she could feel her whole body respond. She'd been kissed tenderly, sweetly, hungrily, but never like this. Never with such possession. Never with such command. His tongue explored the inner walls of her mouth, stirring a heat within her. Jackie pulled off his shirt, arching into him, and braced herself as he pulled her close, knowing how staggering his casual pats could be. She didn't have to worry. The tenderness with which he held her was nearly her undoing.

Clay stepped back, his voice hoarse. "I want you."

She wrapped her legs around him, drawing him close. "I got that impression."

"I'm too old--"

She placed a finger against his mouth. "You're certainly not old enough to be my father unless you were doing very naughty things in elementary school."

"I was big for my age."

Jackie brushed her mouth against his, indulging in the succulent taste of his lips. "I bet you were."

His hand slipped to the curve of her neck. "I might as well enjoy this."

"Yes."

"Unfortunately, I picture Drake trying to hang me by the balls and I'd be forced to kill him. A very messy end."

She draped her arms on his shoulder. "Drake's not here."

"I know."

She leaned close and whispered, "And he doesn't have to know." She kissed him again.

Clay smiled against her mouth. "Are you trying to get me into trouble, Mischief?"

"Trouble can be fun."

"Hmm. Especially when you're causing it." He deepened the kiss. It soon became more reckless, more thrilling, more dangerous.

Jackie pulled away with wide eyes.

"Am I scaring you?" he asked.

"Yes."

He looked mildly embarrassed. "I'm sorry."

"No." She held his face in her hands. "It's wonderful. Keep going."

He kissed behind her ear. "It can't work between us." His lips moved to the curve of her neck. When the rough hairs of his five o'clock shadow brushed against her skin, her toes curled. "You're not my kind of woman."

She tilted her head to the side, inviting further exploration. "You're not my kind of man."

"Hmm."

"Ever heard that variety is the spice of life?"

"Don't worry. They vary. They're just not like you."

Jackie rested a hand on his chest, wishing he'd stop talking and kiss her again. "And I've never been with a guy like you."

He stopped her hand from descending. "Probably for a reason."

"Why?"

"We don't match."

"I think we match pretty well."

He tweaked her nose. "Yes, Mischief, you would." He glanced down at his wet clothes. "I think I need to put something on."

"Good."

Jackie jumped down from the counter after he had left. He was right. They were wrong for each other. All wrong. But she didn't care. She'd been going out with guys who were right for her and she'd never felt like this. It was time to break a few rules.

Clay returned to the kitchen. His mouth dropped. Jackie turned. Her mouth fell open.

"What are you doing?" he demanded as she stood at the sink wearing just her bra and panties.

"I thought you said you were going to put something on."

"Yes, my *clothes.*"

"Oh." She folded her arms, heat burning her cheeks. "I suppose I misunderstood you." She cleared her throat and gestured to the sink. "I'm washing the dishes."

"I can see that."

"Sure, and a lot more," she mumbled.

"Red suits you."

"Thank you." She lifted her chin, gathering courage. "So, do I put something on or do you take something off?"

Clay leaned against the fridge and let his eyes travel the length of her with slow, masculine pleasure. His voice deepened into huskiness. "Naked would have been better."

She furrowed her brows. "What?"

"You washing the dishes naked."

"Perhaps another time. For now I'm wearing a matching bra and panty set, which, for me, is rare. I got them at Divine Notions." She struck a pose. "Do you like them?"

Clay moved from the fridge and gradually came toward her. She'd once wondered what it would feel like to be his prey, and from the smoldering look in his eyes, now she knew. "I'm not sure yet, let me see." He fell on his knees.

Jackie looked down at him, uncertain. "What are you doing?"

"I want to do a closer inspection." He rested a hand on her hip while the other made a sensuous path up her side to her bra strap. "Nice fabric." His finger traced a pattern on the bra. "This is embroidery, right?"

She could barely speak so she only nodded.

He cupped her breast. "So how much of this is padding? No, don't say anything. Let me find out." He slowly lowered the strap. "You'd better stop me if—"

She unlatched the bra and tossed it away.

He stared for a moment, then raised his eyes to hers. "You have just enough."

She bit her lip and whispered, "For what?"

"For this." His mouth covered her breast with the effect of lava over ice, his tongue doing things to her nipple she couldn't even describe. He wrapped his arms around her. She arched into him until the fire raging inside her forced her to her knees as well. She pulled his shirt off, then went for his jeans.

He stopped. "I can't believe I'm about to take you on the kitchen floor."

"You prefer the table?"

He placed his hand over her mouth. "Be quiet. I'm thinking."

Jackie removed his hand and glanced down. "You can do that while you're wrapping your friend. I promise I won't move."

Clay took a condom from his back pocket. "I guess I have a little optimism myself."

She grinned. "Amazing."

He rolled on the condom. "I'll give you a second to be sure."

She placed her hand on him and finished the deed. "Oh, I'm sure."

He glanced down at her hand. She hadn't bewitched him yet, but she was certainly casting a spell. He had to be careful not to get trapped, to remember to be alert, to not surrender. He drew her close, ready to make a little magic of his own.

Clay skimmed his hand along the length of her, his palm fiery hot as it made its way down between her legs. His fingers softly massaged her center, he then replaced them with his tongue. Jackie stiffened at the unexpected sensation, acutely aware of the wet warmth that was both foreign and exquisite. She was almost too afraid to indulge in a feeling so delicious.

"Relax," he whispered.

She closed her eyes, allowing herself to surrender to the heat of ecstasy spreading through her, causing her to grow damp. "Please," she begged, ready to feel him inside her.

"You're ready?"

"Yes."

"You're sure?"

"Yes," she said, more forceful this time. She gripped his broad shoulders strengthened by the need of her desire.

"Careful or you'll leave marks," Clay warned when her nails pinched his back.

"Sorry," she said without apology. "But tonight you're mine."

He chuckled at her possessiveness, although he felt a sense of his own. The feeling surprised him. Clay prided himself on being a good, but detached lover. One who was always composed and calm, but tonight he felt an unfamiliar sense of eagerness and he wasn't sure how much longer he could wait. His entire body was hard, desperate for release. However, he forced himself to move with a studied patience, determined not to lose control. Unfortunately, some of his control slipped when Jackie pressed a kiss on the sensitive part behind his ear, then trailed a hot path down his neck. He gritted his teeth and entered her a little less gently than he'd planned.

Jackie offered no gasp of surprise or protest; instead, she tightened around him and Clay groaned as more of his control shattered. He sank deeper inside her. A mutual shudder swept through them, igniting a raw hunger both unexpected and fierce in its intensity.

The intensity fueled them. Jackie greedily surveyed every inch of him as though he were an undiscovered island. Everything about him intrigued her—from the raised scar on his back to a tiny birthmark inside his thigh. She never thought the male form could provide such fascination. Clay found as much fascination with her. Although Jackie was certainly not the first woman he'd ever been with, he felt a sense of awe at the way her nipples hardened under the tender caress of his tongue, the wide sweep of her hips and the gentle curve of her behind.

They silently explored each other, leaving no room for subtlety. Their desire cast away all thought of how vulnerable they were to each other. Neither knew, nor cared how much time passed or where they were. The only thing that mattered was being together.

Soon exhaustion overcame them and they collapsed, limp with pleasure. Clay sighed; Jackie began to tremble.

Clay sat up, alarmed. "Are you all right?"

"I'm fine," she said through chattering teeth.

"Then why are you shaking like that? Are you cold? Let me get you a blanket." He left before she could tell him that she didn't need one, that she was just feeling so many emotions she couldn't keep still. Clay came back and wrapped her in a blanket. He carried her to the couch and held her.

"I'm fine, really," she said, even though she knew then that she wouldn't mind him holding her forever.

"Then why are you crying?"

Jackie blinked, trying to get the tears to stop. "I don't know."

Clay became concerned. He'd never been with a woman who'd responded like this. "Are you having regrets?"

She nodded.

He swore.

She laughed at his expression. "I wish I'd slept with you sooner. I've never felt this way. I didn't even know it could be this way. Like living on sparkling cider and finally tasting champagne." She jumped up. "Let's do something else."

"I'm afraid you've discovered all that I can do."

"We could go for a walk or go to a club or do a puzzle. Let's finish your puzzle."

He glanced at his watch. "It's late. You should go home."

"Don't worry. I don't plan to stay the night. I know about your rules, remember?"

He stood. "I suggest you get dressed."

Jackie tossed the blanket aside. "Hey, I'll finish washing the dishes."

He picked up the blanket and dropped it over her head. "Next time."

She pulled it down. "So there will be a next time?" Clay went into the kitchen and pulled on his jeans, pretending not to hear her.

She picked up her bra and fastened it. "Clay, what does this mean?"

"That you're officially over Brian."

She began to dress, suddenly feeling vulnerable and unsure. She couldn't imitate his aloof attitude. "Can I see you again?"

He sighed. "You're supposed to leave the questions for the morning."

"It wouldn't be anything serious," she said quickly. "I know how you feel about relationships. It will just be casual. And think about it, you didn't even have to cook me dinner."

He shook his head. "Jackie--"

"No one needs to know about us, so my brothers won't be a complication, and I know you don't want to get married and I don't want to marry you so there's no agenda. You said I was like you and I don't want commitment, so . . ." Her voice died at the look on his face.

He glanced at a chair. "Sit down."

She did, staring up at him with hopeful eyes. Clay rested his hands on his hips and groaned. Damn those eyes. How could he be the one to crush the hope in them? And he couldn't deny that he still wanted her. That was a surprise. Once was usually enough. This time he'd only awakened an appetite for a little sprite with impish eyes. For a while at least he was hooked. His little mischief maker had enchanted him. What was amazing was that he'd also seemed to have enchanted her. He'd never had a woman look at him with a desire that matched his own. But he had to be careful to temper his feelings. He couldn't allow any weakness to leave him vulnerable to her. Clay sat down, trying to find the right words to say. When nothing came, he took her hand.

She pulled away. "Don't."

For a moment he was hurt that his touch offended her. "Don't what?"

"Don't try to coddle me. If you're going to tell me this was a one-night stand, then just say so."

"Because that's not what you want this to be?"

She nodded.

Me, neither. However, he couldn't make this what she wanted it to be. "You don't know me."

"That's okay. We'll get to know each other more. I like you. We could go to movies, eat out or in—"

He shook his head and smiled ruefully. "You don't understand how this works."

"We'll have sex, too."

"I know, but what you're describing is a relationship."

Jackie vehemently shook her head. "No, no. It doesn't have to be that formal. We just see each other every once in a while, casually. I'd like to get to know you better." It would be a struggle for her to keep her feelings for him a secret when they visited Cassie and Drake for Sunday dinner.

Clay rubbed the back of his neck. "That's sweet. However, the problem is, I don't want you to."

"Why not? Is there something wrong with you?"

"I'd like to think not, but—"

"I won't—"

"Yes, you will." He stood. "You'll want more."

"No."

"Why?" He looked at her curiously. "Why wouldn't you ask more from me?"

"I'll take what I can get."

"That's the problem. You deserve more." He tapped the table. "This is what I was talking about before. You accept the slim pickings, you accept men who talk about their ex-wives and want threesomes—"

"Or sex with no ties."

He hesitated, then said, "I couldn't treat you like the others, Jackie. So don't ask me to."

Jackie was silent a moment. "How about an affair?"

"Why don't you sleep on it and then—"

"I don't need to sleep on it. I know what I feel. I know that I want to see you again."

"How about I call you Friday?"

"I want an answer now."

"Yes."

She blinked. "Just like that?"

"Do you want me to think it over?"

"No, it's just you seemed so hesitant before."

"I just want to make sure you know what you're getting into."

"I'm not sure, but I'm sure it will be an adventure."

"So I'll call you Friday."

"That's tomorrow."

"I know."

She smiled. "Friday's perfect."

***

At home, Jackie fell onto the couch and shut her eyes, not quite sure what she was feeling. What a wonderful night. She curled up on the couch, a bit of fear racing through her as she wondered if her feelings meant more. She brushed them aside; she was going to have an affair with Clay. It seemed unreal, no one would believe her. She sighed—such good news and no one to tell. Usually she would have called Cassie or Adriana, but she would have to keep Clay a secret. It wouldn't be hard. She didn't want their arrangement put under scrutiny. Jackie sighed again. He certainly made up for dinner. Thirty dollars well spent. She sat up and opened her wallet to see what money she had left. She stared. A twenty that hadn't been there before peeked out. She fell back and grinned. Yep, he was definitely sly.

***

Mack walked into the office the next day, surprised to see Clay at his computer. "You're here early."

"Hmm."

"Got a break?" He poured some coffee, then sat at his desk. "What are you working on?"

"Winstead."

"I have that under control."

"I'm just finding some trivial information on him."

Mack frowned. "Why?"

"I want to ruin his day."

"What is this all about?"

"Jackie is the reason Winstead thought we had tape. He was misbehaving and she told him she was undercover with us."

"What do you mean by misbehaving?"

"I'm sure you've done it a few times."

Mack sent him a look. "This is D.C., the city of sex scandals. I'm not important enough to have one, but all my women are willing. Is she okay?"

"Yeah."

"But you're not."

"No."

Mack straightened, uncomfortable with Clay's tone. "Now, wait a second. Winstead isn't a guy you want to mess with."

"He won't know it's me."

Mack was quiet for a moment, then became curious. "What do you plan to do?"

"When you were a kid and you touched something you shouldn't have, what happened?"

"Got my hand slapped."

Clay grinned. "Exactly."

***

Jackie stared at the phone. She wouldn't call him. She would wait until tonight. She was at work. She should focus on work. Clay was merely an extracurricular activity. And what an activity. She straightened her features when she began to smile—she had to remember this was casual. But she did want to thank him for the money. However, she didn't want to bug him, and yet she wouldn't mind hearing his voice. She gripped the phone, then gently set it down. This was stupid. She'd known him for more than four years; she shouldn't feel so awkward about calling him. But she wouldn't be able to stand his cool, aloof tone acting as though their affair didn't matter while she tried to keep her heart from racing. She picked up the receiver, then set it down again. "That man is so .. ." She shook her fists, at a loss for words.

"Who is?" Patty asked, entering the room with a file.

"I can't believe I'm acting this way for a man so wrong for me. He's too, um . . ." Her words trailed off.

"Sexy, intriguing, exciting?"

Jackie glared at her. "Good-bye, Patty."

"No, not yet. I came in here for a reason. Faye identified two Requests For Proposals and she's hoping you can whip something up."

Jackie took the folders, scowling. "I hate writing proposals."

Faye walked in. "I know," she said with regret, "But we need the money."

Jackie glanced at the due date on the proposals and groaned. "There must be a better way."

"Are you sure you don't want to attend the funeral with me? It would be nice to have you there."

"Sure," she said, resigned. "Perhaps it will give me ideas on preparing my own."

Chapter Nine

Mack hung up the phone and turned to Clay. "Milton called. He said his wife is working late. We know when her office closes so we'll do a stakeout."

Clay swore. He'd have to cancel with Jackie. He could send Mack on his own, but they usually did stakeouts together so one of them would stay alert.

Mack looked at him, confused. "I thought you'd be happy to get this over with fast."

"I had a date," he grumbled.

"Tell her it's an important case. She'll understand." He grinned. "Make it sound dangerous and she may even worry about you."

"This woman won't."

Mack sat on the corner of his desk and sighed. "Ah, women." He opened his notebook and glanced at the contents. "Unpredictable creatures. You know, last night—"

"If I want to hear about a man's sexual exploits, which on most occasions I don't, I'll pick up a magazine."

"Speaking of magazines, I submitted to *Swank* once. They turned me down. Perhaps I should try *Cheaters Club*." He snapped his fingers and pointed at Clay. "Hey, maybe you could read the story for me, see where I went wrong."

"Sure, I will. Right after I finish gouging out my eyes."

"This woman must really be important."

"This has nothing to do with Jackie."

Mack stopped and stared "You had a date with *Jackie*? The little brat, Jackie? What an interesting turn of events. Lucky man. Bet you'll have fun. Big things come in little packages."

Clay sat back. Jackie was his business and his business alone. He said in a low, yet polite tone. "You're beginning to get on my nerves."

Mack correctly interpreted the threat under the civil words. "I'll go check the equipment."

"Thank you." Clay stared at his phone for a moment before picking up the receiver. He doubted she'd be very understanding about this. He shrugged. She'd have to learn.

"HOPE Services, Jackie speaking."

"Hi, it's me."

"Hi. I'm glad you called."

Clay hesitated. Did he imagine it or did she sound strangely happy to hear from him? He reminded himself he didn't care.

"How has your day been?" she asked.

"The usual. Um—"

"Thanks for the money."

"You're welcome. I---"

"It was quite a surprise. You didn't have to." She lowered her voice. "You more than made up for the cost of dinner."

Clay cleared his throat. "Uh, thanks. Listen—"

"I thought we could do Chinese tonight."

"Yes, well—"

"You could come to my place. Just tell me what color you want me to wear. I have blue, purple, and tan. I may have green, but I don't think so. What is your favorite color, by the way?"

His voice grew impatient. "Jackie—"

"You don't have to tell me. I was just curious."

He replied with cold silence.

She sighed, resigned. "You're calling to cancel, aren't you?"

"Yes. I have a stakeout. I'd like to close this case if I can and tonight is a good time."

"Okay. I understand. Another time. Maybe tomorrow."

"I'll call you."

"Which means no."

"No, it means I'll call you." He hesitated. "I like black."

"Black? Black is not a color. It's the absence of color."

"I like black."

"Fine, I'll see what I have for next time. Bye."

"Bye." He set the phone down and twirled his pen. Milton would pay big for this.

***

Jackie stared at the stacks of papers on her desk, annoyed with how disappointed she was. It was silly. She'd seen him yesterday, she shouldn't miss him already. She looked at her watch—it was lunchtime, that's all. Jackie grabbed her handbag and stood to go out for lunch; she needed to do something. She decided to visit her eldest brother, Drake, at the Blue Mango, one of the two restaurants he owned in D.C. When she entered the restaurant, she saw that the lunch crowd was in full form. Waiters expertly darted to and fro while the heady scent of gourmet cuisine filled the air. She went to the back office, pleased to see that Eric was there also. As a financial planner, he helped Drake with the books.

Eric saw her first. He usually saw more than people thought, though his gold-rimmed glasses and studious face made him look myopic. Slighter in build and lighter in shade than Drake, they barely looked like brothers.

"Where's the disinfectant?" Eric teased. "A little bug just entered."

Jackie made a face. "Amazing how some things don't improve with age."

Drake glanced up, his intense amber eyes briefly meeting hers. The expression, in contrast to his pepper-gray hair, usually intimidated those that didn't know him well. "Is this a social visit or do you want something?"

"Social," she said.

He gestured to a seat. "Sit down."

She slid into a chair. "I have to write another grant."

"Why?"

"Mr. Hamlick died."

"I'm sorry."

"How?" Eric asked.

"Natural causes." She crossed her legs and swung her foot. "So we need money."

Drake straightened. "I could—"

Jackie shook her head. "Your donation is fine, but I can't have you carrying the entire project. We need someone with lots of money."

"There's K—" Eric stopped then glanced at Drake. He shook his head. "Never mind."

Drake said, "Don't worry, we'll figure something out."

"You don't need to," Jackie said, wishing men didn't always feel they had to fix things. "I just wanted to share."

"Nevertheless, families help each other."

She looked at the framed photos of his wife, Cassie, and their two kids: four-year-old Marcus, who had his father's eyes, and Ericka, nearly two. In a few months he'd add another picture. Family meant everything to Drake.

"Have you eaten?" he asked.

"I'm not hungry. Really," she said when he looked unconvinced. "I—"

He held up his hand at the sound of hurried footsteps racing past. "Cedric?" After a few moment, Cedric Diaz peeked his head inside the room. Though a young man of nearly twenty-one; with black hair pulled back in a ponytail, he flashed a sheepish grin that made him look younger. Drake frowned. "You're late."

Cedric's olive skin developed a red tinge. "I'm sorry. I was getting things ready. Pamela's--"

Drake folded his arms. "I have this bored expression on my face for a reason. It means I don't care."

"Sorry, sir. It won't happen again."

"Good." He nodded, giving silent dismissal.

Cedric waved to Jackie and Eric, then left.

Eric wiped his glasses. "Give the kid a break."

Drake shook his head. "He's not a kid anymore. And he's become distracted these past few weeks."

"His girlfriend is coming to visit for Spring Break."

"I think it's something else." He rubbed his chin. "He's improved a lot and I don't want that to stop. He's going places with or without Pamela." Pamela had formerly worked at the Blue Mango before going on to college. Cedric had decided to forgo college for real life experience. It had put a strain on the relationship. "You've been against that relationship from the start."

"I'm not against it. I realize that they're young and will soon have to make a decision about their future."

"They have a tight bond. I think it will work."

"I doubt it. What happens when she leaves college?"

"They'll get married."

"No, they'll realize they've grown apart."

Eric flashed a grin. "Want to place a bet?"

"I thought you didn't like losing money."

His grin widened. "I don't plan to lose."

"Three hundred."

"You're on."

Drake turned to Jackie. "I can get something put together for you."

She resisted rolling her eyes. Would her brother ever get out of the habit of trying to feed people? "I'm fine, honestly."

Eric said, "Since you're both here, I might as well tell you my news."

They turned to him.

He adjusted his glasses. "My doctor's a little worried about me and wants to conduct some tests."

Jackie stared, his words knocking the air out of her like a punch in the chest. Their parents had died of cancer. She couldn't take seeing Eric weaken and then die as they had.

"What is he worried about?" Drake asked.

"My lungs. He wants to do some tests to see what is going on. I've done X-rays before—there was a shadow and it turned up to be nothing. I'm sure this is nothing."

"Why are you so sure? Why is he concerned?"

"It's a doctor's job," he said "It's just tests."

Drake glanced out the window, his voice barely audible. "Cancer?"

He shrugged.

Jackie uncrossed her legs and sat forward, trying to combat the rising anxiety. He couldn't be really sick. It was all a mistake. "Do you feel okay? You didn't tell us anything was wrong."

"Does he ever?" Drake said, annoyed.

Eric shot him a glance. "I'm telling you now."

Drake began cracking his knuckles, a bad habit he'd picked up after he'd quit smoking a year ago. "I suppose we should be grateful you told us before you were admitted into surgery."

Jackie sighed. "It's amazing that you'd end up with lung cancer." She regretted her words when a look of pain and guilt briefly crossed Drake's face.

Eric scolded her with a glance. "It's not cancer. A little chest pain, that's all. It's just tests."

"Right. Of course," she said quickly.

"And if it is cancer, it's nobody's fault." He glanced at his brother, who'd grown quiet. "Hey, remember, I'm the guy who could get sick in a test tube."

Jackie took a deep breath, wishing she could take it all in stride as he did. But the thought of Eric being sick terrified her. "Does Adriana know?"

His light humor disappeared. "No, and I'm not going to tell her. It would only worry her."

Drake said, "She's your wife, she has the right to worry."

"We've only been married a year and--"

Drake drummed his fingers. "And you don't want the honeymoon to end? Wake up. The honeymoon's over, you're married now. Your battles become hers, she has a right to know. She's going to be upset if this turns out to be serious."

Eric shrugged. "I'm sure it's not." He took off his glasses, then shoved them back on. "I told you because I thought you should know, not so that you would worry."

"You don't want us to worry," Drake said in an ironic tone. He clasped his hands together and rested his chin on top. "Anymore instructions, professor?"

"Just one. You can't tell Cassie."

Drake straightened. "Why not?"

"Because then she'll tell Adriana. They're best friends."

"You want me to keep the fact that my brother may have cancer or some other disease a secret from my wife?"

"Just for a few weeks."

Drake shook his head. "I'll tell her not to say anything, but I can't keep this from her. Cassie and I talk about everything."

Eric's voice was firm. "Well, you won't be talking about this." He looked at Jackie. "And neither will you."

Jackie began to protest. "Eric—"

"I don't want their sympathies. I don't want them feeling sorry for me."

"They love you."

"I know that. That's why I can't put them through what we went through with our parents. Cassie will tell Adriana. Adriana will tell Nina," he said, referring to his eight-year-old stepdaughter. "What will I say to her? I can't promise her anything. Jackie, you know how it feels to be a kid and have a father that's not there for you."

"This is different. Things can be done. Dad wasn't you, you can't think you'll end up the same."

"I don't plan to, so don't worry. If the news is bad, I'll tell her. Otherwise it's just between us. Okay?" When neither replied he looked at Drake. "Okay?" he asked again, more firmly this time.

Drake nodded reluctantly.

"Jackie?"

She sent Drake a look of resignation, he gave a slight shrug. Then she said the word she knew she'd regret. "Okay."

***

"Get the camera off her ass," Clay growled as Mack focused the lens. They sat in the parking lot of the Hillside Motel under a flickering street lamp, hearing the booming dance beat from a nearby club.

Mack grinned. "She's got a great one."

Clay agreed. Milton's wife, Roberta, was a well-made woman, but he wasn't in the mood to comment. He reached for the camera. "Give me that and you take notes."

Mack moved it away. "All right, all right. No need to get violent."

Clay sat back and sighed. He was bored, but this was part of the job. Roberta hadn't been hard to follow. For a woman involved in an affair, she was very predictable. Hillside was one place she frequented. The kind of place where one key could open four rooms. It was a peach and green two-level building with a rusted railing and crumbling stairs. People rarely went there for the atmosphere. A neon sign from the club across the street reflected in the windows. Clay tapped his pen against the notepad as Mack videotaped the lover parking his car and meeting her.

"There's our Romeo going into the motel," Mack said, watching Roberta's lover.

Clay scribbled down some notes, then glanced up. He saw a man walking toward the pair. He was of medium height with black hair and a long coat. Something about the man's gait put him on alert. It was too fast, too determined. He picked up his binoculars, then swore.

Mack glanced at him. "What?"

"That's Milton."

"What is he doing here?"

"I guess he's finally going to approach her. I wish he'd come to his senses sooner."

"About time." Mack shook his head. "I'm going to miss this case, though."

Clay paused when he saw Milton reach inside his coat. He could feel the hairs bristle on the back of his neck. Something wasn't right. "I don't like this."

Mack agreed. "Don't know why he asked us to come, if he was coming himself."

"What's that in his hand?"

Mack snorted. "Funny, it looks like a gun."

They stopped, stared at each other, then jumped out of the car.

Chapter Ten

Clay asked a bystander to call 911 while Mack raced across the lot. "Drop your weapon," he ordered, holding out his own.

Milton kept his gun on his wife and her lover. "Stay away."

"Milton, you don't want to do this."

The middle-aged man ignored him and stepped closer to the pair. "Roberta, are you happy?"

Under the fading light she looked like a wilting vine with her coiffured bun coming undone. She clasped her hands together. "Milton, please."

"I've loved you all these years. I've given you chances, haven't I?" His tone harshened. "Haven't I?"

"Yes. Yes, you did."

"But you still lied to me. Do you think I deserved that?"

"No, you deserved better. Don't do this, please." Her voice trembled. "Please."

"It's too late to beg."

"Put the gun down," Mack urged. "We can talk this over."

"No! I'm sick of talking. Sick of it! We talked, didn't we? But they were just words. They didn't mean anything." His voice cracked as tears built in his eyes. "I tried to be everything you wanted and I failed. . . I failed us both. I love you and I'll show you how much. I want you all to see what she made me do." He placed the gun against his head.

"Wait!" Clay said. "I need to get your mother on the phone."

"What?"

"I can get her on the phone right now." He held up his mobile phone. "I think she has the right to say goodbye to you since she'll never see you again. I know you want to hurt Roberta, but do you also want to hurt your mom, too? Leave her alone without anybody?"

A series of emotions crossed his face. He glanced at Roberta and spoke with venom in his tone. "But I want her to suffer."

"She'll suffer." Clay kept talking as Mack moved slowly out of view. "When you divorce her and leave her with nothing, she'll suffer. But what will your mother have with you gone? No one visits her but you. You're the only bright spot in her life. Pulling the trigger now is like shooting your mother in the heart."

The gun wavered. Milton looked at him, helpless. "I don't know. Life means nothing."

"At least say good-bye." He held the mobile toward him. "Here. Call her."

The moment Milton reached for the phone, Mack jumped on him and seized the gun. Soon the police arrived and had him in handcuffs.

After giving their report to the police, Mack and Clay headed back to their car. Clay glanced at Milton in the police cruiser. Tears streamed down his face while Roberta flirted with an officer and her lover looked grim. "Poor, crazy bastard," Clay said.

Mack patted him on the back. "Good job, buddy. How did you know his mother would work?"

"I didn't. I Just kept talking until you could make your move."

"Quick thinking."

"Great instincts."

"Perhaps I'll listen to you next time."

"Hmm. How do you plan to get paid for this job?"

"He paid in advance."

Clay stopped and grabbed Mack's shoulder, forcing him to stop. "You didn't think that was strange?"

He shrugged. "I knew the guy was odd. I didn't think he'd try to blow his brains out."

Clay released him. "At least it's over."

"Yeah."

Mack sat behind the wheel and started the ignition. "That little speech would have worked on me. If I decided to put a hole in my head, my mother would grab me from the grave, condemn me for my sin, then weep and tell me how much I'd broken her heart."

Clay put on his seatbelt as Mack merged into traffic. "Mine wouldn't even remember my name. Then she'd say, 'I thought you'd died years ago.'" His stepmother would be annoyed he hadn't chosen a cleaner way to go. He didn't care. He'd given up caring when his biological mother abandoned him at five and his stepmother hated him on sight.

"She would care," Mack said. "You just don't know it."

The last time he'd seen his biological mother was at his sister's funeral. Five years had passed since she'd thrown him out of her house after he'd run away. Despite their shared grief, he didn't speak to her and she didn't try to speak to him. "Yeah, I do know."

***

Funerals are generally thought to be solemn occasions. Mr. Hamlick's proved to be anything but. Jackie couldn't determine whether it was the ceremony or the garish decorations that ruined the appearance of bereavement. She saw his two daughters sitting in the front pew, their names were inconsequential since they rarely used them in public. They preferred the distinction of their husbands' names—Mrs. Daniel Becker and Mrs. Jerome Trent. They were attractive women who had made the mistake of thinking they were still young by wearing low-cut blouses to emphasize their long necks. They had probably been swanlike in youth, but resembled goosenecks now. Their tinted gray hair matched their silver-gray clothes as though fashion rather than decorum had been a priority. Mr. Hamlick had one son who was unable to attend the affair because he was conducting one of his own in Italy with a dancer. Everyone knew his mistress would have waited and correctly assumed he just didn't want to be there.

When Faye and Jackie introduced themselves to the two daughters, they were greeted with cool smiles and minimal interest. Faye and Jackie hadn't expected more.

"Your father was a wonderful man," Jackie said.

"Yes, I know," Mrs. Daniel Becker said. "Will you both be at the burial?"

"Yes."

She managed a tight grin. Not because she couldn't smile wider—she just didn't want to exert the effort.

"Good. I want as many people as possible for the film footage."

A Hollywood director couldn't have staged a better event. Requisite tears and sniffles. No wailers. People crowded together to get into the camera shot. Jackie stood to the side and listened to the drone of the minister. At the most solemn moment, a trio of birds decided to chirp loudly. At last it was over. The crowd slowly dispersed, offering condolences and then asking when the Beckers' banquet would be held.

"You would think they would have more respect for their father," Faye said. "My parents died when I was young."

"Mine, too."

They shared a look of known pain. "Hurts," Faye said.

"It sucks."

Faye nodded, amused by Jackie's bluntness. "Yes, that, too."

"I'm almost sorry I came," she said, disgusted.

"Welcome to the circus," a deep voice said behind them.

They turned to a man of average height and forgettable features except for eyes as blue as cornflowers. "You must admit, it's entertaining," Jackie said, embarrassed that her feelings had been obvious.

Faye measured him with interest. "Are you a guest?"

"A distant relative." He looked at the coffin with sadness.

Her interest dimmed.

Jackie shook his hand, pleased to see the first sign of genuine emotion since the ceremony. "I'm sorry for your loss. I'm Jackie Henson and this is Faye Radcliff."

"Nicolas Douglas. How did you know him?"

"He used to invest in our nonprofit organization."

"Yes, he loved charities. What do you do?"

"Let me give you my card." Jackie opened her purse, then shook her head. "Oh, darn. I'm all out. Faye can give you one." She grabbed Faye's bag, pulled out a card, and wrote her number on the back, knowing he wouldn't use it, but not wanting to put Faye on the spot.

"What do you do?" Faye asked him.

"I'm a detective."

"Oh."

Jackie handed him the card. "Here."

He stuck it in his pocket. "Thank you. You'll be hearing from me."

Jackie smiled. "Good."

He returned the expression, then left.

"You're incorrigible," Faye whispered.

Jackie looked blank. "What?"

"Trying to fix me up at a funeral."

"He's attractive and you need to get out more. You're working yourself to death. You're always in that office."

"Not always. I'm dedicated to my job. We came here for a purpose and that wasn't it."

"Well, our other reason didn't work. I bet he'll call back next week."

Faye draped her handbag strap over her shoulder. "I bet he won't call at all."

She shrugged. "Nothing lost except a business card."

"How can you be so optimistic?"

Sheer will. She'd learned that life had to get better even when everything else seemed lost. She stared at the grave site. It was getting harder and harder to keep that attitude. Now Hamlick was really gone and the shock of Eric's news still lingered. She didn't even know where her parents were buried.

"I want to stay for a minute," Jackie said. "I'll meet you at the car."

"Okay."

Jackie stood alone, the quiet of the cemetery offering little peace. She stared at Hamlick's coffin. "Your children are awful," she said to the box. "But I'm certain you knew that—you never spoke about them much." She folded her arms. "I miss you already. You could have lasted a couple more years, right? But that's selfish of me. I just don't have anyone to talk to."

Jackie looked up at the sky through passing cumulus clouds to the invisible deity above. "Okay, when does it end? Don't you think I have struggled enough? Do you have to test to see how strong I am? You took away my friend. So he was old—I still loved him." Jackie blinked back tears. "But you've taken loved ones from me before. I can take losing the funding. I'll, figure that out. Brian dumping me." She laughed bitterly. "That's nothing new. It's not like you blessed me with a great love life. I accept that. But Eric? No. I can't accept that." She clenched her fists. "I won't accept that. I won't. Do you hear me?"

"There's no one up there."

She spun around and saw Nicolas. "What?"

"You're not talking to anybody."

She folded her arms, surprised. "You don't believe in God?"

"No."

She stared at him, bewildered. "How can you bear not having faith in anything?"

"How can you have faith in something that doesn't exist?"

"I have faith that it does."

"Faith is just something people believe in to make the world feel more bearable. Gives you all the answers and makes you feel safe. Unfortunately, there are no real answers. Science does its best but is as limited as the mind of man. We just fumble through life, then die."

"No, there's more to life than that."

"Some benevolent spirit who helps us? And which one do you believe in? The ones of myths and legends? Or the more modern, acceptable ones like Allah or Jehovah."

"I do believe in God." She brushed aside a tear, then laughed at herself. "I must look foolish to you."

"No, only sad. Life is a series of misadventures—it's easy to cast blame and it's easy to be misled." His eyes swept her face. For a moment she felt as though he were stripping her bare. "You're very vulnerable. Be careful who you trust."

"What do you mean by that?"

He hesitated, then handed her a card. "Do you believe in this?"

She looked at the white card with green printing:

Careless Rapture Ministry
Peace in Surrender

Careless Rapture? It was him? She glanced up, a sliver of fear coursing through her. He didn't sound the same and he certainly didn't look as she had expected. Had he followed her here? What did he want from her? She took a hasty step back.

"What do you want?"

He furrowed his brows, confused. "I only asked a question."

"Why did you call me? Are you trying to make me believe in this? Why did you give it to me?"

"You're the one who gave this to me." He flipped the card over.

Jackie stared at her hasty scrawl. "Oh." She frowned."But I got this out of Faye's bag."

"Do you think she's a believer?"

"No, she's very traditional. It's hard to believe she would buy into this."

"Like I said, be careful. There are a lot of charlatans out there promising the perfect peace."

"That's okay. I'll stick with what I know." She grinned. "So are you going to call her?"

He shoved a hand in his pocket. "Personally, I'd like to call you instead."

She blinked, surprised. "Oh. Well, um ..."

He smiled. "I know. You're seeing someone else." He sighed with mock regret. "The interesting ones always are."

"Faye's interesting."

"I suppose she just hides it well."

"She's very devoted to her job. But give her time and she'll loosen up."

"She's lucky to have a friend like you. So who looks out for you?"

"Besides my two brothers and their wives?"

"Good, so you're well taken care of," he said, like a pleased guardian.

Jackie raised a brow. "I'm not as innocent as I look."

He turned. "No, you're much more."

***

Jackie thought about Nicolas's words as Faye drove her home. "Have you ever heard of the Careless Rapture Ministry?"

"No. Why?"

"Because you had their card in your bag."

Faye frowned. "I don't know what you're talking about."

"I spoke to Nicolas and the card I gave him had the Careless Rapture Ministry on it. Not much else but a symbol and a message of peace."

She shook her head. "I still don't . . . oh, no."

Jackie turned to her, alarmed. "What?"

"I took a stack of cards off Patty's desk and dumped them in my bag to throw away. You know how she likes to try and slip in religious material with our promotional flyers and brochures. I must have forgotten to clean out my purse."

"Can I look now?"

"Please do, and take all the cards out."

Jackie went through Faye's organized bag and took out the cards. "Did she say where she got them?"

"I didn't ask her," she said with regret. "It didn't seem important at the time."

"I know."

Faye sighed, resigned. "So you may be on to something about Melanie's man."

"Yes, I hope so."

"I'm sorry I didn't take you seriously before."

"That's okay. It sounded pretty fantastic."

Faye tapped her finger against the steering wheel. "So what are you going to do?"

"First I'm going to talk to Patty."

"Be careful. You know how easily she gets hurt. Do you think she mailed the card to clients?"

"No, I don't think she'd go that far."

"This is Patty we're talking about."

Jackie glanced out the window, not looking forward to the task. "I know."

***

That night Jackie arranged her CDs, trying to pretend she wasn't waiting for the phone to ring. When it finally did, she tripped over her shoes, hit her knee on the couch, then answered.

"Hello?" she answered, trying to sound casual.

"Did you hurt yourself?" Clay asked.

"What?"

"Did you hurt yourself racing to the phone?"

Jackie rubbed her knee and winced. "I didn't race to the phone."

"Hmm. Sorry I couldn't call sooner."

"How was the stakeout?"

"Fine. The case is closed. How was the funeral?"

"A disaster. A real circus. I'm not sure I saw one genuine teardrop and we will probably not get any help from the family. But on a positive note, Faye met a guy, Nicolas something. I forgot his last name. He seems interesting. An atheist, but I don't think Faye is picky. Something may come of that so the day won't have been completely wasted."

"Sounds interesting."

"It was. Also, I may be getting closer to our invisible man."

"How so?"

"I accidentally gave Nicolas a card out of Faye's bag. She had taken a stack from Patty's desk. I'm going to ask Patty how she got them."

"I already know how."

Her eyes widened. "How?"

"Through the mail."

Jackie shook her head. "No, that doesn't sound right."

"That's how it happened. She has a tendency to attend conferences and put her name down to receive more information. She got on his mailing list."

"You're just guessing?"

"No, I'm not. She told me."

"You came by my place?"

"No, I called her over the phone. I said I was a preacher who was organizing a church for underprivileged individuals. She helped me with some ideas. She was very open."

Jackie sank into the couch. "Oh."

"I thought you'd be glad I was on the case."

"I am."

He laughed at her disappointment. "But you wanted to be a step ahead."

"Just a little. Why didn't you tell me this?"

"I don't usually give clients a play-by-play of everything I do. I get the information they need. When I have enough, you'll know."

"I'm still going to speak to Patty."

"Fine. Ask her about receiving any fliers."

"So when are you coming over? Do you want me to order now or wait until you get here?"

"Jackie—"

She closed her eyes and groaned. "Don't tell me. You can't make it."

"Right now I'm standing in an alley waiting for a guy who thinks he's a pigeon in a police sitcom. But he has information for me so I have to go along with his oddities."

"Sounds exciting!!

"It's not. I think I just saw a rat scurry behind a dumpster."

"If it looks like Brian, say hello."

"Already did."

Jackie laughed. "Thanks." She took down her hair and pulled out her earrings, "So, I guess I'll see you tomorrow."

"Tomorrow?"

"Yes. Remember? Sunday dinner at Drake and Cassie's?"

"Damn, I nearly forgot about that."

"Are you coming?"

He hesitated. "Should I?"

"Yes, I want to see you. I can keep a secret if you can."

He was quiet, then said, "See you Sunday."

"Clay?"

"Yeah?"

Her voice was soft. "Be careful."

"I will."

Jackie hung up the phone and turned on the TV.

A distance away, Clay stared at the phone, then put it in his jacket. *Be careful.* They were odd words to hear. He suddenly didn't feel the March chill still gripping the air. He couldn't remember anyone ever saying that to him. He shrugged, annoyed that he was giving the statement any importance, then turned and walked farther into the alley.

***

That Sunday afternoon, Jackie sat at the kitchen island chopping celery in her brother's kitchen. A rich scent of stew bubbling on the stove and the sweet aroma of biscuits from the oven filled the air. Her sister-in-law, Cassie stood at the counter, scribbling something on a napkin. She wore a pink dress that complemented her full figure and the slight swell of her belly. Cassie was one of those women who managed to look comfortably pregnant—her brown hair was pulled back in a braid while her glasses slid down the bridge of her nose. She absently pushed them back in place.

Jackie smiled to herself, glad to have Cassie as part of her family. She was a comforting woman, someone to confide in and make you laugh when life seemed grim; they were qualities that made her a successful speaker and self-help author. Her other persona, Cassandra—who wore contacts and stylish clothes—little resembled the woman now.

Drake entered the kitchen and checked his stew. He looked at Jackie. "Done with the celery?"

"In a minute."

He reached for the knife. "I can do it."

She pointed the knife at him. "I said in a minute."

He held up his hands in mock surrender. She finished chopping, then pushed the cutting board toward him. "There."

"At last." He added them to the pot, then turned to his wife. "What are you working on?"

"An idea," Cassie said. "Shh, I'm thinking."

He wrapped an arm around her and kissed her neck.

"Behave yourself," she scolded.

"I'm trying."

Eric walked into the room with Ericka attached to his leg. He saw Drake steal another kiss and scowled playfully. "What are you trying to do? Give her twins?"

Drake grinned. "Jealous?"

Eric colored a bit, but said nothing. Cassie elbowed her husband in the ribs. They all knew Eric and Adriana were trying to conceive without success. Immediately contrite, Drake slapped Eric on the back in goodwill. "Has Nina brought any herbs for me today?"

Drake succeeded in smoothing the awkward moment. Nina always put a smile on Erie's face. "Yes, she did. Adriana has it. She'll be in soon. We're growing tomatoes this year."

Ericka let go of her uncle's leg and spun around until she fell down dizzy. She laughed, then stood to start over

"Not in the kitchen," Cassie said.

Drake scooped her up; Ericka giggled, thinking it was a game. "Come on, let's see what your brother and cousin are up to."

Eric walked over to Cassie and leaned against the counter. "What are you doing?"

"Writing."

"On a napkin?"

"A really good idea just came to me. If I don't get it down, I'll lose it."

"You should try keeping pads of paper everywhere," he suggested, being ever practical.

"I try, but somehow I still end up writing on napkins. I know I'm disorganized, but I find it preferable to not having any ideas at all."

"What are we having for dessert?"

"Strawberry cream pie," she whispered, knowing his fondness for sweets. She held out her hand. "You may kiss me."

He did so. "Could you please teach my wife how to cook?"

Cassie laughed. "The only reason Adriana would be in a kitchen is if she'd left a fashion magazine there."

"I know."

Adriana entered the room, draped in a purple peasant blouse, black skirt, and large gold hoop earrings. "Are you talking about me?" she asked, pulling on a strand of curly black hair that fell against her dark coffee skin. A vivacious woman, she owned three lingerie stores that had a growing name, and her own lingerie line.

"We were wondering where you were," Cassie said.

Adriana handed her a small plastic bag. "From Nina's garden."

"It's cilantro," Eric said.

Adriana patted him on the cheek. "Thank you, dear. Since they can't read the prominent label on the front, they'd never know what it is."

Eric turned to Jackie and jerked his head in Adriana's direction. "I have my regrets about marrying her sometimes."

"The feeling is mutual." She rested her hip against the counter. "When I think of all the men I could have married."

He sighed. "And I think of all the women I could be sleeping with."

Adriana stuck out her tongue.

Jackie laughed. "You two are the oddest pair of newlyweds."

"Newlyweds? I feel as though I've known her all my life." He winked, then left.

Cassie folded up her napkins. "I think everyone is here."

"Clay hasn't come yet," Jackie said, then blushed. "I don't think."

"Yes, he has," Adriana said. "He's talking to Drake."

"Oh." She tried to sound nonchalant, though she was disappointed he hadn't said hello.

They walked to the dining room and Cassie announced dinner.

Jackie pulled Adriana aside and said, "I wore the rose design you created. It's great."

Clay appeared behind them. "Is that the one with the embroidered trim?" he said.

The two women turned. Jackie's heart accelerated at the sight of him. His expression, however, was as cool and unreadable as it had always been.

Adriana nodded. "Yes."

"Brilliant design."

"Thank you."

Eric stared at him, curious. "How did you get to see it?"

Clay faltered.

Jackie said quickly, "I took him by the shop and showed him. He wanted to impress a date."

Eric raised his brows. "By wearing women's lingerie?"

Adriana sent him a look. "You shouldn't be one to tease."

Eric smiled, but still looked suspicious. Fortunately, Drake's son, Marcus, came in with Nina, loudly explaining a long story only another child could understand. Everyone headed to the table.

***

Jackie was determined not to meet Clay's gaze though he sat directly in front of her. She wondered what was going on in his mind. Wondered if he felt the desire to be close to her as she felt for him. She glanced at Adriana and wondered when Eric would tell her about his lungs, then glanced at Drake, wondering what he would say if she told him she was seeing Clay. She knew they would both be furious.

As dinner progressed, her spirits dimmed. She wished she had some sign that Clay's feelings had changed toward her. She knew their affair was casual, that anything more was forbidden. Yet she craved for just a look or touch that would signal that she meant something more to him than just a fun night out—or, in their case, in. Then again, she knew that just a touch from him would send her senses reeling and she wouldn't be able to hide what she felt for him.

Jackie helped Cassie clear the plates for dessert then stayed behind in the kitchen, leaning against the sink to gather her thoughts. She was so engrossed in them that she nearly screamed when someone touched her shoulder, and she spun around to stare up at Clay.

He put a finger to his lips and lead her to the pantry. Shutting the door, he said, "I forgot to say hello." He kissed her, his mouth warm and demanding. Jackie made a few demands of her own. When he tried to pull back, she wouldn't let him and he stumbled back against a shelf. A can of soup fell.

"Careful," Clay said. "They'll wonder what's going on in here."

"I missed you."

"I gathered that." He grinned, then ducked out of the pantry.

Jackie returned to her seat a few moments later, glad everyone was involved in a conversation. About what, she didn't care—she only hoped she didn't look "kissed." She caught Clay's gaze and he winked. Jackie sighed wistfully. She'd never noticed, how long his eyelashes were.

Eric asked, "So, Clay, how are you and Jackie getting at it?"

Clay nearly choked. "I'm sorry?"

"How's work? You two have been quiet. I'm trying to draw you into the conversation. Your job must be stressful."

"Oh, it's fine. I'm busy with three cases."

"You do missing people sometimes—what do you think about this Amanda incident?"

"I think they're looking for a body."

Jackie said, "I think there's hope."

"The prognosis doesn't look good."

Cassie spoke up, hoping to change to a lighter topic. "So, Jackie, how is Brian?"

"We broke up."

"Sorry."

"I'm not." She rushed on when Cassie sent her an odd look. "We weren't really suited."

Cassie nodded. "I see."

***

Clay helped carry dishes to the kitchen as Cassie filled the dishwasher. She turned to him and smiled. He smiled back, remembering when she'd first smiled at him. It had been a warm, toothless grin and it was beautiful, making him feel for the first time as though he'd belonged—the stepchild in his father's new family. But her love for him hadn't kept him from running away. He knew that had hurt her, and was glad she had allowed him back into her life after so many years.

"Mom called," she said.

He managed not to cringe. "Why?"

"Just to talk. It wasn't an interesting conversation, but at least she wasn't picking on me. You should try it some time."

"Picking on you?"

"No, talking."

"I don't need to talk."

"Yeah, that worries me. You've been unusually quiet."

"I have a lot on my mind."

Cassie nodded, but looked unconvinced. "You do have someone you confide in, right? I know it doesn't have to be me, but you do talk to someone?"

"I don't need to talk. I can take care of myself."

"I don't doubt it. How about women? Are you seeing anyone?"

"There are women. I got high marks for 'plays well with others.'"

Cassie grinned. "I'm sure you did. But you know the offer is open."

He patted her on the head. "Yes, little sister. I know."

***

Under a starless night, Claudia Meeks drank her fourth beer, then sat on the sagging brown couch in her apartment. She wasn't sure canceling HOPE Services was such a good idea. Perhaps she should have talked to Jackie about it. She was always understanding. She never judged her, even when she made mistakes. Unfortunately, Claudia couldn't talk to her, she'd been sworn to secrecy.

She took one long swallow, then glanced around her dingy apartment. The window didn't close all the way and the heater had been turned off for an inspection she knew would never happen. Who would have thought her life would end up like this? High school band leader and she had graduated top of her class. Well, more like the middle. She sighed and set the beer down. HOPE Services had promised to help her get on her feet soon. She wanted to get on her feet now, not wait—she was tired of waiting. Soon she wouldn't have to. The deal was made. The promise of money was good.

She stood at that sound of a knock and opened the door. She welcomed her killer inside.

Chapter Eleven

Jackie smiled at Patty as she entered the office. She knew she had to choose her words carefully since Patty was quick to take offense. "I'd like to see you in my office," she said.

Patty looked at her, surprised. "Do you need me to take notes?"

"No, I just have a few questions and I know you can help me."

"Okay." Patty followed her into the office and sat down.

Jackie sat behind her desk and chewed her lower lip. She pulled out a card and handed it to her. "What do you think about this?"

Patty looked at the card and shrugged. "I think the design is pretty. You need help designing new HOPE Services cards? Sure, I'll help you. I think the current color is so dull. I'd go with purple myself—"

"No, the office cards are fine. I was just wondering about the message."

"It's a nice message."

"Yes, but not appropriate for the office, which is why Faye took these cards off your desk."

Her lips thinned. "She had no right touching my things."

"But you understand the policy here."

"I understand that I should have been given a warning before she up and took my cards. She's just Ms. Clean Everything. Always so tidy. Her office is like a library." She glanced around Jackie's desk—books were on the floor her desk was filled with old proposals. "Unlike your office."

"Yes, well, I'm not here to accuse you or her of anything. I was just curious why you chose this card."

"Listen, I got it in the mail and I liked the message and the symbol. Looks like a peaceful sign, doesn't it? If I believed in tattoos I'd get one looking like that. But I don't believe in tattoos—"

"So that's why you had it on your desk?" Jackie asked, trying to keep her on the subject.

"Yes. I think everyone should have something to believe in. I liked the thought of our clients surrendering to our help and thought it would be nice for them to carry around. I wasn't trying to preach anything."

Jackie nodded, knowing Patty was still annoyed about the time when she had told her to take down her Jesus fan.

"So you don't believe in the Careless Rapture Ministry?"

"I don't even know what that is."

"There's a possibility it's a cult."

Patty shrugged. "I wasn't encouraging anyone to join it. I just had the cards on my desk. It's not like it has a one–eight hundred number on it or even an address. It's almost like a calling card."

"Yes." That was what was so strange. "Did you receive anything else besides the cards? Like a flier?"

Patty thought for a moment, then shook her head. "No, just the cards."

"Have you received any strange phone calls?"

"Yes."

Jackie sat forward. "What?"

"My ex-husband's wife called me to say—"

"No, I mean really odd."

"No."

"Do you remember any of the clients taking the cards?"

Patty's eyes narrowed. "Why? Are you trying to blame me for some client joining a cult? I didn't do anything but have the cards on my desk. If someone wants to take it a step farther then that's their business and I won't have the blame pinned on me."

"I wasn't blaming you. But you're a key to a mystery I'm trying to figure out."

"I don't remember anyone taking the cards, but you know how busy I am."

Jackie didn't know, but nodded anyway. "Thank you for your time, Patty. I really appreciate it."

"No problem."

Jackie watched Patty leave, then rested her chin in her hand. She still didn't know much about her invisible man—this adviser. It was possible Melanie had taken a card from the office, but that didn't explain how she had gotten involved. Jackie called Melanie and left her number, then stared at the stacks of old proposals on her desk. So far staring was as far as she had come. She couldn't get her mind to focus on writing the new grants. Fortunately, no other clients had called to cancel, but that didn't make things all right. When the phone rang, she pushed the piles aside and answered the phone.

"Hi, Jackie," she heard Cassie say. "Adriana and I are going out for some girl time to hang out. Do you want to come?"

"Sure..."

Cassie paused, then said, "You seemed a little down the other day. Is anything wrong?"

Jackie brightened her voice. "Oh, no. Things are just hectic at work." At least that wasn't a complete lie.

"Yes. I understand. See you tonight."

***

In tune with the changing seasons, the stores in the mall blossomed with spring sales followed by the cacophonous sounds of rustling bags, crying children, harried adults, and flirting teens. Adriana stopped in front of a Nordstrom window display. "Let's go in."

"Adriana, we're window-shopping," Cassie said.

"I'm just looking."

"Then continue."

She wiggled her fingers. "I like looking with my hands."

"All right." Cassie glanced at a bench. "I'll wait for you out here. Try to leave the store empty-handed." Adriana just smiled and went inside.

Since Jackie wasn't much of a shopper, she decided to keep Cassie company. She watched the passing crowd, noticing a child with a drink the size of his head.

Cassie touched her hand. "Jackie?"

She turned to her. "Yes?"

Cassie began to speak, but at the same time an eager voice interrupted her. "Are you Cassandra Graham?" They both looked up at the short stylishly dressed woman with fluffy brunet hair and nervous grin standing in front of them. "I think I went to one of your workshops."

Cassie offered the woman a polite smile. "I'm afraid you must have me confused with someone else."

The woman's face fell. "I guess you're right," she said, looking at Cassie's simple patterned dress. "She's a lot more glamorous." The woman rested a hand on her chest. "She changed my life

"You changed your life, she merely gave you the tools."

"Wow! You even sound like her." The woman narrowed her eyes, skeptical. "Are you certain you're not her?"

Cassie glanced at Jackie, then sighed. "I suppose I should reward you for seeing through my disguise." She held out her hand. "Yes, I'm Cassandra."

The woman was besides herself. She enthusiastically pumped her hand. "Oh, I knew it!" She wiggled herself between them and grabbed both of Cassie's hands. "I love you! I didn't like Fear of Ridicule as much--I know it's for men, but I thought I could get some tips. I didn't, but who cares? *Recipes for Romance* was fantastic! Oh, and that book you did for teens was great! My daughter read it twice and I'm going to buy it for my niece. That poor girl needs it. So, what are you working on now? Will you be traveling to New Jersey anytime soon? I have a cousin there. She loves you, too."

Cassie patiently answered all the woman's questions, signed her address book, then waved as the woman left.

Jackie shook her head, amazed by the onslaught and Cassie's composure. "I'm surprised she didn't ask you when you were due."

Cassie patted her stomach affectionately. "Big girls don't get asked questions like that. People have to be careful." She grinned. "I could be pregnant or just really, really fat. I've made the mistake myself and wanted to dig a hole in the ground." She shook her head, amazed. "Unfortunately, it never fails. When you look your worst, someone will recognize you."

Jackie shook her head. "You could never look bad."

"Spoken like a true relative." She stood. "Come on, let's get Adriana before she pulls out her wallet."

They reached her too late. Adriana ended up buying a blouse, defending her purchase by pointing out that she'd returned six other items. The trio left the mall and headed to the Golden Diner, a pricey restaurant with a home-cooked feel and casual, sophisticated ambience.

Adriana picked at her chicken salad. "I'm worried about Eric."

"Why?" Cassie asked.

"I don't know. He just seems tired."

"It's probably the weather change. Allergies, perhaps? What do you think, Jackie?"

Jackie hesitated. "I don't know. Eric likes to be secretive."

Cassie nodded. "He's used to keeping things to himself, he hasn't learned to be a husband yet. He'll be okay. If it were something serious, I'm sure he'd tell you."

Adriana nodded but her expression didn't change. Jackie affected a casual tone. "Do you think Clay will ever marry?"

Adriana frowned. "I don't think he should."

Cassie nudged her with her foot. "That's not nice."

"It's true." Adriana shuddered. "He's too mysterious---too different."

"This coming from a woman who used to date a man with a pierced lip."

Adriana rolled her eyes. "All I am saying is that there are men you date and men you marry."

Cassie checked off his attributes on her fingers. "He's kind, intelligent—"

Adriana grinned. "And you're not biased because he's your half-brother?"

"I was right about Eric."

"But wrong about Drake."

"I know." She'd nearly lost him because she felt so undeserving after a lifetime of self-loathing. Thankfully, he'd been patient until she came to her senses. "However, I'm not biased about Clay. I have a younger brother no woman should marry. Unfortunately, two women already have married him. Clay is..." She searched for words and found none. "...Clay. He's completely his own person, self-made."

"I admire him," Adriana admitted. "I even like him. I just don't understand him. I mean, what kind of guy becomes an investigator?"

"A caring one." Cassie smiled wistfully. "He used to walk me to school and help me with my homework. Sometimes he'd tell me stories about his big sister."

"What was her name?" Jackie asked.

Cassie thought for a moment. "I don't think he ever mentioned her real name. He had a nickname for her. Rennie. She lived with his mother." She paused. "Now that I think of it, I never met her. She never came to visit and Dad didn't have any pictures of her. At least none that I ever saw. I never considered how that must have made Clay feel. We weren't a family that talked about much. Even when Rennie died Dad didn't discuss it."

"That's awful."

"Dad was distraught, but he never talked about it." She shook her head. "Not that Mom would have let him. She preferred to keep a distance between his past family and his present one. I always wondered how he felt making that decision, taking Clay and not his sister. I never had the courage to ask him. When Clay ran away ..." She sighed. "There were so many unspoken questions when he left. I still haven't asked him many of them."

"Like what?" Jackie asked, trying to sound casual.

"Like what did you do? Where did you go? How did you survive?"

"Aren't you curious?"

"Of course, but I don't want to bring up painful memories. I don't want to give him a reason to leave again. I have this sense that if you get too close, he'll disappear."

"Like a phantom," Adriana said in an ominous tone. "Don't look at me like that, it's true. I've known you almost all my life and I remember meeting Clay. Yes, he was nice. He even bought me an ice cream cone once, but every time I met him he always seemed like a stranger. How is that possible? He's in your life, then out of it, then in again, and you still don't know much about him. You don't even know his favorite color."

Jackie sipped her drink. "Black."

Adriana and Cassie turned to her, surprised. "What?"

Jackie shrugged nonchalantly, annoyed she'd been so careless with what she knew. "He told me his favorite color is black."

"That's not like him to share personal information."

"I was trying to think of a Christmas gift."

Adriana accepted the explanation; Cassie didn't. She flashed a sly grin. "Are you interested?"

"No," she lied. "Just curious."

"Stay curious," Adriana said. "You and Clay"—she cut her hand through the air—"*Never.*"

Cassie waved her fork. "Again, need I point out the kind of couple you and Eric make?"

"We complement each other. Clay's too old for her."

"He's not that old."

"Jackie deserves someone polished, refined, upwardly mobile."

"You're beginning to sound like Drake," Jackie grumbled.

"Because he's right." Adriana sat forward and lowered her voice. "I know he's intriguing. And to be perfectly honest, he was my first crush."

Cassie stared at her, surprised. "You never told me that."

"I know. You don't usually tell your best friend you have a crush on her brother. Besides, I was eight."

"Clay would love to know that."

Adriana pointed a finger at her and said in a low voice, "Don't you dare tell him."

Jackie leaned forward, intrigued. "Why did you have a crush on him?"

"The fact that he was cute didn't hurt. He always knew the right thing to say. If I felt ugly, he'd say I was pretty. If I felt stupid, he'd say I was smart. He never picked on me like other brothers do. His accent also helped and I fell for it."

"When did your crush stop?"

"When I discovered Child of Rage."

"What?"

"A rock and roll band," Cassie explained. "She fell in love with the lead singer, thus beginning her affection for bad boys."

Adriana glanced at Cassie. "Yes, as I am constantly reminded, I had my fair share of bad boys and thoroughly enjoyed myself. The problem is Clay isn't a bad boy."

"Then what is he?"

"I don't know and that's the whole mystery. You should be able to categorize a man so that you know how to deal with him. With Clay you can't. Besides, you want to marry well and he doesn't fit the standards."

Jackie shook her head. "I've dated polished and refined. Unfortunately, I'm not refined enough for them. Remember where I come from? I'm not like you two. You're cultured without effort."

Adriana laughed. "If you only knew. You can marry well, don't sell yourself short. Your brothers married up, so can you."

Cassie frowned. "Did you marry Eric for his money?"

Adriana looked insulted. "Of course not."

"Then stop giving ridiculous advice."

"It's not ridiculous. She can't afford to marry poorly."

"Clay isn't poor."

"I didn't say he was." She squeezed Jackie's hand. "Marry for love. Just make sure he has money."

"I'm not thinking about marriage anyway."

Cassie rested her arm on Jackie's shoulders and gave her a quick squeeze. "If you do, follow your heart."

"And make sure your head agrees with it."

Jackie rested against Cassie and smiled at Adriana, loving them as both sisters and friends. But she felt like a fraud.

***

"Jackie, didn't seem herself today," Cassie said as Drake prepared for bed.

He pulled on a T-shirt. "What do you mean?"

"I'm not sure. She's usually more lively, more playful. Tonight she was subdued. I don't know," she said, frustrated. "I can't put my finger on it."

He closed the dresser drawer. "She's concerned about work."

Cassie shook her head. "No, she's been under pressure before. This seemed different."

He turned off his side lamp and slid into bed, gathering her close. He was exhausted, but always felt most at home in bed with her, with the scent of cocoa butter and her soft curves. "Go to sleep."

"Jackie's different about the same way you are."

He stopped. "What do you mean?"

She gently shook his shoulder. "I know you, Drake. What's wrong?"

He sat up and looked into the open brown eyes that had captured his heart years ago. She trusted him, he didn't want to start lying to her now. He opened his mouth, closed it, then shook his head. He tucked a strand of hair behind her ear. "I can't tell you," he said finally.

"Why not?"

He rested his head against the headboard, his exhaustion turning into worry then guilt. "I just can't." He turned to her. "Don't be angry."

"I'm not angry. I'm hurt, concerned, annoyed, but not angry." She pulled up the sheets and turned off her light. "Fine. If you can't talk, we might as well go to sleep."

He didn't move. She grabbed his hand. "Stop that." He hadn't realized he'd been cracking his knuckles. "Go to sleep."

"Right."

After a few moments she said, "I know what it is."

He waited. "What?"

"You're seeing someone else."

He grinned into the darkness. He could never second-guess what she would say. He released a world weary sigh. "How did you find out?"

"Lipstick on your underwear."

"How did it get there?"

"How would I know? You're the one having an affair." She turned to him, sitting up on her elbow. "You're not very good at this."

"At what? Pretending I'm having an affair?"

"Yes."

He brushed her cheek with his knuckles. "I'll try harder next time."

"Do. It will be more fun that way. It even helps if you come up with a name."

"I know her name. It's Annette. She's a beautiful woman with an unfortunate name. Ow!" he cried when Cassie pinched him.

"Say my middle name is beautiful."

"With a straight face? Ow!" She'd pinched him again. "Okay, your middle name is beautiful."

"And that if there was anything seriously wrong, you would tell me."

His tone grew serious. "Yes, I'd tell you."

"Good. So ends your nightly torture." She pulled up the covers and soon drifted off to sleep. Drake couldn't do the same.

Chapter Twelve

Clay sat in Eugene's bar with Drake, Eric, and Eric's friend Carter, a man with hazel eyes, brown hair, and a deceptively innocent face. Eugene's was a comfortable place that offered good drinks, an occasional exciting game on TV, and waitresses that weren't too hard on the eyes—though Clay would never admit he liked coming more for the company than the drinks. He considered few people friends, and Drake and Eric made up that few. He briefly thought about Jackie, then pushed the guilt aside. It would be over between them before anyone found out. However, Drake looked as though something was troubling him. For one sinking moment, Clay wondered if he knew.

"What's wrong, mate?"

Drake sighed. "Cassie knows."

He lifted his beer. "Knows what?"

"That I'm hiding something."

"What are you hiding?" Carter asked.

"The fact that Eric's doctor's worried about his lungs."

Eric scowled. "Nice to know you're able to keep a secret."

"I haven't told Cassie."

Eric still scowled.

Clay tapped the side of his mug. "Why is it a secret?"

Drake shot his brother a look of disgust. "He doesn't want his wife to know or mine."

"Women talk," Eric said.

"She's going to break me down."

"Lie."

"I can't lie to her."

The three men stared at him, stunned.

Carter finally said, "You're kidding, right?"

Eric grabbed a handful of peanuts and popped one in his mouth. "There are certain social norms Drake never learned. Like lying to his wife."

Drake frowned. "You enjoy lying to yours?"

"I don't have to lie. She doesn't suspect a thing."

"Yet."

"Lying isn't necessarily a bad thing," Carter said.

"It's a means of survival in certain cases. Especially in marriage." He twisted the wedding band on his finger. "Trust me."

Clay leaned forward, ready to impart some wisdom.

"There's an art in lying to a woman. It comes in two forms. One takes careful planning, the other cunning. First you have to establish the situation."

Drake blinked. "What does that mean?"

"How do you know she's on to you?" Eric clarified.

"She asked me what was wrong."

Clay nodded. "What did you say?"

"I said, 'I can't tell you.'"

The men groaned as though they'd just witnessed a bad sports play.

Carter rested his hands on his head and shut his eyes as though in pain. "He's screwed."

Clay shook his head. "No, no, he can get out of this. Listen closely, mate. She's going to ask you again." He pointed at Drake to make the message clear. "Whatever you do, don't say, 'Nothing.'"

The other men nodded. "You're dead in the water if you do," Carter said.

Drake furrowed his brows. "Why?"

"Women don't believe in 'nothing,'" Eric said.

Carter finished his beer. "Yeah. If she asks you what you're thinking and you say, 'Nothing,' she'll think you're keeping something from her. She can't believe you could really be thinking about nothing. Which also leads to the reverse of this."

Drake stared. "The reverse?"

"If she says nothing is wrong, it's definitely something, but she won't tell you what—"

"And that's a whole other story," Clay interrupted.

Drake scratched his head but nodded. "Okay, so I don't say, 'Nothing.'"

"Right. And this is what will save you. Tell her about a situation she knows you wouldn't want to talk about."

"Like what?"

Clay thought for a moment. "Say your prostate's bothering you."

Eric shook his head. "No, then she'll want you to go visit the doctor."

They grunted, acknowledging this fact.

"Work," Carter suggested. "Say you might have to fire somebody."

Drake signaled for another beer. "She'll ask me who."

They fell into silence.

"We need a self-contained lie that won't snowball," Carter said.

"Does one exist?" Drake scoffed.

"Sure. We just have to think of it."

Eric snapped his fingers. "You're worried about Jackie."

Drake thanked the waitress when she handed him his drink. He took a gulp. "She'll ask me why."

"Just say you're concerned," Carter said. "It's an easy out."

Eric nodded. "It's easy to worry about Jackie."

"True," Drake said slowly. "She said Jackie seemed different when they went out—subdued."

Eric frowned. "Jackie subdued? That isn't like her. She must be more upset about her breakup than she lets on."

"I think I know someone who could take her mind off it."

"Stay out of her love life, Drake," Eric said.

"It would just be an introduction. She's not seeing anyone now and I'm just looking out for her."

Clay felt his gut twist.

Drake turned to him and patted him on the back. "Then I have to find a woman for you," he said, his affection for Clay clear in his gaze.

Clay finished his drink feeling like crap. "I'm fine."

"I think you could use a refill," Eric said. "Drake, buy the man a beer."

"Your money isn't working?" he asked Eric, signaling the waitress.

"He gave you good advice. We'll see if it works."

Drake grinned. "I'm not worried. I trust him."

Clay glanced away, unable to meet his gaze.

***

Faye came into Jackie's office on a morning when Jackie had gotten little sleep. She hadn't been able to speak to Clay since the previous Sunday. "Did you read the Metro section?"

"No."

"That Winstead guy suffered some sort of freak accident in his car. There was an acid-like substance on his steering wheel and he singed his hands." She tossed the paper on the desk. "They look like lobster claws now."

Jackie looked at the photo and grimaced. "Ouch."

Faye laughed. "I'm sure he used a stronger word than that." She surveyed the cluttered desk. "How are things coming?"

"They're moving." *From one pile to another.*

"Good. Keep at it. We'll be back on our feet in no time and you'll be happy to hear that I convinced another client to join."

"Do you think we should?"

"We have to. With our present grant we have to serve a certain number of people. If we lose three more clients, we'll be in serious jeopardy. The more we have, the better we look, plus those numbers will help with the grants you're writing."

Jackie tapped her chin pensively. "Do you think we should warn the new client?"

"About what?"

"The man Melanie talked about."

Faye folded her arms. "Has Melanie called you?"

"No." She wasn't sure if that was a good sign or bad.

Faye shrugged. "Then in all likelihood you've convinced her to stay with us and that guy was a passing infatuation. There are men out there that can charm you blind."

"He called me once," Jackie said quietly.

Faye looked at her, stunned, "What?"

Jackie became unsure. "At least I think it was him." She shook her head. What he'd said sounded silly and he hadn't called her since. "Never mind. You're probably right. So has Nicolas called?" Jackie asked, curious about the blue-eyed stranger they'd met at the funeral.

"We went out last weekend."

"Did you have a good time?"

"Yes, it was nice. Well, I won't keep you."

"Wait a minute. I would like a few details, please."

Faye shrugged. "There isn't much to say. Dinner and dancing. The usual."

"Oh"

Faye turned to the door, then tripped on a stack of books. She caught herself on a chair.

"I'm sorry," Jackie said, moving the stack to the wall. She glanced around her cramped, messy office, then back at Faye. She looked out of place in her stylish clothes—as though she belonged in a multimillion-dollar corporation. "Why do you do this? I mean, I know why I'm here, but you grew up so far away from this. You could be at a job that makes a lot more money."

She took a while to answer, her face slowly lighting up as she pondered the reasons. "It's in my blood, I guess. My parents were always involved in charities and I loved helping them. I loved the feeling that I was contributing to making the world a better place. I just followed in their footsteps."

"I'm glad you did."

She grinned. "So am I."

After Faye left, Jackie sagged against her seat. For the first time she felt beaten. She'd tried contacting other possible investors and failed; she'd considered putting a fundraiser together then thought of all the effort that would entail. Her social life was also uncertain—she hadn't heard from Clay in days. Perhaps Adriana was right. They were all wrong for each other and fate was trying to give her a sign.

Suddenly Faye's pleased greeting caught her attention. "Hello, Clayton! What a nice surprise."

She heard Clay's low grumble and rushed to the reception area. He couldn't be here. He wasn't supposed to be here. What if he told Faye about the investigation?

She halted when she saw them. Faye turned to her and smiled. "This is Jackie Henson, our vice president."

Clay shook Jackie's limp hand. "Nice to meet you."

"This is Clayton Dubois, he's interested in the program and—"

"I'd like to speak with you," Clay smoothly interrupted.

Jackie found her voice. "Yes, of course."

She led him to her office then shut the door. "Why haven't you called me?" She held out her hand and lowered her head. "Wait. That wasn't the question I meant to ask you."

"I've been busy."

"What are you doing here?"

"Are you asking out of curiosity or an accusation?"

"If Faye discovers you're a private investigator—"

He sat. "She won't. She thinks I'm a reporter doing an article on non-profit organizations. But thank you," he said sarcastically. "You have this very clever knack of insulting my intelligence."

"It's not hard."

His eyes darkened.

She waved a dismissive hand. "I didn't mean it that way." She was glad to see him, yet annoyed he hadn't called. She shouldn't be because this was a casual relationship, nothing more. "It's just a surprise to see you here, *Clayton*."

"I had to think of a name similar to my own in case you saw me and called me by name."

"I see."

He stretched his legs out and stared up at her, his voice quiet "Do you trust me to do my job?"

"Yes. What have you discovered?"

"Well, I know one thing."

She leaned close. "What?"

"It's a man."

She playfully hit him and kissed her teeth. "You're annoying."

"When I have anything interesting, I'll let you know."

"So why are you here?"

He took out an envelope and handed it to her. "This is Winstead's contribution."

Jackie took the envelope, confused. "But he didn't offer to contribute anything."

"He paid us off. I thought you could put it to better use."

"Oh, thank you." She opened it and looked at the amount. "Goodness." She glanced up, amazed. "Don't you want any for yourself?"

"No."

"Don't you like money?"

"I like money, just not that kind."

Jackie began to grin. "Did you hear what happened to him?"

Clay looked bored. "No."

"He got his hands burned in his own car. Could you imagine such a freak accident?"

"Guess he won't be touching things for some time."

"Yes." She looked at him. Something suddenly clicked. Her mouth fell open. "Clay? You didn't."

He raised an innocent brow. "What?"

"You know what. That's awful." She wagged a finger. "It isn't nice to play pranks, little boy."

"Mischief made me do it."

"Thank her for me."

He pulled her onto his lap. "I plan to." He glanced at the door. "Do people usually knock before they enter?"

Jackie undid the top button of his shirt. "Yes. Why?"

"Because I want to kiss you and I'd prefer not to have an audience."

She pressed her lips on his chest. "I didn't know you were shy."

"I could learn not to be." He drew her close and kissed her.

The phone rang.

Jackie grabbed his jacket and rested her forehead against his chest. "Fate is against us."

"She probably has the right idea."

Jackie grabbed his arm before he stood. "Don't go away, please."

"Answer the phone."

"Don't go away."

He sat back. Relieved, she picked up the receiver.

"Jackie Services, HOPE speaking." She shook her head. "I mean HOPE Services, Jackie speaking."

"Bad day?" Eric said.

Sure. *If you consider trying to make out with your lover when your brother calls.* "Sort of. Hi."

"Hi. I was thinking about your financial trouble and wondered if you'd thought about Kevin."

"Kevin?"

"Yes, Cassie's friend. He's got loads of money. You could ask him to contribute. I didn't want to say anything in front of Drake. You know he hates him."

Jackie slapped her forehead, wishing she had thought of him herself. Kevin, of course. "That's a good idea. Thank you so much."

"Naturally, I'd get a percentage for offering you this suggestion."

She rested against the desk and toyed with her pens. "You'll get a percentage. How does zero sound?"

"Sounds like the amount of sensible ideas that enter your head. What are you up to?"

Jackie stopped. "What do you mean?"

"Cassie said you weren't yourself the other day."

"You spoke to Cassie?"

"No, I spoke to Adriana, which is basically the same thing."

"I'm thinking about work."

His tone grew serious. "You're talking to me, not Drake."

Damn him for being so astute. "Truth is there have been a number of clients who have been canceling our service. One mentioned some adviser who had told her to do so. It has me worried. So I've been preoccupied thinking about this mysterious adviser." She crossed her fingers, hoping her explanation would fool him.

"Have you thought about having Clay look into it for you? He helped me out once."

She tried to sound surprised. "That's a good idea."

He suddenly laughed. "And I'm sure you thought about it before I did."

"What does that mean?"

"It means whatever you're up to I'll keep it between us. Bye."

"Bye." She slowly hung up the phone, then looked at Clay guiltily. "That was Eric. I think he's on to us."

Clay shrugged. "By the time he figures things out, we'll be over."

She made a face. "You don't need to sound so pleased about it."

"Aren't you pleased? I doubt you want to explain me to them."

"No, but—"

"Then relax."

She wished she could, but the thought of him out of her life was a gloomy prospect. He'd been in it only a short time and had already become a staple.

"So, what's a good idea?" Clay asked.

"That I go to Kevin for help."

Clay frowned. "I think you should stick with proposals."

"You don't like Kevin either?"

"I know his sort," he grumbled. "Just don't feel grateful if he says yes."

She raised an innocent brow. "I'll be very grateful if he says yes."

His jaw twitched. "How grateful?"

She winked. "Maybe give him what you don't have time for."

He leaned back, his eyes dark and unreadable. "You're doing it again."

"Doing what?"

"Trying the 'Mack' approach."

"I was only teasing."

"I don't like that kind of teasing. If you want to start a relationship with Kevin, go ahead. I won't like it, but I won't stop you. However, you're making that crucial mistake again by trying to manipulate me instead of telling me what you want. I don't play games, little girl."

This time the reference stung with its accuracy. "I want to see you more."

"I know. That's why I came over."

"You just wanted to give me the money."

"I could have mailed it."

Her eyes fell, shame crawling over her skin. He was right. He'd made an excuse to see her. "I'm sorry. I guess—"

"You want more."

Her eyes flew up. "No, this is fine." She pushed herself from the desk. "I'm glad you came by. Let me just schedule a meeting with Kevin, then we'll go to lunch."

"I'm not sure about Kevin."

She laughed at his grim expression. "Unlike you, I know how to handle him."

"I'm coming with you."

She was inwardly thrilled at the prospect, but merely shrugged. "Suit yourself."

Chapter Thirteen

Kevin Jackson was a wealthy man who'd once been Drake's romantic rival for Cassie's affections. A playboy by nature and a rogue by choice, he spent his spring and summers on his Maryland estate just an hour drive out of D.C. On ten acres of land, his magnificent home boasted a private lake and landscaped row of trees. Jackie and Clay waited for their host in the sitting room under a large, vaulted ceiling, trying to get comfortable on furniture more suited for form than function. A few moments later, Kevin entered the room, an attractive man of easy confidence and excellent dress. He flashed a big smile.

"I see you brought an escort," he said to Jackie with mock dismay.

"I'm just the driver," Clay said. "Pretend I'm not here."

"That won't be hard. I'm used to ignoring drivers." He gave Jackie his full attention. "So what do you need?" Jackie explained the situation. Kevin asked her pointed questions that hinted of a fine business mind behind his quick smile and handsome face, and finally said, "I'll think it over."

Her enthusiasm died. She'd hoped to get an easy yes. "Okay."

"You're disappointed," he said, catching the passing expression. "I know what you wanted to hear, however—"

"I understand," she said, trying to appear professional though she wanted to stomp her foot in frustration. "But consider this. We could name something after you for longevity purposes."

"How about a venereal disease?" Clay muttered.

Jackie pinched him.

"Thank you. I'll tell you my decision in about a week or two. But enough about business. How is your brother Drake doing?"

"Oh, he's great."

He frowned with regret. "I was hoping for some good news." He rested back and grinned at them. "So what's going on between you two?"

Jackie's eyes widened; Clay stiffened.

His grin broadened. "Oh, I see I've hit a nerve." He rubbed his hands together with pleasure. "Does anybody else know?"

Jackie opened her mouth then closed it. Clay merely stared.

Kevin raised a knowing brow. "I won't tell anyone." He released a dramatic sigh. "Seems I'm always a step too late. I was hoping to get to Jackie myself. But you wouldn't like that."

"Neither would Drake," Clay said.

"And you think he'll approve of you?" he scoffed. "He may not like me, but I've got the background to shut him up. I like to use that advantage on occasion. You, on the other hand, have nothing."

Clay's tone hardened. "I make a decent living."

"What's a decent living nowadays? A hundred fifty thousand?"

Clay didn't respond.

"The truth is, you're good enough for a pal, but not for his sister." He shrugged. "But you don't have to face that because this isn't serious, right?"

Clay blinked lazily. "What do you think?"

Kevin glanced at Jackie then back at Clay. "I think you're in over your head."

Jackie spoke up. "We're just having fun."

"Fun? So which McDonald's has he taken you to?"

"You're not being fair."

He shrugged, then took Jackie's hand and kissed it. "When you want some caviar and champagne, come by."

Clay leaned forward. "Listen—"

Kevin shot, him a glance. "I thought you were just the driver."

"I'm also a part-time bodyguard."

Kevin let Jackie's hand go. "And a full-time something else."

Jackie spoke before Clay could. "Thank you for seeing me. I hope to hear from you soon."

"Don't worry. You will." He stood. "Clay, I want to show you something." He left the sitting room and told his assistant to keep Jackie occupied, then led Clay into the garden. They were greeted by the sound of rushing water from a fountain of a lion roaring.

Clay shoved his hands into his pockets. "What do you want to show me?"

"Some common sense. You seem to have lost yours."

"Are you trying to sound clever, or do you have a point?"

"I'm a jerk. I know that. My escapades with women are legendary. But I understand them."

Clay flashed a cold smile. "Are you warning me off? Drake would be proud."

"I'm advising you. You're going to hurt her."

"And you wouldn't?"

"No, because she wouldn't fall in love with me."

"Flash enough cash and she might."

Kevin stared at him a moment, then said, "You don't understand women at all."

"I understand them enough."

"Then let her go." His eyes gleamed. "Unless you can't."

He shrugged. "I like having her around."

"I can help you beat Drake. I could set you up with an income twice his salary."

"How often would I have to kiss your ass?"

"I have plenty of people who do that so you wouldn't have to."

"No, thanks."

"Of course you don't need my help."

Clay stilled. "What?"

"I did a little investigating on you. You've made some very profitable investments. So why the pretense? Because it doesn't fit the image? Don't worry, I understand the importance of image." He folded his arms. "But I can't figure yours out. Is it easier to be an outsider than to belong?"

Clay turned to the house.

"The image will rule you if you're not careful."

He spun around. "Has yours?"

"No, I created my image, yours created you." He walked past him. "Let's go inside. Jackie's waiting and this is about as deep as I get."

"Do you want Jackie?"

Kevin grinned over his shoulder. "Not as much as you do."

***

Jackie and Clay drove back in silence, the Maryland hillside soon making way for city buildings. Jackie rolled down the window. "There's no reason to be upset. You know Kevin likes to flirt."

He changed lanes. "I'm not upset and he wasn't flirting."

"It doesn't matter anyway."

"Stay away from him."

Jackie checked her wrists and ankles.

He looked at her curiously. "What are you doing?"

"Trying to find my chains. For a moment there you sounded like a jailer."

Clay glanced at his rearview mirror, embarrassed. He wasn't a jealous man and he certainly wasn't a possessive one.

"I've lived life this far," she informed him in a curt tone. "I don't need instructions."

"You're right."

She saw his jaw twitch. "You're still upset."

"I'm not upset." He tapped the steering wheel. "He was right about Drake. I'm good enough for a mate, but not for you."

"Drake isn't important. Besides, he can't look down on you. You both ended up on the streets at sixteen and worked your way up."

Yes, but he escaped. I'm still there. He stopped in front of her building.

Jackie smiled. "Oh, by the way, I'm wearing black."

"What?"

"I'm wearing black."

He looked at her, confused. "Your top is blue."

"Underneath."

He caught on and grinned. "Really?"

"You won't know until we reach my place."

"I don't get a sneak peek?"

She stepped out of the car. "Why settle for a sneak peek when you can see the whole thing?"

***

He had her on the bed and naked before he even noticed the color. "Where are your—"

"In the side table."

Clay opened the drawer, grabbed a condom, and began to rip it open. He stopped. "Hang on. I didn't know they made this brand anymore." He flipped it over. "It's expired." He shifted through the drawer, amazed. "All your condoms have expired."

She sat up and searched through with him. "Are you sure?"

He lifted another one. "I think this one's made out of sheepskin."

"I guess it's been a while since a man's been here." She fell back on the bed. "Great. No condoms."

"Is there a drugstore nearby?"

Jackie jumped out of bed and grabbed a shirt. "Yes."

"You don't need to come with me."

She threw his shirt at him. "I want to make sure you'll come right back."

"Stay here. Don't worry. I'll be right back."

***

He didn't come right back. He would have—with a box of condoms and a spring in his step—if he hadn't seen Tanya and her boyfriend through a bar window. He halted and peered closer just to make sure it was them. It was. He swore fiercely, then considered his options. He could walk past, pretend he didn't see them, and have a fantastic evening with Jackie, or get Tanya safely home in her father's arms and close the case.

He pictured Jackie waiting for him and started walking. He actually had a woman waiting for him. The last time that had happened he'd been in his late teens and accidentally lost the keys after handcuffing his date to the bed. That was an accident, this was on purpose. Jackie was in her bedroom, naked, waiting for him. His body responded to just the thought of it. Yes, he would pretend he hadn't seen Tanya. He knew she was in the general area, that was enough. He stopped, his sense of duty taking hold. He couldn't do it, he couldn't leave her. He kicked the side of a building. "Damn it!"

"Brother, you okay?"

Clay spun around and saw a wino grasping a brown bag in the shape of a bottle. He took a deep breath. "I'm fine."

"You need to just chill." He held out his crumpled bag. "Want some?"

"No, thanks."

He nodded and sauntered off.

Clay rested his forehead against the cool brick building. This would definitely make Jackie reconsider Kevin's offer. He wouldn't blame her. He gritted his teeth and dialed Jackie's number.

"Are you lost?" she asked.

"Umm. No." He glanced at the bar, noticed how the shadow of a tree reflected in the window, its budding leaves blowing in the slight breeze. "You're not going to like this."

"Probably not. What is it?"

"I've just spotted someone I've been looking for. It's part of a case."

She didn't reply. He closed his eyes, waiting for the blast. She finally said, "All right. I'll wait for you."

He paused. She wasn't supposed to say that. "What?"

"I said I'll wait for you."

Perhaps she misunderstood. "This is a case. It may take hours."

"It's a Saturday night. I'll be up."

He'd expected anger, maybe even tears. He would have welcomed it. Not this quiet acceptance. He suddenly realized he didn't want her to wait for him. He didn't like how it was beginning to feel like a real relationship. "Jackie, I don't think you should—"

"Good-bye, Clay. I'll see you later." She hung up.

He began to dial her number again, then stopped. He couldn't deal with her right now, he had to think about Tanya. He dialed Mack's number, then told him the situation and location while watching the pair eat their appetizer. That was a good sign—they didn't look as though they would be leaving soon. If all went well, it would be easy. He wasn't optimistic. When Mack came, they watched Tanya leave the table and head to the bar. With the pair separated it was a good time to go into action.

Clay walked past the table and glanced at Frank, Tanya's date, a slender man of indeterminate height, a nose too wide for his face, and a stubborn chin easily knocked out of joint. Clay approached the bar and rested a foot on Tanya's stool. She looked a lot older than seventeen with her short black hair, tight clothes, and heavy makeup, which was why the bartender had fallen for her fake ID. "Tanya Patten?"

She turned around. "Yes?"

"It's time to go home."

She screamed.

Frank leaped to his feet and flashed a knife. "What do you think you're doing?"

Clay jerked his head at Tanya. "I'm taking her home."

"She doesn't want to go home."

"That's too bad. I suggest you put that knife away before you hurt yourself."

"I'm not going back to jail."

"If that knife touches me, you won't make it to jail." Clay spun around when he heard a soft sound behind him. He grabbed Tanya's wrist before she struck him with a beer bottle. His dark eyes pierced hers. "Don't," he said, his eyes as cold as his voice. She dropped the bottle; it shattered on the ground. He turned back to Frank. "She's going home. Play your cards right and her father may be lenient."

Police sirens pierced the air. Tanya screamed, "Run, Frank! Get away."

He hesitated, then ran out the back door.

Clay held out his hand to help her down from the stool. She ignored it and stared at him with disgust. "You're a bastard. You don't know anything about love, just money." She spat in his face, then stormed out the front door.

A heavyset man with tired eyes came up to her. "Tanya, you had us worried."

"I'm sorry, Daddy, but I love him." She saw the police cuff Frank and screamed again. "No! It's not fair. Dad, do something. Frank!"

Clay frowned as Mr. Patten led her away without looking at him or Mack. "You're welcome," he muttered.

Mack shrugged. "His thanks will come in the form of a check. That's good enough for me."

They watched Patten's gray Jaguar drive past. Tanya flashed them a rude gesture.

Clay sighed. "So much for the damsel in distress."

Mack said, "Don't try to play the white knight and you won't be disappointed."

"Yeah. Want to hear a news flash?"

"Sure."

"I postponed a great evening to return her home to her family and I'm a bastard."

Mack patted him on the back. "Welcome to the club." He looked at his watch. "There's enough time to get back to your date."

Clay walked over to the police to give his report.

***

I should just go home, Clay thought as he rode the elevator to Jackie's place. That's usually what he did after a night like this—get a beer then crash on the couch. It was exactly what he would do once he left. He stared at the door a few moments before knocking.

She opened the door with a smile. "Did everything go well?"

"Yes."

"Good."

He stepped in, then halted at the sight. On the coffee table were pretzels, popcorn, and chips. Next to it, a cooler. He lifted the lid and saw beer on ice. He swore.

She frowned at him "What's wrong? Isn't that the right brand?"

"It's the right brand." He sat, then said with regret, "You're beginning to know me."

"Is that a bad thing?"

Clay lifted a can and shook his head, amazed. "For me, yes." He grinned up at her. "Thanks."

"You're welcome." She curled up beside him. "What happened?"

He hesitated. He didn't usually talk about a case. But, strangely, he wanted to talk to her; he didn't analyze why. In broad terms, he told her about the case and what had happened tonight. "And then when I tried to help her down from the stool, she spat on me. Now—"

Jackie stiffened. "She did what?"

"Relax, I've had worse."

"What's her name?"

He laughed. "Are you planning to cause a little mischief?"

"You're not the only one allowed to play pranks. What's her name?"

Clay rubbed the top of her head affectionately. "I can't tell you, so forget it."

She turned on the TV and they watched it together in silence. Clay fell asleep, but a half hour later, he woke up. The TV was on low and Jackie rested beside him. He hadn't meant to fall asleep. How many beers had he had? He glanced at the coffee table and saw only one. Weird. He didn't usually let his guard down like that. He looked at Jackie sleeping peacefully, enjoying the feel of her next to him, and the faint scent of her papaya cream lotion. He brushed his lips against her forehead. He didn't want to wake her but knew it was best to go. He gently nudged her and watched her eyes flutter open.

"I'd better go," he said.

"You can stay if you want," she muttered against his chest.

"No. I didn't mean to fall asleep."

"That's okay." She looked up at him. "I tried to carry you to bed, but you were a little heavier than I thought."

He gazed down at her sleep-heavy gaze and wanted to kiss her—another part of him wanted to stay. He knew he couldn't. "It's the thought that counts." He stood.

"Why won't you stay?"

"It's better this way. It doesn't blur the lines."

"Between an affair and a relationship?"

"Yes."

"So you've never just slept beside a woman before?"

"No."

He handed her the box of condoms. "For next time." He put on his jacket. "I'm sorry. I shouldn't have come back here."

"I'm glad you did." She noticed his frown. "Why don't you like me saying that?"

He opened the door. "No reason. Look, I have to go."

He kissed her briefly. She watched him walk down the hall. "You mean, you have to run," she whispered.

Chapter Fourteen

The first thing Clay saw when he entered the office was Brent hovering over a newspaper, holding a large magnifying glass against his eye.

"What are you doing?" he asked.

Brent glanced up briefly. "Looking for clues." He frowned at the magnifying glass. "But I think this thing is broken. It makes things look smaller. I thought it was supposed to make things look bigger."

Clay took the magnifying glass and placed it on the page.

Brent looked down and smiled. "Oh, yeah. That's better."

"What are you looking for?"

"Clues. You know, to that Amanda girl's disappearance."

"And you think they're in the paper?"

"Yeah." He tapped the paper. "See, this is a photo taken of Amanda's mother. She's sitting in Amanda's bedroom. I'm looking to see what kind of girl she was—is."

"You didn't believe the detailed profile given on the news?"

"Nah. That's just common stuff. The basics. You know, a good student, quiet, soft-spoken. You can really tell a lot about a person from their bedroom."

"And what have you found?"

He looked at Clay, amazed. "You're really interested? Do you think I'm on to something?"

No. "You might be."

Thrilled by the prospect, Brent sat straighter. He ran a hand through his hair, causing it to stick out at various angles. "I think I already have a theory. But let me tell you how I came to my conclusion first."

"All right."

He pulled out a pad. "I created a list of all the things I saw in her room and what they could mean. Like, I wrote down mugs. She had a lot of them. Which means she's a caffeine addict. She has to have coffee to survive, which is normal for a college student, right?"

"Or it could mean she just liked to collect mugs from different states, which could mean she likes to travel or likes to collect."

"Oh, yeah. That, too. I also wrote down psych books. She had a lot of self-help books and ones about depression. So she must have been depressed."

"Or a psychology major."

"Right, that, too. But this is what led me to my theory. The posters. Band posters. I wrote down the names of all the groups. She also had rave fliers. So though she was shy, she liked to party. I figure she's a true music devotee from the amount of CDs she had—has. Here, have a look." Clay swiftly surveyed the photo of Mrs. Heldon sitting forlorn in her daughter's room. "You agree?"

"Hmm"

"So are you ready for my theory?"

Clay nodded.

"I think she fell in love with one of these rock stars and ran off to meet him."

"Interesting. Why do you think that?"

"Her love of musicians. Usually only teenagers have a poster worship like this, right?"

"Not necessarily, but let's not debate that. No, I wonder why you think she ran off when all the evidence points to a possible abduction? It looks as though she left in a hurry."

"I don't know. I was just trying to go with my own thinking. Not what the media says." He folded his arms. "So umm what do you think?"

I think you're strange, but have potential. "Tomorrow we're going out."

His face lit up. "On a case?"

"Yes."

"Cool."

Clay walked into his office. Mack came up behind him and shut the.
door. "Tell me I'm losing my mind. Tell me you didn't say you were going
to take bubblehead boy on a case."

"I'm just taking him out of the office. He has a curious mind."

"You found it?"

"He may surprise us."

Mack sat down. "It's all an act, you know."

"What?"

"That cynical PI you try to pull off. You're a closet optimist."

"No need to be insulting."

He shook his head. "You'll need all the patience in the world to survive
Brent."

"I'm not worried."

Mack shook his head again. "I read over-your interview notes with
Melanie."

Clay tensed. "And?"

He handed him a file. "And after some searching, I think you've uncov-
ered Jackie's invisible man."

Clay took the file and set it on his desk.

"Are you going to tell Jackie?"

He turned to his computer. "No."

Mack shrugged, though he wondered why.

***

Clay considered himself a patient man. He almost lost that patience
when he saw Brent the next day. Brent was dressed in black trousers, a gray
shirt, and black jacket, and resembled an extra on a bloody gangster film.

Clay rubbed his nose, then sighed. "What are you wearing?"

Brent glanced down. "Um, slacks from—"

"No, I mean I can smell you and I'm not supposed to."

Brent looked at him, confused. "What?"

"You're wearing cologne."

He smiled. "Oh, that. It's Desire. You like it?"

"No"

His face fell. "Oh. I could wear something else next time."

"Follow me. " Clay walked into his office. "Sit down."

He hesitated. "We're not going out?"

Clay lowered his gaze and his voice. "Sit down."

He did.

"When you leave this office, you represent a business."

"Right. Hodder Investigations. So are we going out or not?"

Clay picked up a pen and twirled it.

Brent held up his hand. "No more questions. Right. I got it."

"What is our job?"

"To investigate."

He nodded. "Yes, and that requires what?"

"That we be investigators."

"And that means?"

"You know, this question thing would be a lot easier if it were multiple choice."

"Consider it an essay question and answer it. What does being an investigator mean?"

He looked at Clay with a blank expression.

"It means we must be invisible. You don't take your dress code off a TV screen or have your scent enter the room before you. You want to blend in unless you're acting in character."

He nodded in agreement. "Yeah. Yeah, I know about that. I had a girlfriend who took Method acting once."

"Hmm. I'm going to give you a mystery and let you figure it out."

His face lit up. "Really? What?"

"Why do you want to be an investigator?"

"It seems like a cool job. Speaking of cool, I like that twirling stuff you do with your pen. Could you show me how to do it?"

"Try and concentrate."

Brent put two fingers on either side of his head. "Right."

"Why else?"

"You get to meet different types of people."

"You basically get three varieties: jerks, sad sacks, and liars. Why else?"

"'Cause I want to be like you and Mack. You guys are so cool. You know everything and nothing gets to you."

"Not---"

"No disrespect, but let me finish." He rested his elbows on his knees. "I don't think I was meant for much. My parents wanted me to go into the family hardware business. But I want more. I want to help people, not tell them the best wrench to use. That's why I took criminal studies. I see the people you help and you can't tell me that doesn't feel good. I appreciate this chance to prove myself." He tugged on his jacket lapels. "One day I'll be Brent Holliday, investigator."

Clay sighed. "No cape required."

"What?"

He stood. "Never mind. Let's roll."

Brent proved to be a good listener once he settled down. His retention skills, however, proved to be a problem. After a few hours Clay needed a break and headed for a restaurant. He saw a familiar face in the waiting area—a tall, dark-skinned girl with big earrings. Clay remembered when she used to work at the Blue Mango with her boyfriend, Cedric.

She recognized him and smiled. "Hi, Mr. Jarrett."

"Hi, Pamela. What are you doing here?"

"Spring break."

"Lucky girl."

He felt Brent shifting back and forth like an eager puppy waiting for attention. "This is Brent."

She smiled at him. "Hi."

He only grinned.

"So what are you two doing here?" she asked, to break the silence.

Brent smoothed his hair back and puffed out his chest.

"Taking a break from a case. Clay and I are working on important business."

Clay shoved his hands in his pockets.

"What?" she asked, intrigued.

"It's confidential, but it involves a missing person."

"Oh. Sounds exciting." Her tone was polite interest but not amazement.

Brent didn't notice. He shrugged nonchalantly. "It's part of the job. So what do you do?"

"I'm still in school. I got my associate's degree in culinary arts and restaurant management. I recently transferred to the Art Institute of Pittsburgh to complete my bachelor's."

"You're really going places. While you're in town I could show you around."

"I have a boyfriend."

"Oh, you do, huh? What is he majoring in?"

"He's a waiter at a top restaurant. The Blue Mango."

"He's a part-time student?"

She hesitated. "No, he's not in school."

"Why not? Can't he afford it?"

Her smile became less polite and more forced. "No, he just likes his job."

"I see."

Clay tapped him on the shoulder. "We'd better grab a table."

Brent nodded. "I'll catch up with you." He turned back to Pamela. "Must be hard for you."

She furrowed her brows. "What do you mean?"

"What do you and your boyfriend talk about?"

"A lot of things."

"You'll end up making more money than him. A pretty woman like you shouldn't have to carry around a man."

"She doesn't have to," a low voice said.

They turned to Cedric. Pamela took his hand and smiled. "This is Brent."

He held out his hand. "Investigator. Graduated from George Washington."

Cedric looked at his hand in disgust. "Good for you."

"So you're a waiter."

"Yeah."

"You always planning to do that?"

Cedric took a step closer. "What's it to you?"

Brent took a step back. "Just trying to have a civil conversation."

"Fine. Let me say a few words." He punched him. Brent crashed into the wall, then slid to the ground. "Is that clear enough for you?" He took Pamela's hand and left.

Clay helped Brent to his feet. "You should have left when I told you to."

Brent gently probed his jaw. "I didn't know she was dating a thug."

"How many times were you shoved in a locker in high school?"

Brent turned, surprised.

"You tried too hard to be smooth, to actually be smooth. In all things, just be yourself."

***

Pamela looked at Cedric as they strolled down Sixteenth Street. "Are you going to talk or brood all day?"

"That guy was a—"

"Yes, I know what he was. He's not here right now I am and I'll be leaving soon."

Clay stopped walking and pulled her close. It was amazing how fast a week could go. "I wish you didn't have to leave."

"Only two more years."

"Then what?"

"Master's, maybe, but I'll stay here."

He brushed his lips against hers. "I was hoping you would say that."

"Why?"

"You know I would never want to get in your way," he said, his words coming out awkwardly. "I want you to be whatever you want to be. I just like having you around."

"I know. It's been hard."

He dug into his pocket. "I bought you something to take back with you."

"What?"

He pulled out a little black box and opened it. It was a ring with a diamond so small she could barely see it. She thought it was beautiful. "Will you marry me?"

She clasped her hands together, knowing the importance of his offer. She lifted moist eyes. "But I don't want to get married."

Hurt and disappointment flashed in his eyes. "What?"

"At least, not yet."

His eyes fell. "Oh."

"It's too soon."

He shook his head. "Not for me." He looked at her, his eyes pleading for her to change her mind. "I know I want you to be my wife."

"I'm not ready to be a wife."

He turned and walked away. She walked silently beside him. After a moment she said, "But when I am ready, the only wife I'll want to be is yours."

"We love each other, right?"

Pamela nodded.

He stopped walking. "Then say yes. We don't have to get married now. Just wear the ring so I know you're mine."

"I don't need a ring to belong to you."

"The other guys need to know."

She folded her arms and tilted her head to the side. "The other guys know because I tell them. Don't you trust me?"

"Yes," he said, unable to rid himself of the disappointment inside.

Cedric had a hard time concentrating after Pamela left. So he wasn't surprised when he was called into the manager's office. However, he was surprised to see Drake there instead of the manager, Lance. That wasn't good. "What's wrong?" Drake asked him.

"Pamela left yesterday."

"She's left before."

He shifted awkwardly. "I asked her to marry me and she said no. She's not ready yet. It sorta put me off my rhythm."

"You're still young."

"I'm a man."

Drake nodded. Yes, he was a man and it wasn't fair to brush away his pain because he was so many years removed from this moment. He shoved his hand in his pocket and pulled out a little action figure. For reasons he couldn't understand, Marcus had a habit of slipping things in his pocket "to keep Daddy company." He set the figure on the table, then leaned back in the chair. "I wish I had something to say to you to make you feel better, but I don't. But remember, today's disappointments may be tomorrow's joys. What you want now may need time to simmer like a good stew before it's ready. Okay?"

"Okay. I didn't mean to cause trouble."

"Fine, then get back to work." Drake watched him go, then picked up the action figure and placed it back in his pocket. For the first time in his life he hoped he'd made a bet he wouldn't win.

***

"Did you see Brent's eye?" Mack asked Clay the next day. "Someone did us a favor and punched him."

"He was trying to be smooth with the wrong woman."

Mack laughed. "And she punched him?"

"No, her boyfriend did. He makes some bad decisions, but has he told you his theory on the Amanda disappearance?"

"That's she's a groupie—"

Clay waved his hand. "Forget about that and think about her leaving."

"The police are on the case and they're not doughnut eating imbeciles," he said.

"No one is saying they are."

"Then let them do their job and we do ours."

Mack was right, he couldn't get distracted. He had other things to figure out. Like Patty's cards.

***

Jackie sat on her couch, working on a possible new budget, when the phone rang. She picked up the phone, happy for the break. "Hello?"

"Still looking for me?" a familiar voice asked.

She gripped the phone, anxiety creeping up her spine. "Who is this?"

"You know who I am. You just don't know my name."

Jackie tried to sound glib in an effort to hide her fear. "Oh, it's Rumpelstiltskin."

He laughed. A low, chilling sound. "A sense of humor. Very nice. Unfortunately, that's not my name. Melanie knows it, though. She could help you."

"I will find out who you are and I will stop you."

He clicked his tongue with mock sympathy. "Such anger. Pity, in someone so young. No wonder Melanie gave me your number. She wants you to experience the same peace she has."

"My peace will come when I find you."

"Yes, that's right. However, you will not find me on your own. Since you've made no progress so far, let me help you. Melanie will tell you who I am if you get to her before she leaves."

Jackie's heart began to race. "Before she leaves?"

He replied with the dial tone.

Jackie called Clay. "He called me again."

"What did he say?"

She wrapped the cord around her hand. "He said I should see Melanie before she leaves."

"I'll be right over."

***

Melanie lived in a section of southeast D.C. where tourists and most taxis didn't venture. Jackie and Clay walked up to the brick complex, where a cracked cement walkway led a path to Melanie's first-level front door. Her lawn sprouted more weeds than grass. Through an open window above, they heard a baby crying while two adults shouted obscenities at each other. Jackie knocked on the door. No one replied.

She turned to Clay. "Break it down."

He glanced around the complex, his sharp eyes taking in a used needle on the ground and the stripped car, left like a disregarded skeleton on the street. "She may be out."

Her tone hardened. "Break down the door or I will." Clay looked at Jackie's stubborn face and smiled. "I'd like to see you try. It may prove amusing."

She walked away and then ran toward the door. He casually held out his hand and stopped her. "Breaking down the door is only one way," he said patiently. "But there's an easier way." He pulled out a thin wire and picked the lock. He opened the door. They found Melanie lying face up next to an empty bottle of pills.

Jackie rushed to her and checked her vital signs while Clay called an ambulance. She was still alive, though barely. "You have to hold on," she urged, awkwardly cradling her.

Jackie had faint memories of her mother, kept alive by photos and the stories her brothers told. One thing she remembered were her mother's arms as she lay in bed; they were skinny, like twigs at her side, and they used to lift her up and hug her. She remembered creeping into the room one day and laying her mother's head in her lap and humming as her mother used to, hoping that if she could hum enough her mother could get well like magic tears or a kiss had done in a fairy tale. Jackie felt that desperation now, wanting some magic act to prevent the death that was destined. She turned to Clay. "We could try to make her sick."

"The drugs are already taking effect."

"We have to stop them somehow."

Melanie's eyes drifted to hers. Eyes once so clear were now dazed and unfocused. "What for?" she whispered through cracked lips. "It will come soon—the peace, the rapture. He'll come for you, too. He'll save you."

"What is his name?"

She smiled weakly. "I told him about you. You're like the rest of us."

Jackie resisted the urge to shake her. "What is his name?"

"Name?"

"Your adviser. You can tell me now. He told me so."

"He did." she said, uncertain.

"Yes." She stroked Melanie's forehead. "It's all right now."

Her face relaxed. She took a deep breath, then said, "His name is Emmerick …" Her voice died away. A few seconds later, so did she.

Jackie stared at the wide, sightless eyes. She turned to Clay, who stood with his hands on his hips and no readable expression on his face. Her sense of helplessness ignited into rage. She wanted to scream and shout at him for not stopping this, for being so busy with other cases that he hadn't prevented what had happened. She wanted to pound his chest, cause him some pain, to get some emotion on his face. At that moment she hated him for being so calm, for being so distant.

She stood and faced him. "Don't you care?"

"Of course I care."

"Then show it."

His eyes searched hers. "What do you expect me to do?"

"Feel something."

He merely looked at her.

Jackie gripped her hands. "Sometimes you--"

"Hate me? Do I disgust you with my heartlessness? Don't worry, I inspire that in a lot of people, but I don't have the luxury of coddling you and trying to make everything okay. It's not okay. This world isn't okay. You've seen death before so you know it exists. People die sometimes by their own hands. I'm not a hero sometimes I'm too late."

His words shamed her with their truth. She could hear the pain in the distant syllables of his words ringing with the bell of remorse. It was unfair to blame him.

Jackie briefly shut her eyes and took a deep, steadying breath. "This wasn't supposed to happen! We were supposed to save her. She wasn't supposed to die in this place." She looked around at the dirt on the wall;

there was the smell of damp carpet from last week's rain. Tears filled her eyes. It was a dreadful place to die, but many people died in places far worse. "I failed."

He touched her shoulder. "You didn't fail."

She shrugged his hand away. "Yes, I did."

"No, you—"

"You don't call this failure?" She pointed to Melanie's lifeless body. "What would you call it? A miscalculation?"

"She killed herself. You couldn't have stopped that."

"Yes, I could have."

"Sometimes people have a despair that cannot be reached. You couldn't have—"

Jackie pounded her fists against her thighs. "I needed time. He stole that from me. He killed her and I still don't know anything about him. Neither do you." She studied his face a moment. "Do you?"

He nodded.

"How long have you known?"

Long enough. He'd met Melanie and realized she was in pretty deep. It would take a major intervention to combat the brainwashing. What she said was familiar and in his gut he knew then who her messenger was.

"His name is Lamont Emmerick. At least, that's one of his names. He grew up in Michigan, the second son to a factory worker and teacher. His parents were happily married. He graduated from a local Detroit college and made his way west. Lived in California, then Washington. Never stayed in a place longer than three years. He had worked as an insurance agent before following his 'calling.'"

Jackie's anger dipped into a dull anger that radiated in the back of her mind, slowly heating itself as she felt her limbs tremble. She wanted to shatter something, presently his face. She could barely get the words through her teeth. "Why didn't you tell me this?"

"Because he's a dangerous man."

"Did I hire you to be a damn bodyguard? You bastard. You knew all this time and you didn't tell me. You let her die. You're right—you're no hero, you're a traitor."

"She was in too deep, like a trapped fly in milk Emmerick isn't the type of man you can reason with. I didn't want you ... I wanted to protect you."

"I don't care. You should have told me."

"I couldn't."

"Why not?"

He walked to the window and ran his finger against the ledge. "Because I hadn't stopped him," he said simply, wiping the dust from his fingertips.

"What do you mean? How could you have stopped him?"

He captured her eyes. "By killing him the first time I had a chance."

Chapter Fifteen

Jackie needed only to look at the shadows in Clay's eyes to know what he meant; they almost reached out to her, chilling her heart with their remote sadness. She slowly fell to her knees, feeling ill. "But she doesn't have any marks on her. How could it be the same man who killed your sister?"

"He only beat his wives. His style hasn't changed much. Suicide is the preferred method of peace. I'll have to verify a few things." He disappeared into the next room.

She wished he wasn't so calm. Didn't he know how cold it seemed? She wanted—no, needed—some burst of emotion: pain, rage, hurt, anything. She, thought of Adriana comparing Clay to a phantom. What was going on in his mind? "I can get someone else to help me," she said when he returned to the room.

He raised a brow. "Are you firing me?"

"Yes."

"Too bad."

"Clay—"

"Then let me do my job."

"You've done your. job. Now that I know who he is—"

Clay spun around so quickly, she jumped. "You're going to stay away from him until I say so."

"Don't tell me what to do."

"You're a smart woman, don't spite me just because you don't like instructions."

She bristled at his tone. "I—"

"I know what he's capable of." He pointed to Melanie. "This is nothing."

"He can't—"

"I want your promise." He grabbed her arm. "Promise."

"You're hurting me."

"Promise."

He released his grip. She rubbed her arm; he noticed the motion and felt guilty. He reached for her—she stepped back. "Trust me," he said.

"Only if you tell me everything from now on. I don't need protection from the truth."

"Okay." He walked around the bare room. Along the wall, the carpet threads were unraveled. He picked up a scrap piece of paper and pocketed it.

She bit her lip. "Shouldn't you leave it for the police?"

"She was poor and this is a suicide. There won't be an investigation."

"But he—"

"Won't be connected to this. There are no pamphlets connected to him. She died by her own hands." He lifted up the carpet. "He's not going to be easy to catch."

Jackie shifted from one foot to the other. "When do you think the ambulance will get here?"

"Tuesday, if we're lucky."

She shot him a look. "That's not funny."

"It's a bad neighborhood. People here steal the tires off police cruisers." He saw her staring at the body, all her emotions ready to become tears. "I'll get him for you," he promised in a soft voice.

She met his eyes. "We'll get him together."

***

Clay stared at his computer screen and swore. It was too easy. All the information about the Careless Rapture Ministry was on their Web site. It didn't make sense.

He twirled his pen. "Why does he have a Web site?"

Mack looked up from his desk. "Who?"

"Emmerick." Clay tapped his pen against the computer screen. "Why does he have a Web site?"

Mack took off his reading glasses. "Exposure? Connection to his followers?"

Clay considered that for a moment, then shook his head. "But he targets low-income individuals. Most wouldn't have access to the Internet. Why not stick with fliers and the one-on-one approach? This is unnecessary, so why does it exist? Why expose himself? Why not keep it underground?"

"Ego?"

"Yes, he has one. But I don't think that's it."

Mack saw a certain look in Clay's eyes and pinched the bridge of his nose. "Don't get too deep. Our job is to find out more about him. Find out where he is. We're not hired to draw up a psychological profile."

Clay ignored him. "There wasn't anything in her apartment. Not a booklet, pamphlet, card. Nothing to connect Melanie to him."

"Perhaps he was afraid."

"She killed herself. Why would he be afraid of that?" He ran a tired hand down his face. "He's not acting in character and I don't like that."

"Perhaps she cleaned everything up herself before she killed herself. It's not unusual for victims to set things in order before they die."

"Yes, but why leave nothing? No note. No reason. If this is part of their ritual, wouldn't she be proud of what she had done?" Clay leaned back, baffled. "I want you to get ahold of Nicolas for me."

"The police won't touch this."

"They may be able to help."

"I used to be a cop, remember? He can't help you."

"I still want to talk to him." Clay twirled his pen. "I want to try."

***

Nicolas listened to Clay's story as they sat in the back booth of a cafe with three coffees between them. Nicolas shook his head after Clay finished. "Have you heard about a girl named Amanda?" Nicolas asked. "She's been missing for nearly three weeks. We would have forgotten about her except that she didn't have the decency to be some ordinary girl. She's Senator Heldon's niece. Do you know what that means? It means we've got the flaming government on our ass and the media thinking they are damn detectives and putting the public in a frenzy."

Nicolas took a sip of his coffee, his blue eyes sharp. "I don't need to tell you how this works, but I'll try. No one cares about some ex-hooker who got herself involved with a nutcase and decided to kill herself. If she came from a good family? Maybe. Had some looks? Possibly. What you've just told me is a sad story. This city has a lot of those." His eyes darted between them. "I don't want to leave you high and dry, though." He took out a card and shoved it across the table to Clay. "I think reporters are scum, but he's one of the few that doesn't twist our words in print. Perhaps he could write a story and get some interest." He lifted his mug. "Good luck."

***

Unfortunately, they had no interest. Steve Reinfeld of the *Post* listened, his long face and intense features kind, but once Clay finished, he rubbed his thin chin and shrugged. "Nice story, but it's not news. People won't care. If it was a slow news day, perhaps. But with this disappearance of Amanda Heldon still a hot topic, your story wouldn't get the space the size of a personal ad." He pulled on his goatee. "News is important information with an entertainment factor. You have to package it right. Give me a juicy angle related to what's happening now, maybe I could help you out then. Otherwise, let it die."

Later that day, Mack and Clay sat in their office in low spirits, appropriate with the drizzling rain. Clay twirled his pen. "You know how you said we weren't in the business of storytelling?"

"Yeah."

"Well, what if we were? How would you tell this story?"

"Homeless preyed on by killer."

Clay shook his head. "No. He's not a killer in the traditional sense."

"Cult leader recruits disenfranchised for new reign."

Clay shook his head. "No, that won't work either. How can we catch people's interest?"

Mack went online to check the Web site again.

Clay rubbed the back of his neck. "There has to be something we can get him on."

"Does he like women? I could arrange a prostitute to visit him."

"No."

"Drugs?"

"No."

Mack frowned good-naturedly. "If you really wanted to get him, you would have said yes. You're so damn ethical."

"No, I just want something more."

Mack clapped his hands together and pointed to the screen. "Great. This might interest you."

"What?"

He turned the monitor to Clay. "He's written a book."

"So?"

"So, if you've written something, don't you need to publicize it?"

"You're suggesting we offer him some publicity?"

"Yes. Get the bastard out from under his rock."

Clay thought for a moment. "TV or radio?"

"TV. I know this woman who's eager to get some ratings on her local news show. It's public television, but at least it's some exposure. We could set it up as a debate. But do you think he'll fall for it?"

Clay began to smile. "Yes, he will."

That evening, Clay stared across the restaurant table at Jackie, amazed. "I thought you'd be happy."

She nearly choked on her drink. "Happy? I can't believe you're going to help publicize his book. I want to see him behind bars."

"He will be, but as I've said, he's not easy to catch. This will make him visible—underground he's more dangerous. He may expose himself and then people will see what he's about and may stay away."

She angrily bit into her sandwich. "Or be intrigued."

"Don't you trust me?"

"Yes, I trust you. I've told you I trust you. The problem is I don't trust him You've admitted that he's clever." She rested her forearms on the table and leaned forward. "What will you do when you see him again?"

"Debate him."

"What if he makes you lose your temper on TV?"

"I don't lose my temper," he said softly.

She set her sandwich down and folded her arms. "What was your sister's name?"

"Rennie."

"No, her real name."

He frowned. "Does it matter?"

"Yes, the more you avoid it, the more power you give it. When Melanie did not say Emmerick's name, she made it almost sacred."

He squirted ketchup on his fries.

"What was her name?"

He shook his head. "It doesn't matter now."

She watched him for a moment, then said, "Cancel the show. You're not ready."

A flash of irritation crossed his face. "Of course I'm ready. I've always been ready to see him again."

She narrowed her eyes. "Is this about my case or your revenge?"

"You saw Melanie."

"Yes, she killed herself." She paused. "Rennie didn't."

He pushed his plate away. "You hired me to get him for you and I'm going to."

"I hired you to get a name and address, not become a vigilante."

"It's just a TV show."

No, it wasn't, and he knew it, too. That worried her—he wasn't prepared. When someone didn't know their weakness, they were vulnerable because they didn't know how to protect themselves. Clay wouldn't even admit to any. Whether it was arrogance, conceit, or denial, he was in danger, but she knew she couldn't stop him.

He grinned, trying to lessen her unease. "I can take care of myself. Don't worry about me."

"Fine." She grabbed a handful of jelly packets. He gently covered her hand with his. "Take two."

She smiled, chagrined. "Bad habit."

"I know," he said quietly. "I've been hungry, too." His dark eyes showed a sensitivity she wouldn't have expected from one made so cynical by life. It felt good to be with someone with whom she didn't have to explain everything. But the shadows were still there. No matter how many times she was with him, a part of him was still a stranger. He had warned her that the relationship wouldn't be enough. She would make it so.

Two days later, she knew she couldn't. It wasn't enough. Jackie pulled on her nightgown as Clay prepared to leave. The sex was always great, but somehow this time less fulfilling.

She sat on the bed and drew her knees to her chest. "Am I the only woman you're seeing?"

He hesitated, then said, "Of course."

She nodded. "Just curious."

He sat beside her and sighed, resigned. "Go ahead and say it."

"Say what?"

"Whatever's on your mind."

She bit her lip. "Why won't you stay?"

His gaze sharpened. "You know why."

"Yes, I do. But I don't understand why. I can understand if someone doesn't want you to stay, but what about when someone does?"

He pulled on his shoes. "You're doing it again."

"I'm not trying to manipulate you. I'm trying to figure you out."

"You don't need to figure me out." He walked to the door.

She jumped to her feet. "What are you hiding?"

He turned to her and began to smile. It wasn't a pretty expression. "What are you searching for? Whatever you need, I can assure you I don't have it."

"Why are you so certain?"

"Because I know you."

She folded her arms. "A few weeks ago I would have believed you, but now I'm not so sure. You're a quick talker with the eloquence of a hustler that convinces people to believe you. I know—I do it myself sometimes. I did it with Winstead. But there are a lot of things you don't know, things you wouldn't even admit to yourself."

He opened the door. "I'd better go."

"Don't you mean *run*?"

He stopped and closed the door with a soft click. "What do you mean by that?"

"You're used to running away."

He stared at her with hard, dark eyes. "Are you calling me a coward?"

"Why? Because you're scared?"

"I'm not scared of anything."

She didn't flinch under his intense gaze. Instead, she smiled softly. "I'm not sure if you've noticed, but I'm not afraid of you."

"Maybe you should be."

"Why?"

"Because you can't handle me. And I'm not going to change."

"I don't want to change you."

"Why do you want me to stay when you know I always leave? Why do you want to figure me out when I don't want you to? You're spoiled and—"

"I'm spoiled?" Her voice cracked in disbelief. "You're spoiled, too. We give to outsiders, but when it comes to relationships, people have to follow our rules. We like getting our own way. You get everyone to do exactly what you want. Heck, Cassie is afraid to ask you any questions because you've made it quite clear that if anyone gets too close, you'll leave. That's your control. And you're always in control."

"I---"

Jackie waved her finger. "Just listen, then you can reply."

He rested against the wall and waited.

"I wanted you to stay because I foolishly thought it would be nice to wake up with you beside me. Simple as that. I wasn't trying to put a lead around your neck." She pointed when he opened his mouth. "I said listen."

Clay folded his arms.

"You were right in the beginning—I'm not your kind of woman. I care whether you're safe or not, I care whether you're tired or upset. I can't help myself." She rested her hands on her hips. "Let me tell you a few other things you won't like. I worry about you. I know I'm not supposed to, but I do. I think about you at work, I think about calling you for no reason except to say hello or to hear your voice." She walked up to him. "Oh, and guess what? You're not going to like this, but I'm going to enjoy telling you this." She grabbed his collar and pulled him down. "Sometimes I love you and sometimes I could kick the crap out of you." She pushed him aside and stormed into the hallway.

She went into the kitchen and grabbed a box of crackers and spreadable cheese, slamming the cupboard and fridge as she did so. She sat and ate her way through the contents. Clay came into the room a few moments later.

She looked at him with mock surprise. "You haven't left yet? You'd better leave before the sun rises. I'd hate to be accused of trying to change you, and there's that distinct fear I may grow too attached to you. I know you wouldn't want that."

"Can I speak now?"

"I'm not sure. Do you need instructions?"

He sat and grabbed a cracker.

"Aren't you going to leave?"

He spread cheese on the cracker. "You wanted me to stay a moment ago."

"Who cares what I want?" she said. "You'll do what you damn well please anyway."

He placed another cracker on top.

"Not all women want a man to fight their battles for them," she continued, "There are little battles that women fight alone. Sometimes a woman just wants a man to be there, be a strength she can draw from when her own begins to wane, be a comfort when she feels unsafe with the thoughts in her mind. But you wouldn't understand that kind of battle because you fight yours alone."

"If you need—"

"No, I don't need you. There. Don't you feel better? You're free. She glanced at the stack of crackers and frowned. "Are you building a tower or a large cracker sandwich?"

He placed another cracker on top of the stack.

She took the cracker off and ate it. "At least the sex is good so we can still have an affair. I just had a brief lapse in judgment."

"I disagree," he said, in a voice so low it came out as a grumble. "I think you judged me very well."

"I'm not judging you."

"Unless I misunderstood you, I'm supposed to read your mind. I'm supposed to know when you're scared or frightened or whatever, and act according to the invisible guidebook of handling women's woes, right?"

"Don't—"

"I'm not finished."

She bit her lip.

"Wouldn't it have been easier if you'd told me why you wanted me to stay? Do you think if you were scared that I would walk away?"

"No, but--"

"That if you were worried I'd ignore you?"

She shook her head.

"So you're angry at me for something I wasn't even aware of." He shook his head, disgusted. "Just like a woman not to tell me the truth."

"Just like a man to be totally blind to it," she countered.

"And what would that be? Being the dumb male that I am, I can't figure it out on my own."

Jackie raised a brow.

Clay waved a dismissive hand. "Besides love."

"You can't just brush that aside." She paused. "Wait, I'm wrong. Yes, you can."

He twirled the knife between his fingers. "I didn't ask you to love me."

"No, that was my misfortune."

He set the knife down.

"I wanted you to stay because you wanted to, not because I needed you to."

He stood, restless. "Exactly. You wanted me to be someone I'm not."

"I wanted to give you an excuse to stay."

He took a deep breath, trying to keep his voice level. He would not lose his temper. "I don't need an excuse. When I want to I'll stay."

"No, you won't. You wouldn't dare risk being that vulnerable."

"I need to leave." He walked to the door.

Jackie jumped to her feet. "Yes, run. Run away from what you're afraid of."

Clay spun around, his temper ignited. "I'm only afraid of one thing and that is—" He abruptly stopped. "I think we've both had enough of this."

Jackie sat back down and grabbed another cracker. "You're right. Bye."

Clay stared at her. He hadn't expected it to end like this. He'd expected it to end clean, swift. This felt as though some bodily organ had been ripped from him, leaving its veins and ligaments dangling. A part of him whispered that he should fight for this, another told him to let go. She didn't give him a chance to decide; she stood. "It's been fun. Good night." She went to her bedroom and slammed the door.

Clay stared at the cracker crumbs on the table and the cheese hardening on the knife blade, then grabbed his jacket and left.

In her room, Jackie didn't wait to hear the front door close before she began pulling the sheets off the bed. She didn't want his scent on anything. She wanted to wash him out of her life. She wanted to forget him. She pulled off the duvet, the pillowcases, the sheets, tossing them on the floor with more force than necessary. Once finished, she stared at the bare bed. She'd stripped it clean, but she knew it was not enough. Nothing would ever be enough to erase the memories. She fell on her bed, face forward, determined not to cry.

Clay walked out into the still night and headed to his car. It was over. He and Jackie were through. He was fine with that. Everything eventually came to an end, he was old enough to know that. However, it was the first time he'd ended a relationship and felt as though he'd been dumped. Funny how she'd wanted to know what he was afraid of. He shook his head at the irony. His biggest fear was being kicked out. It amazed him how often he was.

Chapter Sixteen

Clay stepped into the Channel 23 TV station and walked through the plain building as though heading to his past. He was about to face the man he'd demonized and killed in his dreams. Once he reached the studio, he saw the camera operators working on the equipment and setting up the lighting. He spotted the makeup artist powdering the host's face, then glanced at the three chairs on the stage. His eyes traveled to the far side of the studio. Then he saw him.

The years hadn't altered him much. Emmerick was still a slim man with skin the color of crushed coffee beans. He had refined features that seemed to crowd in the middle of his face. The Afro was gone, replaced by gray braids that hung down his back. His brown eyes had become more watchful than arrogant—they would have to be to keep him out of an asylum this long. The problem with Emmerick was that he wasn't crazy. That was what made him dangerous.

Emmerick turned and saw him. Clay nearly grinned at the shock of recognition that flew across the older man's face. He waited as Emmerick came toward him, stealing himself against the anger that had begun to rise. Age had slowed his gait, but not rid it of its strength, its purpose. Whatever that purpose was.

Emmerick held out his hand. "It's been a long time."

Clay ignored the friendly gesture and folded his arms. "Yes."

"A part of me is not surprised to see you here."

"We were destined to meet again, you'd say," Clay said in an ironic tone.

"Yes, destiny—"

"Save your breath, old man. Your tune hasn't changed and I'm not in the mood to listen to you sing."

Emmerick nodded and backed away. Clay allowed the makeup artist to powder the shine off his face, and nothing else. Soon the host approached them with the requisite plastic smile, her hair effectively pulled back to give her attractive blond features a professional appearance. She explained how the show would progress as they were fitted with microphones. Then they were directed to their seats. Clay sat across from Emmerick, ordering himself to be still. He knew the camera would exaggerate any telling signs of unease and he would not allow Emmerick that advantage.

"And five, four, three, two..."

"Hello, I'm Amy Brennan, thanks for joining us at *Just Talk*. Today we are going to discuss the growing trend of alternative religions in the District. Our two guests are Lamont Emmerick of the Careless Rapture Ministry, the author of *Divinity for the Spirit*, and investigator Clay Jarrett, a Christian."

Clay sent her a look. He hadn't mentioned any religious affiliation. It was clear Amy had her own agenda in mind. He had to be careful not to fall into it.

"Now, Mr. Emmerick, tell us about your ministry."

"My belief is an all-encompassing encounter with the good of the universe. Living in harmony with the various spirits that surround us."

"And Mr. Jarrett, you disagree?"

"I don't disagree with people's beliefs unless it causes harm to others. Emmerick encourages those who are ill to forgo treatment."

"But there are other faiths that don't believe in using traditional science to heal," Amy said.

"He has gone one step further by encouraging patrons to choose death."

Emmerick smiled. "We are all going to die eventually. My belief is that if the universe has touched you with disease, you should surrender. It is in that state of giving when your rapture will come."

"So you think those that have cancer are meant to die?" Amy asked, intrigued by his smile.

"Instead of seeing it as a curse, you should see it as a blessing. An invitation to surrender to divine peace. Science interferes with the natural order of things. Would they have lived years ago?"

"We used to have a high birth-mortality rate," Clay said. "That has changed because our knowledge has changed."

"We also keep those people stuck to life support as vegetables for our own benefit, not theirs. Where is their sanctity, where is their peace?"

"Not all people end up as vegetables. Some come out of comas."

"And some don't."

Clay could feel his patience thinning. "It is not your job to tell people what—"

"People do it every day," Emmerick interrupted smoothly. "Rabbis, priests, and yogis teach followers how to live, how to seek the sanctuary of the spirit that we all desire. It is our right to have that. I am a messenger like them: Am I to be persecuted, as they would have been years ago, because my beliefs are currently not popular?"

"Your message is self-serving. You target the weak—those that are destitute, ill, alone."

"Because they need the message more. No one sees them. How many homeless people do you pass on the streets without looking them in the eye? They are invisible to us. I'm sure you understand that intimately." He smiled with cruel confidence.

Clay didn't reply.

"But I see them. The universe sees them and they are made part of a world that would throw them aside." He leaned forward, his eyes lit with a private knowledge. "The truth is this is a personal vendetta. You already have a bias against people like myself."

"What you are doing is—"

"Perfectly legal. Not all people believe in my practice." He paused like a seasoned speaker. "Your sister did, however." He turned to Amy. "She had been a follower of mine and she died. Tragically. But her death is not a tragedy. It was a release from a life filled with suffering. She was ultimately rewarded for her loyalty and obedience."

"To you or to your universe?" Clay quietly asked.

His gaze pierced the distance between them. "You should know the answer to that. You used to be a believer once."

Amy jumped in. "Is that true, Mr. Jarrett?"

Clay didn't reply right away, almost feeling the camera coming in for a close-up. "Yes."

Emmerick nodded, pleased with the acknowledgement. "You came to me with nothing. A lost teenage runaway lacking education, little hope of a successful future, with your own traditional beliefs in shambles. I taught you how to survive, didn't I?"

"Yes." Clay couldn't say much else without betraying himself, without admitting that Emmerick was prodding a wound he'd thought he'd healed. He knew how Emmerick worked, that he would prod that wound until fresh blood seeped through.

"Everyone had turned you away, but I didn't. I gave you something to hope for." He turned to Amy. "He was one of my best recruiters. One of the most powerful speakers around." He looked at Clay. "I was proud. You were the son I never had."

"You weren't my father."

Emmerick clasped his hands in his lap, unperturbed by the venom in Clay's tone. "I was a father figure. Like Rennie was a mother figure to you. I gave you guidance. Just because you turned against the faith doesn't mean you need to start a crusade to destroy it."

Amy piped up, seeing a perfect angle. "So, as a former member of the Careless Rapture Ministry, were you involved in any, as you would say, harmful activity that causes you to be here today?"

"The ministry had a different name then," Clay said. "The name is as changeable as the beliefs."

Emmerick shook his head as though disappointed. "Your bitterness hurts me. I would suggest you try my book to ease you of your anger. You were always one for anger." He pulled down his collar to reveal a thin scar. "Do you remember when you gave me this? You'd wanted to kill me because of your sister's passing. I had to talk you down from your rage. I saved your life as you did mine and that brings me to my book. The lessons the universe teaches us."

It went steadily downhill from there. Emmerick combated Clay's every statement with some damaging information from the past. He was better than Clay had remembered—too subtle to seem threatening, with a calm, patient manner that didn't allow Clay to argue with him without Clay looking aggressive. So Clay retreated by using vague terms and neutral statements. Soon the program was over. They ceremonially shook hands, both knowing Emmerick had come out the victor. Defeated, Clay left the studio.

A half hour later, he sat in the silence of the Church of Holy Spirit. The silence allowed his thoughts to punish him. The majestic vaulted ceiling hung overhead while a European stained-glass altar with gilded images of saints and kings faced him. He watched an old woman kneel before the brass candles and bow her head, and gripped his hands to keep from being consumed by the memories of Melanie, Gabriella, and Rennie, who'd never get the chance to be old. He'd failed them all and now Jackie, too. He'd lost her when he'd started to treasure what they had.

She was right. He had run. He'd run before he destroyed what he held dear. Alone, he was safe. Everyone was safe. He loosened his fists. There was no need for pity. His life was a series of choices and he would not regret them all right now. He had to think, to plan. The thin scar on Emmerick's neck flashed in his mind. He did try to kill him, and didn't regret it. But Emmerick had been wrong—his sister had been alive then. Clay had tried to kill him when he'd come into his room one night and tried to betray his trust in a way no father figure should. He saw his evil then and wanted to destroy him.

That night Emmerick had persuaded followers to tie up Clay and then Emmerick had beaten him with his fists and his words. Clay had almost taken pleasure in the blows. His own father had never touched him, but somehow the pain felt right, the hurt a comfort. It made him own his feelings of worthlessness. At that moment he understood his sister, why she chose the worst men, why his love could never be enough for her. He'd lain there waiting for death to come so that the pain would subside. Morning came instead.

In the church, he leaned back and stared up at the ceiling, feeling as insignificant as the building meant to make parishioners feel. His life always came to this. To sitting alone.

He briefly rested his forehead on the pew, pressing against the hard wood, then he stood and turned. He halted. Jackie sat three rows back, staring at him. The tenderness in her gaze twisted his heart.

He wanted to touch her. To tell her he was sorry about the other night. To ask for another chance. Instead, he asked, "What are you doing here?"

"I followed you."

He walked to her and trailed his finger along the length of the pew. "You were at the station?"

"Yes."

So you saw my defeat? "I'm working on a new plan."

Jackie touched his hand. "I don't care about a new plan. I don't care about Emmerick. I care about you." She held his hand in both of hers.

Clay tried to pull away, tried to resist the pull to be near her.

She wouldn't release it. "You'll have to make me let go."

He sat, too tired for another battle. She didn't speak; he didn't want to. Soon the silence seemed to diminish the pain and his haunting thoughts melted away.

"What happened when you ran away?" she asked. "What did you do? How did you survive?"

He sniffed. "Didn't you hear? I was part of a cult."

She let his hand go. "There's no harm in trying to find a family when you don't have one."

Clay rested his forearms on the pew in front of them. "I stayed with my sister for a while, then went to England to see my mother."

"How did you get the money?"

"Sold some things I shouldn't have—not drugs, so you can get that look off your face. There are other ways to make quick money, which I did, and went. It didn't work out, so I roamed a bit. Then I met a man who asked me how old I was. I lied, he gave me a job as a courier. I transported things to the islands. One trip there, I helped a guy in a barroom brawl; he happened to be a PI and said he could use me. I returned to the States, met up with my sister again. At that time she was with Prince—Emmerick. He was an impressive speaker. I was in awe at first. Until I saw what he was. I lasted two months, then left. My sister didn't beg me to stay and I never saw her again." He smiled without humor. "A free and easy life of fun and travel."

Jackie rested her head against his shoulder.

The simple gesture made his throat close, preventing words. He could only wonder, *Why, Mischief? Why are you here with me?*

A shaft of light spread down the aisle as someone entered the church. He heard Jackie sigh and something in him sighed with her. He took a deep breath.

"Come by Saturday and I'll cook you dinner."

She sat up and stared at him. "What time?"

"Say, eight-thirty?"

She winked. "I'll be there."

Chapter Seventeen

When Clay entered Hodder Investigations the next day, Brent came up to him with such enthusiasm, he knocked over a pad of files, spilled coffee, and tripped over the desk.

"Calm down," Clay said. "What's wrong with you?"

Brent grabbed paper towels and mopped up the mess. "I saw you on the show."

Clay shoved a hand in his pocket and nodded. "Hmm."

Brent threw the paper towels away, then looked at him, his eyes filled with awe. "Were you really in a cult? Or were you just in character, 'cause, man, if you were in character, that was awesome."

Clay walked into his office. "I wasn't acting."

Brent followed. "So you were really in a cult?" He hit his forehead with the flat of his hand. "I can't believe it. Not someone like you. I thought cults were only for gullible losers."

Clay put his jacket on the back of the chair, then sat. "An apt description."

Brent shook his head. "Nah, not of you." He sat and leaned forward. "Watching that show was like watching a movie where the apprentice meets his master after years have passed. I mean, the way you watched him as he tried to goad you. You didn't even flinch, hard as steel. Nothing he said could get to you."

Odd how it hadn't felt that way.

"Did you ever think about creating your own cult? I'm not into the crazy sacrifice stuff myself, but wearing hoods could be cool." His eyes widened as a thought came to him. "Not white hoods or anything like that. No way." He snapped his fingers. "Hey, they don't have to be hoods at all. How about robes?"

Mack looked up from his laptop. "How about you shut up and find something to do?"

Clay turned on his computer. "No, it's all right. Let him talk." He couldn't hide his past now; he didn't want to. He found Brent's interest intriguing. He could see how unripe minds could be a kind of drug for a man in want of power. A willing follower is a great intoxicant—that was how Emmerick had captured him. He'd been like Brent. Less eager, but just as curious, just as determined to prove himself.

Emmerick had been a good man to emulate. Clay had learned his stillness, his patience from a master of his craft. Emmerick was a keen observer of emotions, the neon signs to a person's inner workings. The key to their mind—and their mind was the greatest thing for a leader to possess.

Clay had felt the power of that control as his protégé. One word from him could send a grown man into tears, make a woman kneel before him, or make a group tremble. Clay had mistaken it for reverence; he'd later learned it was fear. At the time the difference didn't matter; no one would have called Clay a brilliant man. His teachers had laughingly referred to him as someone with unknown potential. They didn't know what to do with him. He wasn't the cleverest person, but with control he didn't need to be. Emmerick's community made him somebody, told him he was good at something. Clay could make people listen and believe.

He could twist people's thoughts, make them do as he wanted. As a recruiter for the community, there was the thrill of gathering more for the flock. He'd gotten satisfaction in being the wolf among the sheep, lurking undetected on the regular city sidewalks, watching people pass, ready to capture another gullible mind. It had taken practice, but Clay had been a quick learner. He'd learned to modulate his voice, his tone, his manner, and to keep his gaze steady without intimidation. He was a big man and had to learn to put people at ease with a smile and a glance that said, "Trust me."

"Umm, Clay?" Brent asked in an odd tone.

"Sorry?"

"I asked what was it like?"

"Not very exciting. At the time he owned a property in upstate New York where we all lived. My sister and his other three wives lived in the main house. The others lived in trailers. There were about twenty of us. There were no books, no TVs, or radios allowed. We refused to have our minds poisoned by the outside. We just studied devotion to our leader and his cause."

"Did you have orgies?"

Clay sighed. "No."

"No freaky stuff like child brides, drug parties, or drinking?"

"No."

Brent frowned, disappointed. "Then what did you do all day?"

"Mostly worked on the message. Created fliers, kept people in order. Those who began to question too often were dealt with swiftly and mercilessly. It was for their own good," he said sarcastically.

Brent scratched his head. "Doesn't sound like much fun."

"It wasn't meant to be fun."

"Then why did you fall for it?"

I wanted a family. I wanted to belong somewhere. "I wanted a purpose and the community gave me one."

"Why do you call it a community?"

"Sounds better than a cult, doesn't it?"

"Yes, I guess. How did you escape? I heard it's almost impossible to escape a cult—uh, community?"

"Not impossible. The trouble is how a community traps your mind, not your body. Like an elephant that learns to stay."

"What?"

"An elephant trainer teaches a baby elephant not to escape by chaining the animal's leg to a huge log so strong that the infant soon gives up trying to escape. As the elephant grows he becomes so used to captivity that even if the trainer ties a stick to its leg, the elephant won't try to escape. The trainer has the elephant's mind and the elephant has no idea of its strength."

"Wow."

"It's escaping the poison of your thoughts that's the true test. There were no chains or bars. We stayed because we were supposed to. To leave was to be a traitor, to turn against God. A betrayal like that lingers. You're left with nothing. No family and nothing to believe in. You're an outcast in every way." He twirled his pen. "I like to say I left, but in truth I was kicked out."

Mack stared, amazed, as though seeing Clay for the first time. "So you really tried to kill him?"

"Yes."

"Why?"

He stopped twirling the pen a moment, then continued. "He was a perverse man and I took exception to it."

"How do you get kicked out of a cult?" Brent asked. "What happens?"

"I can only speak of my experience. I was ceremonially stripped naked and left in a field."

"What did you do?"

"I went back to my old life working for a PI. He was kind enough to give me another chance." He skipped over how he'd stolen some clothes off a clothesline, shoplifted a bag of beef jerky from a market, and slept under newspapers trying to avoid the police and combat the hunger and despair that followed him.

"You know, you should think of writing a book yourself," Brent said.

"No, thanks, I'd rather not put my past into print."

Mack clasped his hands behind his head. "You know you're going to be a curiosity now. I bet people will come up with cases just to meet you."

His statement wasn't far from the truth. But instead of cases, overnight they had received various religious material from people professing their beliefs and offering Clay their faiths in hopes he would find peace.

Clay looked at the stacks of mail on his desk and Mack's. He looked at Brent, who was helping them get through them. He frowned. "I'm beginning to think the show was a bad idea."

Mack slit open an envelope. "Not necessarily. This is interesting. At least people are aware of Emmerick."

"And me." Some considered him a soul in torment, others a lost man— all wanted to help him.

"Whoa," Brent said, staring at a picture. He handed it to Mack.

Mack gave a low whistle. "It's not all bad. Look at this."

Clay took the picture. It was a photograph of a woman kneeling. She wore only a cross around her neck.

"She wants to share the love of the Holy Spirit with you."

Clay lifted a brow and handed Mack the picture.

He tucked the photo in his pocket. "I'm keeping this."

"The rabbi's prayer was beautiful," Brent said. "Think I could take that? My grandmother would love it."

"Go ahead," Clay said. He looked at the letters, prayers, and books. "I don't understand this."

"I do," Brent said.

Mack rolled his eyes. Clay ignored him. "Explain it to me."

"If you think about it, this is what life is all about, right? Being connected to each other and helping each other out."

Clay shrugged, amazed by Brent's simplistic view. A part of his cynical mind had to admit that it made sense. "I'm just glad it was a small local show. I couldn't take any more attention."

"You're just used to being a loner." Brent tapped his leg with a letter opener. "I was thinking last night."

"Really?" Mack said.

"Yeah," Brent said, unaware of his sarcasm. "I thought about why Clay joined that cult and now I know. In a group you matter, you're somebody."

He opened another envelope. "I'm not lying. If you created a community, I'd join it in a heartbeat."

Clay looked at him, alarmed at the thought. "Don't say things like that. It's foolish."

"It's true, though. I trust you. I know you wouldn't create something that would harm people."

Clay stared at him with growing unease, but an idea had begun to form in his mind.

***

Mack shook his head after Clay told him his idea. "Too risky."

"It's worth a try. You saw Brent. He's eager and he's ready to prove himself. He wants to know what investigating is and this is a perfect opportunity to use him."

"Brent is eager, but he isn't ready yet."

"He doesn't have to meet him. The contact could be through e-mails initially. That way we can monitor what he's being exposed to." Clay picked up his pen and twirled it. "He's the perfect bait to draw Emmerick out. To—"

"Brent would be meat. Think about who you're considering. He has the intelligence of a tadpole. If you want to get to Emmerick by e-mail, why not do it yourself or have me do it?"

"No, because eventually I want them to meet and Brent has the mind of someone he'd be drawn to."

"He's not smart enough to use on an idea like this."

Clay tapped the pen against the desk. "He's loyal. You heard him. He would do anything for me. He'd do exactly what I tell him."

"If he remembers. There are too many variables to take a risk of him getting involved with a guy like Emmerick. Brent talks big but you and I know he has a lot to learn and could be easily influenced by a man used to preying on people. Emmerick's good. I saw him with you. If you put Brent out there, it would be a battle for control over his loyalty—his mind. Are you certain you would win? Brent could be a casualty of your revenge."

"You think that's what this is about?" he asked quietly.

Mack's eyes met his. "Isn't it? I know you want him."

Clay sighed. Mack was right—this was becoming more about Emmerick than about anything else. He couldn't allow himself to lose focus of what he was up against, what he was really fighting. He couldn't risk Brent becoming entangled with Emmerick. He had to think of another way to penetrate his weakness.

"You're right. I do want him."

"We'll get him, but you'll have to be patient." Mack rubbed his chin. "Actually, your idea has given me another one. Emmerick has another weakness we can use against him. His ego. You know how his system works. What if we created a division of the ministry and wanted his advice? We could trap him."

"How?"

Mack told him the idea; Clay began to smile.

***

Jackie scolded herself as she rushed over to Clay's apartment. She was late again. She'd torn her closet apart trying to find the perfect outfit for her dinner with him. At last she decided on a cream blouse and green skirt. She wondered what he would cook for her and hoped it wasn't anything that splashed. Anytime she ate pasta she ended up getting sauce on her shirt. She raised her hand to knock.

He opened the door before she had a chance.

"Sorry I'm late," she said.

He opened the door wider. "That's okay. I expected you to be."

Jackie stepped into the dimly lit room and heard the soft sound of jazz playing in the background. She turned to him with amusement in her eyes. "Are you going to practice your seduction scene on me?"

He closed the door. "I don't need to practice. It's already been perfected." He led her to the dining room.

She sat down, impressed by the maroon tablecloth adorned with fine china with a gold trim. The room held a subdued elegance, except for Laura sitting on top of a bookshelf.

He followed Jackie's look. "She helped me pick out the pattern."

"I should be jealous, but she has an excellent eye." She sniffed the air. "Everything looks great, but I don't smell anything cooking."

"I know." He set a bowl in front of her filled with melon balls, pineapple chunks, blueberries, mango, and a sprig of peppermint.

She looked at it, confused. "Fruit salad?"

"Hmm. It's up to you whether it will be dinner or breakfast."

Chapter Eighteen

Her head snapped up. She stared, speechless.

As the silence stretched, so did his patience. "What do you say?"

"Have you ever eaten blindfolded?"

He blinked. "I'm sorry?"

"Have you ever eaten blindfolded?"

"No."

"Let's try tonight." She stood and grabbed a dishtowel. "Sit down."

"But you haven't answered my question."

"Don't worry, I will." She went behind him and folded the dish towel. "Close your eyes. " Clay crouched down. Jackie wrapped the blindfold around his eyes. "Okay, now I'm going to put a piece of fruit in your mouth and you guess what it is."

He hesitated, then said, "All right."

"Open your mouth. Now what do you taste?"

He chewed a moment. "Pineapple."

"Good, and this?"

"Cantaloupe."

"And this?"

He frowned. "That's not on," he protested, using a typical British phrase meaning she wasn't being fair. "That's two fruits."

"What are they?"

"Honeydew and blueberry."

"Very good."

"I try." He opened his mouth and motioned with his hand. "Keep it coming."

Her heart stirred at the ridiculous yet vulnerable picture he made. His mouth open, as trusting as a child.

"Try to guess this." She brought her mouth to his.

He licked his lips when she drew away. "Tastes like Mischief."

"Does it taste good?"

He pulled her onto his lap. "Delicious."

"Do you want more of it?" she whispered.

"As much as you can give me."

She took his hand. "Then follow me."

He lifted his hand to his face. "Can I take the blindfold off?"

"Not yet." She took his hand and led him down the hall.

"Ow!"

She turned and saw him rubbing his forehead, the ceiling lamp swinging behind him. She winced. "Sorry about that."

"My fault," he grumbled. "That's what happens when you have a Lilliputian guide."

"A what?"

"*Gulliver's Travels.* Never mind."

Jackie led him to the bed and gently pushed him to sit down.

"Now wait there. I'm going to strip."

He reached for the blindfold. "I'd like to see this."

Jackie grabbed his hand. "No, just imagine it. We're using different senses tonight. I'm taking off my top right now."

"How?"

She paused. "How?"

"Yes. I want a better description. Are you pulling it over your head or one arm at a time?"

"One arm at a time."

He nodded. "Okay."

"Now the bra. It's paisley and fastened in the back. I'm having a little trouble, but . . . there. Got it. I've tossed it aside. Now I'm slipping out of my shoes."

"How?"

"How else does one take off high heels?"

"You could bend over and take them off, which presents a very nice image, or rest against the drawer and bring your foot up to pull it off, or you could kick them off, or—"

"I stepped out of them," she interrupted, annoyed.

"Listen, if you're going to be my eyes, I want important details."

"I don't think how someone takes off their shoes is an important detail."

"Did you miss the memo? Men are visual creatures."

"Tonight, try to *listen*. I'm removing my skirt by unzipping the back and slipping it off my hips. Now just listen and imagine."

He heard the soft material fall to the ground, the scratchy sound of her stockings, then the elastic snap of her panties as she stepped out of them.

She came toward him. He smelled the tangy, crisp scent of jasmine and orange blossoms he'd first remembered in his office. He reached for her, his hands brushing her breast. "Just take off my pants and I'm a happy man."

She unbuttoned his shirt. "No, I want to enjoy this, too." She pulled back his shirt and rested her hands on his chest.

It was the first time he realized how much he liked the feeling of her hands on him. She didn't have the delicate fingers one would expect from an imp—they were little fingers, but seemed to soothe the darkness within him, tame the anger underneath, and stirred feelings in him he couldn't articulate. She was a true enchantress, bewitching him with merely a touch and a scent. He felt her nimble fingers move to his trousers. In moments, he was naked and felt her warm body against the length of his, ready to gratify a growing hunger as she slipped a condom on him.

He drew her close, ready to indulge in the sweet liquid center between her thighs. A deep healing peace suffused through his body, ridding him of the clinging despair that had become a toxin. It had been a part of his spirit so long that its exit was almost painful. Its passing left him briefly hollow, but her love filled the empty space inside. Her hope, her optimism, her passion defeated any lingering doubt or fear that joy could never be his.

Tonight he felt joy, that seemingly elusive creature kept so long out of reach. Being a man of few words, action was his language, and this night of lovemaking was his pledge—that he would treasure her, honor her, care for her. It was the first time he tried to communicate with his body this way, so there were times his embrace was awkward or his kiss fumbled. But Jackie understood every word. She interpreted the heart-rending eloquence of his feelings as he held her, as he moved inside her. As his hot lips seared a path along her shoulder. She closed her eyes, reveling in the wonder of a passion she'd only known in her fantasies. Even her fantasies couldn't compete with the delights of a real man. How sexy imperfection could be.

They held each other after the lovemaking ended, languid with pleasure.

He finally said, "I'm hungry."

"Me, too." She took off his blindfold and gazed at an amazing, wonderful sight. The shadows were gone.

He furrowed his brows, confused by her expression. "What?"

"Your eyes."

"What about my eyes?"

She cupped the side of his face. "They're beautiful."

***

The next morning Clay squinted at the sunlight seeping through the blinds. He stretched out his arm to feel the warm body lying next to him. The space lay empty and cold. He turned, surprised, then sat up. He hadn't expected to wake up alone. He glanced around the room. There was no sign that Jackie had been there. Not even a lingering scent. But he knew last night had been real. He ran a hand down his face, feeling the stubble on his chin. Had it been too real for her? Had she discovered she didn't want to develop a serious relationship with him? He swore, a heaviness entering his chest at the thought of her fleeing him in the night.

He pulled on his pajama bottoms and walked into the kitchen. It was out of habit; he wasn't hungry. He looked sightlessly through the cupboards and fridge, wondering what to do. So she'd left him—he'd survive. He decided to clean Laura's cage.

"She left," he told the bird. "The one woman I invite to stay and she leaves."

Laura chirped.

"I know you stayed, but you're an exception. Besides, you'll fly away soon enough." He lifted her. "Come. Give us a kiss."

She gave him a peck on the lips. He heard the door open and turned.

Jackie stood in the doorway, her hip resting on the door frame. "Yes, I'm definitely jealous."

He set Laura down and stood, his mood suddenly buoyant. "I thought you'd gone."

"Is that why you're giving my morning kiss to a bird?"

"If you'd stayed in bed you would have gotten yours, too."

"I'll know better next time."

He frowned, noticing that the jacket she wore fit like a long coat. "Why are you wearing my jacket?"

She took it off and hung it in the closet. "It's a chilly morning."

"Where have you been?" He hated how possessive those words sounded. "Not that it's my business."

"I've been for a walk."

Clay went to the kitchen, his appetite returned. "Have you eaten?"

"Not yet."

He pulled down a box of cereal.

She frowned at it. "What is that? Molded bark?"

He poured the contents into a bowl. "Weetabix."

Her frown increased. "Keeps you regular, does it?" She patted him on the back as she went to the fridge. "I suppose you have to worry about things like that at your age."

"Yes. By the way, your bottle is heating on the stove."

"I'm having fruit salad."

"Need me to mash it up for you?"

"Using your face may cause some amusement."

He sat and clicked his tongue. "Careful, little girl. It's dangerous to tease me in the morning. I'm not much fun."

Jackie wrapped her arms around his neck and kissed his cheek. "Oh, I think you are."

They sat down at the table for breakfast.

"I took your keys and put them on the coffee table," she said. "I just wanted to get out for a bit." She placed a key on the table. "I've made you a copy of my key."

"Good." He put the key in his pocket. "There are a few items I'd like to steal."

"My panties are in the top drawer."

"I'm more of a garter man."

"I don't own any garters."

He raised a brow. "Then I suggest you get some."

They fell into silence, then she said, "So."

"So?"

"Do I get a key to your place?"

He glanced around. "I don't think there's anything worth stealing."

"I'm serious."

"So am I... Well, there is my Benny Hill video collection. I'm rather fond of that."

"You don't want to give me a key to your place?"

"I don't like surprises," he said, effectively answering her question. "I'd feel uneasy not knowing if I'd come home and find you here."

"Oh." Her tone was sharp. She stared at her fruit salad, feeling her temper rise. Clay was right. She didn't like the word no in any form. But then she remembered the pleasure of last night and the joy of waking up with him in the morning. He had given her so much already at this point, it would be selfish to ask for more, to disregard the gift he'd given her. She smiled wryly, thinking of how she'd changed. The Jackie of before would have argued, but the Jackie now accepted it. Accepted him.

"Do you want your key back?" he asked.

"No." She smiled at him so he had no doubt everything was fine. "It's yours."

After breakfast they went to see the cherry blossoms spreading their pink and white petals along the Tidal Basin. The sun painted the gleaming rotunda of the Jefferson Memorial a brilliant white and reflected its rays on the tranquil waters.

Later they went to the National Museum of Natural History, staring in awe at the eight-ton African bush elephant that stood at the door entrance under the rotunda. They marveled at the Hope Diamond and made their way around the Insect Zoo. At the museum store, he bought her a dragonfly brooch, which she immediately pinned to her shirt. She bought him a puzzle of an hawk. They planned to work on it once they got home.

They walked hand in hand, their spirits high, but Jackie's enthusiasm began to wane as they walked back to his place.

"What's wrong?" he asked her.

"We have to tell them."

His joy dimmed a bit, too. "Yes. Don't worry, I'll handle things."

Jackie playfully elbowed him in the ribs. "We're a couple now. We'll handle it together."

"Right. Together." He smiled at her then turned. He halted so abruptly, a man collided into him. The man looked up at Clay and held up his hands, offering a ready surrender. "I'm sorry. I wasn't paying attention."

Clay smiled, trying to lessen the man's unease. "It was my fault."

The man took a hasty step sideward. "No, it was mine." He hurried away.

Jackie's mouth kicked up in a quick grin. "Do you usually scare people like that?"

He ignored her.

"Why did you stop like that?" Jackie asked. "Are you okay?"

"Only if I'm hallucinating." He looked at something in the distance and swore. "No, I'm not."

"What do you see?" Jackie groaned. "Oh, no. Don't tell me. Another case."

"No, it's not." He headed to the building. "Fortunately, this is something I can ignore."

A woman called his name. "Clarence!"

He kept walking.

Her voice grew louder. "Clarence!"

Jackie searched through the crowd and saw an older woman struggling with a suitcase, waving at them. "I think she's calling you."

He shrugged. "I know she is. I don't care."

She stared at him, confused. "But she wants to talk to you."

"Yes, but I don't want to talk to her,"

Jackie tugged on his hand. "Come on. She's an old woman."

"Not that old."

The woman caught up with them. "Clarence," she scolded. "Didn't you hear me calling you?"

He slowly spun around and flashed a cold smile. "Yes, Mum. Unfortunately, I did."

Chapter Nineteen

Jackie stared at the woman in shock. This was Clay's mother? This woman with fine, delicate features wearing dangling gold earrings and jeans that showed off a slender build that could shame any woman half her age? The woman smoothed down her shoulder-length hair, dyed—intentionally or unintentionally—an unfortunate shade of orange. The color matched her high-heeled shoes.

She held out a ringed hand to Jackie. "I'm Bertha Graham," she said in a harsh British voice with a hint of island lilt. "And you are?"

"None of your business," Clay said. "What are you doing here?"

"I came to see you."

"Are you dying?"

"No"

He began to leave. "Then come back when you are."

"Clay!" Jackie said, appalled. "You can't speak to your mother like that."

He sent her a glance, but didn't reply.

Bertha said, "I see you've been out shopping."

He blinked, bored. "At least your eyesight hasn't faded."

"Clay," Jackie said, embarrassed by his rudeness.

Bertha took no offense. "I want a second chance."

"I'm a little too old for a mother right now."

"We could be friends."

Clay ignored the statement and glanced at her bags. "Where are you planning to stay?"

"With you."

He shook his head. "Try again."

Her ruby lips thinned. "Clarence Jarrett Graham, am your mother and—"

Clay held up a hand. "Let's clear up a few misunderstandings. First, you're under the misconception that I don't know who you are. I do. So you don't need to remind me. Second, my name is Clay. You will call me Clay and no variation of that. Third, my last name is Jarrett, not Graham."

"So you're ashamed of your father as well as myself? You won't even bear his name?"

"It's no loss to him, I assure you. He has other children." His tone hardened. "What are you doing here?"

"I want to talk to you."

Clay folded his arms and said patiently, "You can talk as much as you like, woman. You're just not going to stay with me."

She threw up her hands, exasperated. "Are you always going to hate me for making a few mistakes?"

"Your mistake was showing up here. You can correct it by leaving. You left me at five, so it shouldn't be hard to do."

"I divorced your father, not you. I left you with him because a boy needs his father."

"A mother helps, too."

She sighed, tired. "I'm here now. Let me try to make it up to you."

"You can't."

"Has your heart become so cold?"

His hands fell. "Yes. The night you kicked me out to roam the streets of London without tossing me a pound, my heart broke and mended as stone. Congratulate yourself on a job well done. You taught me a good lesson. I learned then that I'd never have anything to do with you. That hasn't changed. I'll let you know when it has. Jackie, are you ready to go in?"

Jackie shook her head. "We can't just leave her here."

"Sure we can. There are plenty of men on the street. She'll pick one up eventually and go home with him."

Bertha slapped him—hard.

Clay smiled as though she'd given him a peck on the cheek. "Ah, the warm tingly feelings of a mother's love. Oh, yes, that brings back happy memories."

"Mind your tongue."

He opened the front door. "Come on, Jackie."

Jackie walked up to him and whispered, "I can't leave her here. As much as you despise her, she's family."

"Not mine."

Jackie clenched her fists. "I can't leave her."

A flash of hurt entered his eyes, soon replaced by a cool, unreadable look. "Okay."

She grabbed his arm before he turned. "I'm not taking sides."

"That's fine." He went inside.

She turned to Bertha. "Give me a moment," Jackie said, then raced into the lobby. She jumped in front of Clay before he entered the elevator. "You're angry with me."

"Doesn't matter." He tried to move around her.

She blocked his path. "Yes, it does. You matter a lot to me."

He swore when the elevator doors closed. He pushed the UP button.

"Clay, talk to me."

He pushed the button again.

She grabbed his hand. "You're so eloquent with everything else except with how you feel. Talk to me, please."

He briefly shut his eyes. "I don't know how," he said in a harsh whisper. "Just go. It's all right."

"It's not all right if I'm hurting you. Tell me if I'm hurting you."

He pressed the button harder.

Jackie seized his shirt, wishing she could penetrate his thoughts. "Take this opportunity. You have a chance to change things. Your mother wants to know you." She let his shirt go. "My mother is dead."

"You can have mine if you wish." Clay stepped inside the elevator. "Personally, I don't think it's a fair exchange." He turned in time to see a look of pain cross her face. He had wounded her with his careless remark. He softly swore and stepped out of the elevator, gripping her shoulders. "I can't deal with her. Better yet, I don't want to. Do you know how long I've been trying to destroy the memory of her?" He let her shoulders go. "I can't pretend I want to know her—even for you."

She looked at him helplessly. "And I just can't leave her."

"I know. It's not your way." He pushed the button again. "We both have to do what we have to."

Her eyes filled with regret. "It was a beautiful day."

The elevator doors opened. He stepped inside. "At least I've got my puzzle to keep me company."

Jackie smiled weakly as she watched the doors close.

***

Jackie schooled her features as she approached Bertha. She didn't want to reveal the mixed feelings she had toward a woman who had caused Clay so much pain. "I guess you'll be staying with me."

"I'm not surprised, really," Bertha said. "That one always did have a wicked temper."

"You came as a shock. He has to get used to you." Jackie walked to her car and opened the trunk. When she picked up the suitcase, she nearly toppled over. "What do you have in here?"

"A few bits and bobs."

Jackie slammed the trunk shut, then muttered, "I think you mean rocks and boulders."

Once they reached Jackie's place, Bertha quickly made herself at home. She dumped her suitcase and the various items inside all over the living room. She refused the offer of a quick snack of beans on toast, lit a cigarette on the stove, then stretched out on the couch as though she were lady of the manor. "Nice place." She glanced around the living room. "Bit odd, but it suits you."

"Thanks," Jackie said warily, stunned at how quickly her small place had been taken over by a seemingly harmless-looking woman of more than sixty. "I only have one room."

"Never mind, love. I'll just stay here on the couch till I sort things out."

"Right." She nodded uncertain. Knowing Clay, that could take a while.

Bertha dragged on her cigarette, then tapped the ashes into a saucer, Jackie had put out for her on the coffee table. "I will sort them out. Don't you worry yourself."

Oh, but Jackie would worry. A lot. She opened a window to keep her place from smelling like the inside of a bar. "Perhaps in a week he'll calm down and you'll get a chance to talk to him."

"Yeah, perhaps," Bertha said with little concern. "Mind if I turn on the telly?"

Why ask? You'd do it anyway. "Oh, no. Go ahead."

Toward evening, Bertha had gone through a pack of cigarettes and nearly all the contents in Jackie's fridge. Jackie could see how she could inspire Clay's resentment. Though not maliciously so, she was completely self-absorbed. Bertha was an attractive woman now and must have been a striking beauty in her youth; she was used to the attention that attribute had given her. She seemed the type of woman who would have no use for children, only adding to the mystery of why she'd had them in the first place. However, she was Clay's mother and Jackie found it difficult to think of throwing her out. The only way to get rid of her was to reconcile the two.

"Why did you come?" Jackie asked her as she cleared the dinner dishes. "What do you want?"

Bertha lit another cigarette from the stub of the last. "A second chance, like I told him."

"I don't believe you and neither will Clay."

She smoked in silence for a few moments, then said, "Well, as I've gotten older I've begun to look back on my life and . . . Why are you shaking your head?"

Jackie sat in front of her. "That won't work either. Try the truth."

Her lovely features soon looked defeated. "You want the truth, love? The truth is, I'm bloody lonely. My last chap ran off. I have no other family left except Clarence—Clay." She frowned. "I can't get used to that name. Clay. Imagine having a nickname that reminds you of dirt when you have a good and proper name like' Clarence."

"You've left the subject," Jackie said.

Bertha thought for a moment. "Oh, yes. I don't want to die alone." She set the cigarette down and gazed in the distance. "So I want to set things right." She rested her arms on the table. "I remember when me and his father split up," Bertha said. "Clarence—Clay--and his sister clung to each other and wept. I'll never forget his little face in the window, he was such a pretty boy with eyes that took up his whole face. Nearly broke my heart seeing him crying as he pounded on the window while I drove away. I didn't visit him. I didn't think I needed to. A boy needed his father and he had a good one." She lifted the cigarette and took a long drag. "Oscar was a bore, but a decent bloke. Have you met his father?"

"Yes, he seems like a nice guy."

"Dull as dishwater. You're probably wondering why I married him then. Well, here's a nice piece of advice. Never marry a man just because the sex is great. You can't spend all day in bed." She flashed a smile that echoed her son's. "Trust me. I've tried."

"So you didn't see Clay because he was with his father?"

"Yeah. Oscar was well off. When he married that posh tart of his, I thought, 'Now he's got a mother. Why would he ever need me when he had her?'"

"Did you really send him away when he came to you?"

"Yeah." She grimaced. "God, I didn't know he was only sixteen. The years can just fly by you know and I'd gone on with my life. Sure he was skinny, but so tall and had the same gritty voice he has now. I thought he was a grown man. 'Sides, I didn't know what to do with him and my current bloke didn't take to him. It was a mistake. I know that. But he's never given me a chance to apologize."

"Did you really try?"

Bertha grinned ruefully. "You have such a cute, innocent face, but I can't fool you, can I?"

Jackie shrugged. "You can try, but it's a waste of time."

"Truth is, I was a selfish cow. It's the guilt that's got to me now After Rennie's death, I disconnected from life for awhile. I shouldn't have been surprised with her death. I knew her recklessness would lead to a tragic end. She never listened to any bit of sense and didn't have any of her own, but it didn't make her death any less painful. You'd think her funeral would have brought Clarence—I mean, Clay—and me closer together. It didn't, though." She stared at her cigarette. "I think a part of him blames me." She shrugged. "And perhaps the fault is mine for not guiding her more. But I did my best and that's all a mum can do, isn't it?" She inhaled, then exhaled. "I like my men. I admit that, but our Rennie chose the worse of the lot. The type of man you'd scrape off the bottom of your shoe is the kind she'd fall for. Every time. Without fail. I couldn't understand it. I didn't understand her."

She shifted back in her chair and adjusted her shoulders as though trying to rid herself of the weight of the past. "So what's with you and Clay?"

"Most of the time, I don't know."

She waved her cigarette in understanding. "He's a tricky one, he is. Even as a baby, he was an odd little thing. Almost never cried. Even if I forgot to feed him, I'd just find him in his cot munching on his fist."

Jackie only nodded, wondering how a mother could casually mention forgetting to feed her baby.

"So what does he do?"

"He's a private investigator."

She tapped the cigarette ashes. "Successful?"

"I'd say so."

"That's good. He's not quite bright, but he works hard."

Jackie stiffened, taking offense. "I think he's very smart."

"Fortunately, his looks save him. Thank God for that. Imagine having a son who's ugly and stupid."

"He is not stupid. He's one of the most intelligent men I know."

Bertha grinned. "Love him, do ya?"

Jackie ignored the question. "Actually, he's helping me with a case right now." She hesitated, then said, "We, um, we met Prince again."

She furrowed her brow. "Prince? Am I supposed to know him?"

"Yes, the man Rennie married."

She sniffed. "You call that a marriage? Running about half naked with leaves on your head and picking passages out of the Bible? Besides, a man that needs more than one wife is making up for something. Most men fool themselves into thinking they can satisfy one woman, let alone four. She wasn't a wife."

"It was real to her."

She shook her head, amazed. "Prince," she said with disgust. "Bet you he calls his willy 'Sir' or something equally daft." She dragged on the cigarette, her face becoming pensive. "I don't remember seeing him at the funeral. But I don't remember much then. I'd had a couple of drinks to get me through it."

"He's the leader of the Careless Rapture Ministry. We're trying to shut him down."

"Why try? Rennie failed."

Chapter Twenty

Rennie failed? Bertha's statement echoed in Jackie's mind an hour later. Clay never mentioned that Rennie may have tried to defeat Emmerick. Had he not known or just failed to mention it to her? And if he hadn't known, how would Bertha have gotten that impression? Had Rennie contacted her during the time she was with Emmerick? Was there much more to her death than anyone realized?

Someone knocked, interrupting her disturbing thoughts. Jackie raced to the door, thankful for the break from Bertha.

Cassie smiled. "Hi."

She hugged her. "I'm so glad you're here."

"I'm just stopping by."

"Please, come in," she said in a low voice, "I need your help."

"Why?' Cassie asked as Jackie hastily pulled her inside. She closed the door and nodded at the woman sitting on the couch. "Clay's mother is here."

Cassie blinked, then laughed. "Funny. It sounded like you said Clay's mother is here."

"I did."

"What?"

"He was going to leave her wandering around D.C. because he dislikes her and I couldn't let him do that, but I can't keep her here indefinitely. I don't know what to do."

Cassie patted her hand. "Calm down. I'll see what I can do."

Jackie walked farther into the apartment. "Bertha, this is my sister-in-law, Cassie. Clay's half-sister."

Bertha stood and shook her hand. "Yes, I can tell. You both have your father's forehead."

"Oh, thank you," Cassie said, without taking offense. "It's nice to meet you. I'll be right back. Excuse me." She went to the bathroom.

Bertha pulled Jackie aside and whispered, "She's a big girl, ain't she?"

Jackie's eyes flashed. "She's pregnant."

"Thank goodness for that. 1 thought she was one of those fatties you see waddling down the pavement. You Americans like to eat. I saw one woman so large I don't know how she fits in the toilet." She waved her cigarette. "I'm not sure she'll lose all the weight once the baby's born, though. Shame, she has such a pretty face."

"Her husband thinks she's beautiful and so do I."

"Oh, she has a husband, does she? That's a surprise. So many women don't nowadays. Do you think he'll stick around?"

"He's my brother."

Bertha took a long drag and squinted her eyes. "Is that supposed to be an answer?"

Jackie counted to ten. She was trying hard not to dislike her, but Bertha was making that difficult. When Cassie returned, Jackie led her away before she could get into a conversation with Bertha. She took her to the bedroom, closed the door, and leaned against it. "Well?"

Cassie sat on the bed. "I can't believe that's Clay's mother." She shook her head, amazed. "Wow. Dad's taste sure did change," she said, thinking of her own more refined mother.

"Your tastes would change, too, if you'd married her."

"How did this happen? How did she end up here with you?"

"It's complicated," Jackie said, not wanting to mention her relationship with Clay just yet. "The question is what should I do with her now?"

Cassie grinned mischievously. "I could call Dad and tell him his ex-wife is in town." She rubbed her hands evilly. "Oh, wouldn't Mom love that?"

"Do you think you could persuade him to talk to her?"

"Sure, Dad would talk to her and—"

Jackie shook her head. "No, I mean Clay."

She grimaced. "I don't know. Getting Clay to do something he doesn't want to is nearly impossible."

Jackie clasped her hands together as though in prayer. "Please try. You're his sister."

"His *little* sister. How often does Drake listen to you?"

Jackie sat down beside her. "I know, but you have to try."

"All right. I will." She opened her bag. "Before I forget." She handed her a box.

Jackie opened it. A glass angel sat inside among purple tissue paper.

"Drake's been worried about you so I thought this may cheer you up, and if you're happy, he's happy."

"Drake's worried about me?"

"Yes, he hasn't been himself lately and when I finally confronted him he said he was worried about you." She playfully pinched her arm. "He loves you a lot, you know that."

Jackie held the glass figurine in her palm, knowing it had been given to her based on a lie. Drake was worried about Eric, not her. But Cassie wasn't to know that. Her heart broke that she couldn't tell Cassie the truth. Not about Eric or Clay. She felt like a fraud, a traitor to their friendship. She set the figurine back in the box. "I can't accept this."

"Why not?"

"Because I don't deserve it."

Cassie put her arm around her shoulder. "Of course you do. I know how painful a breakup can be, but your worth doesn't depend on how others treat you."

Cassie's kindness was painful. Jackie hung her head, ashamed. "I'm a terrible friend to you and Adriana."

"You're a wonderful friend. We don't expect you to be upbeat all the time. It's okay to be unhappy sometimes. We're there for you."

"No, it's not that." She shut her eyes. What was the use of saying anything when she couldn't express the truth?

Cassie lifted her chin. "I don't mind that you're seeing Clay." Jackie looked so stunned that she laughed. "You wear your heart in your eyes."

She covered the offending feature. "How embarrassing."

"There's no need to be embarrassed." Cassie removed her hand. "And there's no reason to be ashamed."

"He doesn't love me."

"I know."

Though Jackie knew the truth, hearing Cassie say it made it hurt more. "But give him time. He may not be swift, but he's not stupid."

"He's not stupid at all," she said hotly. "Why does everyone imply that he is?"

Cassie sent her an odd look. "I was just teasing."

She waved a hand. "I know, sorry. Bertha just annoyed me with a similar remark."

"Bertha would try the patience of a monk."

"You've only just met her."

"Yes, and I heard everything she said while in the bathroom." She stood. "I won't tell Drake."

"Thank you."

"But tell him soon. I don't believe in keeping secrets from those you love. Someone always gets hurt."

***

Clay was chopping apple bits for Laura when someone knocked on the door. He ignored it and handed Laura a piece of apple instead. "If it's Jackie bringing over that woman, they can stay outside," he grumbled.

The person knocked again. "Clay, it's me. Cassie." He paused. It couldn't be. She'd never stopped by before.

"Clay?"

It sounded like her. "Um. Just a minute." He glanced around his messy place and went into action. He shoved his unwashed dishes in the cupboard, pushed the scattered newspaper under the couch, kicked his clothes and shoes into the closet, plumped his couch pillows, then opened the door. "What are you doing here?"

She laughed at his gruff tone. "Don't worry. I won't stay long."

"I don't mind that you're here," he said, quickly. "I just, umm . . . How are you doing?"

"I'm fine." She waited for him to invite her in. When he continued to stand and stare, she said, "It would be nice to sit down, though."

He promptly stepped back, opening the door wider. "Sure, right. Come in."

She poked him in the arm. "Clay, it's just me. You don't have to be nervous."

He shut the door. "I'm not nervous."

"You're tugging at the hem of your shirt with those fidgeting fingers of yours." She sat on the couch and grinned up at him. "I remember you used to twirl your fork at dinner and drive Mother crazy."

He returned her smile. "Fortunately, I stopped doing that. I didn't do it on purpose, though."

"I know."

"She didn't."

Cassie sighed. "Yes, well, she didn't understand either of us."

Laura flew onto his shoulder.

Cassie pointed, curious. "What is that?"

"That's Laura."

"I didn't know you have a bird."

"I didn't until recently."

"Can I stroke her?"

"Sure, she's very friendly."

Cassie stroked the bird's head. "She's beautiful."

Clay fell silent, then asked, "Do you want to see what she can do?"

"Sure."

He got a stick and held it out. Laura jumped on it. "Okay, now, dead parrot."

Laura hung upside down and closed her eyes. Clay laughed and turned to Cassie. "Isn't she brilliant?"

"Yes," she said, happy to see him so pleased with himself. "Like her owner."

"I don't own her. She's just visiting." Laura flew back onto his shoulder and he gave her another piece of apple. "Good girl."

"I'm glad to see you're not alone for now."

"I'm fine."

Cassie sent him a knowing look. "I wouldn't say that."

He sat down next to her and pushed an empty beer can out of the way with his foot. "Why not?"

"I met your mother."

He sat back, his voice becoming neutral. "Did you?"

"Yes, I went by Jackie's and . ." She searched for words, ". . . she's an interesting woman."

"You needn't be kind on my account. I have a few adjectives and 'interesting' isn't one of them."

Cassie playfully patted his cheek. "What a mother. You poor thing."

"Have you come to listen to my horror stories?"

"I can imagine most of them. Bet she put your diaper on backwards and fed you steak when you had no teeth."

"Close."

She nudged him with her elbow. "I was thinking of calling Dad."

He flashed a wicked grin. "And tell him Mum's in town? Let me do it."

"Only if you'll do one thing."

His grin fell. "She's not staying here."

"She doesn't have to stay here, just talk to her."

"What good will it do?"

Cassie tucked a strand of hair behind her ear. "Mom and I aren't the best of friends, but we understand each other more and I could only do that by talking to her. By getting to know her better."

"I don't want to know her."

"That emptiness will never go away until you do." She grabbed his hand. "I don't want you to 'run away again. I like having you in my life."

His eyes slid away though his heart responded to her sincerity "You have Drake, you don't need me."

"I have a husband, but brothers are nice to have, too. And the kids love their uncle Clay."

He glanced down at their intertwined fingers. He didn't know how or why they always connected. "Did Dad ever look for me after I left?"

"I don't know. You'll have to ask him."

He shook his head. "I think I already know the answer."

"You're probably guessing wrong." Cassie pushed up her glasses then said in a cautious voice, "When Mom said you were useless and that's why your mother left you, she was wrong. Cruelly, dreadfully wrong."

He smiled, embarrassed by the knowledge in her eyes. She knew how much his stepmom's words had hurt him. How they still lingered. "You remember that?"

"I remember a lot of things. This is going to be hard for you to believe, but people like having you around."

"Until the tide turns."

"Do you think the tide will always turn against you?"

He glanced toward the window. "It usually does."

"Perhaps you need to be more flexible."

"Maybe." He leaned back. "You've never come by before."

"I've never been invited."

He nodded. That was true.

"Will you be coming this Sunday?" she asked.

He squeezed her hand. "Promise me she won't be there."

"Okay." She kissed him on the cheek, then left.

Clay sat on the couch, staring at the blank TV screen. He'd tasted the joy of belonging, but now it had reached the point of leave or be left. He couldn't let Jackie choose between him and her brother. Besides, when it came down to it, he knew what her choice would be-- or, rather, what it should be.

He went to the window and opened it. "It's time to go." He rested Laura on the windowsill. "Go on. Goodbye." She turned to him and chirped. He pointed, then flapped his arms. "Go on. Be a good girl. Go away." She jumped off the windowsill and soon became a dot against the sky.

Chapter Twenty One

When Jackie arrived for Sunday dinner, she peeked in the playroom and saw Nina and Marcus on the ground, while Ericka sat in Clay's lap watching a film. Tears streamed down the children's faces.

She glanced at Clay, then asked them, "What's wrong?"

Nina wiped her eyes with the back of her hand. "Charlotte died."

"Who is Charlotte?"

Marcus sniffed. "The spider. She died."

"Died," Ericka said.

Clay kissed his niece on the forehead, then set her on the conch. He stood and walked toward Jackie. "They have seen *Charlotte's Web* more than ten times and they cry every time. I don't understand it."

"Are you still angry with me?"

"For what?" he asked sarcastically. "For leaving me to spend time with my mother? Not at all I just want to turn you over my knee."

"Have you told anyone?"

Clay raised his brows. "That I want to spank you?"

She hit him in the arm. "About us."

"No, I'm hungry."

She frowned. "What does that have to do with anything?"

"I want to eat before I'm kicked out."

"No one is going to kick you out."

Drake announced dinner—a delicious meal of deep fried fish with sun-dried-tomatoe vinaigrette. After a few moments of idle chatter, Drake said, "Jackie, I know a guy I'd like you to meet."

She cut her fish. "Thank you, but I'm already seeing somebody."

"Who?"

She could feel Clay's gaze. She hesitated. "Just someone. It's nothing serious."

"I'd still like to know his name."

Her voice firmed. "It's not important."

"Of course it's important. We always know who you're going out with."

"If it was serious, I'd let you know."

Drake's amber eyes became more intense. "If he doesn't want us to know who he is, then he's hiding something. I don't think you should go out with someone like that."

Eric spoke up. "Drake, leave it alone."

He sent Eric a look. "Oh, yes," he drawled. "I forgot. You're in favor of keeping secrets."

"What does he mean by that?" Adriana asked.

Eric pushed up his glasses and scowled. "It means he thinks he knows what's best for everyone else."

"How's that chest pain?" Drake asked.

Jackie saw the hint of red stain Eric's face. "It wasn't his smoking that caused the chest pain," she said.

Drake lowered his eyes.

Eric sent her a look of censure. "Don't do that."

"Why not?" she said. "He doesn't have the right to tell us what to do anymore. Drake, we love you, but sometimes we want you out of our lives so we don't feel we have to pay for the weight of your sacrifice."

"My sacrifice was a gift," Drake said quietly. "You don't owe me a thing."

Jackie saw the look of hurt and regretted her words. "Then why does it always feel that way? Like you're our big brother and our father, too. You have to let us make our own mistakes."

"It's my duty to know---"

"No, it's not."

Clay sat forward. "There's no need for this discussion. Drake, she's seeing—ow!" He rubbed his shin where Jackie had kicked him

But he'd already caught Drake's attention. "You know who she's seeing?" he asked.

"He's just speculating," Jackie said. "Because he saw me with someone. He doesn't know for sure." Drake ignored her. "What did he look like? Is he a decent guy?"

"Listen, mate, the truth is—ow!" He glared at Jackie. "Don't kick me again."

"While you two play games," Cassie said, "Eric can answer a question." She rested her elbow on the table and cupped her chin. "What is this about chest pains?"

Adriana waved her fork. "Yes, I'd like to hear about that, too."

Eric glanced at Nina's worried little face and shrugged "It's no big deal."

"What is it?"

"I'll tell you when we get home."

"You'll tell me now."

His jaw twitched. "I have to get some tests done. My doctor's curious about some things."

"What things?"

"My lungs."

Cassie toyed with her earring. "And why haven't you had these tests done yet?"

"My schedule's busy and I don't have time."

"You can make time," she said softly, her words revealing an underlying command.

Cassie looked at Clay and Jackie. "Have you two come to a decision?"

Clay nodded. "Drake—"

"I'm a grown woman." Jackie glared at Clay. "It's none of his business."

"You're his business."

"When I was a child, yes, but not anymore."

Eric took off his glasses and held them out to Drake.

"Perhaps you need these to see."

Drake frowned. "See what?"

He shoved his glasses back on and sent Jackie and Clay a significant look. "What's in front of you."

Drake's eyes darted between them. "No."

Adriana's mouth fell open. "I don't believe it."

Cassie quickly interpreted the look on her husband's face. She said, "Nina, take Marcus and Ericka into the playroom, please. Yes, you can take your dinner. Adriana, could you help them?"

"But I want to hear--" Cassie sent her a look that changed her mind.

Adriana stood. "Come on, children."

Once the children were gone, Cassie said, "Now, let's be rational about this."

"I'll be rational," Drake said, his voice holding a cold edge that contrasted the fire of anger in his gaze. "Have you been seeing my sister?"

"Yes," Clay said.

No one spoke, waiting for the explosive impact of his admission. But Drake didn't explode. He kept his voice level, his gaze steady. "Get out."

Clay pushed back his chair and stood.

Eric, Jackie, and Cassie began to protest. Drake sat back and waited.

Cassie said, "You're both angry, but don't be hasty. Sit down, Clay." She saw him look at Drake. "This is my house, too. Please sit."

He did.

Drake stood. "Then I'll go."

"No," Cassie said.

"Honey, I think I prefer he left. And since I respect you, I'll give him five minutes to get out of my house."

Clay said, "Just let me explain."

"You don't need to explain anything."

"Listen, mate—"

Drakes eyes flashed. "I'm not your mate. And I know how you treat women."

"Jackie's different."

"I know, she's my sister."

Clay picked up a fork and twirled it, his tone ironic. "And I'm not good enough for her, am I? Because I was once on the streets. Because I was once that drunk walking around in a daze?" He pointed the fork at him. "You see in me what you could have become, an ill-educated brute who lives on his wits alone. I have no degrees, no schooling past part of the eleventh grade. I get my grammar wrong and have trouble with numbers, but unfortunately my disadvantages don't stop me from feeling what I do for you sister."

Drake fell silent, the tension radiating through the air. No one made a sound except when Adriana slipped back in her chair. "You're wrong," Drake said in a soft tone. "I never saw a brute. I never will. However, what I see is a man who thought screwing my sister meant more to him than being my friend."

The words hit their mark, Clay pushed back his chair, ready to leave.

"That's not fair," Jackie said. "I made a choice, too."

Drake turned to her. "Does he plan to marry you?"

"It doesn't matter. It's not about what you want for me, but what I want for myself."

"I am—"

"I want you to stay out of my life."

Drake cracked his knuckles, then said, "Sure, but first you have to get out of mine." He left the table.

The rest of them sat in silence. Finally, Eric stood. "We'd better go." Adriana followed him.

Jackie, Clay, and Cassie sat at the table covered with a half-eaten meal.

"I should have gone," Clay said.

Cassie stared at the table. "Be quiet."

"We're sorry," Jackie said.

Cassie looked up, surprised. "Do you think I'm upset about you two?" She shook her head, disappointed. "You should know me better than that. Your relationship is your business. And I'll deal with Drake. No, that's not it at all." She picked up a plate and stacked it on top of another. "What I found interesting was that neither of you were surprised by Eric's news. You both knew and didn't tell me."

"Cassie—"

"I'm sick of excuses. I thought you trusted me. Didn't I keep the secret about the two of you? Didn't I prove I could keep others? I thought we had a real bond; you made me feel stupid." She stood.

Clay grabbed her hand, desperate not to lose her trust as he'd lost Drake's. "You're the only reason I stayed, please don't—give me another chance."

"I'm not kicking you out of my life, Clay, I just realized you never came in." She went into the kitchen.

Clay felt sick. The depths of his despair carving out his insides leaving him empty. He couldn't look at Jackie as the anger of Drake's words and Cassie's hurt echoed in his mind. He grabbed his jacket and left.

Jackie caught up to him as he walked along the quiet street under the whistling trees and the scent of spring wafted from daffodils and forsythias. The light of a lamp post embraced the dark shadows along the sidewalk.

"I did consider him a friend," he said.

"It's okay."

"No, it's not. I hurt him." After a moment he said, "Laura flew away."

Jackie touched his sleeve tenderly. "I'm sorry"

"It was time for her to leave."

"How did she escape?"

"She didn't escape. I opened the window for her."

Jackie kicked a pebble into the grass. "So you encouraged her to go?"

"Yes."

"Do you plan to do the same with me?" she asked in a low voice.

He stopped. "Will I have to?"

She nodded. "Yes."

His voice became harsh. "Drake will never—"

Jackie made an impatient gesture. "He's not my guardian. I don't care what he thinks."

He didn't believe her, but just for tonight he wanted to. He began walking again. "Is that woman still at your house?"

"If you're referring to your mother, yes, she is."

"I'll meet with her."

Jackie spun around and grabbed his arm. "Oh, good. We can—"

He tucked her arm through his. "I'll meet with her alone."

***

As Jackie and Clay walked in silence, Bertha stood at the window smoking, regretting her life choices as she waited for Jackie to return home. Bertha hated the silence that allowed her thoughts to weigh on her and welcomed the loud ringing of the phone. She stubbed out her cigarette and answered. "Hello?"

There was a pause, then a persuasive male voice came on the line.

***

Cassie woke to the sound of movement downstairs. When she glanced at the empty space beside her, she knew what it was. She found Drake in the kitchen. He stood at the stove stirring something in a pot, its sweet aroma scenting the air.

"It's two in the morning," she said, blinking against the bright lights.

"You're supposed to be a sleep."

"So should you."

"I'm not tired." He turned to her. "You've been crying."

"I know."

He drew her close and kissed her forehead. "I'm sorry."

"It's only partially your fault."

His voice cracked. "My fault? What's my fault?"

She bit her lip, then said, "About Clay—"

"He betrayed me."

"How?"

"I invite a man into my home, my family, and he sleeps with my sister."

"I don't see why you're upset, you're sleeping with his."

He sent her a cold glare. "Are you trying to be funny?"

Cassie bit the inside of her cheek to keep from grinning. "No. But if you really think about it, it's no big deal. They are both adults. What did you want him to do? Ask your permission?"

"Yes."

"Don't be absurd."

"My intentions for you were always honorable.. From the first moment I saw you, I wanted to marry you, to provide for you. He's not offering her any of that."

"Perhaps that's not what she wants."

He turned off the stove. "But that's what she deserves. He's not . . . " He trailed off.

"Good enough for her?"

Drake opened the cupboard and grabbed two bowls. "Don't put words in my mouth."

"Then give me a few of your own."

He set the bowls down, then rested his hands on the counter. He hung his head with remembered pain. "I saw my mother work herself to death because she had a husband who couldn't provide. Dad was a good man and he tried, but—"

"Your mother loved him and I don't think she regretted her choice. But the point is Jackie isn't her. She's stronger than you think."

He straightened and poured the green banana porridge in the bowls. "How well do you really know him?"

"Why is this all of a sudden an analysis about Clay? What if Jackie seduced him?"

Drake handed her a bowl. "She wouldn't."

Cassie grabbed a spoon, then sat at the kitchen island. "How do you know?"

He sat beside her. "I know my sister."

"You don't know her as a woman and I can assure you that's a different thing."

"I know her more than I know him."

Cassie glanced at the ceiling, amazed. "I can't believe this."

"What?"

"Are you trying to sound like a snob or is this accidental? Drake, what is this really about?"

He scooped some pudding, then set it back down. "He deceived me."

"You deceived me," she countered.

He had the grace to look embarrassed. "I had a reason."

"So that made it okay?"

"No. It was Eric's secret and I didn't feel it was right for me to tell you I told him it was wrong, but he didn't listen."

"So did you ever consider that maybe Clay was keeping Jackie's secret?"

"You mean she didn't want to tell me?"

"I know she didn't."

Drake captured Cassie's gaze. "So you knew about them and didn't tell me?" He shook his head. "I never thought our marriage would come to this. To deception and keeping secrets from each other."

"It doesn't have to again."

"No."

She saw his hand twitch in the odd way it did when he wanted a cigarette. She knew many things about him, yet also knew there was still so much to learn. Cassie touched his hand. "I know Jackie hurt you, but her words were foolishly spoken."

"Yet clearly understood." He turned to his wife, his eyes bright with pain and confusion. "I did everything I could for them. Why do I feel at times as though they despise me?"

Cassie held his hand to her chest, wishing she could help him understand. "They don't despise you, but sometimes they come to you as a friend and you treat them like children."

"I only give them advice. That's what I've always done."

"Sometimes they only want you to listen, to be there, and not try to guide and help them. Drake, you have to let go. Come, I want to show you something." She led him to the family room and pointed to a portrait they'd had taken last spring: Cassie, Drake, Marcus, and Ericka. "You're the head of a different family now."

He stared at the portrait a long moment, the pleasure of what he had warring with the pain of letting go. He turned to Cassie, surprised that his love for her continued to grow and change with each new year. He pulled her into his arms, Holding her close, feeling the new life inside her move. She was right. He had to let go.

***

Jackie absently typed her proposal, trying not to think of how Clay and Bertha's meeting would be. She was imagining a number of scenarios—most of them bad—when the phone rang.

"Drake was right," Eric said without preamble. "I should have told Adriana. She's furious."

"She won't speak to you?"

"Worse."

She bit her lip to keep from laughing. "Ouch. No sex. Sorry. I know how much you like that."

"Yes," he said grimly. "Unfortunately, so does she."

"For how long?"

His voice rose in surprise. "Does it matter? Next time I'll risk worrying her and give myself a reason to comfort her. Anything is better than this."

"You'll survive."

Eric gave a world-weary sigh. "I'm almost a shell of my former self."

She slipped out of her shoes and wiggled her toes.

"Does your brain still function?"

"Partially. Why?"

"I need your advice."

His tone changed. "You didn't have to hurt him, you know."

"I didn't mean to. I just...He made me so angry and he had no right to mention your chest pains."

"I don't need a champion. I can fight-my own battles and that wasn't one of them."

"He can be such a bully."

"He loves us," Eric said. "An annoying, aggravating fact at times, but it's true."

"I doubt he'll ever talk to me again."

"At least not this century."

"Don't be mean," Jackie said.

"Then stop feeling sorry for yourself. He has every right to be mad at you. He needs time."

She sighed. "You're right. Besides, Drake's not my only problem."

"What else is there?"

"Clay's mom. She's here in the States and she wants to reconcile with him. Since she's staying with me, I don't know what I'll do if things fall apart."

"It's getting crowded?"

She rubbed her forehead. "You know how it is with visitors."

"Expensive."

"This is not about expense, this is about family. They're meeting today and I'm not sure everything will go well." She pulled on her shoes again. "I want things to work out."

"Stay out of it."

She sighed. "I can't. If he just gave her a chance, I think—"

"Stop thinking and listen. Are you listening?"

"Yes."

"Paper and pad ready?"

She rolled her eyes. "Eric!"

"No need to get testy, pest. Here's my advice. Leave things alone. If it doesn't work out, you'll be in the same position I'm in." He paused. "I suggest cold showers."

"How come you don't feel the same way about Clay as Drake does?"

"A simple equation. One, because I'm not Drake, plus one, I know you, which equals Clay didn't have a chance."

"You make me sound devious."

"Aren't you?"

Jackie laughed. "Only sometimes. Bye." She hung up.

A few moments later, Patty peeked her head inside the office. "You have a visitor."

Jackie checked her calendar. "Who?"

Kevin entered and spread his arms wide, looking very much like the wealthy playboy he was. "Me."

She stood and hugged him. "This is a nice surprise." She hadn't seen him since she and Clay had visited his house.

"I'm glad. I want to talk to you about my decision. Grab your bag. We're going out."

Jackie soon found herself in the backseat of his Lexus as the driver took them around the city. "I was impressed with your program," Kevin said. "I read your materials and did a little research. I even met with your boss."

"And?"

"I can't donate."

Her face fell. "Why not?"

He tugged on the cuffs of his sleeves. "I didn't like her shoes."

She blinked, confused. "Why?"

"They didn't match her job."

"What are you talking about? What do her shoes have to do with anything?"

"You've never noticed Faye's shoes or the earrings she wears?"

"I know they're very nice, that's all."

He patted her on the hand as though she were a misguided youth. "Oh, yes. I keep forgetting you were poorly educated. Here's a little lesson. Her shoes cost eight hundred dollars."

"Shoes don't cost that much," she said in disbelief.

"Of course they do. Her earrings were perhaps three hundred, which isn't much by itself, except when you consider her salary."

"That doesn't mean anything. She comes from a wealthy family."

Kevin thought for a moment, then shook his head. "I bet she checks price tags."

"Is there anything wrong with that?"

"When you're rich, you don't have to. If you want something, you buy it. So how can she afford those shoes in a job like that? Does she have a boyfriend?"

"No."

He shrugged. "It's none of my business, anyway."

"I'm sure there's a reasonable explanation," she said in defense.

"Perhaps."

"But it's the reason why you won't contribute?"

"Sorry, babe. I don't like questions when it comes to money. I'll give you a little something to put a smile on your face, but I can't be an investor."

Jackie drummed her fingers on her knee. "Damn."

"Is that the best you can do?"

"I could call you a dirty name."

"Say it with conviction and I'll take it as a compliment."

She made a face.

Kevin stretched his arm the length of the seat. "Let's go to lunch. How about the Blue Mango?"

She narrowed her eyes, knowing what he was up to. "No."

He tapped her on the shoulder. "Oh, come on. I like irritating your brother. I'd love him to see you with me."

"I don't think he's there anyway." She sighed. "Right now I think he dislikes me as much as he does you."

"Impossible. He loves his family." He removed fun from his trousers. "How's Cassie?"

"She's fine." She slanted her eyes at him, unable to ignore the certain note in his tone. "Do you still--"

"Love her? Probably. I don't think about it much."

Jackie glanced out the window, then said, "Of all the women you've met, why her? She's pretty and funny, I know, but—"

"Isn't that what love is? Loving someone for reasons you can't explain?" He cupped her face. "Don't look so tragic, little one. I'm not suffering." He flashed a devastating grin she was forced to return. "I'm happy for her. I think your brother's a jackass, but he's the perfect man for her. I could have offered her money, but not a family life. I don't want to get married and have kids." He shivered at the thought. "I enjoy my life. Truly." He paused. "But I can see that love is making you suffer."

"I'm not suffering."

"At least trying hard not to." He looked out the window and shook his head. "Women get it all wrong. They fall in love with unsuitable men. Clay is the wrong man to fall in love with." He turned to her. "I, however, make a better alternative."

She looked doubtful. "Why?"

"I'm better looking, rich, classier, and I like to be loved."

"Don't you mean adored?"

"Yes, that, too." His hand fell to her shoulder. He lowered his voice. "How would you like time away?"

She lifted a sly brow. "Is that an invitation to something that would get us both in trouble?"

"Yes."

She tilted her head flirtatiously to the side. "Where would you take me?"

He leaned toward her "Where would you like to go?"

"Into Clay's mind."

Kevin frowned and sat back. "That sounds like a dull place."

"It's not."

"Come away with me. Think about it. A vacation on a Greek island."

Jackie narrowed her eyes. "You do like to cause trouble. I bet your mother gave you everything you wanted."

"And more, but this isn't about me. Some shaky waters could spur Clay into action."

She shook her head. "Tempting, but no."

"Why not? You could make Clay jealous and Drake would be thrilled you're seeing Clay and not me."

"I don't want to play games."

"Games can be fun."

"I'm too old for games."

He rested a hand on his chest and released a sigh. "I suppose the problem is I'm not. Perhaps that's why I'm all alone."

"I'm not going to feel sorry for you."

Kevin made his face look like that of a hurt puppy. "I'm a poor, lonely bastard—I mean, bachelor—in need of sex—excuse me, love. Lots and lots of love."

Jackie laughed and playfully hit him until he smiled. "You're dreadful."

"I try."

"We could never work. You remind me too much of Drake."

He stared. "What?"

"That's why you can't stand each other. You're the flip side of the same coin."

"I offer you a weekend getaway and you insult me?" he said, offended.

"You're both used to commanding subordinates, you both like to help when you don't need to, and you both would spoil me rotten."

He held up a hand. "Enough. I may be sick."

"Don't be angry."

"I'm not. Life's too short. I may never speak to you again, but I'm not angry."

She smiled and turned away.

"So what will you do?"

"About funding?"

"No, about Drake. What are you willing to risk?"

"Risk?"

"If you had to make a choice and lose either Drake or Clay for the rest of your life, who would you choose?"

Chapter Twenty Two

The long days of spring settled over the city in a sun-soaked breeze that washed the leaves and grass a brilliant green and polished the stone buildings. Bertha and Clay sat under a tree eating lunch he bought from a street vendor.

"Thanks for seeing me," Bertha said at last, breaking the silence that had stretched between them since he'd picked her up.

"Hmm." He watched her light a cigarette while he took a bite of his hot dog.

"Nice weather."

"Can be until it hits May, then the city is a humid monster."

"You hate the heat. Why do you stay?"

He shrugged. "Cassie." He said her name though it caused pain.

"Family's a good thing. I was seeing a bloke with five kids."

Clay leaned back on his elbow. "He dumped you for his wife, did he?"

Bertha glared at him. "I don't see married men anymore."

"You've made a lot of wives happy."

"Will you continue to be my judge and jury?"

Clay sat up and stared at a passing jogger. "Why did you want to see me?"

She hesitated, then said, "I'm lonely."

He turned to her, surprised. "Honesty. Wow. That's a nice change."

"I've changed a lot." She inhaled, then shook her head. "Well, maybe not a lot."

"So after he dumped you, what happened?"

"Sorry?"

"You've been dumped before and you've been lonely before—that has never sent you running to me."

"I bet you're a successful investigator."

He looked bored. "Answer the question."

"All right, the truth is I got a letter."

"From who?"

"A friend of yours. He didn't give me much information, he just said you needed me."

His eyes widened. "And you believed that?"

Bertha took two nervous puffs, then said, "I wanted to."

The truth of her words startled him. "So you came all this way because some guy said I needed you? Do you have the letter?"

She placed the cigarette between her lips and opened her bag. The cigarette bobbed up and down as she spoke. "Got it in here somewhere. Ah, here." She handed him the letter.

Clay read through the letter, instantly recognizing the language. It spoke about his work as an investigator and how stressed he was. How helpful it would be for her to see him. He folded it back up, then said in a neutral tone, "And you came all this way to help me."

"Some sons would be pleased."

He absently tapped the letter against his knee. "Yeah, some."

"I didn't kill Doreen."

Her name, so long unspoken, hit him like a blow—it twisted his insides, then miraculously subsided. He had wanted to blame her for not being a better mother, for not raising a daughter that thought more highly of herself, but the anger wasn't there to fuel that blame. There was nothing to feed it anymore. "I know," he said. He took the cigarette out of her mouth and stubbed it out. "No wonder you're so skinny. Eat your hot dog."

She took a bite, he nodded in approval, then they sat quietly and finished their meal.

***

Later that day, Clay stormed into the office and slammed the letter on Mack's desk. "You're either a meddling old woman or a raving lunatic."

Mack gripped the arms of his chair, his eyes wide. He'd never seen Clay show such temper. "What did I do?"

"My mother appeared on Saturday. Do you know anything about that?"

Mack scratched his nose. "I could lie, but it seems you already know the answer to that."

"Yes, I do know the answer." Clay held up three fingers. "And I tried to come up with three different scenarios to explain your lack of judgment. One, that you're suffering from an untreated form of syphilis and you're going mad; two, that you naively thought I was a masochist in need of more pain; or three, you really wanted to discover how much physical torture you could endure."

"How about number four? That I'm your friend."

Clay stared. "You're my what?"

"Friend. I wanted to help you out."

"You're my friend?" He said the words as though he'd never heard the term before.

"Hard to believe, I know." Mack rested his glasses on the desk. "Look, buddy, I was worried about you. After Gabriella's death you were burning out. I thought you needed a catalyst, and that talk we had about mothers got me thinking. Megan drafted the first letter—"

Clay's eyes darkened. "You told your daughter about me?"

"As I've said, I consider you a friend. I know you don't feel the same, that's fine." He sat back. "Aside from a friend, I thought I was in danger of losing a good partner and wanted to help. I shouldn't have interfered, but when Megan mentioned contacting your mom, it sounded like a good idea. And if your mother hadn't sounded so willing and eager, I would have forgotten the whole thing. She does love you."

Mack considered him a friend? Clay sat at his desk, amazed. *Not just a partner, but a friend.*

"I'm sorry I stepped over the line."

Clay stared at the black screen of his computer. "Fine. I won't kill you this time."

"Thanks for the reprieve."

"But if you—"

"It won't happen again." He smoothed out an eyebrow. "How did things go?"

"As well as could be expected. You've never met my mother."

"No. Only in e-mails."

"I'll have to introduce you. Should prove interesting."

He swung back and forth in his chair. He'd gained a friendship just when he'd lost one. But he didn't want to lose it. He picked up the phone and called Eric. When he answered, Clay said, "Hey, Eric, I'd like a word with you and Drake. Are you free to meet at Eugene's Wednesday?"

"I'm free. I'm not sure I could get Drake to come."

"I'm not in the position to ask any favors, but if you could try drinks are on me."

"I'll see what I can do."

"Thanks." He hung up, then stared at the phone. He wasn't certain what he would say, but he felt he had to try something. He looked at Mack. "Are you free Wednesday?"

"If free drinks are included, sure."

"They are."

Mack grinned. "I'm already there."

***

Wednesday night at Eugene's was full of women who'd come for free drinks and the men who'd come to see them. But in the far corner of the bar, four men sat quietly with a bowl of pretzels and their drinks: Mack, Clay, Eric, and Carter. Drake had yet to show.

Finally Eric set down his drink and looked at Clay. He looked pale, but grim. "He said he'd come."

"Could be stuck in traffic," Carter said.

Clay glanced at the door. "Hmm."

Mack grinned, trying to ease the tense atmosphere. "You've certainly got women trouble. Jackie *and* your mother."

Clay nodded. "Thanks to you lot."

"What's your mother like?" Eric asked.

"I know I'm supposed to be kind."

"Is she like Angela?" he asked, referring to Cassie's acid-tongued mother.

"I'd say worse."

"I don't think worse is possible."

Clay took a long swallow, then set his glass down. "It is."

"She's mellowed out, though," Eric said, trying to be fair.

"Let me say this. My mum could walk into a bar and leave with a man within ten minutes."

The men looked at him.

"Ten minutes?" Carter asked.

"You could set your watch. She'd love a place like this."

"Do you have a picture of her?"

"No, but if you check the dictionary under the word—"

"Hey, hey, hey," Carter said "You might not like her, but she's still your mother. Have some respect." He ordered another beer.

Eric glanced at his watch; Clay glanced at the door.

"Have you ever made love to an older woman?" Mack asked.

Carter shook his head.

"Define 'older,'" Clay said.

"At least ten years."

He shook his head.

Eric absently rubbed his chest. "I have." He smiled in memory. "She was great."

Mack nodded. "Me, too. Twenty years older and she knew everything."

"I'm impressed," Eric said.

Clay lifted his drink. "So am I. By the way, I've changed my mind."

"About what?" Mack asked.

"You're not meeting my mother."

Mack laughed; it sounded forced.

"So why Jackie?" Carter asked.

When Clay didn't readily reply, Mack spoke up. "He's liked her since—"

Clay shot him a glance. "Mind you don't choke on your beer."

"I'm not drinking beer."

He lifted his glass. "You will be."

Mack grabbed some pretzels.

Clay tapped the side of his glass. "I just like her, that's all." He looked at Eric. "I'm good to her."

Eric rubbed his chest, the corner of his mouth kicking up in a grin. "I know."

Carter straightened. "Hey, I see Drake."

Mack glanced at his watch. "About time."

Clay sat back and took a deep breath as though preparing for battle.,

Drake approached the table, his eyes briefly meeting Clay's before he signaled a waitress. He began to sit when his eyes focused on Eric. "Are you okay?"

Eric nodded. "I just need some air." He stood, then grabbed his chest and collapsed.

Chapter Twenty Three

The hospital waiting room held a quiet that made minutes feel like hours. Jackie shifted in her seat, wishing there was something she could do. Drake was withdrawn, Clay unreadable, Mack checked out an attractive female doctor, Carter tapped his foot, and Adriana looked near collapse. Cassie had stayed home with the kids. Though Drake had tried to reassure Adriana with what little he knew from what Eric had shared, she still looked anxious. They all were.

Desperate to offer comfort, but having no words to say, Jackie sat next to her and took her hand.

Adriana snatched it away. "Don't touch me," she said with such anger Jackie winced.

"Why not?"

"You lied to me. You knew something was wrong and pretended that everything was fine." her eyes filled with tears. "Even when I asked you, you lied."

"He wanted me to keep it a secret."

"And that makes it all right?" She turned away. "I thought we were friends. I was wrong."

"He's my brother and—"

"And your loyalty may have cost him his life."

Drake spoke up. "Don't blame her."

Adriana moved her gaze to him. "Of course not. The tribe leader will shoulder the blame. She won't face anything as long as you're here."

"Be fair," Clay said.

Adriana rolled her eyes. "Yes, come to her defense. I mustn't blame Jackie. Poor little Jackie was only protecting her big brother. She shouldn't be accountable for her actions. It doesn't matter that she was supposed to be my friend. That's not important." She stood, wrapping arms around herself as though cold. "But you wouldn't understand. She's good with men. With men she can use that smile, those eyes, that cute, petite little figure and everything is forgiven." She turned to Jackie. "But I can't forgive you. I thought we were friends. I thought we had a bond like Cassie and I do. A bond where we make fun of each other, give advice, get annoyed, but we *never lie* to each other. Never about the important things." She let her hands fall and stared at Jackie in a new way. "Perhaps that's why you have no female friends. Maybe you don't know how to be a friend." She looked at Drake. "And you don't know how to let anyone into the clan. You made those Sunday dinners a sham." She threw up her hands. "None of it was real. We're not a family. It's the Hensons and the rest of us. Three against two."

"Three against three," Clay said.

"Three?" She sniffed. "I don't think so, Mr. Neutral. You don't count because you don't want to. Not really. You haven't invested in us. None of us know how long you will stay around. It'd be nice, but we all know Clay will do what he wants. A family? That's funny. We're—"

"Enough." Clay's tone was quiet but effective. "Nobody in this room is perfect. However, we don't get together to pretend we are. We do so because we're family and, strangely enough, enjoy each other's company." He glanced at Drake. "Nobody's perfect. Yeah, I might leave. Drake's protective of Eric and Jackie, Cassie will try to make everything all right, Eric will keep things to himself, and Jackie will get her way most times. But you're part of this family, too. You're the one no one wants to worry."

He sat beside Adriana. "Tonight we need you to be strong. If you want us to share things with you, we need to know you'll be able to handle it. Yes, we made a mistake by not saying anything. And if anything seriously happens in that operating room, I won't forgive myself. But for all the mistakes we've made, it doesn't measure up to the one Eric made by not going to the doctor when he should have." His eyes pierced hers. "By not telling you."

***

When they were finally allowed to see Eric, Adriana went alone. He looked worn, but he was alive and that was all that mattered. His chest was bandaged from where they had inserted and removed a tube that drained water from his lungs. His glasses were gone and that made him look much more vulnerable somehow.

"Hi," she said.

"Hi."

"I'm mad at you."

He smiled weakly. "Still? Haven't I been punished enough?"

She leaned against the bed rail and shook her head. "I'm serious, Eric."

His smile faded. "I know."

"I just told everyone off in the waiting room."

"I thought I married a woman with better manners."

"You didn't." She gently touched his forehead. His skin felt cool from the air-conditioning. "What am I going to do with you?"

"You can get me a new pair of lungs. If you can't manage that, just get me out of here."

She gripped the railing, unashamed of her tears. "I'd give you my heart if it made you well." Her voice fell. "You scared me."

"Love, I'm sorry. I didn't want you to worry about me."

"I'm worried now."

He reached for her hand. "I'm sorry."

"Are you sorry that you're sick or sorry you lied?"

He shook his head, his voice firm. "I didn't lie."

"Silence can be a lie. Do you know why I married you?"

"I suspect you're going to tell me."

"I married you because I wanted you in my life. I wanted you in my daughter's life."

His eyes pleaded. "I don't want Nina to see me."

"Too bad."

His tone hardened. "I don't want her to see me like this."

"So far you've done exactly what you've wanted and it hasn't done this family any good. As a husband and father it can't only be about what you want, but about what your family needs. And that means your wife needs to know when you're sick, as does your daughter, because we love you." She stopped and lifted a mischievous brow. "By the way, have you considered how much this emergency room visit will cost us?"

He looked startled, then fiercely swore. "I should have thought about that."

"Think about it the next time you decide to forgo a visit to the doctor. You don't need to pretend or protect me from the truth. I might be flighty sometimes, but I'm far from weak."

"I'd never call you weak." He smiled. "You look beautiful."

"You can't see anything, can you?"

"Hardly."

"Where are your glasses?"

He nodded to the side table. "So considerate, how they put things out of reach."

"They're busy." She put the glasses on his face. "There, that's better."

"Yes." He searched her face. "So you'd give me your heart, huh?"

"Yes."

"Well, you already have mine."

***

Adriana walked past the waiting room, then stopped, turned around and entered. She stared at the small group. She sat down and crossed her legs. "I apologize for my display earlier," she said primly. "However, to ensure that this never happens again, I want to offer you a warning." She turned to Jackie. "To the one woman in this group, I promise if you lie to me again, your access to Eric will become greatly reduced and you won't go out with Cassie or me again." She looked at Mack and Clay. "To the two single men, Eric will no longer visit Eugene's bar, and as the owner of a lingerie store where my clientele happen to be attractive eligible women, I will make sure when they hear your names they will shriek in terror."

"You don't even know me," Mack protested.

"I know your name and your face. That's enough." She turned her attention to Drake and Carter. "To the two married men in the room, since I know your wives, I will conspire to make your lives miserable." She stood and smoothed out her skirt. "That's about it. Eric is waiting to see you now." She left the room. They heard her high heels click down the hallway.

Clay looked at Carter. "Can she really do that? Make your life miserable, I mean? Are wives that powerful?"

Carter nodded. "Yes."

"Sort of puts me off the idea of getting one."

Mack raised a brow. "Never knew you had that idea. Why do you have that look on your face?"

Clay shook his head. "I just had a thought, but now it's gone. I hate that."

"Wives aren't so bad," Carter said. "It's nice to come home to someone who loves you."

"Get a dog," Clay said.

"Hey, in some cases it's the same thing," Mack said. The men laughed; Jackie shook her head. "Come on, boys."

They all entered the room. Drake was coldly polite to Clay in an effort not to do anything to upset his brother. They were all happy to see Eric up and alert.

Clay lifted the sheet. "Nice legs."

Eric frowned. "The attached foot can kick your ass."

"Not right now."

The men ribbed each other—trying not to make Eric laugh too much—Jackie watched in the distance, unable to join in. She couldn't forget that they were in a hospital as she glanced at the white tile floor, faded peach curtains, and Eric lying in a steel bed with tubes attached to him.

"Where's the brat?" Eric asked.

Jackie stepped forward. "I'm here."

"Aren't you going to say anything?"

She didn't know what to say. That she loved him? That she wished he were well? That the phone call saying he was in the hospital had terrified her? That she wished she hadn't kept his secret? He had teased her and indulged her. Told her tales of faraway places—castles, kings, and spiders who caused mischief as they sat alone in whatever shelter Drake could find, trying to keep the hunger at bay with wordplay.

She looked at Drake, who'd given up so much for them. Her anger becoming an understanding that a part of her would always appreciate and feel guilty for his sacrifice. But she now saw more than her two big brothers. She saw men, husbands, and fathers. Their circle had expanded and their roles had changed. Adriana was right—they weren't the three Hensons against the world anymore. They didn't need to be. The thought lifted her heart.

"I want everyone to leave the room," she said.

"A gnat is giving instructions?" Eric said.

"Is that what that buzzing sound was?" Clay asked.

Drake patted her on the head. "She's cute."

"I said go," Jackie said.

They stared at her in a playful challenge.

She folded her arms. "Okay, then I'll tell Adriana—"

Mack held up his hands. "Say no more. We're leaving right now." He smiled at Eric. "I think you'd better get well soon or your wife will have something to say about it."

"Take care," Clay said.

Drake just patted him on the shoulder and Carter made a sign only Eric could interpret, then left.

"So did Adriana tell you off?" she asked. "She gave us a wicked tongue lashing."

"Yes. I have the scars."

"Serves you right."

He rested his head back. "I'm a sick man I could use a little sympathy."

"You're not getting any from me."

He became serious. "Have Drake and Clay talked?"

"No."

"I thought my unfortunate collision with the ground might initiate conversation. Give them time." He lowered his gaze. "He tries, you know, but it's hard for him to shake the father role. Be easy on him."

"I didn't mean what I said."

"Yes, you did, and I understand. You don't want to feel you need his approval. You want him to let go. But don't hate him if he never does."

Jackie made a face. "It really is eerie how well you know us."

"Middle-child syndrome. Before you leave, try to talk to him, even if he pretends to ignore you."

She rolled her eyes with mock exasperation. "Will you always tell me what to do?"

He smiled. "Yeah, brat, I will."

She left and saw Clay and Mack in the waiting room.

"Where are the others?"

"Carter went home and Drake is outside with the smokers, smelling the air."

She laughed. "That's a good one."

Clay shook his head. "I'm not joking. Go see for yourself."

She left the emergency room under the bright lights of the hospital entrance, heard the roar of an ambulance, its red and blue lights piercing the
dark. She saw Drake standing against a tree near a man who was smoking.

Jackie walked over and stood beside him. She didn't touch him and she
didn't say anything.

He shoved his hands in his pockets.

"It's a nice night," she said

He nodded.

"Do you remember this song?" She began to hum one of her mother's
favorite Jimmy Cliff songs, "Sitting in Limbo," which was exactly what they
were doing. But as she hummed that quiet simple song, for a moment
everything was all right.

He briefly closed his eyes with a soft smile of remembrance. "Yes, I
do."

She flexed her foot. "I'm sorry I didn't tell you about Clay—"

He sighed. "I know why you didn't."

"You've been our guardian and our strength for so long. I don't want to
disappoint you, but I want to live my own life."

He rested a hand on her shoulder. "I've always wanted the best for
you." He tweaked her chin and smiled. "But only you know what's best for
you,"

She hugged him. "I'll always want you as a part of my life." She glanced
up at him. "Just not such a big part."

"I understand. Come on. Let's go inside."

***

Eric was released within two days and expected to make a full recovery
if he followed his doctor's orders. They would all make sure he did. At
home, Jackie was pleased that Bertha no longer spent all her time on the

couch. She went out during the day and sometimes in the evening, always coming back at a reasonable time.

In a good mood, Jackie sat in her office, researching a new homeless shelter.

Patty rushed in. "You won't believe it."

"What?"

"Claudia Meeks is dead," she said, as though it was a juicy piece of news instead of a tragedy.

"How?"

"Suicide. Nobody had seen her leave her apartment, but that wasn't unusual so they didn't take notice. The poor thing had begun to smell. A neighbor called the police and there she was on the ground with her beer bottles all over the place and a bottle of pills. Guess she couldn't take it anymore."

Another victim of Emmerick. "When did you learn all this?"

"This morning. Claudia's mother called."

"I thought her mother was dead."

"Only in Claudia's eyes, I guess--she sounded alive enough to me. She wants to speak to you about her. She wonders if you could meet her at the apartment."

"Okay."

Patty turned, then stopped. "She sounds like a rough woman, so I'd be careful."

"Thanks." Jackie stared at the closed door, then called Clay. "Another client is dead."

"Suicide?"

"Yes. I'm going to meet her mother—"

"Okay. Be right there."

***

Mrs. Meeks wasn't as rough as her voice would suggest. She was an older woman with black hair and a streak of gray. She made them weak tea, which Clay fed to a plant and Jackie still held. The place was otherwise bare except for a couple of beanbags.

"Do you mind if I walk about a bit?" Clay asked.

"No, go ahead," Mrs. Meeks said.

"Thanks."

Mrs. Meeks turned to Jackie. "Thank you for trying to help Claudia. She told me a lot about you."

"I'm sorry," Jackie said, "but we weren't aware of you. We didn't know her mother was alive."

"I'm really her aunt. Her mother died of an overdose. But I've raised her most of her life, so I'm like a mother, right?" She didn't wait for a reply. "I couldn't believe it when they called me. Claudia had sounded so hopeful. To kill herself was against our beliefs."

"Sometimes beliefs change."

"No," Mrs. Meeks said firmly. "There was no indication she would take this route. I just don't understand it."

"When she spoke to you, did she sound different somehow?"

"No, just happy, like I said. And hopeful. It is all so strange."

"She didn't mention any new friends?"

"No."

When she became quiet, Jackie asked, "Why did you want to see me?"

"Because I found this." She handed her a card---Careless Rapture. "What is it? Is it some sort of drug like Ecstasy?"

"No, it's a cult."

"Claudia wouldn't join something like that."

Clay came back in the room. "She didn't leave anything."

"No." Mrs. Meeks squinted at him. "Haven't I seen you somewhere before?"

He hoped not. He didn't want to be connected to his *Just Talk* appearance. "I don't think so."

"I'm sure I have. Have you ever modeled cologne?"

Clay furrowed his brows. "No."

She looked at Jackie. "Doesn't he look like a cologne model? Like he'd wear something called Intense?" She turned to Clay and measured him with her eyes. "You could be a model, you're very good-looking."

Jackie glanced at Clay and bit her lip to keep from laughing.

Clay said, "I'll be outside."

"I didn't mean to embarrass him," Mrs. Meeks said after he'd gone.

Jackie smiled. "That's okay. It was nice to see."

Chapter Twenty Four

"Don't say anything," Clay said as they walked to his car.

"I'll try not to." Jackie lifted a bouquet to her nose.

"What's that?"

"Mrs. Meeks gave me these plastic flowers. She said Claudia would have wanted me to have them." She rested them in the backseat. "What do we do now?" she asked, buckling her seatbelt. "We have to stop him."

"Why didn't Claudia tell her aunt about Careless Rapture?"

"She was secretive. Everyone is. Melanie was the only one to speak about him."

"Why? Why the secrecy? It just seems strange. She was honest about everything else."

"Perhaps she didn't want to be talked out of it. I kept you a secret."

"No, this is different. It's wrong somehow. I'm just not sure how."

Jackie rolled down the window. "You know, your mother said something very interesting about Rennie."

"What?"

"She said Rennie had tried to stop Emmerick and failed."

Clay frowned. "Rennie never tried to stop him."

"Then why would she say that?" She shook her head. "I don't think she made it up. Something must have happened to give her that impression."

"What could it be? She wasn't there. Maybe she was just talking and you misunderstood her."

"No, I didn't. She knows something."

"I doubt it. She was completely pissed at the funeral."

She turned to him, confused. "Pissed?"

"Drunk. And she didn't stay around long enough to learn anything. She was probably delusional."

"We can't just write her off, though. We need to know why she thinks that, even if it turns out to be wrong."

"I guess that's my cue. I'll pick her up and have her stay with me."

Jackie clapped her hands together, thrilled. "So your talk really brought you two together? I'm so glad! She wouldn't talk to me about it and I didn't want to ask if she didn't want to talk, since she's the type who would talk if she wanted to. So I just wondered about what had happened and couldn't stop thinking about it, and didn't want to bother you because I know how you are and since she was still at my place I guessed that things were still on shaky ground so—"

He covered her mouth. "Breathe."

She removed his hand. "I'm just so happy that you're learning to understand each other. An important bond is building and you can—" She stopped and scowled. "There's that annoying grin of yours. What did I say that's so amusing?"

"Nearly fifteen years of discord and you think a couple of days have made us friends? That we will bond? It's amazing how set you are on happy endings."

"It's possible."

"My mother is coming to stay with me, that's all. I can't have you suffering anymore."

"Thank you. That kind of consideration deserves a reward."

"What?"

"Don't worry." She winked. "I'll think of something."

***

Jackie went to Adriana's lingerie shop, Divine Notions, and stood outside the door, wondering if she should have gone elsewhere. She took a deep breath, then opened the door. When Adriana saw her, she said something to her assistant and came over.

"What brings you here?" Adriana said.

Jackie sighed, relieved. Her words were casual and her expression was warm. Their friendship had remained intact. "I need a garter belt."

"First time?"

She nodded.

"Oh, good. This will be fun."

Jackie ended up with a black garter belt and a short, see-through red skirt with two matching bras. At the counter Jackie asked, "Have you ever heard of shoes costing eight hundred dollars?"

Adriana nodded. "Yes."

"Would you be able to recognize a pair?"

"Probably. Why?"

"My boss likes to wear expensive shoes and I was wondering how she could afford them."

She handed Jackie her bag of purchases. "Why not just ask her?"

Jackie stared at her, appalled. "I couldn't."

"Sure you could. All you do is compliment her on her shoes and hint at wanting a pair."

Jackie gripped her bag. "I've never asked about her shoes before, she wouldn't believe me."

Adriana began to grin, interpreting the silent request. "You want me to do it?"

Jackie blinked her eyes outrageously and smiled. "Please?"

***

Thirty minutes later, Jackie nodded at Faye, who stood by the copy machine. "There she is."

Adriana glanced at her shoes. "Then you have a problem."

"What?"

"She might wear expensive shoes, but those are screaming Payless."

Jackie rested a hand on her hip. "Oh, great."

"That jacket, however, is something else entirely. Excuse me." She walked to the copy machine. "Faye Radcliff?"

Faye turned to her with a professional smile. "Yes?"

"Hi. I'm Adriana Graham, Jackie's sister-in-law. She's told me so much about you, it's a pleasure to meet you finally. Right now I'm on a mission to get her out of these boring clothes and I couldn't help but notice your jacket. It's gorgeous. Where can I get one?"

"You can't. It's from a celebrity giveaway."

"I'm jealous."

"Don't be." She lowered her voice to a conspiratorial tone. "I admit to being a fiend when it comes to giveaways and estate sales. I may not be rich, but I can dress like royalty. You should see my closet."

Adriana grinned. "You should see mine."

"Can you get inside?"

"Hardly. I'm debating on whether to leave my husband any space at all."

She laughed. Jackie stared at Faye, amazed. She'd never seen her so open and friendly before. "There's another estate sale coming up soon. I could give you the address and we could go together and get Jackie something."

Adriana sighed with regret. "Thank you, but my husband would kill me."

"Think about it. Jackie has my number."

"I certainly will. It was a pleasure to meet you."

Faye nodded, then returned to her office. Jackie walked Adriana to the elevators. "Sometimes I wonder if I'm missing the female gene," Jackie said.

Adriana pressed the DOWN button with a smirk. "Clay doesn't think so."

"You know what I mean. The ability to chat about clothes and shopping. I could never make a quick friend the way you did."

Adriana shrugged. "Oh, that was idle chatter. That shouldn't be confused with a lasting friendship." They stepped into the elevator.

She sent her a cautious glance. "Like us?"

Adriana adjusted her necklace. "We're getting there. Does this place have a cafeteria?"

"Yes."

"Great, then you can treat me to coffee." She playfully nudged her. "All good lasting friendships begin that way."

Jackie and Adriana chatted for half an hour before Adriana returned to work. Jackie finished her biscotti. A man slid into the chair in front of her. She glanced up and tried not to groan out loud.

"I finally got you alone," said William Chavis, the accountant who wouldn't give up asking her out.

"I'm about to leave."

"You can spare a few minutes. It won't hurt you."

"No, but you want to go out with me and that's impossible because I'm seeing someone."

He sat back, undeterred. "Until there's a ring on your finger, there's still hope."

Too tired to argue, Jackie had two cups of coffee with him. He proved to be just as boring as she'd feared. She struggled to keep her eyes open as he shared his hobby of collecting pens. "How would you like to see my collection?"

"Perhaps another time."

"You're a hard woman to know."

"Yes, but my boss is single," she said, hoping to redirect his interest.

"Faye Radcliff. She certainly doesn't act it."

"She's dedicated to her work."

"I want a woman dedicated to me."

Jackie stood. "I'm afraid you won't find her at this table, but good luck."

***

Clay wasn't used to living with someone. He wasn't sure he ever would be. Bertha had been with him a few days and he still felt uncomfortable with the situation. He would have preferred a bird—a bird didn't ask for money, talk to him when he wanted to be silent, or try to make up childhood memories he was certain had never happened. Though he appreciated the attempt.

He walked into his apartment, wondering if he'd find the familiar smoking figure on the couch. She was either there or out somewhere, she never told him where. Since she was usually out, he hadn't had the chance to talk to her about his sister. He would try tonight. First, he needed to unwind. Walking past his mother, who was stretched out on the couch, he went straight to the fridge, opened it, and scowled. "Mum, stop drinking off my beers," he grumbled, grabbing the last one.

"Do you realize you have an empty birdcage?" she called.

"It's not empty." He popped the top of the can and took a swallow. "I just have a really tiny bird inside. Can't you hear it? It's singing right now."

She kissed her teeth. "Cheeky monkey."

He sat down. "What are you watching?"

"Rubbish."

He picked up the remote. "So we can change the channel?"

She snatched it away. "No, it's good rubbish. How was work?"

"Fine." He took another swallow, then set his beer down. "What did you know about Doreen?"

"Blunt, aren't you?"

"I'm curious."

"About what?"

"You told Jackie that Rennie failed to stop Emmerick."

She dragged on her cigarette and squinted her eyes. "Did I?"

"Yes. Why did you say that?"

She exhaled, surrounding herself in a cloud of smoke. "Probably because it was true."

"How do you know that when you weren't even there? Rennie barely spoke to you. There were no phones in the house and—"

She tapped the ashes of the cigarette in her new Lincoln Memorial ashtray. "Rennie didn't tell me."

"Don't say—"

She shook her head. "No, that Prince fellow didn't tell me- either. It was some woman. I don't remember her name. One of his wives, maybe, or a friend. But she said Rennie had betrayed the trust. That she had tried to stop them. She'd left the main house and moved into one of the trailers and that had angered Emmerick. No one could think of any other reason for her behavior except your leaving."

"Why didn't you say anything?"

"I don't believe we were talking at the time and she was already dead." She reached for his beer; he moved it out of the way."Come on, just a sip."

"No. Keep talking."

"Personally, I'm not sure that is real helpful now."

"Did the woman say how Rennie tried to stop him?"

"She tried to go to the police."

"The police?" That was definitely a break from community code. What would have prompted that? What would she have on Emmerick that the police could have used?

The phone rang; Bertha grabbed it before he had a chance to.

"Yes?" she said. "Okay, meet you there." She hung up and stubbed out her cigarette.

"You're going out again?"

"Yes."

"Who is he?"

She shrugged. "Just a man."

"Yes, I know *what* he is. I worked that out myself. What's his name?"

"You don't need to worry."

Clay folded his arms and shook his head. "Amazing how history repeats itself. You claim to come all this way to see me and in less than two weeks you've already met a man."

Bertha took out her compact and applied foundation. "It's not like that."

"Why won't you tell me a little about him? I would like to know what guy is so enamored with you that he has you out almost every night, calls at three and five in the morning, and has you coming home with less money than you left with. I thought the man was supposed to pay. At least some of the time."

She snapped her compact closed. "I'll be back late."

"You can't keep this up. You're playing a dangerous game."

Bertha stood and grabbed her handbag. "The same one you are." She opened the door. "You can't stop him."

"Watch me."

"No time, love. Bye." She left.

Clay stared at the door, then took a long swallow. He refused to be upset. Bertha could do what she bloody well pleased—he wasn't her guardian and she was old enough to take care of herself. He had other things to think about anyway. Clay set his beer down and swore. A life he had once prided himself on keeping so simple, so easily managed, was now so complicated. He had a brother-in-law who felt betrayed, another whose health worried him, a half-sister who wouldn't speak to him, a visiting mother, a case that continued to make no sense, a partner that had turned into a friend, and a girlfriend. He actually had a *girlfriend*. How had this happened?

He rested his head back and ran a tired hand down his face. In moments like this, he wished he hadn't let Laura go. He could have used her silly tricks or bright chirping right now. But he'd never see her again. She was probably part of someone else's life now, bringing joy into it, and they'd be smart enough not to let her go. He wouldn't regret his decision. It wasn't like him and he still had better things to do with his time. He had to think. He had to focus.

He unpacked the puzzle of the hawk Jackie had given to him. It was the best exercise in creating order out of chaos that he could think of. It calmed his mind. He loved the search for the right piece, slowly seeing the picture come together. If only he could do the same with this case. In essence, it was over. He'd discovered who the invisible man was. But as Mack had mentioned, he couldn't let it go because it was about revenge. Clay couldn't let it go until he avenged Emmerick's silent victims.

First, there was Rennie, whose death may not have been due to a beating that had gotten out of hand or an accident on the stairs, but intentional murder. Then there was Melanie, the only one of the HOPE clients who spoke about the Careless Rapture Ministry. Althea was supposedly a victim, though she had just disappeared, and now there was Claudia, who had killed herself only days after sounding so hopeful to her aunt.

Clay fitted a piece that formed the hawk's wing. Emmerick hadn't called Jackie in a while. He couldn't figure out why he had started in the first place. Harassment wasn't his style. Plus, Jackie wasn't the type of woman he liked to target.

He shook his head, frustrated. He had the pieces and they didn't fit together—he'd have to start from the beginning. Mr. Hamlick's death and the clients canceling. He believed the key started there.

Clay quietly worked on his puzzle, thinking about his setup with Mack. Getting Emmerick to talk to new recruits would be easy, but not the end. He knew there was another piece he was overlooking and he needed to find out what. He needed to know more about the company. Suddenly Clay thought of an idea and the one person who could help him. He groaned.

***

Kevin was enjoying a dip in the sauna with two attractive dancers when his assistant told him Clay was on the phone. He excused himself, then answered. "I don't believe it. You're taking me up on my offer?"

"No." He sighed with regret. "I'm afraid I could use your help."

"No need to flatter me."

"I'm not trying to. Jackie told me you're not donating."

"No. I---"

"You don't have to explain. It's your money and that's your business. I just want you to pretend that you might be."

Kevin frowned. "Pretend?"

"Yes, let them think that you will. I don't care how you convince them, just do it."

"Why?"

"Because I want to see if certain pieces begin to fall into place."

Two days later, Clay received an expected call from Jackie. "Faye is beside herself," she said excitedly. "Someone really big and influential is thinking of donating, isn't that great?"

"Wonderful," he said, pleased with Kevin's fast work.

"The thing is, he wanted to take her out and since she's sort of awkward and wants to really impress him, she invited me along. I thought we could make it a double date."

"A double date?" He frowned. "Isn't that something where two women chat while the men look at each other and do nothing?"

"Yes."

"I'll have to make sure Clayton Dubois is available."

"Clayton Dubois?"

"Yes, the other man you're seeing. Remember, she doesn't know who I really am. That night I am Clayton Dubois, a reporter who writes about nonprofit organizations for *Outline*, a local newspaper. We have been seeing each other casually since we met in the office, after we both discovered an interest in pygmy art."

"I don't know anything about pygmy art," she protested.

"Does she know that?"

"No."

"Good. We've had about two dates that were very uneventful. One was at a Japanese restaurant, where you had your first taste of tofu. The next date was a lunch date at a little deli off of Sixteenth Street. We don't remember the name, but the food was delicious."

"Why does all this matter?" Jackie asked, doubtful.

"If you readily supply information, people tend to believe you. Add details and they'll trust you."

"You've really thought this through."

"Lying takes a certain amount of planning. Besides, deceiving people is part of my job."

"Well, it's not part of mine," she said, becoming anxious. "I hope I don't slip and say something I shouldn't."

"Talk about the company and you won't have to worry. Oh, and by the way . . ."

"What?"

"Expect a big surprise."

Chapter Twenty Five

Jackie had expected a lot of things when she and Clay walked into the lush elegance of the Silk Garden restaurant, but nothing would have prepared her for Kevin sitting next to Faye. Jackie turned to Clay and jerked her head in the direction of the pair. "Did you know about this?"

"Aren't you happy to see him?"

"No. And I find it disturbing that you are." Clay had a different, more aggressive energy. Everything about him tonight was disturbing.

He took her arm. "Come. They saw us. We might as well say hello."

They approached the table and everyone introduced themselves. Jackie glanced at Kevin but managed to keep up the charade. After a light chat and appetizers, Faye excused herself and went to the restroom.

"Don't you women usually do that in pairs?" Clay asked, once Faye had gone.

"Not tonight," Jackie said. She looked at Kevin accusingly. "I thought you told me you wouldn't donate. You said you didn't like her shoes."

"I changed my mind when I thought about her face."

"This had better be about business."

Kevin raised a brow. "It is. I consider all women my business."

Jackie shook her head, determined. "I won't let you do this. I can't let you toy with her. She's a kind woman, just as dedicated to HOPE Services as I am. She is committed to its success."

Kevin grinned. "Tonight I *hope* to see how committed."

"Don't you dare." She turned to Clay, exasperated. "Say something."

Clay sipped his water. "Remember to wear a—"

"That is not helpful!" She scowled at him.

"What is the worry?" Kevin said. "I am just enjoying the company of an attractive woman. I may have misjudged her and I am interested in donating to your company. Is that a crime?"

She narrowed her eyes. "I'm not sure. What are you up to?"

"Ooo, this sounds like a heated debate," Faye said, returning to her seat. "What have I missed?"

"Jackie was just sharing all the good HOPE Services has done over the years," Clay said.

"Yes, she's very devoted to our mission." Faye smiled kindly. "I knew she was perfect from the first interview and we have so much in common. We both lost our parents and are devoted to helping other people. We balance each other out. I tend to think one way and she thinks another. She is definitely my right hand. I'm thrilled to have her as part of our little team."

Clay nodded. "And things have been running smoothly?"

"Yes."

"Except for a few cancellations."

Jackie stiffened, wondering what he was up to.

Faye merely shrugged. "Yes, a few clients have chosen not to continue with our program, but that is to be expected."

"It is my understanding it happened in a quick succession and has tapered off rather abruptly."

Faye thought for a moment, then said, "There seem to be two times a year when people make big decisions. First, the New Year brings a lot of change. People make resolutions to change their lives, sometimes in little steps and sometimes dramatically. Second, spring is also a season of renewal. I can't explain why there was a sudden pattern, but I can only guess that clients decided to make life changes for themselves."

"HOPE Services, I assume, is made up of more than you two."

"Yes, we have a psychologist, counselors, social workers, and health educators that help with the design of the program. And of course we have the food service team that delivers to our homebound clients. Our office handles the administrative aspect. Most of the work is done out in the field."

The waiter approached with their various dishes. Clay took a bite of his curry shrimp and said, "You have an administrative assistant, correct?"

Faye nodded, liberally spreading soy sauce on her rice. "Yes, Patty Jayson is a great help to us. She was there when Latisha was in charge."

"So she knows the organization well?"

She hesitated. "Yes. Very well."

"Why did you hesitate?"

She sighed. "Patty has good intentions, but sometimes she doesn't know the proper decorum."

"She told me that a client, Claudia Meeks, had committed suicide."

"Yes, that's what I mean. A disclosure like that is unsuitable behavior. I'm not surprised she told you about that. However, I prefer to keep things like that within the office."

"How did you feel about it?"

"It was a tragedy." A flash of sadness crossed her face. "The lives of our women are hard and at times their despair leads them to desperate acts." She managed a smile. "It's not common, fortunately."

"Jackie told me your clients may have been targeted by a cult."

She glanced at Jackie. "I admit to disregarding that theory until one of our clients was heavily entrenched in it. It seemed Patty wanted to improve the lives of our clients by relating a message from the cult to them. I am pleased to share that we have not heard of any other such cases."

"Can we talk about something more interesting?" Kevin said.

"I thought you wanted to know more about the program," Clay said.

"Yes, but I am feeling neglected."

"Donate a nice amount," Jackie replied, "and you'll never feel neglected again."

"His donation is important to you?" Clay said.

"Donations are key to a nonprofit."

Faye agreed. "But especially after Mr. Hamlick's death."

"Yes, his passing hurt us."

"Both emotionally and financially," Faye said.

Kevin said, "Stop being a reporter for a moment so we can enjoy our meals."

"I am enjoying my meal, but I can't ignore this opportunity."

Faye frowned. "Opportunity?"

"If I can garner sympathy for this Claudia woman, I can work an angle that may tug a few heartstrings and open a few pocketbooks. Perhaps I could write that due to a cut in funding, HOPE Services had to face the possibility of reducing services, which lead to the death of Claudia Meeks."

"But you could get into trouble," Jackie said.

"Why?"

"Because that's not true."

"How do you know that?"

Jackie lowered her gaze, wishing she hadn't said anything. "I spoke to Claudia's mother."

Faye looked at her, startled. "Her mother? I thought her mother was dead."

"I'm sorry, I mean her aunt. She raised her."

"I still don't understand. Why you would have an exception to Clayton's story?" Her eyes widened with eagerness. "Think of the publicity. We could use something like that."

"Her aunt may see it and not agree with what is printed. Couldn't she sue for libel or something? She said Claudia didn't sound depressed, that she had sounded hopeful. We can't write a story and say she was otherwise."

Faye looked so unhappy, Jackie felt bad for dashing her hopes.

"I could work on a different angle," Clay said.

"Don't worry about an angle at all," Kevin said. "I'm here now and I am seriously interested in donating. Woo me."

***

"I think it went well," Faye said as she and Jackie touched up their makeup in the ladies' room.

"I'm sorry about Clayton."

She waved a dismissive hand. "Oh, don't worry. That's how reporters are. Always seeking a story, and he only meant to help us. I'm very excited about this, I think he can give us the right amount of publicity. And if not, with Mr. Jackson's help we wouldn't have to worry anymore." She powdered her nose, then dropped the compact in her purse. "He's taking me home."

Jackie tried not to grimace. "I don't know if that's wise."

Faye looked at her, surprised. "You sound worried."

"He has a reputation."

"I know about his reputation."

"Then be careful."

Faye suddenly grinned. "You sounded like a big sister just then. I never had one."

"Me neither."

She hesitated. "You know, your sister-in-law gave me an idea. I know we went to the funeral together and we're here now but we've never gone out just to have fun." Her gaze fell. "I'm not saying I'm the most exciting person around, but why don't I take you to that estate sale I was talking about? You could get some great clothes. It would be fun and, to be honest, I would love to give you some tips. You could come by my place for lunch. I always go on a full stomach, ready for the hunt, and then we'll drive over together. What do you say?"

Jackie smiled, thrilled with the idea. "Sounds like fun."

***

"Why are you grinning like that?" Clay asked Jackie in the car.

"I think I've made a friend. Faye and I are going out."

"Remember to take a bouquet of roses and a bottle of wine."

Jackie playfully hit him. "This is serious. My first female friend outside of the family. That's a big step."

"Hmm. I liked her."

"You sound surprised."

He drummed his fingers on the steering wheel. "I am."

"I'm glad you like her. Most men don't seem to."

He frowned. "Why do you say that?"

"Because it's true. She doesn't date much and when I mention her name they seem less than enthused. Her date with Nicolas went only so-so and when I mentioned her to William he nearly shuddered. I think she's just awkward with men."

"Or perhaps she doesn't like men."

Jackie thought for a moment, then her mouth slowly fell open. She vehemently shook her head. "No, that's not it."

"How do you know?"

"I just do," she said firmly.

He grinned. "You just don't like that it doesn't fit your fairy-tale world."

"That's not true. Faye is very reserved, that's all."

"Kevin will loosen her up. If he doesn't—"

"That doesn't mean she's gay, that means she has taste."

Clay raised a brow. "I thought you liked Kevin."

"I do. But I don't care if he does donate, I don't want them together. He's terrible for her."

Clay shrugged.

She rested her arm on the door frame. "Why did you mention Claudia?"

"I was being a reporter."

"You played the role too well. I nearly revealed too much."

He patted her on the knee. "You were perfect. We work well together."

She beamed at the casual praise. "Thank you." She glanced out the window. "How is your mother?"

"I wouldn't know. I hardly see her. Nothing new there."

Jackie didn't reply, knowing it was best to leave that topic alone.

***

At work the next day, Patty shoved letters into envelopes, slammed cabinet file drawers, and hit the stapler as though she were killing flies.

"What's wrong?" Jackie asked.

"I wish that woman would stop telling me what to do." She whacked the stapler again.

"She is the boss."

"She's Ms. Nosy, that's what she is." She patted her hair. "I can tell people about our clients if I want to. Suicide isn't our fault. Besides, I don't see the-harm in telling people the truth."

"You have to be careful when talking to the media."

Her neck began to move like a snake. "Are you going to tell me off too?"

"No, personally, I appreciated you telling me."

"Yeah, yeah." She stood and grabbed her handbag. "I'm taking a break."

Jackie shook her head and went to her office. She sat at her desk and began to clean up a mess of files and papers when the phone rang.

"I had expected more of a challenge," a familiar chilling voice said. "I thought you were supposed to protect people. To look out for them."

She gripped the phone, fear clawing its way up her throat. "I do."

"Not very well, it seems."

Her tone turned sharp. "What do you mean?"

"You lost one."

"Who? What are you talking about?"

"You lost one of your family." The line went dead.

Jackie dropped the phone. It clattered to the desk, unnoticed. She knew who he targeted—the disadvantaged, lonely, or sick. Who in her family could fit that profile? With trembling fingers, she called Eric.

"Hello?" he said.

She nearly wept with joy at the sound of his voice. "Eric. I'm so glad you're there. Are you okay?"

"Yes, of course," he said impatiently. "What's wrong?"

"I was just a little worried about you," she said, barely able to keep the phone steady. "Umm, is Adriana at work?"

"No, she's here. Do you want to speak with her?"

"No, that's okay. And Nina's okay, too?"

"Yes." His tone sharpened. "What's going on?"

She didn't want to worry him. "I just wanted to make sure you're all doing well."

He paused, then said, "You're lying to me."

"Try to give your mind a rest. I was just checking in on you. Oh, there's another call. I have to go. Bye." She hung up.

Jackie called Cassie next and got the answering machine. She called her cell phone. Still no reply. Would Emmerick target her? It was possible. She was so open and friendly, he could trick her by pretending to be a fan. What if he'd scheduled to meet her somewhere and abducted her? But why? Why? She grabbed her bag. She couldn't worry about why right now. She had to make sure Cassie was all right.

A few minutes later she stood in front of Cassie and Drake's house. She knocked and rang the doorbell. She waited. And waited. Jackie took a deep breath. She wouldn't panic. Just because Cassie wasn't home didn't mean she was in danger. She had to calm down and think. Oh, why couldn't the nanny be at home? Then she'd know Cassie's schedule. But she'd probably taken the children out to the park. Perhaps she had a performance. Jackie paced the front step, rejecting the idea. Cassie hadn't scheduled any until the autumn. She took out her mobile and called Drake.

"Have you heard from Cassie?" she asked once he'd picked up the line.

"No, should I have?"

"I guess not," she said, trying not to alarm him, though her stomach felt it had been squeezed to the size of a pea. "I thought we had an appointment today and she isn't here. Did she tell you she was going out?"

"No, but when she's not writing she sometimes meets with people. She has her own schedule."

"Right. Well, if she calls you, could you tell her to get in touch with me?"

"Sure." He paused. "You sound worried. Are you in trouble? Do you want to talk to me about it?"

"No, it's a woman thing."

"Okay, but you know if there's anything—"

"I know. Love you. Bye."

She sat on the front step and dialed Clay. Once he picked up she said in a rush, "I can't get a hold of Cassie. I don't know where she is and I think Emmerick might have her and if he does this is all my fault and Drake will never forgive me and I'll never forgive myself—" Tears. choked her voice. "We have to do something or--"

"Slow down, slow down," he said. "What are you on about?"

Jackie took a deep breath. "Emmerick called me a few moments ago at my office and said he had someone from my family. I thought of someone Weak and then thought of Eric, but he's fine. So are Adriana and Nina, and then I thought about Cassie and she's not home and I can't get a hold of her and Drake hasn't heard from her and it will be all my fault because I didn't tell them—"

"Breathe. She could be running errands and not have her phone."

"And what if she isn't? Oh, god, what if he hurts her and—"

"He doesn't work that way," Clay assured her, his calm voice attempting to break through her panic. "He's trying to scare you."

"He's succeeding."

"Go home and I'll meet you there."

"But—"

His tone was patient. "Go home and I'll meet you there."

She brushed away escaping tears. "Okay."

Clay set the phone down and turned to Mack. "That was Jackie. Emmerick called her."

"Great, everything is on schedule. Action time?"

"Exactly."

***

Jackie's mind flooded with terrible scenarios as she whizzed through the traffic. She would never forgive herself if anything happened to Cassie. Never. More disturbing thoughts gripped her as she rode the elevator to her apartment. She nearly screamed when her mobile phone rang. She scrambled through her handbag and grabbed it.

Cassie's voice came on the line. "Hi, Jackie. Drake said you wanted to speak to me."

Her knees buckled with relief, but she managed not to slide to the ground. "Oh, I'm so glad you're okay."

"Why wouldn't I be?"

She sagged against the wall, wishing she could hug her. "I don't know. I was just thinking about you and wondered if you were doing okay."

"I'm fine. How about you?"

She stepped out on her floor. "Good."

"Now tell me why you're worried."

"It's a long story. I promise to tell you later."

"I'll hold you to that promise."

"Don't worry, when this is all over I'll tell you everything."

She hung up, then entered her apartment. She flopped on the couch, all her energy gone, and jumped up when someone knocked on the door. She opened it and smiled at Clay's grim features. "That bastard was just trying to scare me. He doesn't have Cassie. Everybody's safe."

"No," he said quietly. "Not everybody."

A shiver of fear crept up her spine. "What do you mean?"

"He has my mother."

Chapter Twenty Six

Jackie looked at Clay, renewed fear creeping into her eyes. "He has your mother? Are you sure?"

"Yes." He came in and shut the door. "Fortunately, had expected that."

She watched him drape a garment bag over the couch, perplexed. "How?"

"His tactics haven't changed. I knew she was seeing a man. When he started calling at three and five every morning after she'd spent a night out with him, I made a guess as to what was going on. The phone calls are part of the community trying to get to you. They keep you tired and hound you so you don't have a chance to think."

"Why would she get involved?"

"I'm not quite sure yet. Either she's fallen for his charms or he's fallen for hers. My guess is the former." He zipped open the garment bag and handed her a purple robe with hood.

She held it up. "What is this for?"

"We're going to join a ministry," he said, taking off his jacket.

"A ministry?"

"Yes."

"But look at us. I'm sure people will remember a figure as big as you. And I won't know what to do. "There's no way we'll be able to fit in."

"Don't worry. The masquerade won't last long. But remember this: When you're there, you are not to drink or eat anything. Keep your eyes lowered, not only so he won't see your face, but because it is a sign of humility. Only listen in spurts, count sheep if you have to. He modulates his voice to keep your attention and you'll find yourself listening even when you don't want to."

She knew Clay's calm should reassure her, but it worried her more. "Are you sure you can beat him?"

"No, but I can't afford to fail."

Jackie pulled on the robe. "How will we know where he is? Where she is?"

"This isn't accidental, Jackie. It's all been planned meticulously. This is April. A holy season to him. A time of annual awakening. He invites a select group of Careless Rapture believers to come celebrate. It's invitation only."

"But we weren't invited."

He showed her a card. "Of course we were."

She took it from him and read its inscription. "How did you get that?" She looked up at him.. "I don't understand."

His penetrating gaze locked hers. "I don't want you to know too much, your innocence will keep you safe. Just trust me."

She took a deep breath. "I do."

* * *

They drove under approaching storm clouds to a dilapidated cabin in the Virginia mountains. Jackie saw three other cars and a van parked along the gravel drive. There were no other houses for miles.

"I'm nervous," Jackie said, fiddling with her robe. "Why did he call me?"

"My guess is that he first spoke to Bertha at your house and assumed she was your relative. He wanted to scare you."

"Why?"

Clay shook his head, frustrated. "I haven't worked that out yet, but I will." He knocked on the wooden door: A robed figure answered. Clay said something in a low voice she couldn't decipher before they were let inside. About ten other robed figures sat cross-legged in a circle in the empty room. The sickly glow of candles cast shadows on the walls and wooden floor. She heard the hushed sound of rain.

It reminded Clay of his first gathering, where the wind whistled through the cracks and he'd first heard Emmerick's powerful voice.

That same voice spoke now. "Glad you could join us, friends," he said. "Please sit and join the circle."

Jackie resisted turning to Clay for guidance and did as she was told.

"Now feel the energy rise up within you. Embrace the light. Awaken your senses."

"I call for a new awakening," Clay said.

Emmerick paused and removed his hood. "I know that voice."

"Yes."

"It's the voice of a traitor."

Clay removed his hood. "Or the voice of your conscience."

"How did you get in here?" he demanded.

"A little trickery."

"I will not have you pollute this sacred gathering." Emmerick pointed at Clay. "Remove him."

Two hooded figures stood, flashing large knives with the promise of malice.

Clay said, "You disappoint me, Emmerick. I thought you were a man of your word."

"I am. However, we both know you are not. You are a man of action. I wanted to level the playing field."

"I've changed."

"Very well." He made a motion with his hand and the knives disappeared. The guards sat.

"I know you have my mother."

"Your mother?"

"Yes," Clay said. "You made a little mistake thinking she was part of Jackie's family."

"I don't know what you're talking about," he said simply. "Yes, I have a new recruit, whether she is your mother or not is immaterial. She came of her own free will."

"As Rennie had?"

"As they all do. You should know that. I do not need to use force. I am a messenger of a higher power. That power allows me to—"

"Indulge in extreme megalomania."

Emmerick clapped his hands in exaggerated applause. "Congratulations. That is a large word for a man like you.'

"I've learned to read."

"Then did you read anything about the Messiah complex? I believe you are suffering from a form of it yourself. Are you still tortured by the death of your sister and that other, what was her name? Gabriella? Have you been spit on lately?"

Jackie started.

The group turned to her. Clay spoke quickly to redirect their attention. "Those are my demons, you have yours. I believe Rennie knew about them and that's why she tried to stop you."

Emmerick hesitated. "How did you . . . Well, it doesn't matter anyway," he said, unconcerned.

"What did she know?"

"Why rehash the past? I can't be tried for her death twice."

"So you admit to killing her?"

His cool voice chilled the air. "I admit that she's dead."

"At your hands."

Emmerick clicked his tongue in pity. "Have you come to avenge her, my boy? Does the anger linger still? You will never have peace as long---"

"I think I know why you did it," Clay interrupted. "Perhaps she knew about your little habit. That though you enjoyed your wives you had a preference for boys."

"I do not have a preference in the way you are trying to imply. Men, of course, are the stronger sex, therefore given the bigger responsibility of this ministry."

"It wasn't the mission of the ministry that brought you into my room that night. You became my traitor." Clay's words fell like stones. "I tried to kill you for betraying a trust I had believed was sacred. I can only guess that she saw you and knew she couldn't be married to you anymore."

He shrugged. "All conjecture."

"No, I think that was the truth. And I think you knew you were in danger of losing control. You had me kicked out, because to have someone leave would topple your kingdom. She was a strong force and people would have followed her."

"No."

"Your surrender philosophy is a lie."

"It is an ultimate truth," he said with conviction. "But you approach it with blind eyes. You see yourself as a god. You who think you can save others and torment yourself when you don't. Isn't there something debase in a man who thinks so highly of himself?" He addressed the group. "There is true power in surrender. To accept things as they are."

"To choose death instead of life," Clay said gravely.

"Death chooses us. I welcome it. But why are we arguing opposing philosophies? If you do not believe, then why are you here?" He smiled with confidence. "You can't do anything to me."

"I can charge you with kidnapping."

His smile slipped. "What are you talking about?"

"I'm talking about Amanda Heldon. The young woman everyone thought was abducted."

"I didn't---"

"Kidnap her? No, not originally. In the beginning, she came to you willingly. A colleague of mine pointed out the possibility that Amanda may have run off to meet someone." He paused. "I basically dismissed the thought until I came upon your Web site. Now, why would you need a Web site? You targeted the poor, the disillusioned, the sick." He snapped his fingers. "Ah, but to fund such a group you need money, don't you? By attracting a wealthier demographic you could continue your work. Ask them to donate their money to the cause. They would willingly empty their pockets since they are just as eager for peace as the wino on the street.

"So I had a missing girl and a Web site. There was a picture of Amanda's mother in her room. If you study the picture you can learn a little bit about Amanda. She loved bands. She had posters everywhere. Most of the groups I didn't know, except that one peeking from under the bed sounded familiar. At first it looked like a Rave poster, then I looked more closely. It had an innocuous statement splashed across the top with just *Careless Rapture* at the bottom. Very clever of you not to use the word 'ministry.' No one paid attention. It could have been one of the many bands she liked to listen to. Only, I knew what it was. Do you want to tell me what happened or should I guess?"

Einmerick folded his arms, amused. "Enlighten us."

Clay took no offense to the condescending tone. "A girl like Amanda is perfect for you. Eager to please, eager to do well. Lonely and shy. She needed a friend and through e-mails you convinced her you were one. You invited her to meet you and you never let her go."

"She's decided to stay on her own. She's a true believer. She knows the dangers of the outside world."

"Yes, a month with you would convince her of that. But if she's a true believer, let me see her face."

Emmerick lifted a candle, then stood behind one of the robed figures and lifted its hood. Amanda stared at him with dark green eyes that looked like marbles—no emotions. That was not a good sign. He would have to approach her carefully. She was apt to be more loyal to Emmerick than she would be to him. Emmerick moved to another figure and removed its hood.

"Oh, and I believe this is the one you call your mother. However, they're both mine."

"I can't allow that."

"You'll have to." The candle cast dark shadows against his face. "Then again, perhaps I could do you a favor and let you have one of them." He flashed a malicious grin. "You've always wanted to play hero. Here's your chance. Persuade one of them to leave with you. It will be fascinating to see my former protégé use the techniques I taught him. You were talented when it came to persuasion. So who will be your choice?" He stood behind Bertha. "Your mother? The one Rennie described as a slag? The one who left you? The one who hurt you by throwing you out when you needed her most? The one who always chooses the nearest man over you? Isn't it ironic that she did it again? Left you for another man?" He rested a hand on his chest. "Me."

Emmerick moved to stand behind Amanda. "Or there's the senator's niece. That would be a great victory. Think of all the cheers and adulation you'd receive when you returned her home. But will she leave with you? You're a stranger. I've told her a few things about you. How you deceived me. That you have an anger you barely tame. That you would use her to penetrate my world. You're still just a poor runaway inside. With her you could finally belong. You've always wanted to belong—"

Someone coughed. Clay blinked, pulling himself out of the sticky web of words Emmerick had started to weave around him. He'd begun to listen to Emmerick's words and got caught up in the mind game—the challenge of outwitting him. But that wasn't why he was here.

"You can't win," Emmerick said. "They won't betray me. They won't betray this ministry." He set the candle down. "So make your choice. Here's your chance to be a hero."

"I don't want to be a hero."

"Of course you do. You've always wanted to be the one who charges into battle. The one who fights alone. You want to save, you want to be somebody important."

"Yes, I used to. But now when I charge into battle I don't fight alone."

"So you refuse my challenge?"

"I suggest you surrender," Clay said.

Emmerick made a motion with his hands. The knives appeared again. "And if I don't?"

"I wouldn't be surprised because you don't believe in surrender—peaceful or otherwise. A true charlatan."

"All messengers must accept the labels their present society will hurl at them. Surrender should not be confused with succumbing to one's opposition. I don't believe in this kind of surrender."

"You don't believe in a surrender of any kind." Clay folded his arms. "I believe you had a life-saving triple bypass a few years back. Why hadn't you surrendered to your fate then?"

He started, surprised, then cleared his throat. "There are moments when—"

"You surrender."

"I refuse."

"Then my friends will make you."

That was the signal for Mack and the others to remove their hoods. Nobody moved.

Emmerick smiled at the look on his face. "Were you expecting your friends to show up?" He motioned to one of the guards, who opened a closet. "Don't worry, they did."

The guard led Nicolas, Mack, and Brent into the center of the room, their faces scraped and bruised, their hands tied behind their backs while masking tape covered their mouths.

"No!" Jackie screamed, as a member grabbed her. She fought him until he put a knife to her neck and ended the struggle.

The followers removed their hoods and stared at Clay as though he were a traitor.

"I'm afraid you're all alone," Emmerick said.

Clay stood as though his plan had fallen on him and left him paralyzed.

"Thanks for sending the entertainment. You kept my followers busy while we awaited your arrival. The youngest one proved especially interesting."

The implication of his words broke through Clay's paralysis. He lunged at Emmerick. Three members wrestled him to the ground. One pressed his head against the floor as though he wanted to crush his skull. He could feel grains of dirt pressing into his cheek.

"Such anger," Emmerick said, disappointed. "Let him face me."

One held Clay's hands while another grabbed his collar and forced him to his knees.

Emmerick stared down at him with cold disdain. "You shouldn't have tried to defeat me."

Clay glared back, but said nothing.

"Why are you here? I was good to you."

"You betrayed me," he snapped.

The acid in his tone melted the mask Emmerick wore, revealing the pathetic old man behind it. An old man with wounds as deep as his own. "I loved you. Was it wrong for me to show that? You were my son, like my flesh and blood." He waved his fist. "I depended on you, I gave you everything, taught you all I knew. I clothed and fed you—you betrayed me. I didn't kill your sister. I didn't kill anyone. I released them, there's a difference.

"Be ashamed of yourself, for being nothing, for accomplishing nothing, for not using the talents given to you. Together we could have created a ministry that stretched the world. But you were too arrogant. Too proud. You had to be alone. But who have you saved? Your life is littered with the names of the dead, and look around you now—you've betrayed all those who have trusted you. Look at them. Look what you've done to them." He grabbed Clay's chin and forced him to look around the room. "This is your fault. You led them here." He let him go and wiped his hands as though he'd touched something dirty. "Fortunately, I am a compassionate man. I have the power to forgive. I will allow you to leave with one of these people, though the choice is rather simple. Your mother, Amanda, your friends, or her?"

Clay looked at them, then lowered his gaze. "I won't choose."

"How about I make it easy for you? I'll give you your friends and your female companion in exchange for the other two."

He didn't raise his eyes. "No."

"Put aside your pride—they mean nothing to you. Your mother doesn't want you and neither does Amanda. Make your choice!"

"No."

Emmerick made his tone more indulgent. "You're really not in the position to be greedy. If you haven't noticed, you're at a disadvantage here. I can have them toss you out of here and leave you with nothing. I have before."

Clay kept his gaze lowered.

"Or we could play a game of persuasion."

Clay met his eyes. "I can't outwit you."

"And I can't fight you. That leaves us at a crossroads."

"I have a solution."

He raised his eyebrows. "What?"

"If you let them go, I'll surrender."

His voice faltered. "You'll surrender?"

"Yes."

"I don't believe you."

"What do I have to lose? I haven't amounted to anything, I've hurt those I care about; all I've ever wanted was to feel as though my life meant something. If you've truly forgiven me, you'll give me that chance."

"Very well." He handed Clay a small vial.

"Clay, don't," Jackie said as he opened the vial. "Your life does mean something. Let go of me!" she yelled to her guard.

He held her tighter, his knife pressing against her throat with such force that blood seeped through.

Clay noticed the blood. "Keep still. He'll hurt you."

"I don't care," Jackie said, feeling the hot sting of the knife wound. "Don't do this, please. We can find another way. There has to be another way."

"There isn't. If I do this he'll be forced to keep his promise." Before she could protest, Clay drank the contents.

Emmerick motioned with his hands and the guards released them.

Jackie ran to Clay as the vial dropped to the floor. She gripped his arm, tears filling her eyes. "Why?"

"I'm okay," he said.

Emmerick smirked. "Yes, you will be for the next half hour."

Mack came up beside Clay. "Let's get you to a hospital," he said, trying to sound calm, though he wasn't.

Brent took his other arm. "You're going to be okay. Come on."

Emmerick looked at Clay with amusement. "And once again you have your chance to be a hero." He clicked his tongue. "Unfortunately, you did a rather foolish thing. I've released your mother and Amanda, but as you've noticed neither has made a move toward you, They are loyal to me. Their minds belong to me. I hold their truths. So here is your great contribution and, in the end you've discovered your life was worthless." He smiled cruelly. "No one is worth dying for." He went to the door. "Come, followers."

No one moved.

"I said come."

One of the guards turned to Clay and fell to his knees, the other followed, and soon all the members fell on their knees, their heads bowed to him.

Emmeriek, stared, stunned. "Get up! What are you doing! He is a traitor. I am your leader, your adviser. Get up, I say!"

No one moved.

Nicolas approached Emmerick. "Seems they've lost faith in you. In the face of such kindness one can easily spot a fraud. You're under arrest for the abduction of Amanda Heldon." He read him his Miranda rights as he led him away.

Clay looked at all the bowed heads. "No, you mustn't do this."

One member, a young pimply-faced youth with wide gray eyes said, "We'll do whatever you say. We want to honor your sacrifice."

"Then make my death mean something by living life fully by being free. Go into the world and be free. The world is yours."

Amanda cautiously walked toward him. "But why did you do it? You could have taken your mother. You don't even know me."

"I do know you. I've been you. You saw his Web site, right?"

She nodded.

"And he sent you e-mails telling you how clever you were and how you weren't alone. He seemed like a friend."

She nodded again.

"So you met him. It was in a crowded place because you would never meet with a stranger alone. You talked and ate and then you don't remember a thing."

"Yes," she whispered.

"And you woke up groggy, frightened. You felt foolish, didn't you? You're a smart girl, how could you fall for this? He told you a lot of bad things about yourself," he said, aware of how Emmerick would have controlled her mind. "But they're not true."

She wrapped her arms around his neck. "Thank you."

Brent pulled on his arm. "Come, we have to go."

They all went outside. The rain had stopped, drops of water dripping from the roof and off the trees. The followers bowed to him one by one, then drove away in the van. Amanda went with the police.

"I'm not afraid to die," Clay said, as Jackie clung to him and Mack sent him worried glances.

"We're not going to let you," Brent said.

As Mack opened the door, Clay took a moment to lookout at the gathering mist as it swept past the cabin. Like a phantom, it enveloped the field and trees in a hazy scene as though trying to relegate it to memory. He let the haunting memories of those he'd lost mingle with it. Suddenly a sharp pain penetrated his skull. He stumbled to his knees.

Mack swore, catching him before he hit the ground. "What's wrong?"

He couldn't speak, the pain squeezing his jaw shut.

"Emmerick said reaction time was a half hour," Mack said.

Jackie touched his face. It felt sticky and cold. "Then why is he going down so fast?"

"Maybe he's allergic," Brent said.

Bertha sent him a look of disgust. "He just drank poison, you daft twit."

"I know, but Emmerick said—"

"Either Emmerick lied or mixed it with something else." Mack struggled to lift Clay into the car. "Somebody, help me," he cried.

Brent came to his side. "Call an ambulance."

"An ambulance won't reach us out here."

"They can meet us somewhere."

Mack staggered to his feet. "There isn't enough time. Let's lift him One, two, three."

Clay cried out in agony. Their hands felt like knives piercing under his skin. "Let me die," he whispered through parched lips.

"Ignore him," Jackie said. "Get him in the car." After an effort they got Clay inside the backseat.

"We need to call for help," Brent said.

Jackie took out her mobile phone, then swore. "I can't get a signal."

Mack sighed. "Get in the car."

Brent looked hopeful. "There was a house a couple miles back. They'll have a phone and they have a field. I think I saw a field."

"So what?"

"It's big enough."

Mack turned away, irritated. "Get in the car and shut up."

Brent seized his arm, determined. "Just listen. It's big enough. I know where it is. Let me drive."

Mack shoved him away. "Stop talking and get in the damn car."

"But I know the way. Give me the keys."

"No!"

Brent grabbed Mack's collar and pushed him against the car. "I know you don't like me very much, but I don't care. Let me do this. I can help."

Mack's eyes clashed with his. "Let me go," he said with cold anger.

Brent tightened his grip. "First, give me the keys."

"Give him the keys," Jackie said. "I don't know what he's talking about but he's the only one here with an idea."

Mack reluctantly handed Brent the keys. "You'd better be right."

Brent jumped into the car and started the ignition. "Don't worry, I am. The field's big enough."

Mack clenched his teeth. "For what?"

Brent only smiled and sped down the gravel drive.

Chapter Twenty Seven

Brent was right. The field was big enough for the MedEvac helicopter to land. Within ten minutes, Clay was whizzed away to the nearest trauma center.

Clay didn't remember much after leaving the cabin. He remembered moments of agonizing pain, times he wished they would just let him die. Then the pain stopped. But his throat felt like sandpaper, his tongue like a stone in his mouth. He couldn't open his eyes and moving his limbs felt like needles sticking into his flesh. After a few minutes, he realized someone held his hand. The hand was warm, firm—too big to be a woman's. He squeezed the hand to make sure. Yep, it was a man's.

"That's my boy. Jackie, he squeezed my hand. That's the way. Keep squeezing. You always did have a strong grip."

Clay's heart pounded. He knew that voice.

"Come on, do it again," his father said. "Can you do that for me?"

He squeezed his hand again, wishing he could open his eyes so he could see his father's face. To his annoyance tears seeped from under his lids and spilled down his cheeks instead.

Oscar Graham clumsily wiped his son's face with a tissue. "You're going to be okay. Just rest. I'm here."

Clay kept hold of his father's hand and drifted off to sleep.

***

As evening set, the sun lengthened the shadows in the room, bathing the area in a rosy-peach hue. Jackie adjusted Clay's bedclothes before she headed to the cafeteria for something to eat. She'd been in the hospital since he'd been admitted. When he finally opened his eyes, she wanted to be the first person he saw. She wanted him to know he was never alone. Someone knocked on the door and she turned. "Come in."

Nicolas entered the room. "How is he?"

"They've had to give him drugs to stimulate his heart, but he's going to recover." The doctors weren't certain, but she was.

He set a small potted plant on the side table next to the cards and flowers Clay had received. "I can't believe he did what he did. I keep seeing it in my dreams." He shook his head. "It was foolish in a way. We could have come back for Amanda. We could have come up with another plan."

"Yes, but by doing what he did, he freed them all. Not just one."

Nicolas fell silent, staring at the oxygen mask over Clay's mouth. "You're right."

"Good."

He stood by the bed, then turned to her, his eyes a startling blue in the dying light. "I still don't believe in God or souls and all that stuff, but he helped me to gain a faith of a different kind. In my job I've seen people do cruel things to each other." He shook his head, grim. "I'd lost my faith in the goodness of man. In dignity, in honor, in truth, even in love. He gave those back to me. When he wakes up, thank him for me."

"Thank him yourself."

"Can he hear me?"

"He can squeeze your hand."

"That's just a nerve impulse."

"I believe he can hear you, however, you can believe whatever you want to."

Nicolas rested his hand on the bed next to Clay's. "I still don't know why you did it, but thanks anyway." He wasn't sure whether it was because he wanted to believe or if it actually happened, but Clay's little finger moved to touch his.

Days later, Clay opened his eyes and regained his speech. He'd lost some vision in his left eye due to nerve damage and his left hand trembled a bit, but otherwise he was expected to make a full recovery. Although pleased with the constant flow of well-wishers, he wished they would stop—until Drake entered the room holding Marcus.

Marcus bent over to kiss him on the cheek, then asked, "Is your boo-boo all better?"

"It's getting there."

"Don't you know poison can kill you?" Drake said.

Cassie entered the room with Ericka. "He wanted to make sure you knew that," she said to Clay, and kissed him on the cheek. "Next time just read the label."

He smiled, his eyes drinking in the sight of them as though they were the very antidote needed to make him well. "I'll remember that."

Drake glanced at Jackie. "Is she taking good care of you?"

"Yes. Umm, about—"

"Good. I want you well enough for it."

"For what?"

"You still owe me a drink."

"Did I hear the word 'drink'?" Kevin said, coming into the room. "What are we celebrating?"

Drake's smile fell. Kevin ignored him. He turned to Cassie and gave her a big kiss on the mouth. Drake's frown increased. Kevin pinched Marcus's nose and Ericka's chin, making the two children giggle. Kevin finally turned to Drake and said, "Oh, I didn't see you there."

Cassie grabbed Drake's arm as his eyes darkened.

"We'd better go. Take care."

Jackie wagged her finger at Kevin after they'd left.

"You're terrible. Must you annoy him?"

He shrugged without remorse. "Hey, he got the girl. I have to come out with something." He walked over to the bed. "So how is the patient?"

"Recovering," Clay said.

"Are the nurses treating you well?"

"Yes."

Kevin raised a devilish brow. "How well?"

"I haven't died, so I'd say very well. I have one nurse who's very kind."

Kevin leaned forward with interest. "What's her name? I'd like to thank her."

"His name is Roger."

Kevin jerked back. "You have a male nurse? What they hell are they thinking? You nearly died. You should get the best—a woman. Who the hell wants to wake up to hairy arms and no chest? I'll get you another one."

"I don't need another one. He's good. Besides, if need a woman, I have Jackie."

Kevin glanced at her and winked. "Yes, that's true."

"Thanks for stopping by."

Kevin looked embarrassed. "Yes, well, they've been writing about Amanda's rescue and I thought I'd stop by and see the hero."

"He's not here." Clay held out his hand. "By the way, thanks for helping me out that night with Faye."

Kevin shook his hand, then frowned, concerned. "You're acting nice. This isn't like you."

"I know." He smiled. "Doesn't suit the image."

Kevin returned the expression. "Right."

"It's likely the drugs talking, but consider stopping by when I'm out of here."

Kevin hesitated, shocked by the casual offer of friendship. He finally said, "I will."

***

Three days later they released him. "At last," Clay said as the nurse helped him into a wheelchair. "I'm finally going home."

"You have to take things easy," Jackie said.

"I will."

"We'll make sure," Bertha said, standing behind him.

Clay sent Jackie a look of panic, then turned to Bertha. "How long are you planning to stay?"

She patted his arm. "Never you mind."

"But—"

"Come on," Jackie said. "We'll discuss it later."

Clay smiled as he passed through the glass doors of the hospital. He was ready to breathe the fresh air, see the sun. However, once outside the sun almost blinded him with a bright flash. And another. Voices began to attack him like a swarm of bees.

"No comment," Jackie said as she and Bertha pushed past the photographers and reporters who assaulted them with questions.

"How's he doing?"

"Has Amanda come to visit?"

"Will you testify at Emmerick's trial?"

"Can't we get just one statement?"

Without comment, Clay, Bertha, and Jackie all ducked into Jackie's car and sped away.

A good distance away from the ambush, Clay rolled down his window. He rested his head back, letting the wind brush his face. "So I'm still here."

Bertha patted his shoulder. "Yes, and you'll live a long while yet."

He turned to her as she sat in the backseat. "How did you meet Emmerick?"

"I heard him on the phone."

"So you heard a man's voice on the phone and decided to meet him?"

"I guessed who he was and wanted to help. I wanted to know more about the man Rennie had loved and tried to betray."

"And you couldn't tell me this?"

"Would you have let me?"

"No."

"A part of me was intrigued by him. I suppose if I really admitted it, I felt as though I needed him. Some of what he said made sense. However, what you did made even more sense. I realized one thing I never gave you and Rennie: I never made you feel as though you mattered. I'm sorry for that."

He shrugged and turned.

"Clay," Jackie said, amazed. "Your mother is trying to have a heart-to-heart moment with you. Don't you care?"

He glanced at Bertha, then pulled something from inside his bag. "Here." He tossed her a small box of chocolates.

"Oh, ta, love," she said, thrilled. She ripped the box open.

He turned to Jackie. "There. We've had our heart-to-heart moment."

Jackie shook her head. "I don't understand you."

He grinned. "Yes, you do."

"Emmerick's not a bad-looking fellow," Bertha said.

"Amazing how you notice the important details," Clay said.

"Yeah, one thing I found interesting."

"What?"

"How different he sounded on the phone."

Chapter Twenty Eight

The recovery of Amanda Heldon made Clay a minor celebrity. He found his picture in major newsmagazines and was interviewed for three news programs—one on Internet predators and two about cults. A literary agent contacted him about writing a book and another talked about a movie deal.

Mack grinned at him as he entered the office. "So how does it feel to be a hero?"

"I'm not a hero."

He waved a newspaper. "This says you are. All the papers do."

"The papers like to make up stories. I'm an ordinary guy that did a job. Amanda was the hero for surviving him. I'm glad she's safe. It almost makes me believe in happy endings."

"Almost?"

He knew Mack couldn't understand him. Mack, Brent, and Clay received one hundred thousand dollars each for Amanda's return. Clay was glad for the money, but his true reward was the picture of Amanda in her parents' arms. However, he wasn't satisfied and he wasn't sure why.

"This is great for business," Mack said. "This case has put our business on another level. We can double our fee and work less. Why can't you be happy?"

Clay wanted to and was annoyed that he couldn't be. He didn't know why. Emmerick was going to trial, no one had quit HOPE Services in weeks, and there had been no more suicides. "I should be happy."

"But you're not."

"No. Perhaps I'm too cynical. Clean-cut endings annoy me."

Mack patted him on the back. "Take a break and enjoy the limelight a little. You deserve it."

"You do, too. You kept me on track."

There was a knock on the door, then Mack's daughter Megan peeked her head inside. She was as blond as her father, with devious blue eyes. "I'm looking for two heroes."

Mack stood and gave a grand bow. "At your service."

Clay shook her hand. "It's a pleasure to meet you. Your father speaks highly of you."

"I'd say the same." She sat on the corner of Mack's desk. "So who is the guy out front?"

"Our court jester," Mack said.

Clay raised a brow. "He saved my life."

Mack shoved on his reading glasses and grunted.

"His name is Brent Holiday," Clay said.

Megan glanced toward the door. "He's cute."

Clay grinned. "He's also single."

Mack sent him a look. "There's a reason for that. He's not the brightest bulb in the box."

"That's okay," Megan said. "Clever men are hard to keep track of." She kissed her dad on the cheek. "You taught me that. I'm going to introduce myself. I'll be back." She left the room.

Clay clasped his hands together, pleased. "Payback time, mate. I hope she marries him."

"Why?"

"Because you'll have to pay for the wedding."

Mack groaned. "No, that won't happen. Megan wouldn't do that to me."

Clay's sudden good humor died. He twirled his pen solemnly.

Mack sighed. "Let it go, will you?"

"I want to, but the puzzle doesn't fit." He swore. "It's very annoying."

"What doesn't fit?"

"Why was Melanie the only one who talked about Careless Rapture? Emmerick talked about Gabriella and Tanya instead of her."

"I told him about Gabriella and the Tanya incident because I wanted to use that information to trap him."

"Yes, you gave him the ammunition he wanted, which doesn't make sense because Melanie's death would have been better."

Mack swung back and forth in his chair. "Do you think he might not have known about her?"

"That's possible."

"Which would make you wonder why someone would want you to believe she was involved with him."

"And why his voice sounded different on the phone."

Mack frowned. "What?"

"My mum said he sounded different on the phone than in real life. Jackie agreed. They said they couldn't put their finger on why."

"An imitator?"

Clay twirled a pen. "Why?"

Mack sighed. "Damn, just when I thought it was over."

"It will be. Just let me work out some scenarios."

Megan entered the room, grinning. "I have a date. Brent and I are going out this weekend."

Clay nodded. "Have fun."

"What will your mother say?"

Megan stuck her hands in her back pocket. "I have good taste?"

Clay tossed his pen down. "Of course!"

Megan and Mack looked at him, confused. "What?"

He pointed at Mack. "Your ex-wife." He pointed at Megan. "Your mother." He joined his hands together. "It fits. I just have to find out why."

"What are you talking about?"

"The present and the past."

"Someone who knew Emmerick is trying to blame him for the deaths of the others?"

"Yes, and it's someone who knows him well." He sent Mack a significant look.

Mack understood immediately. "Let's get on it."

***

Sunday dinner at Cassie and Drake's was full of loud voices, laughter, and food. Drake had made Clay's favorite dish—Toad in the Hole. He'd added some spices, stating that English food tasted like paste.

As they tucked into a dessert of soursop ice cream, Eric tapped his glass and held up his hands. "I have an announcement."

Everyone turned and listened.

"We're pregnant."

Adriana stared at him, stunned. "No, we're not."

"Yes, we are."

"I should know."

"Yes, you should," he agreed. "You've missed your period for nearly three months."

"You've kept track?" Adrianna's face burned with embarrassment, along with the other women at the table. All too shocked to move.

"It's simple mathematics." He took a sip. "You haven't bought a new box of tampons in that amount of time."

"Eric!" she said, her voice barely audible, but clearly revealing her shock.

"The likelihood is it will be a boy."

"You are---" she couldn't finish.

Eric continued undeterred. He turned to Clay. "Do you have what I requested?"

Clay tossed him a pregnancy test box. Jackie looked at him, amazed. He held up his hands. "I don't ask questions."

Eric handed it to Adrian. "We might as well find out."

"You delight in public humiliations. I know we're not to keep secrets, but this..."

"I'll be the one humiliated if I'm wrong." Eric was oblivious to daggers coming from the women, and the men remained silent.

Adrianna grabbed the box and stood. "An excellent incentive." She left. Cassie and Jackie followed.

"What is it with women and toilets?" Clay asked. "And what's with you keeping track of your wife's cycle and announcing it like that?"

Eric shrugged unconcerned then glanced at Nina, who looked both excited and anxious. He crooked his finger. "Come here."

She did, her eyes wide.

"You know that no one can replace you, right?"

She nodded, though her eyes filled with tears. "You're my family and anyone would be lucky to have you as a big sister."

Marcus piped up. "I'm a big brother."

Clay grinned at him "Yes, we know."

Eric took Nina's hand and patted his leg. "I'm nervous. Let's wait together."

She smiled and climbed onto his lap.

Drake rested his arms on the table. "How long does a pregnancy test take?"

"You're the father of two."

"Cassie always knew first."

After more than a few minutes, the women returned to the table and sat.

Drake frowned when no one spoke. "Well?"

"You were wrong," Adrianna said.

Eric looked crushed. "Oh."

She held up the stick and smiled. "It's going to be a girl," she predicted.

***

Jackie went to work thrilled with the news.

"I'm going to be an aunt four times over," she told Patty. "Adriana is expecting."

"Shame they can't stay babies long."

Jackie walked past, not wanting to deal with Patty's changing moods.

She went into Faye's office and raised her hand to knock, pausing when she heard a man's voice in the room.

The same chilling voice she'd heard on the phone. She opened the door.

Chapter Twenty Nine

Only Faye sat inside.

Jackie stared, speechless.

Faye set the receiver down and stared at her concerned. "Is there something wrong?"

She pointed to the phone. "It was you?"

"On the phone?" She nodded. "Yes."

Listening to her deep, husky voice, Jackie could easily understand how Faye could lower it to sound like a man's. "But why?"

She shrugged. "Don't look at me like that. It's not what you think."

"Then what is it?"

"Sit down, you look as though you're about to faint. Let me get you something to drink."

Jackie sat. "I'm not thirsty. I just want to understand."

"Wait here." Faye left and came back with a glass of orange juice. She handed it to Jackie.

Jackie took the glass. "What is going on?"

Faye closed the door and went behind her desk. "I wanted to help you. I knew what my husband was up to and I wanted you to stop him."

She stopped with the glass, to her lips. "Your husband? Who's your husband?"

"Emmerick, of course?"

Jackie set the glass down. "You know about Emmerick? How can that be? You don't wear a ring."

"Our faith doesn't require such tawdry symbols."

"So you do know about Careless Rapture. Why didn't you tell me?"

Faye stiffened. "I have a certain image to maintain. I couldn't afford you looking down on me because I was involved with such a revolutionary man."

"Why didn't you stop him?"

"Because I couldn't. I'm not like you, Jackie, I don't have that passion that fuels you to do what you do. Betraying him was the hardest thing to do."

"But the phone calls, why?"

"I wanted to make it personal. I wanted you to specifically focus on what a threat he was."

Jackie shook her head, trying to make sense of it all and failing. She lifted the glass.

The door burst open, startling them both. Clay, Mack, and Nicolas stood in the doorway.

"What is this?" Faye demanded.

Clay took Jackie's glass. "Did you drink this?"

"No."

"Good." He turned to Faye. "Why don't you drink it for her?"

"I'm not thirsty," she said.

Jackie stood. "What are you doing here? What's going on?"

"This is Emmerick's wife," Mack said.

Jackie nodded. "I know. She just told me. She was also the voice on the phone. She wanted us to catch Emmerick. We were having a calm chat about it all before you three burst in here like vigilantes."

"You wanted us to catch Emmerick?"

She nodded. "Yes."

"So he could cover your crime."

Faye adjusted her blouse. "I don't know what you're talking about."

"I'm talking about your revenge."

"Don't be absurd. Who would I want to avenge? I have no enemies. Ask anyone. I wouldn't hurt anyone."

"I think you made a mistake," Jackie said. "If you'd just let her explain, I'm sure everything will be clear."

Nicolas jerked his head in Jackie's direction. "Nice to have such a loyal colleague. Very helpful, too. You knew Jackie would never suspect you. Plus you have one big thing in common—She lost her parents, too."

Faye shrugged. "It is no secret that my parents died."

"Yes, I knew," Jackie said.

"Did she tell you how they died?" Nicolas shook his head. "I doubt it. She likes to share how they were kind and generous people who helped the poor and she was right. You told me that same story on our date."

"If you can call being bored to death a date," Faye said.

Nicolas ignored her, his blue eyes on Jackie. "Did she tell you about Tyrone Davis?"

"Who?" Jackie asked.

"The crazed drug addict who shot her parents while he was high. Isn't that correct?"

Faye stared, but said nothing.

"Her parents had been helping his wife and two daughters when he entered the apartment demanding money," Clay explained. "When they tried to talk to him, he shot them point blank, then took the thirty dollars they had between them. He went to prison to serve a life sentence, but that couldn't compensate for the loss of your parents. It's something you never truly heal from." He nodded. "I understand that kind of loss."

Faye met his eyes. "I know you do," she said quietly.

"But you went on with your life. You had to. With the loving guidance of your grandparents you were determined to continue your parents' work. You honestly take pleasure in helping others. I'm not sure how you met Lamont, but you did—as a college student, perhaps? You fell for his charms and his message. He had reinvented his ministry so you became his only wife under your particular religious order."

She raised her chin. "We've been married longer than most traditional couples."

"You are to be congratulated," Mack said dryly.

"But life wasn't easy because of the constant travel, and you were running out of money," Clay said. "You're the one who suggested your hometown of D.C. With your degree you were lucky enough to get established positions in nonprofit organizations, while he continued his work. Unfortunately, the marriage began to hit a rough patch when you discovered Emmerick had other uses for his new recruits."

"It was disgusting, the hours he would spend online with young men and women. Bringing them home. But he is a genius and sees the world through different eyes."

"You didn't worry about him too much because you'd received a lucky break. HOPE Services needed a new president and you were hastily hired through a friend of Latisha. The same friend who made sure Winstead got rid of her. The same friend who was involved in your ministry. She made a very good administrative assistant."

Jackie's eyes widened. "Patty?"

"Yes, Patty," Clay said. "Together you knew a program like HOPE Services could suit you, since it had been established for a while and the grant funder didn't look too closely at how things were run. So you were able to create two financial books and siphon money from some of the phony clients you created. Ah, but there was one problem. You needed a vice president.

"Enter Jackie Henson, a deceptively harmless young woman who had a passion to help the disadvantaged. You underestimated the depths of her passion, so you hired her. And immediately knew your mistake. Yes, she was ambitious like yourself, but she was also very involved with the clients. Fortunately, at the time she couldn't meet with them all since you kept her busy with proposals, various fund-raisers, and handling day-to-day operations."

Faye leaned back and smiled coldly. "You're a very good storyteller."

"Since you're enjoying this so much, let me finish."

She nodded. "Go ahead."

"Everything was fine until you met Althea Williams and Claudia Meeks. You couldn't believe it when they came to your office. They looked so similar. You discovered they were sisters. And you had a niggling feeling that you had met them before. That you knew them."

"You did," Mack said. "You knew them and you also knew their father. Would you like to take a wild guess who that might be?"

Faye blinked.

"Tyrone Davis. The sight of them angered you. They had done nothing with their lives, making your parents' sacrifice a complete waste. You couldn't bear it. And that's when you snapped."

She shook her head. "No, I didn't."

"Perhaps you didn't snap," Clay said. "You put your mind to better use. You started a plan. It all began with Melanie. Poor, lost Melanie. She was the key." He rubbed the back of his neck. "It always bothered me that Melanie was the only link to Careless Rapture. That she was the only one who mentioned an adviser. Why hadn't anyone else? Of course, now it makes sense. It was because she was the only one connected to it. She was to be your explanation for the deaths of the others.

"Manipulating Melanie wasn't hard. She was an eager follower and suffered from a paralyzing depression and lupus. Your deep, husky voice easily fooled Melanie to thinking you were a man. You didn't have to meet her, you used the phone as your tool. It was easy to get her to do as you pleased. She hungered for a message that told her, her suffering would end, that the universe would be kind. So, in addition to Patty, you had another follower.

"You sent Patty the bag of cards, knowing she would harmlessly set them on her desk. That was to shift the blame once Jackie began to look into things. Now with Melanie involved in Careless Rapture, you had to focus on your true victims—Althea and Claudia. You tell them of a get-rich-quick scheme you want them to be a part of. They listen, ready to do as you say. Now here comes the next puzzle piece: the clients canceling service. You convince Melanie to cancel service to prove her loyalty to the ministry while you convince Althea and Claudia to do so because you can't tell them about the scheme as president of HOPE Services—it would be a conflict of interest. You'd give them all the information once they canceled their services. They did."

"Enter stage two," Nicolas said. "Chaos. Clients are suddenly canceling service for no reason. Five in three weeks? Why? You knew why, but you wouldn't tell anyone. Jackie wasn't to know that only three of the five were real clients anyway. But she had fallen for your initial ploy anyway. She was worried about Melanie and her involvement with an adviser. With Jackie focused on Melanie you could focus on the others. Then you had a stroke of luck—Mr. Hamlick died.

"Your source of funding was in jeopardy. So you had Jackie look for funding to divert her attention. Althea was already dead, but since she'd already canceled services, she'd fallen off the radar and no one would notice."

"But how?" Jackie asked.

"Poison. They trusted Faye so she slipped something in their food or drink. All three women were found with a bottle of pills to make it look like a suicide. However, Melanie was the only true suicide. You knew exactly when she was going to do it, which was why you called Jackie to complete the story. To believe in the danger of the Careless Rapture Ministry.

"You were fine with Althea. But you made a mistake with Claudia. You didn't know she had family. You didn't know she had an aunt she spoke to, which would refute the Careless Rapture theory. But still you didn't have to worry. No one would suspect you. And yet you were nervous about Patty's big mouth and Jackie wasn't as convinced about Claudia's suicide as you'd hoped. You saw that at the restaurant."

"This is all so ridiculous," Faye interrupted.

"But you knew another way to distract her," Mack said. "Bertha. You didn't know she wasn't a relative of Jackie's, but you had spoken to her about the ministry one time and she was another perfect foil. You scheduled a meeting with her and Emmerick. And they hit it off. But you were used to his extramarital activities and didn't take much notice. So when Jackie began to doubt, you made that last taunting phone call about having a family member to send her in a panic."

"It worked," Clay said. "And we were all set to bring Emmerick down."

"If I'm not mistaken, you did." She clapped her hands. "Good job."

"But something bothered me. And it began with the phone calls. It wasn't Emmerick's style. Then Jackie and Mum talked about how different he sounded on the phone. Which made me think that the man on the phone and the man in life were not one and the same.

"But who would want to imitate him? Who would know so much about him? Who would know his habits, his speech patterns, his schedule? I remember asking my brother-in-law if wives were really powerful. I can see that they are." Clay leaned against the desk, his eyes piercing her cold stare. "I understand revenge—"

Faye leaped to her feet, her words like ice. "You don't have the balls for revenge; you don't have the brains for it." She came around the desk and stared at them with contempt. "So are you going to arrest me?" she said to Nicolas.

"But why?" Jackie asked.

Faye saw the look of pain on Jackie's face and her mask of disdain briefly crumbled. "I didn't know innocents like you still existed. I don't know how you can live so hopeful when your life has been as cruel as mine. I tried to live life and forgive, but I couldn't."

"But he's serving his time."

Faye looked as though she wanted to spit. "Serving his time? Do you consider getting a master's degree serving time? Do you call three square meals, an exercise facility, and library, plus the ability to remarry suffering?

He has a better life in prison than he had on the streets." She toyed with her necklace. "When I saw his daughters walk into this office like the same useless and disgusting trash he is, I couldn't bare it."

"And you hate trash," Mack said, glancing around the pristine office.

"Yes, I do," she said simply. "Especially the type that breathes. The type that fills the city streets and ghettos of this city. Some move forward. But others continue to live off the backs of others like parasites. Althea and Claudia were like their parents—they would have died eventually. Claudia from cirrhosis of the liver; Althea would be shot by an angry boyfriend. I couldn't wait that long." She turned to Jackie. "You wanted to help them, but you couldn't have. You didn't know what they were really about. They were greedy and disobedient. They wouldn't show up for sessions and if they did they would have attitudes. As though society owed them something."

She sat. "So these were the two precious girls my parents had gone to visit." A cold smile spread on her face. "I enjoyed killing them. Taking pictures of their bodies was the best. I think I spent around four rolls of film. Every week I sent a picture to him. I wish I could have seen that bastard's face when he saw them. His dear dead daughters. I hope the images haunt his mind."

Nobody spoke.

Nicolas came toward her.

"I never trusted you," she said.

His blue eyes pierced hers. "The feeling was mutual." He handcuffed her. "You're under arrest for the deaths of Althea Williams and Claudia Meeks. You have the right to remain silent..."

***

Jackie sat alone in the office. She could hear the phone on the front desk ringing. There was no one there to answer it; Patty had been taken away for questioning. Instead of her dreams of expanding HOPE Services, she faced two empty offices and the likelihood that all funding would be cut. Two women she'd come to see as allies in this struggle against poverty and degradation were in fact enemies. Why hadn't she seen it? Was she really that foolish?

She remembered Winstead's words that nobody cared about helping derelicts. If the very people who set out to help them used funding for their own purposes, perhaps he was right. Perhaps nobody really did.

Clay came into the room. "Jackie?"

She looked up at him, but didn't really see him He walked toward her troubled by the sadness in her eyes. It looked too much like hopelessness, as though the realities of life had finally shattered the light of her soul.

"Did you know about Faye all along?" she asked.

He shook his head. "No. The dinner with Kevin gave me suspicions of her involvement, but I never thought Faye would intentionally hurt anyone. I didn't realize the·extent of her involvement until Mum mentioned how different "Emmerick" sounded on the phone. I also could never get over why Emmerick was acting out of character by harassing you. Things didn't seem to fit, then I saw Mack and his daughter. Suddenly, I thought about how the past affects the present and how things can be connected. At that moment things began to click."

"Oh," she said with little interest.

He sighed.

"Come on," he said. "Let me take you home."

Chapter Thirty

Jackie woke up just as the sun began to spread across the city. She sat by the window in Clay's apartment, wrapped in a blanket. For two days now she'd been huddled like a broken animal. She didn't speak or eat or sleep, either sitting on the couch or by the window. She knew she had not been good company, but she didn't care. She only wanted to hide.

She felt as though she could no longer trust anyone. She was afraid to. Afraid that her judgment would be wrong, again. So deadly wrong. How could the face of evil appear as a friend? Despite the beauty of the coming day, she could only see shadows, the danger. She wanted to hide forever. Life held no joy—it was a soup that offered no sustenance. A meal only enjoyed by the simple, those who could not differentiate between water and wine. She'd tasted life's bitterness and could consume no more.

What hope was there when such cruelty existed? How could she run a program promising something she no longer believed in? She knew there was no ultimate sanctuary and there would always be pain. Jackie closed her eyes.

She opened them when she heard tapping on the window. She glanced to see what it was and gasped. "It can't be." She raced to the sleeping figure in the bed and shook him. "Clay, wake up."

"No," he grumbled.

She shook him harder. "Please! This is important."

"Can't it wait?"

"No."

He reluctantly sat up. "What is it?"

She pointed to the window. "Look."

He squinted at the window and saw a yellow and blue budgie. He jumped out of bed. "I don't believe it." He opened the window. "Laura?"

The bird flew onto his shoulder and chirped.

Clay removed Laura from his shoulder and sat on the bed, staring at the bird in wonder. "This has to be a dream."

Jackie clasped her hands together, the sight of the bird edging away the fears and doubts she'd started to cling to. But it wasn't Laura that removed them. It was the gentleness with which Clay held Laura, the way he stroked her head despite the slight tremor of his hand. How she trusted him; Jackie understood, for he treated her with the same tenderness. With him she always felt safe and cherished. She laughed to think how she'd once thought him so cold and unfeeling.

Jackie rested her cheek against Clay's bare back and closed her eyes. At that moment she felt one with him. There was no difference in age, no difference in height, no difference in experience, no difference at all. She felt the depth of her love for him and it filled her heart with courage. The courage to live and trust and dream. Jackie sat up and stared at the bird, thankful for its return. "I knew she would come back."

Clay turned to her and an unknown tension eased. He'd been afraid he'd lost her to the sadness that had haunted him all his life. But no . . . she was free. They both were. "You knew it, huh?" He smirked. "Is that because that's how fairy tales end?"

"Yes." She smiled with such unmitigated joy, he felt his heart move. He knew then that he loved her. He loved her in a way that gave him strength, that made him feel fully alive. It replaced the pain he'd long carried with him—a once trusted companion. Now he felt hope. He shook his head. He'd never felt that before. He'd been searching for it and seeing it out of reach. Now it was here in this room, in his heart.

He no longer had to sit in a church to find a quiet sanctuary. He had only to look at Jackie to find safety and peace in her bright gaze. His mischief maker had completely bewitched him, and he felt no shame or fear in that knowledge, just a firm belief that that was how it was supposed to be.

He set Laura on his dresser drawer, then grabbed his clothes. He began to whistle.

"I've never heard you whistle before."

"I'm talking to Laura."

Jackie stared at him. "You're acting strange."

He stood and opened the door. "It's probably because I'm in love with you."

She leaped out of bed and followed him into the kitchen. "What?"

He searched inside the fridge. "What would you like for breakfast?"

She tugged on his arm, wanting him to look at her. "Who cares? What did you just say?"

Clay put a finger to his lips. "Quiet or you'll wake Mum."

She threw up her hands. "I don't care. She doesn't get up until noon anyway." Jackie stood in front of him, blocking his access to the fridge. "Did you say you loved me?"

He gently pushed her to the side. "I said I'm in love with you. It's an ongoing sickness."

"I have it, too."

He nodded. "Yes, it's very important to love yourself."

"Clay," she said, exasperated with this playful mood. "I'm in love with you."

He waved a hand as though fending her off. "I know." He turned to the sink.

She wrapped her hands around his waist, again resting her cheek against his back. "What are you going to do about it?"

He shrugged. "I don't know."

She took a step back and frowned. "What do you mean you don't know?"

He looked at her a moment, then handed her his keys.

She stared at them, confused. "Do you want me to go somewhere?"

"They're the keys to everything I own. My place, my car, my job, the safety deposit box where I keep my girlie magazines—collector's editions."

"Why are you giving them to me?"

"They're yours."

Jackie grasped them to her chest, feeling the grooves bite into her palm. "They're mine?" she said breathlessly.

He trapped her against the fridge, his heart reflecting in his eyes. "They're yours. Which means all that I have is yours. It means you taught me how to live, how to breathe, how to feel. You taught me that being a man isn't about being alone, it's about risking being wrong, trusting. It is about knowing when you're weak, knowing when you need help, and asking for it. It means I want to wake up to you every morning and go to bed with you every night. It means I'll never run away again because with you I'm always home."

Jackie stared at him speechless.

"I'm asking you to marry me, in case you're not sure."

Jackie gazed at the keys, running a hand over them as though they were diamonds. She looked up and said, "The answer is yes."

He lifted her in his arms and held her tight, then closed his eyes and whispered, "Thank you, Mischief."

"For what?"

Clay drew back and smiled. "Helping me believe in happy endings."

***

Clay stood by his office window as a fierce February wind swept through the city, touching trees and buildings with frost. He opened the window, inhaling a freezing blast. He loved the winter. How it chilled his skin and made the air feel as though it could break. He still had the holiday picture postcard Cassie and Adriana had sent of the new family members, Julie and Geoffrey, dressed like reindeer. Eric had been right. He'd gotten his boy and three hundred dollars for a bet he and Drake had. Strangely enough, Drake didn't seem very upset about losing. He was too proud of how Jackie had managed to keep HOPE Services running. As president, she had reorganized the entire company, inspiring corporate companies to invest in her endeavors.

In the spring, Clay and Jackie hoped to move into their new town house where Laura and her new friend Howard would have a large room to fly around in. Plus, they'd have a nice guest room for when his mother visited in the summer.

"Brr! It's freezing in here."

He turned as Jackie entered the room, bundled in a red winter coat and a hat she had pulled down to her eyebrows. "Are you ready to go home?"

Home. He loved that word. He shut the window, then took her hand. "Yes, I am."

About the Author

National bestselling author Dara Girard is an award-winning, multi-published author of more than twenty novels. Dara loves to travel, eat French pastries and hear from readers.

You can write her at:
contactdara@daragirard.com
or
P.O. Box 10345
Silver Spring, MD 20914

If you'd like to receive a reply, please send a self-addressed stamped envelope. And remember to visit www.daragirard.com to find out more about her current and upcoming books..

If you enjoyed *Careless Rapture* don't miss....

Table for Two (Book 1 in Henson Series) A woman who's given up on love meets a man who is hard to resist.

Gaining Interest (Book 2 in Henson Series) A savvy woman with a weakness for bad boys meets a man who definitely isn't one. Or is he?

The Daughters of Winston Barnett An immigrant father of five daughters has to deal with their love lives and ambitions.

The Sapphire Pendant A woman retrieves a priceless heirloom and discovers a family secret and precious love.

Honest Betrayal A woman marries for convenience and uncovers secrets in her husband's past.

The Lady Next Door and Other Stories a collection of five short stories.